Quinlan's Secret

· THE ELDERS BOOK TWO ·

Cailyn Lloyd

Quinlan's Secret

ISBN-13: 978-0-578-66464-4

Cover Art by Rose Miller

For Haley, Carson, Charlotte,
Scarlett, Maddie, and Isla
Little monsters, every one of you

One

"By the way, it's haunted," the man said, standing by the bar, shuffling paperwork.

"What? Now you tell me?" Josh Abelson looked at the old guy critically for any hint he was joking. Greg Fitzsimmons had been odd from the get-go, quirky and humorless, an aging hippy from another era with long grey hair pulled back into a man-tail, his face a craggy testament to a life lived hard. Fitzsimmons was the former owner of this tavern, a rundown corner bar with battered plank floors, cheap stools, and oak woodwork darkened by age and decades of smoke.

The old guy put a hand on his shoulder. "No big deal. Adds a little character to the place."

"What do you mean, exactly, by haunted?" Josh asked. Why was he asking? He didn't believe in ghosts. It was probably just a legend, a story told over beers and passed down over the years. Why tell him now? They had signed papers, the sale closed. The tavern was his.

Fitzsimmons shrugged. "The usual. Noises and shadowy figures in the basement. The occasional footsteps overhead when no one's up there. The waitresses won't go in the basement. I'm surprised you haven't heard the rumors." The old guy put a finger to his nose like he was going to pick, then snatched it away at the last second. Yuck.

Rumors? *Yeah, right.* Josh stifled a chuckle. "I don't believe in any of that nonsense—"

"Yeah, neither did I. They seem harmless enough though."

"They—?"

"The ghosts." Fitzsimmons said, his stony expression unwavering.

The guy had to be pulling his leg. What did it matter? Josh planned to gut the place and convert it to a stylish brew-pub. The bones of the place were sound, the foundation solid, the location ideal. The neighborhood had run down over the years, but now young affluent couples were buying the old houses in this sleeper community and renovating them or tearing them down and building anew.

He hadn't asked the neighbors about the place because when he reopened, he had no intention of welcoming the old crowd: a bunch of Boomers who, like the owner, sat around bitching about their wives, politics, and the useless Millennial generation. Josh was GenX and thought the younger crowd was just fine.

Fitzsimmons looked around. Oddly, Josh detected no nostalgia in that last glance. "Well, Mr. Abelson, it's all yours. I hope it's everything you ever imagined." He let out a humorless laugh that sounded vaguely creepy and slapped his hand on the bar. He turned and walked toward the front entrance.

"It will be." Josh closed his eyes, listening to the receding footsteps. The door banged shut a moment later.

So long, weird old dude!

The tavern was silent, the late afternoon sun shining through grimy windows. It didn't look like a dream, but it was. After twenty years of legal practice, Josh had exhausted all interest in his profession and longed for a new career, a second life. He probably had enough money to retire now if he wanted, but at forty-eight, he wasn't yet ready for a life centered around yard work, a fishing boat, or golf.

Owning a tavern had become the dream over the years. Instead of being tied to a rigid schedule in a professional office, he would hang out at the bar when he wanted. Let others do the work when he needed a break. Come to know his clientele, hopefully establish a diverse group of regulars. Manage a kitchen—even if he had no clue what he was doing yet. He was a quick study and had a knack for learning new skills. He'd spent weeks driving around, meeting and talking to bar owners, picking their brains, trying to learn any and every detail about the trade, and was already well-schooled in the general specifics of running a business.

Josh surveyed the barroom. Undoubtedly elegant once, the luster was long gone. The oak bar, almost forty feet in length, had been sorely neglected. The back bar, also oak, looked equally shabby, marred by stains, the finish cracked and darkened with age. The floors were maple, the ceiling embossed tin, the walls paneled with some once-popular crap from the '80s. The place looked beyond salvage but Josh had a gift, the ability to envision the woodwork restored, the walls finished in plaster with oak accents, booths, tables, oak bar stools; he could see it all in glorious detail in his head.

The building itself, built in 1854, was brick and had been a bank originally. The tavern, with all the ornate woodwork, came later in that century. Upstairs, over the bar, lay a large apartment that hadn't been lived in for decades, a space Josh intended to renovate as well. He and Kiera, his girlfriend, planned to live in the apartment after the tavern opened when they needed to stay close at hand. They had talked about living together but couldn't decide who would give up their house. Perhaps they would sell both houses and buy a new place. For now, Kiera thought the apartment was a perfect interim solution and they would worry about it *after* the bar was up and running.

Josh wandered around the room for a few minutes, dreaming, picturing the floor layout, the booths, the tables, the decor. He felt good, a sense of accomplishment. He had focused on a goal and gone for it with his usual vigor, the way he'd built a practice from scratch and turned it into a thriving law office.

A name engraved dead center on the back bar caught his attention:

Thorson Kuenlang

Probably the carpenter. Maybe the original owner. Worth checking out.

Josh eyed himself in the bar mirror. Dark hair, brown eyes with some early age lines. Not bad looking—quite handsome according to his girlfriend. Was he nuts doing this now? He would know soon enough.

He walked down the stairs to the basement—a dingy, poorly lit hole filled with all manner of junk: old taps and kegs, broken stools and tables, a pool table, a couple of slot machines that might be a hundred years old, cases of empty beer and soda bottles—apparently, the old guy didn't believe in chucking anything. It looked like a hoarder's dream and smelled of mildew, oil, stale beer, and neglect. Christ, there could be a ghost lost in there somewhere. The haunting was a quirky story and one he could use for a little added atmosphere. Every old place, it seemed, had a ghost. It was virtually a rule.

Tomorrow, everything would change. A crew would throw this junk into dumpsters and haul it to a landfill. All but the slot machines—those he would restore for period decor in the bar. The paneling upstairs would go as well, along with every stick of furniture in the building. Another crew would gut the second floor to the studs.

Just then, a stack of broken chairs tipped and clattered to the concrete floor.

"Holy shit!" Josh started and then laughed. Must be the ghosts welcoming him to the bar. He hadn't chosen a name yet. Suddenly, *The Haunted Tavern* popped into his head. It had a certain raw appeal. He made a mental note to check to see how common the name was.

The Haunted Tavern?

Maybe.

He couldn't wait to share the story with Kiera.

Two

Ugh.

Kiera O'Donnell opened one eye and screwed it shut an instant later. With her head clamped in a migraine-like vice of her own making, the room was far too bright. Too much chardonnay. The tequila chaser hadn't helped. When would she learn?

At forty-six, *never* seemed the reasonable answer.

Something was snuffling around her waist.

Where the hell was she? She cracked an eye again, just slightly. The living room. Laying on her sofa. Her flat screen in the corner hanging over the gas fireplace, playing some game show with the sound off, and the doorway to her study, a room that saw very little use these days.

Ghost pawed her. He was a black flat-coated retriever-border collie mix without a name when she rescued him. When she let him out at night, he disappeared in the dark except when light reflected an eerie crimson from his eyes, hence the name Ghost. What time was it? He probably had to go out.

"Shit!" Ten o'clock. She had planned on storm chasing today. Crap. Was it too late?

She sat and held her head in her hands, trying to stave off the pain of being upright. The ache was intense, and a sudden wave of nausea rolled through her. Kiera let Ghost out and went to the bathroom and peed. Looked in the mirror. She looked like shit, her mousy brown hair a rat's nest on her head, a pillow imprint on her face. People said she was attractive—when she wasn't hung over. Nice eyes and cheekbones, a sexy mouth, or so Josh thought. Right now, her mouth tasted like death. She ran the electric toothbrush around her teeth with little enthusiasm, then dumped four Advil into her hand and washed them down with tepid tap water.

She wanted to fall into bed and sleep for a few hours, but Ghost needed to be fed and she needed to check the forecast even though she couldn't see leaving the house and driving anywhere with this awful hangover.

She opened her laptop and tried to focus as she brought up the *Storm Prediction Center Convective Outlooks.*

Damn!

Moderate Risk. A special notation over western Wisconsin for an enhanced risk of strong tornadoes.

Why did she do that last tequila shot?

Like that made any difference.

She couldn't drive the way she felt. What to do. What to do...

Kiera decided on a plan: take a Sumatriptan, her migraine med, and grab two hours of sleep. She would just have time to make the target area.

Josh would be tied up all day, so she fired off a quick text saying she was chasing and would be gone until dark, maybe later. He knew the drill.

★   ★   ★

At one, Kiera dropped her camera bag in the back seat along with a water dish and treats for Ghost, then mounted her laptop on a swivel table bolted between the seats. She brought up weather models, a satellite image and a surface plot of temperatures, wind barbs, and dew points. Her initial target was Osseo near Eau Claire, but she would refine that as she drove west on US 10.

The trip went quickly. Kiera drove too fast and alternated her attention between the road and the laptop, watching the satellite and surface data, looking for the chasing sweet spot where the perfect conditions converged and created atmospheric violence. It seemed like a perverse hobby, wishing for bad weather, but the weather would happen regardless so she might as well be there to observe it.

A tornado watch went up over most of western Wisconsin. Her focus remained on Osseo. Everything pointed to that area: the surface map, shear profiles, the satellite images. Her mind worked like a computer, absorbing the data and turning it into a forecast in her head, the driving and the forecasting running on autopilot at some level. All the ingredients were converging in one place and she was heading right for it. It was a rush, a blast of adrenaline, watching the road disappear under her wheels as the clouds exploded ahead into crisp towers of cumulus—the nimbus tower to her west twisting like a gigantic corkscrew as the updraft rotated.

Heading into the storm with the rain core on her right flank, the base of the thunderstorm lay ahead, hidden by trees. The trees soon gave way to open fields and the dark saucer-shaped base lay another ten miles ahead. A tornado warning popped up on the computer screen for the storm, probably just a radar signature, but it meant conditions were prime. She saw a storm spotter sitting at an intersection with a **SKYWARN** decal on his car door but no other chasers on the road, which seemed odd. It was a big day. There should be chasers everywhere, unless they were behind the storm, trying to play catch-up—a bad place to be for visibility and good photography. Here, ahead of the storm, with the sun to the west, any tornado that formed would likely be backlit and far more photogenic.

Low, ragged clouds danced and rotated beneath the storm base. A clear wedge appeared in the cloud base, eroding the back edge. The rotation in the lowered base—the wall cloud—accelerated. A thin funnel spun slowly down. She turned right on a dirt road and hit the accelerator until she was going seventy. Bracing Ghost with her arm, she slammed on the brakes, stopping at a great vantage point. Kiera pulled her camera, a Sony Alpha A7 with a Tamron 28-300mm telephoto lens, from the backseat.

The spinning funnel was due west, about a mile out, and moving east. This was a dangerous spot and she knew it.

Touchdown!

A burst of dirt spun up, the circulation traveling ten feet before dissipating. The chase was afoot. The vortex had reached the ground once and would likely do it again, maybe several times before the tornadic circulation was fully established.

Another spin up of dirt.

Kiera snapped a half-dozen pics. She knew she needed to move, but suddenly decided to sit tight. She had never been this close!

Lightning hit the ground a hundred feet away with a deafening crash. Temporarily blinded, she blinked and saw a funnel snake most of the way to the ground, heading right for her. She really should move.

The funnel skipped along the ground, a tenuous vapor appearing and snaking in tangled loops, evaporating then reappearing again.

Kiera stared, mesmerized, but she didn't move. Nope. She sat there, playing chicken with a tornado even though a road heading east, the logical option, lay a mere fifty feet ahead.

The tornado touched down again about a hundred yards out and the thin drill-bit funnel cut a path toward her. She imagined it lifting and skipping over her at the last second, a strong gust rocking the RAV4, nearly pushing it over maybe. Instead, Ghost barked and broke the spell.

"Shit!" She could be stupid but she couldn't risk harming him. Some might argue she had already put him at risk but in truth, storm chasing wasn't that dangerous. Reversing quickly out of the tornado's path, the circulation crossed the road right where they had been parked moments before.

"Holy shit!" Too damned close! Still, it was an amazing moment. The tornado plowed east, kicking up debris, sending all manner of vegetation flying.

Kiera shifted into gear and gave chase, turning right and paralleling the tornado as it touched down again and grew larger. She hit the gas and roared ahead to get a better vantage point ahead of the swelling funnel, making a quick call to the National Weather Service to report the tornado.

The next ten minutes were electric. The funnel grew to almost a hundred yards across. Power flashes lit the blackness under the storm base as the tornado ripped through power lines. She drove on, stopping at good vantage points, alternating camera modes between still photos and clips of video. The twister ripped a barn to shreds in an explosion of debris. Kiera caught it all on video, jumped in the RAV4, and tore ahead of it again.

She snapped dozens of photos and kept just ahead of the funnel as she watched the radar and the GPS, trying to anticipate the storm and the roads, staying in the sweet spot just ahead of it.

Five minutes later, the funnel thinned and tilted to the north, evolving to rope stage, the final gasp before the tornado dissipated. The storm was also changing shape, becoming more of a squall and less a supercell, a long dark shelf cloud stretching north and south of her location. The terrain here was far more wooded, making it difficult to observe or photograph storm structure anyway.

Kiera stayed with the storm for nearly an hour but it evolved to a linear gust front—a squall line. It wouldn't spawn any further tornadoes and the clouds weren't particularly interesting. She checked her position. While she had mapped her course carefully, she didn't really know where she was. It was easy to develop a myopia when chasing, keeping track of road options while ignoring the bigger picture. Happened all the time. Couldn't keep track of everything. Thank God for GPS.

She broke chase and steered toward Stevens Point and the interstate thirty miles ahead, enjoying the lush green landscape dotted with barns, silos, and farm homesteads. Her phone pinged repeatedly as friends and other chasers called or texted, wondering how she had done. They could wait. She'd post the pictures and a chase report to her website in the morning. It was a great chase and the pics would attract a lot of interest on the internet. The National Weather Service would probably want them as well.

The drive home was often tough. The excitement and adrenaline of the chase waning, the ride home seemed much longer than the trip out. Post-chase fatigue set in. Now, her mind was free to wander, and not always in useful ways.

What was that stupid stunt with the tornado today? Why did she do it?

Kiera didn't know. She had always played a little fast and loose with her life, but didn't feel she had a death wish. Still, Ghost apparently had more common sense than she did.

Kiera glanced at him, curled up on the seat, asleep. She knew in her heart that he was more than a dog, a surrogate for the child she would never have. He had willingly become a support animal, sensing when she was down or agitated. He would attack playfully or clown around, had ways of cheering her up.

She was prone to depression, had been since her teens. It had crept back a few years ago as life had slowly chipped away at her happiness. Her father had died two years ago of a senseless coronary, a shock but not a total surprise. He had been an overweight guy in his fifties who refused to exercise or see a doctor regularly. His father had died at sixty-one of a coronary and, either in denial or acceptance, her father had refused to worry about the possibility. Her mother had been dealing with breast cancer at the time. A year later, the cancer took her life. She had an older sister, Megan, but they were polar opposites and had never gotten along well.

Throw in a divorce and somehow, her life had just slowly slipped off the tracks. She lost interest in her career and considered a return to school to seek out a new vocation. A couple of chardonnays after work morphed into a bottle, plus the odd tequila chaser now and then. At least she had the presence of mind to Uber home. Soon, she pretty much had her own Uber guy, a humorous dude named Jake. What was the point of taking a car to work if you never drove it home?

Last December, she had walked into her boss's office and resigned her position as a project archeologist with a cultural resource management firm. She no longer needed the money, one of the awful ironies of her parents' passing. After her mother's estate had been settled, she probably never needed to work again. She had a vague plan to sort her life out—whatever that meant—but worried she might meander through life doing nothing meaningful instead.

She was a bit of an adrenaline junkie and her position in archeology hadn't been the least bit exciting. She had plenty of hobbies: skydiving, storm chasing, running—including the occasional marathon—but the best chasing was over for the season and a bum ankle after a jump and a bad landing last spring had nixed the running and the skydiving for a while.

Josh was the one bright facet in her life. They had been dating for six months when her mother died. He had been wonderfully supportive, encouraging her decision to quit her job. And why not? He had just done the same. He thought they would lead a charmed life from here on and live happily ever after. Almost six foot and handsome, a sensitive, kind soul, he was an awesome catch and he had a cute butt. She smiled. Maybe she would get the fairy tale.

She was excited about the tavern, though for now, the project was still an intangible. Kiera didn't really know what to expect. While it was originally Josh's dream, she had gotten swept up in it, would be a full partner, and planned to tend bar when they opened. It was something new and different and exactly what she needed right now.

Still, the grey cloud of depression appeared far too often. She had the blues. An emotional funk that she had struggled through on and off for the past few years. An increasing malaise, the feeling that age was creeping up on her, with the certain knowledge she would never have a child of her own. She was infertile, unable to conceive thanks to a rare uterine malformation, a birth defect undiagnosed until she tried to conceive. Kiera had wanted children until doctors determined she couldn't have any of her own. Now she was no longer sure. Or maybe her doubts were simply rationalizations to minimize the profound sadness she experienced at times.

Melancholy was the word for how she felt.

She hated the feeling, the sense of impending doom, a sure sign of depression.

Might be time to see her therapist again.

Three

At six the following morning, Josh stood by as two large trucks dropped dumpsters in the back lot of the tavern. He wasn't a morning person, but these people insisted this was the only available time for a drop off. Six o'clock.

Assholes. Who gets up at five in the morning?

Much of the world, he discovered. The roads were filled with cars and people going this way and that. Who knew? Even in his office, he had never started before nine.

The heavy containers dropped with a metallic clatter and the trucks pulled out as his crews arrived for their first day on the job. While he was adept at carpentry, plumbing, and electrical work, the renovation was too big and too complex for one person. He had hired people to clear the basement and another crew to gut the second floor. A third team would remove all the paneling from the bar area. He had always enjoyed doing electrical work—he and his ex-wife had flipped their first home and had done the work themselves.

After setting up his tools, he began installing a new 400 amp service panel in the basement next to the existing service that was so old, it still used twist-out fuses instead of breakers. He wore noise-canceling headphones and jammed a '90s alt-rock mix to shut out the racket as crews tore into his building and dragged the junk out of the basement. The floor was otherwise covered with a thick rime of dirt, the air dank and smelling of mold, mildew, and old beer. Josh couldn't wait until they finished.

He was warming to the idea of the *Haunted Tavern* but needed to do some research to determine the extent the name had been used or abused in the past. Most of all, he needed stories. Perhaps the old guy knew some stories. Josh decided he would do well to research the tavern personally—a building this old had to have history. Find some old photos to hang on the wall. An old sepia of the bank would be awesome.

His phone vibrated. A text from Kiera.

How's it going, babe?

Busy putting the new elec panel in. How was the chase?

Awesome! A solid 3! Great pics!

An F-3 tornado was no small deal. An F-3! Jesus, the woman knew no fear. They had started dating almost two years ago and spent much of their waking time together. They hadn't made the commitment to living under one roof, but it seemed close. She didn't hint, she wasn't pushy, but he sensed it was time. Marriage was another matter. His previous marriage had imploded three years ago in an acrimonious divorce but he had been mostly lucky.

Lillian, his ex, was an attorney as well and they made about the same amount of money. Nevertheless, Lillian tried to gouge him out of vindictiveness, but the judge was having none of it. In the end, they sold the house and their stuff and walked off with equal shares of cash. Their children were both in college and seemed relieved that their parents, also known as the Bickersons, had finally split. Afterward, he wondered why it had taken so long for them to realize the obvious: the marriage had been over for years, virtually every emotional tie severed. It was a failure and he hated failing. Some counseling had taught him to be more pragmatic. Still, he had resolved to never marry again, a resolve that was slowly weakening as Kiera became more deeply ingrained into his life.

Josh texted: *Dinner?*

Yep. When?

Make it 7. Finnegan's?

Yep. C ya!

Finnegan's was an Irish pub across town, a cozy little place with four tables and a couple of booths, well decorated and authentically themed, with Irish beers, ales, and stouts. It was one of their go-to places for dinner. The food was decent but nothing to write home about. They liked the atmosphere and had plans to go with a similar old-world theme, only bigger and better, with a pro chef and a wider selection of wines and beers.

He went back to the electrical box and finished mounting it to the concrete wall, humming to Green Day's *Time of Your Life*.

He needed to run temporary lines to each floor so the crews would have power while he rewired the building with new Romex and conduit where the electrical code required it. Technically, he couldn't wire the building himself but he had a friend, Pat Merrill, a journeyman electrician, who would sign off on the inspections.

He was bending conduit when he heard a shout from the far corner of the basement, even over the headphones. A moment later there was a loud crash as something hit the floor amid a billowing cloud of dust. There was more yelling and hand-waving as the dust began to settle.

Josh ripped his headphones off and dashed over to see what was going on. A guy, one of the demo crew, lay on the floor screaming. A large tank—an old boiler or something—had fallen on his leg and it looked bad. Crushed maybe. Two guys were maneuvering to move the tank.

"Stop! Wait a minute." Josh raised a hand. "Moving it may make things worse. Somebody dial 911."

While one of the guys made the call, Josh knelt and took the guy's hand, checked his pulse—which was strong and steady—and tried to calm him while they waited for the EMTs to arrive. He was just a kid really, maybe twenty-five, fighting to compose himself.

"Take it easy. EMTs are on their way. What's your name?"

"Adam."

"Hurt bad, Adam?"

"Not really."

He winced and Josh knew he was struggling to look strong. The floor beneath his head was gross, a slime of dirt and rusty water. "Somebody have something for his head? A coat? A blanket?"

Moments later, he heard a siren, growing louder. Someone handed him a coat.

"You sure we shouldn't move that?" Bill, the crew chief said.

He could feel the eyes of the others boring into him. "No, I'm not sure, but we should let the pros decide. They'll be here soon enough."

They seemed willing to defer to his judgement. He worried they would exacerbate the injury. Just what he needed, the first day on the job. Christ, he hoped the guy's leg wasn't as bad as it looked, caved in as it was at mid-shin. Definitely broken, maybe shattered.

The EMTs arrived in under five minutes and took control. After ensuring the man was stable, they directed the crew who gently lifted the tank and set it aside. They shooed the guys across the basement and out of the way. They asked for more light—there were only two bulbs hanging in the entire basement. Josh set up several work lights.

While they waited and watched the EMTs work, Josh turned to Bill. "So what happened?"

Bill looked about fifty, with a full beard and grizzled face. "Not sure. Somehow, the tank just fell. We weren't even working on it at the time. Almost like it got pushed."

Josh listened skeptically. Of course they would deflect blame. Didn't matter. While his practical brain worried about liability, Bill was an independent contractor and the liability or workers comp insurance was his problem. He just felt bad for the guy lying on the ground who would likely be out of work for months.

Twenty minutes later, the EMTs had Adam on a stretcher and hauled him away.

Josh didn't believe in omens any more than he believed in ghosts, but an accident like this on the first day felt like a harbinger of bad luck.

No point in dwelling on it.

He had work to do.

★　★　★

Josh walked into Finnegan's just after seven. Kiera waved from the corner booth they both preferred. Somewhat private, with dark paneling and soft lighting, it felt cozy and authentic, almost like being transported to a pub in Dublin.

Kiera was strikingly attractive, he felt, though it might be his hormones talking. She always looked hot to him. His friends judged her as okay, not striking, but he didn't care what they thought, and didn't care for how they talked about women in general. She was halfway through a glass of chardonnay. The woman did like her wine, perhaps a little too well—though she never got stupid or belligerent and she never drove if she drank more than two glasses.

He slid into the booth. "Hey babe."

"Hey sweetie. You look like shit," she said cheerfully.

"Thanks. Rough day." He briefly described the demolition work and filled her in on the accident in the basement.

"How's the guy doing?" Kiera asked, swirling her glass.

"Don't know. Still haven't heard. The EMTs thought he probably had multiple fractures."

"Holy shit. First day. Not a great way to start this project. Feels like an omen—"

Josh winced. "Christ, don't say that! I had the same thought but it's silly. Shit happens, it's a construction site."

"Wow. Mr. Empathy."

Oops. That had sounded callous. "No, I feel bad for the guy, but what can I do?"

"Send him a card, at least." She playfully slapped his arm.

The waitress stopped over and took his drink order for a bottle of Spotted Cow, a local brew.

Josh touched her hand. "I forgot to tell you. After we signed the papers, Fitzsimmons says to me, 'by the way, it's haunted'."

Kiera set her glass down. "Was he serious?"

"Who knows, but it gave me an idea." Josh paused for effect and spread his hands, a curtain opening. "How about *The Haunted Tavern?*"

Pursing her lips, Kiera considered for a moment, then said, "Nope. Too corny. Too Disney."

"Really? I kind of like it. I was going to dig up some old pics and stories, make up a few of my own—"

"Make up your own? Exactly how ethical were you as an attorney?" She looked at him disapprovingly.

"Very. What the hell?" Sometimes she feigned seriousness and he couldn't tell—

"Oh relax, I'm messing with you," Kiera said, putting her hand on his. "I don't know about that name. It might work. Anyone else using it?"

"I don't know."

"Still…it's too in-your-face. How about *Jacob Marley's?* Something a little more subtle?"

"Maybe. I'll think about it." He liked it. Would it be a problem if they couldn't agree? How would they resolve it? Better to change the subject. "So how was the chase?"

Kiera grabbed her phone and let him page through the photos taken in frightening proximity to a nightmare of a tornado. "Jesus."

"EF-3 baby. It was a rush." She smiled like a kid with a new skateboard. It was adorable.

"You're nuts. How come I never see anything like this when I go out with you?"

"Luck mostly." She smiled a smug smile. "And I have the feeling you're bad luck. Ghost and I seem to do better."

He pointed the top of his bottle at her. "That's just rude."

"He doesn't whine as much as you do either."

He was trying to avoid letting the day get to him and wasn't quite in the mood for Kiera's banter. Finally he said, "Did Abbie go?"

Abbie was a friend Kiera had promised to take chasing.

"No. I forgot to call her. She's mad at me too," Kiera said offhandedly.

"I'm not mad."

"Grumpy then."

"Maybe. I'm just worried we're off to a bad start."

She grasped his hands. "It's fine. Just a bump in the road."

It was true but he couldn't relax. He wished he could. He nodded, flashed Kiera a half-baked smile and drained his beer.

He thought: *nothing better happen tomorrow.*

Four

Two days later, Kiera awoke with a clear head when Ghost jumped on the bed and pawed at her face, his none-too-subtle way of telling her he was hungry and had to go out.

"Okay buddy, two minutes. Okay?"

Undeterred, he burrowed his snout between her head and the pillow.

"Alright, alright. God, you're a pest."

Kiera crawled from bed, eyes half open. She walked to the kitchen and loaded the Keurig, let Ghost out and plopped down at the table. She opened her laptop, then her phone rang. It was Willow Monroe, childhood friend, college roommate, flower-child, new age fruitcake, and a genuinely sweet soul. She fancied herself a psychic and dabbled in Tarot, palmistry, and numerology. It didn't seem to help her in the relationship department. Willow went through boyfriends like some women went through purses.

"Hey Willow, what's up?"

"What'd you do, Kiera?" Her tone was playful but accusatory.

"Huh?"

"I'm getting a bad vibe from your Tarot and horoscope. What'd you do?"

"A bad vibe? What do you mean?" Willow could be quite obtuse at times.

With no trace of humor, Willow said, "I see some threat in your life."

"I was chasing a few days ago. I might've been a little reckless."

"Maybe that's it, but I'm not sure."

"I'm fine Willow, but thanks for looking out for me."

"You're my bestie, I have to."

After a little small talk, Kiera signed off. Ghost was barking at the door. In his case, *arf arf* easily translated to "feed me, feed me". She poured kibble into his bowl as he paced restlessly and then stood back as he tore into his breakfast. She fried up strips of bacon and made a sandwich, feeling that the good whole wheat toast canceled out the bad fatty bacon. Life was a series of compromises. Ghost sat vigilantly by the stove with his big sad dog eyes, a subtle beg for bacon. She'd read somewhere that dogs had two sets of eyelids and thus, the ability to make these sad, woeful faces. Ghost was exceptional at it.

She showered, luxuriating in the strong stream of hot water, pampering herself as she had no plans all day. After drying her hair and pulling it into a ponytail, she slipped into jean shorts and a comfy black tee advertising a bar in the Caymans.

Kiera walked out to the patio with a glass of chardonnay and her laptop. She checked her email and caught up on the news, then paged through her investments and sold shares of a stock that looked shaky.

Curious, she typed *The Haunted Tavern* into Google and scanned the results. Other than *The Haunted Tavern* in Kissimmee, no other bar or restaurant had used the name. There were plenty of entries for haunted bars and taverns and numerous haunted tavern tours, but the name was otherwise unused. Still, she didn't much care for it. It sounded cheesy.

She typed *Fitzsimmons Tavern* into the search bar. The first two pages were filled with entries from Yelp, Trip Adviser, and such, all with generally low opinions of the place. With a three-star average out of five, that seemed generous from what she had seen. Then came the *Fitzsimmons* in other cities plus pages about zoning, complaints, and liquor license issues. Then she found a post about the liquor license that included an interesting tidbit: the bar used to be called Quinlan's Tavern. Maybe she would find some ghostly stories under that name.

A Quinlan's Tavern in Boston came up first and filled the first couple of pages. Then came the first promising entry:

On the Fond du Lac road, near Miller's Crossing, James Quinlan kept tavern. Quinlan's Tavern was a great place for travelers. Nothing was more common than to see, a few hours before sunset, a four-horse, white-covered wagon drive up before the tavern and make inquires for the 'old man'. The old man was Mr. James Quinlan. The wagon-yard, with its complement of turkeys, geese, ducks, a drove of speckled chickens, old broken dishes and often, a supply of mud, made the place look rather amusing. Quinlan was a favorite with his guests. His table had the food which most of his guests liked, and his feather beds were delightful places for a weary traveler to sleep.

Had to be the same place. Part of an Auburn County history, the entry was undated. She bookmarked the site for Josh. He had been talking about doing just this, searching the history of the bar and finding some cool photos they could hang as part of the decor. She would do it for him.

She kept digging, turning up occasional references to Quinlan's Tavern in local histories and newspaper clips hidden behind the firewall of Newspapers.com. No matter. She bought a basic subscription and entered *Quinlan's Tavern* in the search bar. A slew of snippets and articles popped up: licensing approvals, bar picnics in the summer, live music now and then, bowling league news, problems with the tavern staying open after hours.

Kiera jumped when she clicked on the next page of results that included an article from April 17th, 1922 with a bold headline:

Five Slain in Gangland Shootout

Trouble came to Miller's Crossing Friday night when members of two rival bootleg crews met at Quinlan's, a reputed speakeasy, supposedly to settle a dispute over territory between west-side Chicago gangs and the Milwaukee mob. The men met upstairs, a fight ensued, revolvers were drawn, and shots fired. When police arrived, they found five men dead upstairs, riddled with bullets...

The article filled two long columns on the front page. Kiera downloaded every aspect of the article, photos, follow-ups, anything she could find. This stuff was absolute dynamite. Josh would love it. Talk about history! How had this story been lost over the years? Almost a hundred years had passed—that was the likely answer.

She waded through article after article about Quinlan's, mostly mundane stuff, until she stumbled across an article from June 9, 1877. The headline crowed:

Quinlan Guilty!

Mrs. Charlotte Quinlan was found guilty of murder, by poison, of her two children, a boy of thirteen and a little girl, a pretty child of ten years. Mr. Bevans, attorney, attempted to set up a defense of insanity...

Three columns of endless detail followed. It was hard to read. The woman had put strychnine in their food and then sat and watched them die. Who could do that? She was also suspected of poisoning two neighbors, though the cases couldn't be proven. She was sentenced to life; Wisconsin didn't have the death penalty, even then. Leafing through more headlines, Kiera found an enigmatic headline:

Do Quinlan Children Remain?

Though they have been in the grave for five years, patrons of Quinlan's Tavern insist the Quinlan children remain, appearing at the end of the bar where they often sat whilst their father worked. An upstairs tenant has reported hearing children giggling on many occasions and has heard footsteps on the stairs. Mrs. Charlotte Quinlan was...

The article included photos of the children and the tavern. By far the most interesting story yet, the article and photographs had earned their own wall and special display. The haunting in the bar had been an abstract until now. The article meant nothing, certainly wasn't a verification of the haunting, but it intrigued Kiera. When they moved in, would they see or hear things?

Kiera quickly flipped forward again, looking for missed tidbits, until 1931 when she found a story dear to her heart. In July of that year, a tornado had ripped the roof off the tavern. The article also noted that tornadoes had struck Miller's Crossing in 1892 and 1878.

Cool! The town is a tornado magnet!

She spent an hour organizing the materials, printing the photos and news clips. She decided to pull a surprise visit on Josh at the tavern to show him the materials and see how they were coming with the renovation. She didn't have Josh's gift of vision when it came to the tavern. She saw a rundown dump that might be better demolished and rebuilt—except for the back bar. That oak woodwork was beautiful even in its neglected state.

Josh's insistence on owning a bar seemed a little odd to her. She had a preconceived idea that all bar owners were drunks and owned a bar so they could be close to and control the source of their addiction. But Josh wasn't a drunk. Indeed, he drank in moderation at all times. Given the amount of chardonnay she had been drinking lately, she had no right to talk.

She packed a quick lunch, ham and cheese sandwiches, beer, wine, and glasses. Ghost stood by the door, imploring her with his sad eyes to take him along.

"I'm sorry, buddy. It's too messy and dangerous for you there."

Kiera rolled the windows of the RAV4 down. It was a beautiful day, the sky deep blue crisscrossed by a few ragged contrails. Not too hot, not too muggy, a Goldilocks sort of day. Some days, she felt guilty being unemployed, felt she should look for work and do something useful. But she wasn't bored and on a day like this, the idea of working again seemed ludicrous. Josh didn't question it and since he had technically retired, he seemed to approve. Still, given that she and Josh were throwing themselves into a new business, *retired* seemed an inappropriate term.

As the tavern came into view, she felt a sudden shadow cross her vision. Armed with the knowledge of the colorful history of the place, it looked a little more ominous and less welcoming. She wondered what Willow would make of the place and decided to have lunch with her soon. They could swing by the tavern and get her read on the building. It seemed odd to even consider the idea and Josh would certainly mock it, but he didn't know Willow the way Kiera did.

Yes, she was weird and new-agey with her crystals and tarot cards, but Willow had an uncanny knack of knowing things and foreseeing events and judging people with prescient accuracy. Josh usually countered these assertions with, "if she's so damned prescient, why isn't she playing the market and making scads of money?" to which Willow would reply, "How do you know I'm not?"

She wasn't and to Josh, that signaled a case closed. He had even bugged Willow for market tips to which Willow would reply, "You're mocking me Joshua. Not nice." And it was true, he was, one of his less attractive traits. It was ironic the old guy had told Josh the tavern was haunted. Maybe Fitzsimmons had been mocking him.

The site was an exercise in mayhem. A large truck was pulling one of the dumpsters onto its bed with a loud screech of metal. An air compressor was running and there was all manner of hammering and banging from within. They had ripped most of the old windows out and dust floated from the openings in a thick cloud from the first floor. Kiera donned a mask and earplugs and walked about in a quick survey. The basement was mostly cleared. Upstairs, they had removed the paneling from every corner of the bar and a crew was sandblasting the varnish from the bar, the back bar, and the floors, a loud and messy job that required hazmat suits for the crew. Still, she knew it was much quicker than stripping all that wood.

She made her way up the stairway, knowing Josh was working up there. The second-floor apartment had been fully gutted, and Josh was pulling wires up through the center wall. He smiled when he saw her. He walked over, pulled his mask down and gave her a kiss.

"Come to help?"

"Yeah, right. You got time for a quick bite?" She held the cooler up. "I have some cool stuff to show you."

"Sure, over here." He had a workbench set up, covered with electrical schematics. He shoved them aside and took the cooler, setting it on the table. Kiera pulled a sandwich and a beer from it and handed them to Josh, then grabbed her sandwich, a glass, and a bottle of chardonnay for herself. She laid the folder in the center of the table.

"What's that?" Josh said. "Great sandwich, by the way."

"You're going to love this. You won't believe what I found."

She laid out the articles and the photos and let Josh peruse them, then poured a glass of wine.

After a moment, Josh said, "Holy shit!" through a mouthful. He had focused on the gangland killings. "This is awesome!"

"I thought you'd like it. I'll have these blown up and framed. They'll look so cool in the bar. Did you know any of this? Did the old guy say anything?"

"Nope, nothing beyond the haunting nonsense."

"I think that's odd. He must've known."

"Explains this though." He showed Kiera a coffee can lid that had been nailed to the floor. Beneath it were two splintered gaps that could be bullet holes.

"Wow, this place has some real history. Maybe the ghosts are real too."

"Yeah right."

"I was thinking of having Willow over, see what her read on the place is."

"Are you serious? I know she's your BFF but she's weird. Of course she'll think the place is haunted." He rolled his eyes. "Gonna throw a Ouija party?"

Kiera slapped his arm. "Don't be an ass, and no, no Ouija party."

He pulled her in and kissed her cheek, smelling of beer. "Sorry babe."

They ate their sandwiches, sipped at their drinks, and leafed through the articles and photos. Kiera envisioned an entire wall of this stuff, plus it would help with promotion once they were open. While they weren't yet married, she had invested in the project and Josh had made it clear he considered her a full partner and was receptive to her suggestions. She was certain of one thing, *The Haunted Tavern* was out. They needed something much more colorful, in keeping with all this history.

"So what about *Quinlan's Tavern*? It's good name, it's historical, and it sounds authentic."

"I don't know. Let me think on it," Josh said. "I better get back to work."

Kiera nodded and gathered up the picnic. "Dinner at my place tonight?"

"Yeah." He smiled a crooked grin, a hint of a leer.

"Good. Plan on staying over."

"Yes, ma'am."

Five

Josh spent much of the afternoon drilling through studs and pulling wires to power lights, outlets, and appliances in the apartment. Mostly an open plan design, the kitchen, an island, and a dining area would be situated adjacent to the upper landing. The bathroom and bedroom would be to the left at the back of the unit, the living room and an office nook to the right on the street end of the building.

It was engrossing work that he often got lost in—checking the plans, drilling holes, pulling wire, nailing everything in place with wire staples. Hours passed, scarcely noticed. At five, his phone alarm signaled time to quit. Kiera had dinner planned for six. He was mostly done with the rough-in. A little work in the morning and he would be ready for the electrical inspector at noon.

He heard somebody coming up the stairs. Bill, the demolition foreman, trudged the last few steps and leaned on the railing at the top of the staircase. Working in the basement, he was huffing from the two-story climb and smeared with dirt.

"Yo, Josh. You gotta come down and see this." His stony expression was unreadable.

"What?"

"Best see for yourself."

Josh bounded down the stairs as Bill walked a lazy pace behind him. When he reached the basement, the change surprised him, even from this morning. The rest of the junk was gone, hauled out and tossed in the dumpster outside. The old furnace had been dismantled and scrapped. The concrete floor and stone walls had been power-washed. Industrial fans were drying everything out. A group of guys stood in the far left corner, beneath a cloud of cigarette smoke.

"So what's up?"

Bill caught up and passed him, pushing to the center of the group.

"This." He pointed down to a metal panel set in the floor. It was steel, or more likely, cast iron, rusted but in decent condition after the power-wash. Four oblong holes that looked like handholds were set in each corner. There were no other marks or foundry stamps in the metal.

"You open it?"

"We can't—"

"What?"

"We've tried pry bars, two guys on each corner, it won't budge."

As if he doubted such a thing was possible, Josh leaned over, grabbed the nearest handhold and pulled. It didn't budge. "Holy shit! Rusted shut?"

"I don't think so. I mean it could be, but we haven't been able to break the seal."

"Maybe it's just a sewer lateral. Might be best to leave it be for now."

"You're not curious?" Bill said. "There are some stories about this place, ghosts and stuff."

Josh wondered if he was the only person who *hadn't* heard the stories. "No. Let's leave it for now."

"You're the boss."

Did he just roll his eyes?

He decided to let it go. No reason to argue it, and he *was* the boss.

⋆ ⋆ ⋆

Josh pulled into Kiera's driveway just after six. Typical of newer homes, a three-car garage dominated the right side of the house, a gable crowned the left end, bookends to a covered entryway and porch edged by a white picket railing. The exterior was tan steel siding with brick accents, the yard thick with twenty-year-old trees—Colorado blue spruces, oaks and maples—all about the same age as the subdivision. Beds of perennials and annuals—honeysuckle, wisteria, hostas, coneflowers, and magnolias—completed the tasteful landscaping around the house.

Kiera was sitting on the front porch, wine in hand. She stood and waved him in, looking hot in short cut-offs and a black tank top. Ghost ran to meet him.

He kissed her cheek. "You look hot, babe."

She scooted away from his groping hand and herded him through the door.

"Just in time, buddy, dinner's ready," she said, closing the door behind him.

"Smells great." The air was redolent with roasted garlic, rosemary, and fresh bread.

The house walls were painted mostly in mid to dark earth tones—tans, olives, and browns. She seemed almost pathologically allergic to white; there was no white anywhere in the house. The furniture was classic oak of excellent quality, what younger people referred to as big brown furniture.

She had laid out dinner on the island. Under the candlelight, the plates and dark green granite countertop looked quite elegant. The meal smelled fabulous: pork roast, asparagus, oven-roasted potatoes, and dinner rolls. The woman was a superb cook. There was wine, of course, a spicy Catena malbec. Ghost sat staring at them, a not-so-subtle attempt to beg, until Kiera told him to lie down.

Kiera said, "So how'd it go this afternoon?"

"Great! I'm just about ready for the inspector." Josh stabbed a potato. "Basement's done. The guys found a manhole or something in the basement floor."

"What's under it?"

"Don't know. We couldn't get it open."

In a spooky voice, eyes wide, Kiera said, "It's where all the ghosts are hiding."

"Yeah, right."

"Speaking of ghosts, Willow's coming over tomorrow. Mind if we stop by?"

Well that didn't take long.

"Seriously?"

"Yeah. If the place might be haunted, don't you want an expert opinion?"

"Willow is hardly an expert. She's a sweetheart, but she's no expert. There *are* no experts," he said with a sweeping gesture. "It's all pseudoscience and superstitious nonsense. I'm surprised that with your science background you give her so much credibility."

"If you knew Willow like I do, you'd understand."

She spoke quietly and looked defensive. Time to back off before he hurt her feelings.

"I know, she's the ghost whisperer. Sorry I'm such a skeptic."

Just then, Kiera's phone pinged. Kiera peeked, frowned, and tossed her phone further down the island in disgust. It slid and fell to the floor.

Josh stopped eating, trying to conceal his shock. Kiera wasn't given to fits of anger. "Problem?"

"Oh, just another one of my sister's guilt trips." Kiera appeared close to tears.

Now he understood. The sister was a nasty shrew, had been since Kiera's parents had died. "Want to talk about it?"

Kiera sat for a moment, regaining her composure. She took a sip of wine and closed her eyes for a moment.

"Not really, but the short version is this: she's complaining because I haven't been to see my niece and nephew in two months and, given how much I ignore her kids, it was probably just as well I never had any of my own."

"Jesus, that's horrible." Josh tried to stay calm. What he really wanted was to grab Kiera's phone and send a big *Fuck you!* to her sister. Kiera couldn't have kids. It wasn't a choice. She hadn't considered adoption because her ex-husband had been an ass about it, insisting he didn't want some reject kid. Josh knew how sensitive she was on the subject. Surely her sister did as well. "Somebody should drop a house on her."

Kiera smiled weakly. "I'd love to."

At a loss for anything better to say, he said, "Maybe Willow can do something."

"Says the guy who enjoys mocking her."

"All in good fun," Josh said. "Who knows, maybe she'll get lucky."

★　★　★

The next morning, Josh decided to start early, rolling out of bed at seven, grabbing a muffin at Mickey D's and arriving at the tavern before eight. The sandblasting crew was already hard at work, disturbing the quiet street. He hoped the neighbors didn't hate him by the time the job was done.

He checked on the crew sandblasting the main floor area. They were making great progress. The bar and back bar were nearly done and two guys had started on the floor. Two more days and they would wrap-up. Then a staining crew would stain everything and seal it with polyurethane. He was throwing a lot of money at this project, but the sooner he opened, the sooner the revenue stream kicked in. With any luck, he hoped to pay off the renovation loans within a year.

He grabbed his toolbox from his Tahoe and hiked up the stairs. He didn't like leaving his tools on site, especially with no windows to protect the place. Odd jobs remained in the bathroom before the inspector showed up to okay his rough-in. Two twenty-amp circuits to connect to GFIs in the box, a couple of kitchen circuits, and he would be ready. Pat Merrill, his electrician friend, would arrive just before the inspector. He set up his phone to play '90s alt-rock through a construction radio.

He pulled the last runs through the walls, two to the kitchen and two to the bathroom, and was nailing the last wire staple in place when he stopped, puzzled. Most of the walls had been plaster lathe. His crew had ripped all of it out and tossed it in the dumpster outside. One wall, between the kitchen and the bedroom, was wood—roughhewn one-by-sixes, probably the original partition.

There was a pattern burned into the raw wood facing the bathroom, like someone had branded symbols into the wood with a blowtorch. He didn't recall seeing them yesterday when he pulled the wire for the lights into the bathroom.

ᚠ ᚨ ᛜ ᚠ ᛈ   ᚠ ᚱ ᛁ ᚲ ᚨ ᚱ

He ran his fingers over it. What the hell?

It looked like writing, but it didn't. He snapped a quick pic with his phone and continued working. The inspector would arrive soon. The enigmatic symbols—whatever they were—left him feeling uneasy, why he didn't know. It wasn't there yesterday, he was almost certain of it. He might conclude Kiera, or someone else, was messing with him, but when would she have had time? Willow was coming today. She would have some ominous interpretation of the symbols, he felt certain.

Pat Merrill and the inspector both arrived ten minutes late, both in a hurry. The inspector found no fault with Josh's work. Josh then called the drywall foreman to confirm they were ready to start in the morning.

With that, he donned a hard hat, goggles, and a mask and started pulling wire into the main floor, along the walls, behind the bar, and up through the joists for the lighting. He couldn't stop thinking about those symbols. Grudgingly, he dumped his safety gear by the door and trudged up the stairs. He grabbed his laptop and performed an image search, but the results were puzzling. They suggested the symbols were runes, specifically *Elder Futhark*, whatever that meant.

A Google search provided a Wikipedia definition: *The oldest form of the runic alphabets, a writing system used by Germanic tribes. Runic inscriptions are found on artifacts, including jewelry, amulets, tools, weapons, and runestones, from the 2nd to the 8th centuries.*

Uh huh. Now he was certain someone was messing with him. One of the guys on the demo crew maybe? There were enough blowtorches on site. He turned to the stairs, deciding to ignore the prank rather than make a big deal out of it. The message probably said, *ha ha fuck you* in runic or whatever.

But his laugh was hollow. The symbols or runes didn't feel like a prank.

They looked ominous; they reminded him of a horror story he read as a kid.

The story didn't end well.

Six

Kiera lay in bed, trying to sleep, as Ghost tried to nudge her out of bed. It was nine a.m. After tossing and turning, trying to shoo Ghost back down onto the floor, she gave up and slid out of bed. She had a vague memory of a dream, a tornado bearing down on her, a monster, and she couldn't get out of the way and the Death tarot card went flying by and Ghost snatched it out of the air. Weird.

She had an hour before Willow arrived, though she would likely be late. Willow's concept of time was fuzzy at best. Kiera took a long hot shower, dried her hair, and looked in the fridge for breakfast. Casting a wary eye at the yogurt, she grabbed the eggs, bacon, and an English muffin instead and threw a sandwich together. She needed a new morning routine.

Willow arrived thirty minutes late. Wearing a bright sundress and a floppy hat, she looked stunning in a way Kiera never would. Her wavy blonde hair and dewy complexion were perfect.

"Willow!"

"Kiera!"

Willow threw her arms out, grabbed her, and gave her a vaguely indecent hug. Kiera had long wondered whether Willow's door secretly swung both ways, but considered it a *don't ask, don't tell* situation. Willow had never actually come on to her, so it was probably nothing. A decidedly touchy-feely type, though.

"You look great!" Willow gushed.

"You too, sweetie. Love that dress." It was a routine they replayed every time they met. "Glass of chard?"

"Please. Let's catch up and then I want to visit this haunted tavern your hubby bought."

"He's not my hubby."

"Might as well be. You two are joined at the hip."

Nope. Not for a while yet. She wasn't ready to remarry. Her ex had been verbally abusive and even though Josh was the polar opposite, she wasn't ready to commit again. Josh seemed in no hurry either.

They sat on the patio, sipped their wine, and shared the minutiae of the past few weeks. Then Willow pulled out her Tarot deck and plopped them down. "Time for your reading."

Oh yay. This part of the routine she could do without. She found tarot readings silly and mildly dramatic but humored Willow to be a good friend.

After shuffling, Willow spread the cards and Kiera drew six of them and Willow then laid them in a straight line down, a universal six-card spread.

Willow turned the top card: *The Devil.* Willow frowned. "You drew the same card the other day."

"What does that mean?"

"You're feeling the temptation of a certain relationship, pastime or other form of pleasure. It might be hard to resist. Question your motives. These sorts of situations aren't usually good news."

Kiera discreetly rolled her eyes. Willow could be so dramatic. She turned the next card: *Strength.*

"That sounds good."

Willow considered, then said, "What you need most is to find the strength and willpower to see you through and achieve what you want. Put your fears to rest and develop a positive attitude and you will persevere."

Kiera nodded. *Uh huh.* Pretty generic, like a horoscope.

Willow turned the third card: *The Chariot.* "This is good. You're worried things are more of a struggle than you expect. Just relax, calm that mind of yours and you'll find the strength to battle on until you succeed."

"I'm not sure being in a battle sounds all that great."

"Shh. Relax. Calm your mind."

Kiera stifled an urge to roll her eyes. Shush? Really?

The next card, *The Hierophant,* looked like a bishop sitting in a chair. "What's that mean?" Kiera asked.

"That's good too. You will receive counsel and honest advice from a wise teacher, priest, or parent—oh shit, I'm sorry Kiera—anyway, someone you have a lot of respect for."

Kiera ignored the reference to her parents but found her words unsettling anyway. While she loved and respected Willow and knew there was more to her psychic abilities than Josh imagined, she considered tarot mere entertainment on par with astrology. There was no good reason to feel uneasy about the reading, but she did.

Willow pointed to the fifth card, *The Fool.* That didn't look good either. She said, "This is about the negative things in your life and the answer is simple: beware of impetuous and impulsive decisions. They may cost you dearly."

Kiera looked down as Willow turned the last card. "Oh great."
Death.

"It's not as bad as it looks. Just relax." Willow rubbed Kiera's fore-arm in reassurance. "This indicates change in your life—"

"Yeah, death's a pretty big change."

"Stop that! It means you may face some turbulence in your life, leaving room for a better future."

"What turbulence?"

"It doesn't tell me that. It's more about embracing life and living every day as though it were your last."

"Yeah, that's reassuring." Willow was fudging her answer to this card, and she was further disturbed by Willow's half-hearted and insincere explanation.

Kiera gripped the edge of the table and pushed back. "That's enough. Let's go to the tavern and then lunch at The Vinery, okay?"

They took Kiera's RAV4 and drove to the bar, gabbing nonstop.

The tavern remained a hive of activity. A compressor was running in the parking lot and dust wafted from the window openings on the first floor. The plumbers had arrived and were hauling lengths of PVC pipe into the basement. The heating and cooling guys had also started and were unpacking what looked like parts of a new furnace in the parking lot. Somewhere inside, Josh was toiling away. It amazed Kiera that all these people weren't tripping over each other.

"What do you think?" Kiera turned to Willow and was struck by her expression: her mouth agape, eyes wide, rigid as if in a trance. "Willow, are you okay?"

When she didn't speak, Kiera touched her shoulder. "Willow?"

Willow jumped, startled. "Whoa." She put a hand to her neck.

"Are you okay?"

Her face was ashen, her lower lip trembling slightly. "No. I'm not. I can't go in there."

Kiera wanted to say 'not funny, Willow' but it was clear she wasn't joking. "What's the matter?"

"I'm not sure. I feel something...I don't know how to describe it. Something's off about this place."

"Power of suggestion, maybe? Just because I said something?"

Willow looked stricken. "Screw you, Kiera."

Now Kiera felt bad. It was the wrong thing to say even if it might be true. Willow took her abilities seriously and was mocked enough as it was. It was the first time Kiera had seriously questioned her. "I'm sorry. I shouldn't have said that." She touched her hand. "I thought maybe you were being dramatic because of the supposed haunting stuff."

Still pale, shoulders rigid, Willow said, "It may be haunted, Kiera, I don't really know. There's something wrong with this place that has nothing to do with ghosts. I can't explain it. I can't even describe it."

"So you won't go in?"

"I don't know. Let me walk around it first."

Her demeanor was unnerving. Willow had never acted like this before. She was prone to dramatics, just a facet of her ebullient style. Not this creepy, spooked and frightened affect.

Willow pushed on the car door and slipped out, never taking her eyes off the tavern. She walked along the right side of the building, then backtracked, and inched along the other side to the back parking lot. Head up and tilted inquisitively, Willow acted like she was trying to receive a wave or listening for an answer from above—a wary curiosity. She stepped slowly back around to the front, approached the door and stood for a moment before reaching out to touch the brick wall.

Her fingers grazed the brick lightly, then Willow yanked her hand away and recoiled as if the wall were hot coals. Her feet tangled and she fell onto the grass in a graceless heap. Kiera ran over and pulled her to her feet. "You okay?"

"No. Let's go."

"Still want lunch?" Kiera stared at Willow, but couldn't tell if she was being dramatic or felt truly disturbed.

"Yeah. I need a glass of wine. And a shot."

"Are you going to tell me what's up?"

"Not yet. Give me a few minutes." Willow stared into space, expressionless.

They drove in silence to The Vinery, a lovely wine and small plate bar that had just opened on Fond du Lac Avenue. Standing in the middle of a strip mall, it was flanked by a dry cleaner and a Dollar Store. Stepping inside was like entering a different world. A large aquarium filled with exotic fish dominated the right wall lined with high tables. The left booth-lined wall was adorned with vines and plants, some plastic, some real. An enclosed glass wine cellar took up most of the back wall, just behind a small tasting bar. It was dark and intriguing and Kiera loved it.

The waitress seated them at a booth and took their drink order: two glasses of chardonnay and a shot of Jack.

Kiera waited for her friend to say something, anything. Her eyes looked glazed, her expression indeterminate.

A moment later, the waitress brought their drink order and watched Willow down the Jack with one swallow.

"You go, girl," the waitress said. "Will you ladies be ordering food?"

"Yes, but give us five or ten yet, please."

As the waitress walked away, Willow said, "It's a *thin place*, I think."

"What?" Kiera was beginning to think Willow had lost it; the bar wasn't especially narrow. "A thin place?"

"It's hard to explain." She paused. "It's a place where the distance between heaven and Earth is narrower...I've seen them described as places in the world where the walls"—she gestured with finger quotes—"are weak, where another dimension seems nearer than usual. They can be religious spots, like the Blue Mosque in Istanbul, but they needn't be. One list I saw included Hong Kong airport and a hole-in-the-wall Tokyo bar. The origin of the idea is Irish."

"Never heard of it. And if it was the meeting of heaven and earth—"

"It wasn't. It was more like earth and hell, I don't know. I still can't explain it. The concept of thin places is spiritual. The feeling I had was dark."

Kiera no longer knew what to think. She had thought of taking Willow to the bar as something of a lark. While she trusted Willow and understood her psychic sense, this reaction was beyond the pale. It almost sounded like lunacy. What would she tell Josh?

She decided she wouldn't tell Josh anything. He would think Willow had slipped off the edge. She wasn't sure she wouldn't agree. The ramblings about heaven and hell and thin places sounded unhinged. On the other hand, maybe she should try to keep an open mind. Research the concept. See if there was some basis for her ideas.

Looking wounded, Willow said, "You think I'm nuts."

It was hard to deny. Any attempt to lie and Willow would sense her insincerity. "I don't understand what you're talking about. I'm sorry, it sounds a little crazy. Explain it to me. Help me understand."

"I don't know if I can." Willow stared off into space, then looked at Kiera. "Have you ever done acid?"

"No. You know I haven't. I figured my chardonnay habit was enough."

"Too bad. It's kind of like that. The thin place, it heightens your senses. You feel more aware—more strongly connected to the universe. As I said, it's usually very spiritual...and illuminating. It's like, uh, a wormhole or something."

"Sounds spooky." Kiera still felt clueless.

"It shouldn't be, but it was today. It was almost like there were two doors, one going up and one going down."

"Can that happen?" Silly question, Kiera decided, given the subject.

"I don't know. I've never heard of it."

"That doesn't sound good."

Willow looked her in the eye. "I don't think it is."

Seven

Kiera stood atop the bar, looking down at the array of black and white photos and old newspaper clippings laid out on the floor, enlarged and framed in oak. From the *Gangland Killing* headline to the earlier stories about Quinlan's Tavern, they were interesting, edgy stories that would give the tavern a cool atmosphere. The display would fill the side wall opposite the bar. With the paneling gone and the plaster restored with a creamy beige paint, she had a stylish period backdrop for her display.

The past few weeks had seen a blizzard of activity. A crew had stained the bar and back bar with a classic oak tint, the floors with a deeper provincial brown—all finished with a thick coating of polyurethane. The walls were finished and painted. Two installers were pulling lines from the basement cooler for the draft beer system. The heating and cooling crew was wrapping up the furnace and air-conditioning systems. Two women were finishing the installation of the ovens and fryers. The windows had been installed and the outdoor sign was going up this week. A Milwaukee TV station was working up a story on the renovation. Neighbors had dropped in and seemed pleased the old building was getting a makeover.

Satisfied with the arrangement, she measured and placed hangers for the frames, mounting and leveling the display as she moved across the wall. She stood back and admired her handiwork. It looked awesome. Josh would love it.

Last wall, finished. Earlier, she had also arranged a small grouping of her storm photographs and a ghost display featuring the stories about the Quinlan children.

She looked at her phone. Almost six o'clock. Time for dinner. She decided to surprise Josh with some takeout from Artesana, a tapas bar that had opened a few months ago.

★ ★ ★

Josh screwed the cover onto the last outlet in the kitchen as Kiera walked in with food. Sweet! He was famished and it smelled great. Ghost came bounding up the stairs behind her, nose in the air, keenly interested in the bag she was holding.

Kiera said, "Tapas. Ready for a break?"

"I'm done. Just need the final inspection," Josh said. Ghost trotted over, snuffling around for affection. Josh scratched under his jaw. "Hey buddy."

"So what's the plan tomorrow?" Kiera set the bag on the kitchen island.

"Inspector will be here at eight. The appliances are coming mid-afternoon. We need to go out furniture shopping to finish the place up," Josh said.

"Day after okay?"

"What are you doing tomorrow?"

"I'm watching a system coming in tomorrow afternoon. Northwestern Illinois looks good so I'm heading home after dinner." Kiera said. "Did you check out the decor downstairs?"

"No, sorry. Let's eat, then I'll walk you down and take a look," Josh said. He pulled a bottle of chardonnay from a cooler and poured some into two plastic cups on the quartz countertop.

"Oh man, I have to do something about this." She scowled at the plastic cup. "I'll bring some glasses and dishes tomorrow."

Kiera laid out the plates: Spanish pork ribs, crab with Manchego cheese, roasted Brussels sprouts, potatoes with aioli, and lamb chops. Ravenously hungry, they ate in silence.

Josh scanned the apartment as he ate. It was nearly complete. The drywallers had come and gone and a crew had painted the walls. The kitchen floor was dark red ceramic, the remainder of the apartment carpeted with a soft plush mid-brown carpeting. Other than the stools they sat on, there was no furniture. Another chore yet to be handled.

Josh wiped his hands with a paper towel, gathered up the containers, bags, and plates and tossed them out the window into the dumpster.

"Shall we?"

Kiera nodded. "Yep, I've got to get going. Sure you don't want to blow off a day and come with? Looks like a good day."

"Wish I could. Too much going on here and I prefer to meet with the inspector personally in case he finds a problem."

They ambled down the stairs with Ghost leading the way. Josh turned into the bar area and stopped, stunned. Kiera had hung the framed articles and photos in an eye-catching display that dominated the wall. Ceiling spots illuminated the art, and wood letters above spelled out *Quinlan's Tavern*. Kiera had a knack for decorating, but the display was exceptional, even for her. It was exciting too—the end now in sight, the culmination of his dreams.

"Awesome, Kiera! Wow, it looks perfect."

"Thanks sweetie," Kiera said, then smiled, looking self-conscious. "You know me, I never do anything half-assed."

"I love your ass, you know that."

"Now, now, little piggy." Kiera stepped over and wrapped her arms around him. "I know you have to work late. I'm probably chasing tomorrow, but we need to get together one of these nights and mess around."

"No argument here," Josh said, though he had been hoping it would be tonight. Oh well. "Day after tomorrow? Furniture shopping, dinner, and sex, okay?"

"Done." She kissed him again and sashayed out the door with Ghost in tow.

Josh admired her receding figure, smiled, and headed down into the basement and the electrical box for the apartment next to the service for the bar. The basement was light-years from the awful mess he inherited when he bought the place. Since he negotiated a great price on the bar and property, he considered the basement cleanup a small price to pay.

A cinder-block room, the main cooler, dominated the center of the room. The heating and cooling gear sat off to the right, the electric panels mounted on the wall just beyond the stairwell. He opened the apartment panel and flipped the remaining breakers to ON, pleased that none of them tripped off, indicating a problem.

He walked upstairs, poured himself a glass of wine and walked around the kitchen, checking the outlets with a meter, checking the grounding, and tripping the GFIs with a ground fault. Everything worked perfectly. He spent another hour packing up his tools, sweeping the floors of wire clippings, knockouts, and strips of wire insulation.

It was unbelievable they had gotten this far in just under a month. He could have used fewer contractors, but finishing quickly would get the doors open sooner and put paying customers at the bar and in the booths. They planned to open before July Fourth, and it looked like they would make it. Get the place established before Fall and he felt certain they would have it made.

He heard a deep metallic clang but couldn't tell if it came from the basement or outside. Josh looked at his phone. Eleven o'clock. Time to head home. He walked down to the basement and switched the power to the apartment off as a precaution. As he turned to leave, a dark shadow in the far corner caught his eye.

He stopped and stared in shock. "What the hell?"

The cast iron hatch or sewer cover was leaning against the wall! Sealed shut when they found it, no one had been able to open it, even with pry bars. Yet, there it stood, the hole in the floor wide open.

A shudder ran down his spine. He scanned the basement, suddenly hyper vigilant. Had someone tried to break in? Josh stepped back and flicked on the rest of the basement lights.

The room appeared to be empty but there were nooks and crannies in the walls, a couple of workbenches, and two cabinets for supplies.

"Hey! Anyone in here?"

The faint sound of traffic outdoors and a slight hum from the cooler fans were the only sounds. He grabbed a flashlight and a heavy box wrench from the toolbox near the stairs.

He walked to the workbenches, flashing the light beneath them, then inched to the cabinets, stopped and listened. Not a peep, a shuffle—

nothing. Standing in front of the first cabinet, he yanked the door open, stepped back, and held the wrench up.

Sighed. Empty.

Same with the next cabinet.

He walked a slow circuit around the basement, easing up to the deep nook where the water line came in. Nothing.

Only the cooler remained. He listened for a moment, flipped the heavy handle and yanked the door open. Quick flash of the light. Zip.

Finding nothing amiss in the dark corners of the basement, he wondered, was someone messing with him? Trying to break-in? Had he interrupted them? But that made little sense. Why open the floor hatch?

Unless they came in that way.

Josh crept to the opening and peered down into the hole with the light, surprised to find the walls of the shaft were rough stone and not concrete like the basement floor. Perhaps twelve feet deep, someone had carved vertical stone steps into one wall of the rock. There were no rungs, but grooves were chiseled into the top edge of each step. Hand grips probably. The iron hatch had rested on a finely chiseled ledge in the concrete floor. What held it in place? It seemed strange. He'd assumed it was a sewer lateral. Now he wasn't so sure.

"Hello?"

A faint echo returned a moment later.

He stepped over to the hatch and tried to move it. He grunted with the effort and had barely budged it. Jesus! It had to weigh two or three hundred pounds. Who the hell had moved it? *How* had they moved it? And why?

He couldn't safely move it by himself, that much was certain. He thought about calling the police, but what would he tell them? The basement was empty. Whoever opened it was gone.

Or were they? He wasn't sure. Could they be hiding down in the hole? He couldn't just leave things. What if they emerged and vandalized the place? Or started a fire? He knew he should go down and check but he was exhausted, tended toward claustrophobic, and felt nervous about exploring it without a weapon.

He mentally checked a list of friends who might still be awake and decided to text Kiera: *You up?*

A moment later: *Yep. Going to bed soon. What you need?*

He phoned her and quickly explained the situation.

"Holy shit! What are you going to do?" Kiera said.

"I can't leave here until morning when I'll have some help," Josh said. "I hate to ask but would you bring me a bedroll, a pillow, and your Kimber? I'll sleep in the bar and keep an eye on the place."

"Sure babe. I'll be there in ten."

Josh left the lights on as a deterrent, locked the basement door and waited at the bar for Kiera. He was a heavy sleeper. He just hoped that if anyone started trouble in the basement, he would hear it and be able to react. Call the cops. Kiera's Kimber Micro 9 was a sweet, deadly little gun, but he prayed he wouldn't need it. The situation left him nervous, angry, and puzzled. It was inexplicable. If it was a joke, someone would get their ass kicked.

There was a light tap at the front door a few minutes later. Kiera handed him a bedroll, two pillows, and the Kimber with two spare clips.

"So what's down there?" she asked.

"I didn't look."

"Really?" Kiera threw him a quizzical look. "Then we're checking it out tomorrow—if I get back early enough. Be safe, babe. Got to run."

She gave him a peck on the lips and dashed back to the car in her pajamas.

After a walk around the exterior of the tavern and then the first floor, Josh unrolled the sleeping bag and settled in, his phone and the Kimber within easy reach.

Moments later, he was asleep.

Eight

Lachlan Hayward stood on the sidewalk and admired the brick Victorian two-story with the corner turret. His old friend, Kenric Shepherd, had always possessed an impeccable sense of taste and the house was no exception. He strolled up the front walk, absorbing the energies from the old structure, still detecting a hint of his friend, even now, a year after his death.

At the ornate period oak door, he stopped and eyed the black keypad suspiciously.

Technology. Lachlan had little use for it. Kenric had gone full-on with technology, trying to become some sort of new-age tech visionary, striving perhaps to relinquish his past. Lachlan considered himself more of an old dog with little need for new tricks. The old ways still served him well and he saw no reason to change.

Ironic that Kenric should die in some collision with his old life. The details of his death were sparse and had left the *Aeldo*—The Elders— shocked and disheartened by the loss of a man they considered the greatest sorcerer who ever lived. Kenric had sent an enigmatic message three days before he died, that he was on the trail of some unnamed foe.

Then came word that he had been killed in an explosion in the States. No one could imagine why he was there or who he was pursuing. Perhaps now they never would know.

Lachlan referred to his mobile phone, one of the few concessions he made to technology for sheer convenience. Their ubiquity and practicality amazed him. A thousand years ago, possession of such a device would have led to a brief trial and death by fire. Occasionally, they dispensed with the trial.

The code, given to him by the attorney, was 7774. He recognized the numbers as Kenric's birthday: July of 774.

The lock clicked. Lachlan turned the handle and stepped into the foyer. A dining area lay to the left, a sitting room to the right. He was struck by the exquisite decor, pieces of museum quality that Kenric had somehow held onto over the years. Victoriana and equally impressive Tudor pieces, all brilliantly situated in a harmonious arrangement with a positive Qi any practitioner of Feng Shui would appreciate. It just felt right. Peaceful.

Some pieces were much older. Figurines from Neolithic Europe. Ancient Roman Pottery. Greek artifacts. The house was a veritable museum, a house that now belonged to him. Kenric had named Lachlan as sole beneficiary of the estate: the house and furnishings, a small property in North London, and several bank accounts, including a numbered account in Switzerland.

He had been here almost a year ago to sign probate papers, transfer the mortgage, and arrange to maintain the utilities until he could take possession of the house, but hadn't been allowed inside at the time. Surprisingly, there was little evidence anyone had been in the home since, even though Lachlan knew the FBI and ATF had gone through the building with exquisite precision. Lachlan assumed they had taken it apart and put it together again in an attempt to determine Kenric's involvement in the explosion at the MacKenzie house. That it was so neat now suggested they wanted to conceal the target of their search.

With a discerning eye, he noticed amulets placed discreetly around the first floor. For all his talk about relinquishing the old ways, Kenric had still practiced them religiously, it seemed. He wondered what the authorities had made of them.

Lachlan stood and absorbed the energies within the house. There was little on the first floor; evidently Kenric had spent little time there. He sensed more energy above and below.

Lachlan climbed the stairs with vigor for a man his age—his fitness a matter of some pride and more than a little magic. He stopped at the top landing with a start at the mess that greeted him.

The upstairs had been remodeled into one large room with a loo in the corner and a cot where Kenric had evidently slept. So Spartan, so typical of the man. It was here, Lachlan assumed, that Kenric had performed his *modern alchemy,* as he liked to call it.

The room had been professionally ransacked, the agents very thorough in their work. Lachlan assumed three or four desktop computers must have once sat on the plywood sheets supported by sawhorses arrayed along one wall. They were gone. All that remained were scattered cords, dangling power cables, and dark monitors which evidently weren't needed. So much for a careful, discreet search.

The nearby oak desk had been thoroughly searched as well, the drawers left open and mostly emptied other than stationery and office supplies. Lachlan also found a few academic articles, papers, and class outlines—items that hadn't interested the FBI apparently. On the opposite wall, his eyes fell upon a keyboard and a large monitor on a small table. The computer tower was gone. An empty wine glass and a dinner plate suggested it was the last place Kenric had worked. To the right of the table, a thick ream of computer paper lay on the floor, a printout titled: *MB Translation.*

He sat and reached for it. Flipping through the pages, he was confused by what he saw. Each left-hand page appeared to be hand-written Old English script. The right-hand page looked like a translation into modern English. If this was the last thing Kenric worked on, Lachlan wanted to know what was in it.

After checking the remainder of the room, he carried the manuscript downstairs and laid it on a table in the sitting room, then continued down into the basement. Something there called to him, tugged at the sorcerer in his heart like an invisible but tangible tether. Some facet of the old ways, perhaps the scent of some medicament, or the lure of a talisman.

Clearly, Kenric hadn't fully relinquished his past. The workshop he found in the cellar felt familiar, comfortable. The powders, tinctures, and preparations, the casting equipment, the collection of amulets and talismans—these were the tools of his trade. He wondered what the authorities made of this; these things would have made little sense to them. He also noted the FBI had paid little attention to Kenric's many rare and priceless antiquities. Probably had no clue what they were.

On the workbench sat the plaster remnants of a casting, possibly the last piece Kenric made. It was a piece he hadn't seen in three hundred years, a piece that might be mistaken for a fertility figurine, though it was nothing of the sort. It resonated with the core of the Goddess, the life-giving Earth beneath his feet. She had no other name long ago. Some people now called her Gaia and sadly, most now took her for granted and defiled her with abandon.

It was a powerful talisman. That Kenric felt compelled to resort to such a deeply symbolic figure, a figure usually reserved for the most dangerous and desperate of confrontations, spoke volumes. Why had Kenric needed it? A mystery was emerging here, a mystery Lachlan felt compelled to solve.

Lachlan selected a bottle of fine sherry from the sideboard and settled into an exquisitely comfortable Edwardian armchair. He sipped his sherry and reached for the manuscript. Intrigued, he soon slipped into a routine, reading the modern English translation and ignoring the Old English. If he wanted the full texture and nuance of the original, he could reread it later.

He soon realized it was a *grimoire*, a book of spells and invocations, written in the Mercian dialect by someone with considerable skill in the dark arts. Her skill seemed to advance to a dangerous degree after the halfway point. Then the tone of the text became clear.

Boastful. Belligerent. Smug. Repellent.

A malignant narcissist on steroids.

He read for hours. He had nothing but time.

Much later, Lachlan finished. It was dark. He looked at his watch. Two in the morning!

The last three pages made his hair stand on end. Lachlan read them over and over, then compared the original with Kenric's translation, which was virtually identical. Something about this situation clicked in his memory, a vague impression. It had been a long time ago, hundreds of years in the past.

In the text, a woman—the author of the book—had been buried alive by her husband. Before she died, in her final act, she had cast a dangerous invocation on the husband and his family though oddly, she didn't mention the family by name.

A gruesome story. It could be meaningless nonsense, the ramblings of a psychotic woman who fancied herself a witch, though it was curious that Kenric had translated the book to the last page. He must have given it some credence. Still, what did it matter? This had taken place four or five hundred years ago in England, that much was clear from the narrative.

Was this related to Kenric's death? How? It seemed ridiculous, improbable. Especially in Milwaukee, of all places. Something was missing and Lachlan had no idea what it was. Regardless, this book in Old English, this translation, felt like an important clue.

There was a dark mystery here, the pieces of which would hopefully answer one compelling question: what happened here in Wisconsin? What took the life of his dear friend, a man he considered invincible? What dark force had succeeded where all others failed?

Those unanswered questions sent a cold tremor down his spine.

Nine

Rachel Nash sat on her bed, sorting through her collection of Native American arrowheads and tools. Earbuds in, she was listening to Billie Eilish, humming along quietly to *Ocean Eyes*. She found her first arrowhead three years ago while kicking around a field just outside of town. When she showed it to her father and he explained what it was, she was hooked. She went online and researched arrowheads, intrigued to learn that she held a piece of history in her hand. That lead to an enduring fascination with Native American customs and history.

With forty-seven arrowheads, three shaping tools, half a dozen axe heads and various small stone tools, Rachel was proud of her collection and saw the finding and preserving of these pieces of Native American history as an act of respect. She knew the rules of collecting as well. None of the fields she searched showed any evidence of burials. Collecting on burial grounds was forbidden, and rightfully so.

She felt steps coming down the hall, approaching her room. The door opened a moment later and her mother stood there, holding a glass of wine. At two p.m., she was still wearing a bathrobe and hadn't bothered to brush her hair. She waved a hand at Rachel to remove her earbuds and set the glass on the dresser. Standing at the foot of the bed, her mother fixed an eye on Rachel and said, "I asked you to do the dishes an hour ago. Why are you still sitting here playing with those stupid rocks?"

"They're not stupid and I'll do the dishes in a little while, okay?" She exaggerated the *okay* with enough snark to annoy her mother.

"Don't take that tone with me. I'm getting a little tired of this angsty teen-girl mood you've been in for the past two years. You need to snap out of it." She slurred the last sentence.

"Yes mother," she said with subtle derision.

Her mother shook her head. "Just do the damn dishes. Now!"

As she turned to leave, she tangled her feet, lost her balance, and plopped onto the bed, sending the arrowheads and tools flying every which way.

Rachel didn't even try to temper the anger that exploded up and out of her. "Jesus Mom! Get out! Now! You're nothing but a drunk, an embarrassing drunk!"

"That's exactly the attitude I'm talking about." Her mother stood and pointed a forefinger. "No car for the rest of the summer, you little brat!"

She grabbed her wine and slammed the door on her way out.

Rachel flipped her middle finger at the door and said under her breath, "Bitch!"

Carefully gathering up the arrowheads and tools, making sure none had been damaged, she packed them lovingly into a tackle box. She grabbed her backpack and slipped out the window, hopped on her bike and barreled down the driveway toward the farm, trying to burn off her anger, deciding she could live without the damn car.

Ten

Willow couldn't sleep. Again.

The images she saw at the bar had haunted her since her visit and often appeared as soon as she lay down and closed her eyes at night. She lit candles and incense with soothing scents of lavender and chamomile, completed a thirty-minute yoga session, meditated. None of it was working. Tonight she might have to resort to something more conventional, like Xanax.

She had gone through her literature and surfed the internet, looking at every source on thin places she could find. Nothing she read quite hinted to her reaction at the bar, to the feelings she had, to the images she had seen—phantoms of shadows and darkness, cold and menacing, but surprisingly vague given her strong reaction to them. The images were nothing like her understanding of what these spiritual places might be like. They reminded her of scary dreams she'd had as a child when she was sick with a high fever, nightmares that sometimes persisted even after she awoke.

She focused on an article about the Irish Island, Skellig Michael. It most closely resembled her concept of a thin place:

Skellig Michael was one of the most obscure islands of the known world in the sixth century. Shrouded in darkness, it became a beacon to the world. From places like Skellig Michael, Celtic monks and missionaries carried the Gospel back to the mainland in Ireland and Scotland, and eventually to the European continent. Haunts like Skellig Michael are called 'thin places' by the Irish—not because the land is narrow but because the distance between this world and the next shrinks. A thin place is where the veil between this world and the next is lifted and it may be possible to get a glimpse of what life itself is all about.

They are often marked by human spirits that have gone before, felt the thinness and been changed by it. Thin places not only transcend the senses but transcend the boundaries of time and space. Time seems to stand still, and there is a communion with the human spirits that have walked there before and are yet to walk. All their lives, people walk through these places. Some notice the thinness. Some do not.

The concept seemed to be one of spirituality, that thin places were mystic or holy places. None of this came close to describing what Willow felt. The tavern seemed to be the polar opposite. She had a sense of darkness and danger, that the veil being lifted was the one between earth and hell. Truth be told, she felt lost and adrift. She sighed and reached for the bottle of Xanax and downed two with her tea. While she waited for sleep to come, she logged onto her paranormal forum and posted her question, asking whether anyone thought an opposite or mirror image to a thin place might exist.

If it did, what did it mean? It wasn't like a thin place was a trapdoor or quicksand to another dimension. Clearly, Kiera felt nothing there. So maybe it just *was*. It existed, but unless you were sensitive to its presence, it didn't matter, and didn't represent any danger to regular people like Kiera and Josh.

She wanted to stop worrying, but that wasn't in her nature. Her mother always said she worried more than she should. Perhaps the reason she dabbled in the paranormal and used crystals, scents, yoga, meditation and mindfulness was to control it. And also why she had a prescription for Xanax, useful when she couldn't manage her anxiety by other means.

Truth was, she couldn't possibly know if this place represented a real threat. If it did, what could she do about it? Would something like an exorcism work? She didn't know. First, she needed proof and some history to back her claim. Right now, she had nothing but feelings and intuition. Kiera didn't understand it and she'd given up trying to explain it.

Willow had to know more, even if the thought of returning to the tavern filled her with dread. She needed to satisfy her curiosity and make certain Kiera was safe there.

Even at this late hour, answers to her posted question trickled in. While no one had a definitive view on the subject, they all agreed such a thing was not only possible but likely a reality. The universe was filled with dualities and there was no reason to suspect that thin places would be any different.

Still, it was nothing but conjecture. Since thin places were spiritual places where people could feel closer to heaven and feel enlightenment, there was good reason to believe that some thin places might lead to darkness, fear, and death. They would be bad locations that brought out the worst in people. They might be cold and frightening and dangerous. It was all speculation. No one knew. No one had ever documented such a thing.

She would have to go back. It was the only and obvious answer to learning more about the place. Now that her Xanax had kicked in, it didn't seem like such a bad idea.

Maybe that was the trick. Take Xanax before her visit to take the edge off her nerves.

Would it be enough to calm her? What was the risk?

Willow didn't know.

She was going anyway.

Eleven

Josh awoke at seven to somebody pounding on the door. It took a moment to orient himself and remember why he was lying on the floor of the bar. Oh yeah. Some asshole was pranking him or casing the place for a break-in.

He jumped up, rolled his bag up quickly and tossed it behind the bar, then opened the door to let the kitchen contractors in. Soon the place was alive with the sounds of progress from the installers in the kitchen to the plumbers, hard at work in the bathrooms at the back of the building. A quick survey of the bar and the apartment above revealed no signs of an intruder.

Good. He didn't need any complications or vandalism at this point in the project, though he added an alarm system to the *to-do* list for the day. He hadn't considered neighborhood crime an issue, but it would be stupid to ignore it.

He enlisted Jeff, the plumbing crew chief, and two of his guys to assist in the basement. He described the events of the night before as they trudged down the stairs and pushed the lower door open. Josh reached out and flicked the lights on, still talking about sleeping on the floor of the bar.

Jeff interrupted, "Ah dude. About that iron cover—"

Josh turned and stopped dead, feeling his insides tense and turn cold. The hatch was back in place in the floor, looking every bit like it had never been moved. "What the hell is going on here?"

"Josh, what were you smoking last night?" Jeff asked with a smirk.

"Seriously, guys. It was open last night." But he could hardly blame them for thinking otherwise.

"Uh huh."

They stood in a circle around the hatch. Josh motioned at it, "Let's try lifting it then."

After several minutes of unsuccessful pulling, prying, grunting, and groaning, the three guys peeled off, saying they needed to get back to work, looking at Josh with barely concealed concern for his mental health.

Josh stood there, feeling foolish, doubting his senses—and yet, he knew someone had moved the hatch. The only explanation was that somebody was fucking with him, though if they were, this was Olympic-level fuckery. He should have snapped a couple pics last night so he didn't look like an idiot now.

He couldn't imagine how they'd done it. Glancing at the wall beyond the hole in the floor, he saw a faint, thin scratch in the concrete right where the hatch had rested against it the night before.

So he wasn't crazy.

Security cameras and an alarm system had just risen to the top of his *to-do* list.

After a last glance at the metal hatch, he turned, stopped and looked again. A series of faint scratches along one edge of the metal caught his eye. Except they weren't scratches, but more runes. The marks looked new and untarnished. *What the hell was going on here?*

ᛚᚨᚾᛞ ᚠᚱᛁᚷᛖᚱ

Josh pulled his phone from his pocket and checked them against the photo he took yesterday.

They were identical.

He had no clue what these symbols or runes were about, but he knew someone who would—Kiera. He took a photo of the symbols scratched on the hatch and sent both photos to her. Of course, it could be a prank and she might be part of it. Maybe he should play along and pretend to be freaked out, but Josh then decided he really didn't have time for games.

At that moment, he noticed a patina of dust covering the floor and work benches. Jesus! They had just cleaned the basement. Where had all the dirt come from? Grumbling, he swept the benches and the floor, grabbed his toolbox and walked up the stairs to the bar. Kiera called five minutes later.

Without preamble she said, "Where'd you find the runes?"

"On a wall in the apartment and scratched into the hatch in the basement. I figured you knew what they were. Did you have something to do with them?"

He half expected her to laugh, but she said, "No. I'm too busy right now to prank you. Seriously."

"So what does it say?"

"It's not really a sentence. It's a title that roughly translates to *Land Protector*. A title for a warrior, a king or a god."

"That's weird. So why would this inscription be here?"

"I don't know. Runes tend to come and go in fashion, and they're popular for tats. It's probably nothing."

"That's not the weirdest part of all this. The hatch was back in place this morning."

He heard an intake of breath. "Whoa. That's a little creepy."

She sounded genuinely surprised.

"You had nothing to do with it? You and Caleb?"

Caleb Grenier was his best friend, going back to his college days in Madison. Josh went on to law school and Caleb went into IT. Caleb now was an IT freelancer and worked only when he wanted. He did odd jobs as well, had helped Josh out with the electrical work one day, and had offered to tend bar if needed.

"No! I told you, I don't have time. You'll have to talk to Caleb yourself," Kiera said.

"So, how's it going there?"

"I'm getting a sunburn. Looks like a bust," Kiera said, sounding frustrated. "So what are you going to do about the pranks?"

"I don't know. I can't imagine how they're doing it. Maybe the old guy was right about the ghosts," Josh said.

"Are you serious?"

"No, but I felt a definite shiver down my spine when I saw that hatch back in the floor. If I didn't know better..." He chuckled. "Don't tell Willow I said that."

"I'm gonna—"

"Kiera!"

"Relax. I gotta go."

Josh looked at his phone for a minute and tapped on Caleb's contact. Caleb was a Class A prankster. They'd had a class in undergrad—Josh could no longer remember the course, but the professor had been as boring as shit and droned on while clicking through an equally tedious Power Point presentation. Caleb hacked into his computer and replaced some of the pages with photos of exotic dancers, centerfolds, and for the ladies, an explicit shot of a male stripper. It was a riot. The professor freaked out—the first sign of life they'd seen from him—and threatened them all with expulsion. He got over it eventually.

"Yo, dude," Caleb said. "How's the bar coming?"

"Interesting you should ask, buddy," Josh said. "Someone's been pranking me—"

"Not me. I just got back from Cleveland," Caleb said. "So what's going on?"

Josh briefly described the events in the basement at the tavern.

"Sounds pretty elaborate, dude. I wish I was in on it."

He sounded sincere and the more he heard himself relate the details, the more absurd it sounded. It was too elaborate for a prank.

If not a prank, then what?

Ghosts?

Twelve

Lachlan stood on a grassy knoll in the Kettle Moraine State Forest, focused on the beauty of Lost Arrow Lake while absorbing the energies emanating from the ground he stood upon. He didn't fully understand what the energies were, but Kenric had had a hypothesis. With his interest in science, he concluded the energies arose from electromagnetic waves. He posited that emotions and events left their imprint on the landscape and subtly changed the waves passing through the surface of the earth. A highly sensitive person could read these subtle changes and, in effect, look back through time. At one time they thought the waves flowed through a medium called the ether. Kenric concluded that the waves *were* the ether.

Based on news articles and photos on the internet, he stood on the very spot where Kenric had lost his life: the site of the MacKenzie house and the explosion that had been in the news for weeks. Nothing of the house was visible now. The property had been landscaped and allowed to revert to wild prairie.

At first, the scenery distracted him. The circular lake, the remnant of a glacial kettle, and the deep green forest that surrounded it, made up of sugar maples, green ash, white ash, and American elms plus red oak, red pine, and eastern white pine—identifying trees was a hobby of his. More than a hobby really. He made various tools for dowsing and he carved amulets; it was critical to select the proper wood for each task.

The view was mesmerizing, the air rich with smells of vegetative decay and the scent of pine. He sat cross-legged and closed his eyes, focusing on the faint vibrations flowing through him. Clearing his mind and slowing his heart rate, he slipped into a light meditative state.

This plot had once been farmland. Before that, Native Americans lived in a settlement here, drawn he was certain, by the beauty and abundance of the location. A sinister tone crept in when a Tudor house appeared, seemingly out of thin air. He felt no sense of the effort needed to build such a house. Something dark dwelt there, an invisible presence, concealed deep within. Much pain and sadness had visited the house; the sensations were nearly overwhelming even though he remained dispassionate in his observations to avoid becoming mired in the misery evident here.

He witnessed brief flashes of brutal mayhem in the final hours before the explosion. The visions were muddled and foggy so it was impossible to substantiate the details, though he caught glimpses of Kenric and a blonde woman, likely the woman named Laura mentioned in the news articles. The consequences were clear. She died, Kenric and another man died, the house was destroyed. Nevertheless, Lachlan sensed a residual negative energy now that was faint, barely discernable. No longer present, but not entirely eradicated either. Suggesting that in the end, Kenric had failed, that the entity he faced had been weakened but not destroyed. The vibrations suggested it had gone to ground to recover and strengthen.

For now, a supposition only. He wasn't certain it was true.

The primary question? What really happened here? To learn the full truth, he would need to return with the satchel containing his tools and preparations, aids to help him visualize the exact sequence of events of that night. Hopefully, he would confirm his feelings about the beast that had once inhabited the house.

For now, Lachlan had gained a sense of the evil Kenric had attempted to dispel in the confrontation that cost him his life. Lachlan had also found evidence of the materials Kenric must have utilized back in the basement of the Milwaukee house: amulets in metal and wood, talismans, *sorcerer's blue*—a powder and a complex copper compound derived from Egyptian Blue. Dispensed from a shaker, it provided a modest protective barrier against malignant spirits. Celtic crosses. The Goddess piece.

It hadn't been enough.

Finished analyzing the site, Lachlan now felt Kenric's death weigh heavily upon him after sensing his final moments. He realized he had tears in his eyes. Absurd, really. He hadn't cried in a hundred years. He had such a deep fondness for Kenric. Even here, with the evidence of his death, he could scarcely believe it.

Their friendship had spanned more than a millennium. They had both been born in the eighth century, in Mercia, in central England. They had trained at the same time under Godric, the most revered sorcerer of their time—four years of study, plus an apprenticeship. While Lachlan was the older of the two, Kenric's extraordinary talent presented early and he became the favored apprentice. Lachlan never minded, content with a place in the shadows. A gifted but humble man, Kenric was kind and caring and deserved all the accolades he received. He never made Lachlan feel the lesser man.

As young men, they often collaborated. He smiled, recalling the time they swindled a French nobleman by trading gold ingots for a cache of gems. The gems had been stolen from a baron to whom they owed favors. Several of his squires had been attacked and killed north of Paris by highwaymen in the employ of the nobleman.

The gold? It wasn't really gold. Kenric and Lachlan had performed a mighty feat of alchemy by changing lead to gold. Then as now, alchemy was widely believed to be useless, a fraud. Truth was? It worked, but it was unstable. The gold invariably reverted to base metal within hours; a day or two at most.

They met near Paris, made the trade, then rode all night and hopped aboard a waiting caravel, sailing for England and narrowly avoiding the angry nobleman's army. Kenric and Lachlan returned the gems to the baron and the families of the dead, and the nobleman was murdered soon after by people to whom he owed money.

When he closed his eyes, Lachlan could still hear Kenric's voice as they regaled the Aeldo with stories of their youth. They had chased damsels with wild abandon until Kenric met Laila and fell in love; they had vanquished dark knights and villains with style, and lived by a code that made them exemplars of honor in the Middle Ages. They steered clear of religious conflicts and stayed true to the older Gods of their pagan Anglo-Saxon backgrounds.

He sat for an hour, eyes closed, meditating, saying goodbye to the soul of his dead friend. Who knew what came after? Given his knowledge of magic, sorcery, and the good and evil extant in the world, he believed in some existence beyond this world. He just had no idea what it looked like.

Enough wallowing. Time for action.

If the entity had survived—and Lachlan suspected it had—he had an opportunity for revenge. A base desire, but one he had trouble suppressing. His anger and pain were deep. His dearest friend had died and Lachlan wanted someone to answer for it, be it a person, a beast, or a demon. And by Wōden, he would damn well make them pay.

He couldn't blindly charge in and settle the score though. He had no idea what he was facing. First, he had to find it. Study it, devise a plan to destroy it, and never forget that Kenric had been killed doing the very same thing. Kenric had been more adept at sorcery and still he failed. This situation seemed to fall outside Lachlan's considerable experience in dispelling poltergeists, cleaning out demons, dealing with spirits and wraiths—he might need help.

So many questions.

How would he find this thing? What was it? Did it have a name? Though Lachlan didn't care if it did. He refused to give it a name; he would hereafter refer to it only as the *darkness.*

He knew from the newspaper stories that a daughter and another child had survived the mayhem. He needed to find them, needed to visualize the house clearly by finding pictures of the house prior to that night. He needed to get busy and answer every question.

It seemed like a fool's errand.

Lachlan wasn't the least bit deterred.

Thirteen

Kiera's day was falling apart. She sat at a table in a truck stop restaurant poring over numerical weather models, surface maps, and satellite images. Nothing was happening and it looked like nothing would. Sometimes the weather gods simply refused to cooperate.

Her phone rang. Willow.

"Hey sweetie, how are you?"

"I'm okay," Willow said, breathlessly. "I need to go back."

"What?" *Uh oh.* This sounded like *manic* Willow.

"I need to go back—to the tavern."

"When? Why?"

"Now."

"Willow, I'm in Rockford. Illinois. What's the big rush? What's going on?"

"It's hard to explain. Like last time. It's kind of like facing your fears. Maybe I misread the situation, maybe I didn't, but I have to know," Willow said. "Did you say you researched the history of the place?"

"Yeah, I did. I framed the best stuff and put it up in the bar. If I get back early enough, maybe we can stop down tonight?"

"Okay." She sounded disappointed.

"I'll call you when I'm on the road."

Kiera sat for two more hours before deciding the day was a bust and pulled the plug. Hyped up on bad truck stop coffee, she gathered her things and hopped in the RAV4. She sent Josh a text and tapped on Willow's contact.

Willow picked up on the second ring.

"Dinner?" Kiera asked without preamble.

"Sure. Rustic Pines? Then we'll go to the bar?"

"Yep. Sounds good."

★   ★   ★

Josh sat at the bar and worked on a stack of invoices while the delivery people hauled the appliances up the stairs and installed them in the apartment. The electrical inspector passed his work with flying colors. Perfect. The furnace guys were banging around downstairs finishing the cold air returns and both times when he walked down to check on their progress, he couldn't help but eye the corner suspiciously. But the hatch remained where it belonged, firmly planted in the floor.

Kiera texted at five pm that she was heading back and meeting Willow for dinner. He was welcome to join them.

He texted back: *Sure, why not. Where?*

Rustic Pines 7:30

★   ★   ★

Rustic Pines, on the edge of town, was a classic Wisconsin supper club. Dark cedar outside, plenty of dark pine inside, a big bar with the best old fashioneds in town, and plenty of meat on the menu: steaks, chops, fillets, even venison in season.

Willow and Kiera sat at the bar in animated conversation when he walked in the door. The waitress quickly seated them in a booth and took Josh's drink order. He decided to be a joiner and ordered a glass of chardonnay.

"Bust, huh? The crown again?"

"Cap, honey, the cap." Kiera slapped his arm. "Warm air aloft. It prevents storms."

"Whatever." He purposely rolled his eyes. "You and your weather-geek-speak."

Ignoring him, Kiera said, "How'd the inspection go?"

"Perfect."

"Willow wants to go back to the bar, tonight."

"Tonight?" *Oh great. What now? She freaked out the last time.*

"If you don't mind," Willow said.

"I thought you felt a bad vibe in the place," Josh said.

"I did. It's a long story," Willow said defensively.

"Why not. You and Kiera can check out the appliances upstairs."

Willow sipped her wine and asked, "So what was the deal with the hatch in the basement?"

Josh recounted the events from the night before: sleeping in the bar all night and finding the hatch back in place this morning.

"Somebody's messing with you," Kiera said. "What'd you call it?"

"Olympic-level fuckery."

"I think it's creepy as hell," Willow said.

Josh noticed she had turned ashen. *Here we go.* He couldn't help the smirk at the corner of his mouth. "Sure you still want to go there?"

Kiera nudged his shin under the table and gave him *the look.*

Willow held his gaze. "I have to."

"You have to? Why?" Josh asked.

Something in her manner gave him pause. She said, "Do you know what a thin place is?"

"A narrow house?" A shin kick from Kiera. He looked quizzically at her and shrugged. It wasn't a dumb answer.

"No. It's a place where the space between this world or dimension is particularly close to another world or dimension. In the most accepted sense, it's between heaven and earth."

"And you're suggesting that the tavern is one of these thin places?"

"Yep. But I don't think it's heaven and earth there. It's earth and something else."

Kiera kicked him before he had a chance to speak. He bit his tongue. What could he say? The woman was a fruitcake. Sweet, but nutty. It amazed him that for as practical as she was, Kiera never questioned Willow or her beliefs. That, he supposed, might be the truest definition of friendship.

Finally he said, "What's the something else?"

"I don't know. That's why I have to go back. Thank you for indulging me."

They finished the meal with small talk. Josh agreed to go ahead, open the place and turn the lights on while Kiera grabbed the tab.

When he pulled up, the sun had just set and the sky glowed in soft reds broken by dark rays crossing the sky. Crepuscular rays or something, Kiera called them. As he opened the front door, he had a sudden foreboding he couldn't explain but knew it was related to the hatch in the basement. Must have been the talk in the restaurant. He was not a foreboding sort of guy unless you were talking about the Packers with a minute left in a close game. That was entirely natural.

They had blown more than a few games in the final seconds over the years.

By the time he'd lit up the first floor, Kiera and Willow were walking in the front door. Josh watched Willow with interest. She stepped hesitantly in the door and stopped, looking up as if sniffing the air like a retriever. She touched the door, the wall, then knelt and touched the floor, dead serious in her expression. It could have been comical but he didn't laugh. Between the sudden uneasy feeling outdoors and Willow's sober manner, he wondered if there was something to this, regardless of how he felt about the subject.

Willow walked around the room, looking and touching, stopping at the wall Kiera had assembled, studying each picture. She said not one word. In a first, Kiera raised her eyebrows as if this, finally, was too much. *As if.*

Finally, she shook her head. "Not here. Not this floor."

Kiera said, "Let's go up. I want to see the new appliances. You'll love how the apartment is turning out."

They marched up the stairs. Kiera checked out the kitchen and laundry room while Willow roamed around the apartment, nose up, spacey expression. Finally, she announced, "Nope. Not here."

"Do you like the apartment?" Kiera asked.

"Yeah, it's nice." But her tone sounded insincere.

Josh led the way down to the basement and flicked the lights on. He saw it immediately: the floor in the corner was wide open, the hatch leaning against the wall just like the night before. "Shit!"

"What?" Kiera said.

Josh pointed. Kiera looked and started. "Holy shit, Josh. What's going on?"

"I—I don't know." He couldn't imagine what this meant.

At that moment, Willow shrieked and ran up the stairs.

Kiera turned and ran after Willow. Josh crept towards the opening, half-expecting some annoying friend like Caleb to leap out of the hole and scare the shit out of him. As he reached the square opening, he saw something he hadn't noticed the night before. Without the flashlight, the hole seemed to glow with a faint blue-green light.

What the hell?

He edged to the opening and looked down.

There was some type of lighting. No visible bulbs, but the light came from a passage or tunnel that led away from the shaft. He wasn't superstitious, but he was claustrophobic, and the idea of climbing into that unknown passage made him anxious in a way he hadn't felt in some time.

Kiera walked up behind him. "Willow's in the car, I should—holy shit!" She stood next to him and held his arm. "What the hell is that?"

"I don't know, but I don't think I want to climb down and find out," Josh said, feeling confined just looking at the opening.

"Bullshit!" She said, with a wide grin. "Let me take Willow home and then we're going down there, sweetie."

Fourteen

"Holy shit!"

Sunlight, glinting from a faceted surface, drew her to the runnel where water from storms overnight had rushed through.

Rachel Nash knelt down and picked up the object, a finely crafted arrowhead, the best she'd found in weeks. Turning the stone over in her hand, she saw a bluish gemstone inset. A rare find—she had never seen anything like it. The gem seemed to swirl for a moment, maybe glowed a little, but when she focused on the stone, it returned to dark blue, just as she found it. Weird. A trick of the light maybe.

Rachel snapped a pic of the arrowhead with her phone and dropped it into the pouch reserved for such things in her backpack. Then she decided it belonged in the front pocket of her jean shorts. It looked and felt lucky.

The day was hot and humid; the sun burned like a brand on her skin. She didn't feel she needed sunscreen. Her face and arms were already tanned brown. Besides, not using sunscreen was another way to annoy her mother who continually lectured: *when you're forty, your face will look like a leather handbag.*

Hell. If she turned out like her mother, she didn't want to live that long.

The damp earth smelled musty with a faint scent of lilac. She pulled her shirt off—revealing a tank-top beneath—and tossed it in the backpack.

Rachel knelt down and sifted through the dirt and mud with a small garden trowel. If the rain had washed out one arrowhead, there might be others. In a few minutes, she uncovered another, a rather bland arrowhead, not nearly as nice as the first.

Hunting for arrowheads was her only hobby, an odd one according to her mother, when most girls her age were watching YouTube and fretting about boys and acne. She had few friends and didn't care, content on her own. Her last boyfriend had dropped her a few months back so she wasn't dating. Honestly, she had little interest in boys, and refused to stress over her lack of curiosity; she had enough trouble in her life.

Overwhelming curiosity drew Rachel here. To see these things on the internet was one thing. To hold them in her hand? A thrill, and an adventure. How old were they? Had they taken a deer down? Killed someone in battle?

She dreamed of a career in archeology. Not the antics portrayed in the old Indiana Jones movies, but doing this—the hunting, sifting, digging to find small artifacts that told a story. It was the stories she wanted to learn, even if she had to imagine the histories of the pieces she found. Reading on the internet, she had taught herself where and how to search for them.

Rachel discovered this field by accident. Cutting through the hedge trying to find a shortcut to Sophie Hansen's—they were friends in sixth grade—she had walked across this field of prairie grass and wildflowers. She had stumbled and found an arrowhead, a real beauty, a notched projectile point fashioned from quartzite.

The field was part of an abandoned farm. The barn had mostly collapsed years ago and the area reclaimed by nature. The land and fields were overgrown with weeds, brush, and junk trees. The farmhouse was a wreck: a big old American Foursquare, the paint peeled, the siding weathered to grey, the roof pockmarked by holes. Most of the windows were broken and the back door was missing.

Still, few people ventured inside. The floors were rotting and looked unsafe. Kids at school told all sorts of scary stories about the place, from simple hauntings to infestations by the living dead. Rachel wasn't sure she believed any of the stories. A few years back, Jason Hetner, a high school sophomore, and a few friends had thrown a ghost party at the house and Jason had fallen through a hole in the kitchen floor and broken his arm. That was reason enough to stay out of the house. Rachel wasn't interested in the house anyway and didn't believe the ghost stories.

Her dad thought the farm hadn't been worked in over thirty or forty years. Nobody knew who owned it, but he said the old-timers in town called it Quinlan's farm.

The lucky field lay behind the farmhouse. She gained access and hid her bike in the bushes just past a big sign warning:

NO TRESPASSING NO HUNTING

The field was invisible to the road and she had seen no one else on or near the property. No one ever challenged her and she felt safe here scouring the grounds for new finds. With eager concentration, she hunted through this new vein but decided to take a break after a fruitless hour of search. She pulled a Mountain Dew and a bag of Cheetos from the backpack. As she snacked, she fished the new arrowhead from her pocket.

Rachel was mesmerized by the pearly blue gem. Faint patterns appeared to swirl around the faceted surface almost like a miniature galaxy. Staring at it, Rachel felt she might fall into the gem and disappear, feeling no fear, just a sense of absolute peace. On the back, she noticed fine lines engraved into the stone that could be letters, but unlike any letters she had ever seen:

ᚦᛁ ᚲ ᛗᛁ ᚦ ᛒ ᚠ ᚼ ᛗ

As the sun fell low in the west, she scavenged around a group of boulders, some almost three feet in diameter, that formed a cluster in the corner of the field. She had almost given up hope of finding anything in this spot but dawdled to delay going home.

The continual search for Native American tools and arrowheads was a hobby, but also a refuge. Her mother, once her best friend and confidante, had convinced Rachel that she was beautiful, talented, and destined for great things.

Now she drank. Rachel wasn't sure when her mom's habit evolved from an occasional afternoon glass of rosé to a bottle of merlot by dinnertime. It just happened. She wasn't usually a mean drunk, just useless. She sat and played games on her phone and did little else, other than assigning most of the housework to Rachel and her father, claiming she suffered variously with migraines, Lyme disease, or fibromyalgia. And though she wasn't mean, she wasn't nice either. Rachel had gone from beautiful to *watch the snacks* or *your complexion looks pasty* or her favorite slight: *your thighs are getting a little heavy, dear.*

Two years and she could leave. Two years.

Her phone pinged. Dad.

Home young lady. Dinner time.

Fifteen

It never paid to argue with Kiera. He liked her strong-willed nature—except at times like this when reasonable caution suggested they not rush into things. The woman chased tornadoes for God's sake. Never mind the tunnel being a bit creepy. Who was opening the hatch? Why? Still, he felt reasonably certain the supernatural wasn't a reasonable explanation even with Willow's histrionics.

No. There was a rational explanation even if he couldn't see it. He was more concerned that someone had plans to break in. To steal stuff? Vandalize the bar? If so, they weren't being very subtle. Quite the opposite. How were they moving the damn hatch? Had to be a trick to it. He just couldn't imagine what it was.

Okay, he would do this. He had Kiera's Kimber. It wasn't like a Mexican cartel was trying to break in. Maybe it was a former employee from the old bar who was sneaking back in. Sneaking? Why was he leaving the damn hatch open? Josh made a mental note to ask Fitzsimmons what he knew about the hatch tomorrow. He should have done it today.

Kiera bounced in the door a minute later. "Let's go! I'm dying to see what's down there."

"Slow down, sweetie. I'm grabbing your Kimber. Just in case."

"Whatever. Let's go, scaredy cat."

He grabbed the gun and hurried down the stairs, passing Kiera. No way would he let her go first. It was a matter of basic male dignity.

Thirteen vertical stone steps took him down to the floor of the tunnel. It was silent, comfortably warm, lit by a blue-green fluorescence or luminescence, the source of which he couldn't identify. The walls of dark grey stone seemed to glow slightly. Was that even possible? The tunnel led away, sloping down at an angle, lit throughout by the same light even though no fixtures were evident anywhere along the tunnel. It looked like an old mine shaft and smelled faintly of loamy earth.

Kiera dropped down beside him, wide-eyed. "Holy shit! Cool! What the hell is this?"

Josh was momentarily speechless. He had no idea and certainly hadn't imagined this tunnel going off into the unknown. "I have no idea. That's more your department."

Kiera edged ahead, flashing her light every which way, her mouth agape with awe. Finally, she said, "I'm not sure what it is. The walls are limestone, dolomite specifically. This looks like a natural formation—part tunnel, part cave. Someone made it wider. See here?" She pointed to grooves that appeared to be tool marks. "They cut the rock back in these places."

She pointed to the large rough areas between the tool marks. "This is natural dolomite, eroded over time by running water. Groundwater probably ran along this tunnel and down the slope. This may be an old mine. I don't really know."

"Turn your light off," she said and turned hers off. He followed suit. Kiera scanned and touched the walls. "I don't understand the light source. I think it's some sort of bioluminescence, but nothing I'm familiar with. And I don't understand why it's so clean."

Josh hadn't really noticed but it was. Mostly, he felt queasy and claustrophobic in the narrow tunnel. "Weird, huh?"

"There should be bugs and cobwebs and rodents and dirt on the floor. It looks like someone came through and vacuumed. Makes no sense."

"So the ghosts are neat, maybe obsessive about it?"

She gave him a *don't-be-a-moron* look. "Really? Now you sound like Willow."

"Could this be an old mineshaft?"

"That would be one possibility, though usually, limestone isn't a source for ores and gems. I think this rock is part of the Niagara Escarpment, a ridge of stone that arcs up Door County and atop the Great Lakes, and then down through New York state where Niagara Falls pours over it."

"So?"

"It's just interesting, that's all."

They had walked about thirty feet when Kiera stopped, turned, and said, "This isn't the way to do this. We need better lights, hard hats, and cameras like my GoPros."

"I'm good with that," Josh said. "I'm staying overnight though, just in case."

"I would, until we figure out what's going on."

★   ★   ★

Josh opened the tavern the next morning at seven for the contractors, then ran to Menards. He returned two hours later with bags of hardware and security gear. When he walked into the basement, the hatch was closed, as it had been the morning before.

No surprise this time. Yep, Olympic-level fuckery. He unloaded the bag of hardware, fetched a hammer drill from his toolbox and set to work. After drilling holes in the concrete floor, he lashed the hatch to the floor with half-inch steel straps and six-inch concrete anchors. It wasn't foolproof, but it would take some time to loosen and remove the hatch now.

He spent the rest of the day setting up an alarm system for the bar, placing sensors on all the ground floor windows and doors. He set up small surveillance cameras trained on the bar, the hatch in the basement, the door to the apartment, the upper basement door, and the rear parking lot.

He considered it mostly a wasted day, but they could ill-afford a break-in or any vandalism. Work in the building was winding down. The main bar was finished and ready for business. The kitchen crew would wrap-up by the end of the week. He had hired a chef who was busy building a menu based on the instructions Kiera and Josh had given him.

In the morning, he had interviews scheduled with several people applying for various positions: a line cook, two waitresses, a busser, and an expediter, a position normally referred to as *expo*. He and Kiera would manage the bar starting out.

★   ★   ★

After an eventful afternoon shopping for furniture, Josh was ready to quit. Kiera discreetly grabbed his ass and whispered, "Let's go to my place. I'm hungry."

Even the best-laid plans go awry and they ended up in bed before dinner. After a vigorous and enjoyable round of sex, they napped lightly in the post-coital glow.

Kiera finally slid out of bed. "I'd better start dinner before it gets too late to bother."

"All right." Josh sat up and watched her slip back into her clothes. "I'll be right there."

"Start the grill, please." Kiera said as she pulled two tenderloins from the fridge, set them on a tray, and seasoned them with garlic salt and pepper.

Josh stepped in from the patio a minute later. Kiera was slicing fresh romaine, green onions, a pepper, and radishes on a cutting board. He sat down at the island and fiddled with his phone.

As Kiera set the salads on the table, Josh jumped up. "Shit, shit, shit!"

"What?"

"Fire! By the basement door. I can access the security system and cameras from my phone. I decided to peek and saw this." He showed her the phone. Fire was burning right outside the side door. Kiera grabbed her phone and then yanked Josh by the shoulder. "Let's go! You drive, I'll call 911."

They ran out to his car and sped towards the tavern. As they approached, sirens screamed in the distance. Josh sped up to the front door and skidded to a halt, but the tavern was dark. Kiera jumped out and ran to the side door. Josh ran up next to her.

There was no evidence of a fire.

"Shit! What's going on here?"

What would they tell the fire department? They didn't have to wait long. A fire truck and police squad pulled up and two firefighters and a cop walked over. The cop was Owen Prosser, who had been a client of Josh's in a divorce proceeding.

"Hey, Josh, where's the fire?" he asked.

"Hi Owen, it was right here." Josh reversed the video feed on his phone back to the fire and showed it to them. They looked at the replay and then the door.

"You sure this is the same door?"

"Has to be," Josh pointed to the camera above, then placed a palm on the door.

"It's still warm."

Owen touched it as well. "Yeah it is. But no ash or charring. Weird."

One of the firefighters said, "Might have been a flammable liquid. Sounds like a prank to me."

"I'd have to agree," Josh said. "Sorry to waste your time. Thanks for coming out."

"We should look around, just to be sure," Owen said.

While the firefighters walked a perimeter around the building, Owen, Kiera, and Josh navigated a quick circuit inside. Satisfied that all was well, everyone went their separate ways. Josh and Kiera pulled into her driveway five minutes later.

Kiera handed the steaks on a plate to Josh. "Hurry, I'm starving."

Josh stood out by the grill, drinking a beer, watching the steaks, and fuming over the annoying pranks at the bar. The hatch, the fire, the worries about security were wasting his time when he had far too much to do.

Fifteen minutes later, they sat to eat. Kiera sprinkled shredded cheddar on her salad and eyed Josh. "So what the hell's going on, huh?"

"I don't know." Josh cut into his steak. "Mmm, perfect. I thought someone was messing with me but it's all too sophisticated. Maybe somebody wants the bar to fail."

"Like who? The neighbors?"

"Could be, but there's been a bar there forever," Josh said. "A lot of the neighbors seem to be happy with the project. It was a dump when Fitzsimmons had it. This will be a class act."

"Then we're back to ghosts," Kiera said without a trace of humor.

"No. No ghosts," Josh said, then held up his knife. "Wait a minute. There was this guy at a few of the hearings, worried about noise and traffic, some hipster dude. His name was..."

"What?"

"Give me a minute. Um, Schuster. That's it. I'm giving his name to the cops. He seemed like an angry dude."

"I hope that's it. Until they check him out, you should consider more security, a guard or two—"

"Nope. I'm moving in tonight." He raised an eyebrow. "Wanna join me?"

"Sorry, no," Kiera said. "Not until the bed arrives. You're going there after dinner?"

"I think I should."

"No more nooky?" Kiera pleaded lightly with clasped hands.

"Sorry, babe. That fire call pretty much killed my mood."

Sixteen

Josh sat at the bar and powered up the flatscreen TVs mounted in front of the mirrors built into the back bar so they concealed none of the exquisite oak. He sipped on a bottle of Spotted Cow and tried to shake off the anger he felt over the situation. He should be at Kiera's, in bed and appreciating her feminine wiles. Instead, he was stuck here with an uncomfortable night in a bedroll ahead. He thought about the carpeted apartment above but preferred to be near the center of the building, where he was best situated to hear any intruders. Even with five hundred cable channels, there was little to watch. He finally settled on a *Friends* rerun.

At one am, he clicked the sets off, stepped outside and walked the perimeter of the building with the Kimber in his pocket. The neighborhood was quiet and he felt certain things were secure for the night. The cops had probably scared the asshole off for now anyway.

He arranged the bedroll on the floor with the gun and phone nearby, the phone logged into the security app. Moments later, he was asleep.

Later, he awoke, startled by a noise. He lay there, paralyzed by the feeling that someone or something was watching him. He grabbed his phone, clicked it on and turned to see if anyone was there. The bar was empty, nothing disturbed. He shook his head, annoyed he was lying there awake and had probably overreacted. He scanned the bar with his flashlight then lay back down to sleep. He was just drifting off when a footfall landed above in the apartment, with a slight creak of the floorboard.

Then another.

Josh jumped from the bedroll, tired and cranky, wondering who the hell was trying to creep around upstairs. He grabbed the Kimber and went to the stairway door. Yelled up in his most menacing voice, "I'm coming up and I've got a gun!"

He thumped up the stairs, stopped, and peered through the stair rail at floor level. The apartment was silent and dark but for a slight wash of lights from the street. He flicked the lights on and walked around the apartment slowly, gun pointed ahead of him, cop style.

It was empty and Josh realized how jumpy he had become. It was an old building. Creaks and the occasional groan came with the territory. Why was he freaking out? Possibly the late hour, the empty building and the business in the basement, the stress of deadlines to finish and open the tavern. It all conspired to leave him on edge, worrying about every little detail, every problem, real or imagined. Time to chill out.

Josh walked down the stairs, closing the apartment door. Then he noticed runes burned into the bottom half of the door leading outside, the same door where he'd seen the fire earlier.

ᚠ ᚠ ᛗ ᚠᛈ   ᚠᚱ ᛁ ᚷᚠᚱ

"What the fuck!" Josh spat the words out. He kicked the door, then kicked it again. Too tired to react further and still convinced someone was fucking with him, he sat at the bar and slammed a shot of Jack.

Laying down, he tossed and turned for a long while before falling asleep.

⋆   ⋆   ⋆

Kiera lay in bed with Ghost snuggled tight against her back. This element of being unemployed was her favorite. Other than the demands Ghost made in the morning, she could lounge and luxuriate until noon if she wanted. But she also detected a note of boredom sneaking into her enjoyment of these mornings. She felt lazy. That annoying compulsion to work. Her parents' beliefs passed on to her: people who didn't work were shiftless ne'er-do-wells. Ironic that she could retire because Dad had owned a ridiculously large term-life policy.

On the other hand, the tavern would open soon and she would be working again. Storm season was almost over and her ankle had nearly healed. Maybe she could get a couple of jumps in before they opened.

Her phone rang. Willow. "What's up sweetie?"

"I need to talk to you—about the tavern," Willow said. "Want to come over?"

"No. You come here. I promised Ghost a walk today. We can go to the park, sip wine, and chat."

"Sure. An hour?"

Kiera agreed and rolled out of bed. After a shower, she would pack a small basket for lunch. She hated to admit that Willow was wearing on her. Her fixation on the tavern had grown old and Kiera was genuinely concerned Willow was coming unglued. She tended toward OCD anyway, but the tavern had become a full-blown obsession. Kiera wanted to say something, but Willow grew defensive when her beliefs were challenged.

During a long hot shower, she decided the bar opening would give her a good excuse to step back and let Willow settle down a bit. Then she felt guilty for thinking that way. Willow was her best friend. If she was coming unhinged, she owed it to her to be supportive.

After drying her hair and pulling it into a high ponytail, she packed Cheddar, Parmigiano, and Brie, summer sausage, crackers, and a cold bottle of rosé in a picnic basket.

A few minutes later, Willow popped in the side door. She was wearing a sunhat, denim shorts, and paisley print top tied at the waist.

"Hey sweetie!" She hugged Kiera and knelt down, accepting kisses from Ghost.

Willow stood and said, "Shall we?"

"Yep. Basket or Ghost?"

Willow reached for his lead and snapped it to his harness. Kiera grudgingly grabbed the basket and they walked out, into bright sunshine. Willow always took the dog, never the basket. The walk to the park was casual while Ghost stopped and sniffed every post, pole, or mailbox, leaving his calling card for the neighbor dogs. They gabbed, small talk, commenting on the gardens and landscaping they passed.

The park was quiet, just a few young moms—or nannies—watching small children. They grabbed a picnic table in the shade of a gnarly oak and Kiera laid out the luncheon, then poured the rosé into stemless glasses.

Kiera waited until Willow had eaten a piece of Cheddar and sipped her wine. "What's on your mind?"

"Two things—and I know you think I'm losing it—but please hear me out."

Kiera could barely hide her surprise since she had been thinking exactly that. Finally she said, "Maybe a little. Go ahead." She mimed zipping her lips shut.

"Thank you." She took another sip. "One, there's something wrong with the tavern, I've already told you that and I understand why you don't believe me. I'm not sure I believe it myself."

Willow stared skyward for a moment as if seeking an answer there that eluded her here on earth. "It's not the tavern itself. It's the basement, the hole in the floor. That's the thin place. I'm sure of it."

"Josh sealed it up with steel straps and heavy bolts," Kiera said. "Whatever's down there is staying down there."

"I hope you're right. I'm not sure if that'll be enough. Nobody knows," Willow said. "These places are usually benign. Being in such a place should be an uplifting experience. That...opening? It exuded darkness."

"Well, like I said. It's sealed up. What's the other thing?"

"You should consider an exorcism."

Kiera stopped mid-bite. "Are you serious?"

"Deadly. You need to take me seriously."

"I don't care, but Josh will never consider it," she said, shaking her head. "What's the other thing?"

"I know someone who will do it—"

"No. Now what's the other thing?"

Willow looked away from Kiera's direct gaze with a guilty expression. "Don't be mad."

"What?" She was getting a little heated. Jesus! Willow *was* losing it. An exorcism?

"It's Josh." She pursed her lips.

Kiera felt her stomach tighten. "What about Josh?"

Willow looked, then averted her gaze again. "He's going to cheat on you."

Kiera struggled to reign in her anger; thought she might have a stroke. "How do you know that?"

"His tarot reading—"

Kiera fixed a glare on Willow. "Did I ask you to do a tarot reading for Josh?"

"No," Willow mumbled.

"I trust Josh. Butt out," Kiera said with an edge. That should've been the end of it, but she couldn't help but ask, "So who is it? Who's the other woman?"

"I'm not sure. Somebody he works with maybe? At the bar?"

That struck an odd chord with Kiera. There was a waitress he'd shown an unusual interest in during the interview process. Kiera cut the thought off. It was nothing. Willow was making her question things that needed no questioning.

"Enough of that. I trust Josh. End of subject, Willow."

"What about the exorcism?"

Kiera slammed her glass down. "No!"

Seventeen

One week later, Lachlan Hayward pulled into the driveway of an attractive Craftsman style house in Naperville, Illinois—the home of Dana MacKenzie, one of two people to survive the mayhem the night Kenric died. He discovered the link reading through the many news stories about the event and perusing the police records. The woman had reluctantly agreed to meet after he explained his connection with Kenric, the mysterious Dr. Shepherd who had shown up that night and died along with her father and mother. He sensed Dana was hopeful he could provide some closure on one of the issues she didn't understand: who was Kenric Shepherd and why had he been there?

He rang the bell and a moment later, an attractive, petite woman with dark hair and vivid blue eyes answered the door. He announced himself formally: "Lachlan Hayward here to see Miss Dana MacKenzie."

"I'm Dana." She looked him up and down and pushed the door open. "Please, come in."

She directed him to a comfortable-looking recliner at the end of a semicircle of chairs and a sofa facing a large flatscreen TV. "Can I get you something to drink?"

"Tea, if you have it."

"I do. Give me a moment to put a kettle on."

On a side table, he spied a photo of a man and woman in their forties who shared features with Dana. Lucas and Laura MacKenzie, he decided.

She returned, turned a recliner towards him and sat. "So, Lachlan. Tell me about Dr. Shepherd and leave nothing out. My mother and father died in that house along with your friend and I have no idea why. Well, that's not entirely true, but none of it made any sense. My mother was convinced the house was haunted. That they—we were in grave danger. She sent me away shortly before the explosion. I believe your friend was already dead so I don't know much about him. Please, tell me what you can."

She didn't seem to know much more than he did. Maybe this meeting would be unproductive. He had also debated on just how much he should share with this woman. Then he decided there was no harm in telling her everything he knew. If she talked later, who would believe her?

"You asked for the truth, the whole story. I suspect you won't believe it." He sipped his tea, looking for the right words. "Kenric Shepherd was a sorcerer, a member of a group we call the Aeldo, or the Elders, if you like. Does that sound too fantastic for you?"

"No. Not anymore," Dana said, her shoulders slumped, perhaps in resignation of that reality. "After being at that house, I can believe almost anything."

"Quite. I imagine you would. Kenric was chasing something. I'm not sure what it was. But his pursuit culminated in an explosion at your parents' house. I believe he brought explosives, among other things, feeling he needed to blow the building up to destroy whatever he was pursuing. Why did he do those things? That's what I'm trying to determine."

She eyed him suspiciously. "Doesn't sound like you know much more than I do."

"You may be right, but I think I can get to the truth in time. I'll share it with you when I do."

She looked him squarely in the eye. "Fair enough."

"So now, if you would tell me what you know." Lachlan fiddled with his moustache. "Firstly, was your mother psychic that you know of?"

"She was. I'm sure of it," Dana said, rubbing her forearm. "She wasn't comfortable with it. She was a reluctant psychic."

"Some people with psychic abilities feel that way. Did your mother and Dr. Shepherd ever meet prior to that night?"

"My mother? I don't think so. She would have said something." Dana knitted her brow. "I had the impression my father had. Mom and Dad argued about it one night. Apparently, Shepherd had warned my father about something but I didn't hear the rest of the conversation."

"I see. Was there a book involved?"

"There was. My dad and his brother found a book hidden in the house. It was very old, but I never actually saw it."

The kettle began to whistle. "Excuse me, how would you like your tea?"

"English style. A little milk and sugar, thank you."

Could that book be the one Kenric had been translating? *Very old* was a relative term in the States, but if the book was the same, then was the house also the same? A Tudor house from sixteenth century England? Here? That seemed highly improbable. It might help explain why Kenric had come.

Dana returned with two cups of tea, a small pitcher of milk, and a bowl of sugar.

He prepared and sipped his tea. English breakfast tea. Perfect.

"Do you have any photographs of the house?" Lachlan asked.

"No. But my uncle had a website to document the renovation. I don't know if it's still there, but there were hundreds of photos on it."

"The house was very old though?"

"It was. Tudor-something-or-other."

He paused, sipping his tea. "If you don't mind me asking, how did your parents die?"

Dana looked off into space; she appeared to be struggling with her emotions. "I don't know about my mother. I assumed she was killed in the explosion."

There was something she wanted to hide, he felt it strongly. He waited a moment, then said softly, "And your father?"

A dark expression briefly crossed her face, a micro-expression. She studied her hands. Finally, she said, "I'm not sure. I think my mother killed him. I didn't tell the police that. I didn't think it mattered."

"Given the outcome, you're probably right. Regardless, your secret is safe with me. Do you have any idea why? Self-defense perhaps?"

Dana turned her head and stared into space, visibly fighting back tears. After a moment, she said, "He changed in the last month they were there. Treated my mother badly. He was having an affair. I think he tried to kill her. So yes, I think it was self-defense."

A picture slowly evolved. An ancient piece of witchcraft had gone awry: evil deed stacked upon evil deed, culminating in a presence that grew ever stronger. Had the MacKenzies inadvertently set it free? Is that what set it off? Or had the house itself become the villain? Regardless, Kenric had tried to destroy it, but things had gone horribly wrong. Kenric died, the house had been demolished. Still, Lachlan wondered, had the presence within been eradicated?

That was the critical question—one that might keep him awake at night.

A young blonde girl, about five perhaps, poked her head around the corner and eyed Lachlan with a piercing blue-eyed gaze.

"Leah, come in and meet our guest."

Without the slightest hesitation, Leah walked over to him and put a hand on his knee. She looked thoughtful for a second, then announced, "You're old. *Very* old."

An odd sensation traveled along his leg and up his spine. Was she...?

Dana started and admonished, "Leah!"

"No, she's correct. Somewhat older than Kenric, actually." This little girl was positively bursting with psychic energy. Did this woman know? How could she not?

Lachlan looked at Dana. "Is it okay if I hold her hand?"

Dana nodded. There was a contradictory hesitancy in her expression, an apprehension.

He took Leah's hand, closed his eyes and imagined a cartoon scene in his head with a roadrunner and a coyote.

A moment later, Leah giggled. "That's funny."

He said, "Now you."

The image of a white hare popped into his head, the rabbit from *Alice in Wonderland.*

Looking concerned, Dana said, "What's going on?"

"Your daughter has some psychic ability."

"I know, just like her grandma," Dana said. Another dark shadow crossed her face. "She's my niece, actually. Her father passed several years ago."

"Oh dear. I'm sorry to hear that." He marveled at the resiliency of the human spirit. This family had seen so much tragedy; this young woman had already lost a brother and her parents.

"I should go. I will keep you apprised as I learn more."

As he stood to leave, Leah touched his hand. Looking up, she said in a serious tone, "That thing you're looking for? It's still out there."

Lachlan, startled, sat back down and looked into her eyes. "And how do you know that?"

An adorable child, she adopted a coy expression. "I had a dream about you last night."

"So you knew I was coming?"

She nodded. "Uh huh."

Dana looked stunned.

Lachlan realized she had no idea of the depth of this child's gift. "Next time we talk, perhaps we should talk more about your niece?"

"I would love to."

He said his goodbyes and walked to his car. Leah had a powerful gift, maybe on par with his. Good thing she lived here, away from that place. She would be in special danger otherwise. Whatever Kenric had been chasing would be drawn to her gift. He wasn't entirely certain she wouldn't become a target anyway if he couldn't stop it. It seemed fixated on the MacKenzie family and the last three pages of the book seemed to confirm that.

He needed to return at a better time to talk to Dana, let her know what she was in for. Perhaps provide some guidance to the child.

Mostly, he dwelt on her last words.

It's still out there.

Eighteen

Kiera stood behind the bar, polishing the array of taps and handles.

Two weeks had passed in a blur of activity as they checked off the final details, one by one. Contractors completed their work and a stream of inspectors followed who approved the electrical work, the plumbing, the kitchen, the bathrooms. Josh and Kiera interviewed dozens of people and hired a small but promising group of people to handle the opening night and the first couple of weeks. During all of this, they also found the time to furnish and decorate the apartment and move in, marking another step toward permanency and maybe marriage. As unflappable as she considered herself to be, it all felt a bit overwhelming: the financial investment and risk, a new job, a different relationship, all in a matter of weeks. They were hanging on to their separate houses for now. They still needed to decide if they would live in one house or the other, or if they would look for a new house altogether. Later, when they had time to think again, they'd worry about it.

Kiera had spent an inordinate amount of time polishing the taps, the countertop, the bottles. The doors would open today at four p.m.

and she was equal parts excited and nervous at the prospect. Would they be busy? Or would it be slow at first? Interest seemed high and their Facebook page suggested that quite a few people planned to visit and give them a try.

She and Josh would work the bar, though Josh would also assist anywhere help was needed, plus watching the wait station and the kitchen. Angela, their waitress, also had experience tending bar so she could swing between the two as needed. They felt they could cover almost any eventuality. While Kiera had never previously tended bar, she hired a tutor on Craigslist and spent hours learning to mix cocktails and mixers, pour tap and bottled beers, make dessert drinks, and handle bottles with style while working under pressure. She was outgoing and personable and well-suited to the job. Still, it was quite a change, switching from archaeologist to bartender in just one year.

Would she see any former students or colleagues? That would be interesting, to say the least.

She wasn't sure Willow would come. Things were still strained after their lunch and now, annoyingly, she caught herself looking for any hint of lust or attraction between Josh and Angela. In her mid-twenties, Angela was slim and attractive with long dark hair and vivid blue eyes. She had full lips and an overbite, a feature that most men, including Josh, found sensual for some reason. She knew better. She trusted Josh and wasn't the needy, jealous type. Kiera couldn't understand how Willow and her damned tarot cards had gotten under her skin and left her feeling this way—other than her equally annoying tendency to be right. And if it did come to pass and Josh was that easily led astray, then they weren't meant to be.

Un huh. 'Meant to be' was a silly, naïve viewpoint. They weren't teenagers. They were entering a joint venture. Yes, she was protected legally—Josh had insisted on it—but this would be a lousy moment for a breakup and she didn't have a backup plan if they did.

No, she needed to trust Josh and stop listening to Willow. This anxiety wasn't mindful in any way, shape, or sense. After scolding herself, she would settle down, and then she'd catch herself watching Josh again.

Stop it! Jesus!

At three-thirty, Josh gathered the employees in the bar and lined up rows of shot glasses, asking everyone to call out their favorite shot. As he poured them, he said, "This is a one time exception, otherwise no drinking on the job." He tried to look stern for a moment and failed. "Anyway, a lot of hard work went into this opening and Kiera and I want you to know we really appreciate it!"

The staff clapped. They were a good group: Chef Doyle Lindell, Angela Gelman and Bella Henning on wait staff, and Kyla Penrose working expo or whatever position needed a hand—all of them experienced and enthusiastic. They had been lucky to find them. Kiera vowed then to stop fretting over Angela and Josh. They still needed a busser and line cook, positions they'd fill once they were busier.

"Okay, raise your glasses, everyone. Thank you all. Here's to a great night and many more to follow!"

They all drained their glasses and slammed them on the bar. Josh walked over and unlocked the door. Quinlan's Tavern was open for business.

It was slow at first.

A young couple strolled in ten minutes later. Then some hipster dudes. A few singles drifted in and they all eyed the place approvingly. Close to five pm, a steadier stream of people flowed through the door and by six, they were slammed. The traffic was beyond their wildest expectations and they had only been open two hours! Looked like

Josh had nailed it. The neighborhood was changing to a different demographic and this was the type of place they were looking for.

Two forty-something guys sat at the bar. One called, "Hey, baby-doll. When you got a minute?"

And wow, how Kiera hated being called baby-doll, but reminded herself it went with the job. She would be called plenty of condescending names in the course of this work, she was certain. Instead, she smiled and said, "What can I get you guys?"

By seven, the place was booming. The booths and tables were full, and people were hanging at the bar, waiting to be seated. The opening hadn't been without glitches. The haddock on the menu hadn't been delivered, Bella dropped a tray of glasses, they screwed up orders, and there was a fire on the griddle. The crowd was congenial and seemed to take it all in stride. No one was angry and Bella received a standing ovation for the tray drop.

It was a friendly crowd and Kiera tried to remember all the names. It felt like many of these people could become regulars.

The guy in front of her, Scott Robbins, was tall, good looking, and he knew it. He owned a car dealership in town and seemed to know everyone. Scott was also a bit of a jerk. After one round of drinks, he had become her best friend. A big tipper, he sat there with his wife, acting lovey-dovey, and then flirted with Kiera whenever he had the chance. Despite his slightly creepy edge, Kiera played nice. He would be an influential customer.

As his wife walked toward the bathrooms, Scott leaned in and said, with a wink, "She's almost as good looking as you are. Shot of Jack, please. Get yourself one too."

"No thanks. Boss said no drinking on the job." She poured the shot and slid it to him, avoiding eye contact.

"Your boss needs to lighten up. Who's the boss, anyway?"

Looking up, she smiled and said, "Me."

"Oh. Good to know."

After nine, the pace slowed and the bar thinned to half empty. An older guy, with a well-traveled face and a ponytail sat at the end of the bar, head swiveling back and forth, taking in the details.

As Kiera approached, Josh slid up next to her. "So Greg, what do you think?" Josh turned to Kiera. "This is Greg Fitzsimmons."

Ah, the old owner.

"Nice job, kid. Looks great. Brought the old name back, huh?"

"Yep. So did you buy this place from Quinlan?" Josh asked.

"Nah. Bought it from the bank. Old man Quinlan had been dead for years."

Josh said, "Say. There's a metal hatch in the floor in the basement, under all the junk. Any idea what it's for?"

"Nope. Most of that junk was here when I bought the place. I just added to the pile," he said off-handedly. "Never saw any hatch down there."

"You ever have any problems with break-ins?"

"You kidding? Place was a dump." Fitzsimmons chuckled. "I didn't even bother to lock it half the time."

"So what about the ghosts?"

Fitzsimmons eyed him critically. "Thought you didn't believe in that stuff."

"I don't, but there's been some strange stuff happening in the basement."

Fitzsimmons smirked. "Things moving around down there?"

"Yep."

"Get used to it."

Nineteen

Kiera set the last glass on the shelf and grabbed the furniture polish, buffing the length of the bar to a high shine. It had been another great night. Open for a week now, Quinlan's had been busy every night including Sunday. The kitchen, running near capacity, had found a groove, turning out great food in short order. Early reviews were positive except for a one-star jerk who complained there wasn't enough lobster in the Lobster Mac-n-Cheese. Otherwise, the reviews averaged 4.7 stars across Google, Yelp, and Trip Advisor.

It was hard work. Between the daily cleaning, tending bar, helping the wait and kitchen staff as needed, Kiera felt like she ran every minute for nine hours or more. They had planned on working seven nights a week for the first month or two, until things were humming and they had honed the employees into a finely-tuned machine. It was running so smoothly, Josh handed out cash bonuses as everyone arrived that afternoon. Good people were hard to find and he wanted them to feel appreciated, to know their hard work was noticed and rewarded. He was a great manager, and Kiera felt she meshed well with them, too.

She looked forward to a more relaxed pace, working three or four days a week, as she originally agreed to with Josh. Her investment certainly looked sound. She stopped when she caught Josh and Angela chatting over by the kitchen. They looked a tad too comfortable and Angela had a smitten look as she watched him talk. Blech! Still, Josh didn't seem to be interested and Kiera realized she was being overly sensitive. Josh had been very attentive despite the pace, as if he suspected her surveillance, especially with Angela.

Finished polishing the bar, she grabbed the cash drawer and walked to the office as Josh disappeared down the basement stairs. Just as she set the drawer down, she heard a loud bang followed by a voice barking, "Shit!"

Josh.

She slammed the office door and ran down the stairs, fearful of what she'd find: Josh injured or maimed in some way, crushed under something heavy. She could be remarkably imaginative when she didn't need to be.

Instead, he stood in the corner, looking at the hole in the floor, the hatch off and leaning against the wall.

"Who opened that?" she asked.

"I have no idea, but I will find out." She had never seen him so angry. He kicked one of the bolts into the hole and stormed toward the stairs. "Somebody's in deep shit."

Seeing where his thoughts were heading, Kiera ran after him. "Josh. Slow down. Maybe it wasn't the staff."

"Who else would it be?" He stormed across the basement, looking primed for murder.

"Hey! You've got the camera feed. Look at that first before you go off on everyone."

Josh turned back and stopped, taking a breath. "Shit. You're right. Thanks for talking me down. I was about to blow."

Her voice etched with sarcasm, Kiera said, "Really?"

They walked to the office. Kyla and Bella called 'goodnight' and waved from the front door. Josh plopped down in an office chair and reached for his laptop. Kiera sat and watched him bring up the security software, select the basement cam, and fast-forward from open. At 20:30, the screen went dark and stayed dark until 23:00.

"What the hell?"

"Check the other cameras," Kiera said.

The bar camera ran normally from open to close. Same for the apartment camera and the basement door cam. Josh said, "It looks like an inside job."

"Maybe, maybe not," Kiera said. "The camera could be faulty. Besides, anyone inside the bar could've walked through the interior door and into the basement. We were so busy. I wouldn't have likely noticed."

Josh shook his head. "You're right." He closed the laptop. "I don't understand the point of it."

"Neither do I, but leave it open for now."

He jerked his head and turned to face her. "What? Why?"

"I want to go further into the tunnel, see if it comes out anywhere. See if there's a way someone could break in and rob the place."

He shrugged. "I suppose."

She stared into space. "Even that makes little sense. It's not like they're trying to hide it."

"I know." He grinned. "Must be ghosts. Isn't that what Willow thinks?"

"It is. There might be ghosts here but even I don't believe they're capable of moving a two-hundred-pound iron hatch."

"Neither do I. Anyway, since we're living upstairs now, I'm less worried about a break-in."

Suddenly remembering her plans with Willow, Kiera said, "By the way. Where's my Kimber?"

"Upstairs, why?"

"Willow and I are going to the range tomorrow."

"I thought you were mad at her."

"I was. We're better now." Kiera smiled. "We never stay mad for long."

"So what was the tiff about this time?"

Kiera hesitated and Josh turned with a suspicious eye. "What?"

She sat on the edge of the desk. "Don't be mad."

"What?"

She had built this relationship with Josh on honesty. She decided to fess up. "Willow did a reading on you. She...um...was worried you might...have an affair with a waitress."

"That bitch!" He spit the words out, looking like he might explode.

"Josh!" Honesty suddenly felt like the wrong solution.

Josh pointed a finger at her. "She needs to stay out of my business. You two can tarot all you want. Leave me out of it."

"I told her that."

"But you believed it, didn't you?" He looked mad—and hurt.

"No." But she couldn't meet his gaze. She had screwed up.

"Yes you did. You've been watching me all week." Josh said, shaking his head in disbelief. "Sheesh! I didn't know if I was imagining it or what."

"I'm sorry. Angela's got a thing for you though."

"Half the guys in the bar have a thing for *you*, Kiera. I'm not watching *your* every move." Josh looked her directly in the eyes. "I'm not interested in Angela. I'm with you."

That dropped the final nail in her guilt. He was right. She was an idiot. "I'm sorry, babe." She slid over, wrapped her arms around him and kissed his cheek.

He softened and kissed her back. "Let's lock up and go to bed. I'm beat."

Twenty

Willow and Kiera met the next afternoon at the range. Ned's Shooters Supply sat a mile out of town on the highway, a huge building with almost an acre of guns and rifles, archery gear, hunting supplies, clothing and camo, all under one roof. Kiera wasn't a gun nut but she liked guns. Her dad had taught her how to shoot. He had two daughters and desperately wanted a hunting buddy, and Kiera was thrilled he wanted to teach her how.

She owned six different handguns and two shotguns. Her concealed carry permit allowed her to pack a gun when she hiked alone or went on a dig in a remote location. A girl could never be too careful. She was an attractive woman and always kept an eye out for creeps. It wasn't fair women had to think and act defensively, but it remained a reality in this world.

She ran into plenty of women at the range and it was clear many were there for similar reasons. Willow was an enigma and Kiera never failed to smile when Willow loaded clips, donned protective glasses and earmuffs, and drilled her target with a tight pattern of bullet holes. That peace loving, new-agey flower child was deadly with a gun and could shoot with the best of them. In her case, the motivation was trauma. She had been sexually assaulted in high school and carrying a gun in her purse helped her feel safe when she left the house. It had given her power over the agoraphobia that developed after the assault.

Willow was looking at a Glock when Kiera walked in. She waved and together, they headed back to the range.

"What are you shooting today?" Kiera asked.

"I brought the cannon. I'm feeling a little like Dirty Harry today."

She was wearing a cute aqua-blue sundress and beach flip flops. "Yeah, you look like it."

"Okay, Dirty Harriet then."

They had the range to themselves. It was *Ladies Only* today and usually empty at this time of day. As they set up and loaded their guns, Willow said, "Glass of wine after?"

Kiera rolled her eyes. "Duh. Why would you even ask?"

Conspiratorially, Willow said, "I want to talk about something."

"What?"

"Wait till later, sweetie." She pulled her ear muffs on and waited for Kiera to don hers. Willow turned, adopted a two-handed stance and yelled, "Freeze asshole!"

She emptied the revolver in seconds.

"Jesus, Willow! You weren't kidding." Kiera stood there, wide-eyed, impressed by her brazen approach.

"I warned you." Willow reeled her paper target in, revealing a tight pattern of holes in the head of the bad guy. She smiled grimly, revealing a rough edge to her normally placid demeanor. "Clint Eastwood? Bite me."

Kiera, shooting her Kimber Micro 9, unloaded a clip and reeled her target in, revealing a wider pattern in the torso. A good shoot, but not great.

"Not bad, for a girl," Willow joked.

They spent an hour at the range gabbing, reloading, and shooting at various distances until they had each shot up ten targets. As they packed their guns away, Kiera said, "Where do you want to go?"

"Let's go to The Vinery."

"Sounds good. See you there."

★   ★   ★

They sat at a high table next to the aquarium. Willow ordered a rosé and Kiera, a Sonoma Cutrer chardonnay.

"Okay lady, what's up?" Kiera said, then slapped Willow's arm. "And by the way? Josh has no interest in the waitress."

Willow donned a contrite face. "Sorry. Point taken. I won't do another read. But you believed it, didn't you?"

"Yeah. Thanks to you, I feel like a jerk."

Willow tilted her head. "You still mad?"

"No. You know me. I don't hold grudges or stay mad for long." Kiera slapped her hand. "I will give you shit about it though. Anyway, what'd you want to talk about?"

"The tavern. The opening in the basement floor to be exact."

"As it happens, someone opened it again," Kiera said. "Josh is pissed."

"It's an omen," Willow said solemnly.

Kiera didn't believe that. "No, someone's just messing with us."

Willow clasped Kiera's hands. "Listen, I had a dream last night about that opening. There's a tunnel—"

"How'd you know about that?" Kiera started, feeling her belly tighten.

"There was a tunnel in my dream, but maybe you told me, I don't remember," Willow said with animated hand gestures. "Anyway, have you explored the tunnel at all?"

"Josh and I did, just a little. Why?" A few hackles on her neck went up. Willow had a far off look in her eyes. Almost eerie.

"I saw a boat down there,"

"A boat? In the tunnel?"

"Yes—no. It was in a room and it was so bizarre. A wooden sailboat, kind of like a big canoe with a weird, raised curlicue on each end."

Kiera thought for a moment, puzzled. "Sounds like a Viking longship." She did a quick search on Google and showed Willow a photo.

Willow nodded. "Yep! That's it!"

"That's impossible," Kiera said, disturbed by this tack. "Then again, you did say it was a dream."

"It looked and felt real."

"I'm sure. But the Vikings never traveled this far west. Besides, how would they get a boat into the tunnel?" How had Willow conjured the vision of a longship out of thin air? She hadn't even known what it was.

"I don't know. It was in a large room, a cavern."

"So what does it all mean?"

Willow, silent for a moment, said, "I'm not sure, but it felt spiritual, like a temple or something."

"I wish it were true. It would be the archeological find of the century. A Viking religious site, or a temple, and a longship in Wisconsin? We'd have to rewrite the history of European colonization of North America. The Solutrean hypothesis might actually be valid—"

"Now who's getting carried away. I don't even know what that all means."

Kiera shook her head. "It's not important."

Willow raised an eyebrow. "Did you close it back up?"

"No. Why?"

"Wanna go exploring?"

"Now? I thought the hole in the floor freaked you out?" Willow's shifting moods confused Kiera.

"It does, but I can't ignore the dream. Something down there is calling to me. There's darkness there, but there's also light. And I brought my lucky talisman and a protective amulet."

"Well. I feel much better knowing that." But she couldn't deny that it intrigued her. Whatever Willow had dreamt—some allegorical imagery perhaps—her description was vivid. Now she had to know the truth of it. Her curiosity was compelling.

Besides, they had Willow's lucky talisman.

After an internal eye roll, Kiera said, "Sure. Let's do it."

Twenty-One

Lachlan spent hours poring over images from the MacKenzie Renovations website. The site itself was gone but had been well preserved by the Wayback Machine. A self-professed Luddite, he was learning the finer points of internet search through necessity. He considered himself quite a sleuth as well. Between the book translation from Kenric's office, his knowledge of the house, his visit to the site, and fragments of old conversations remembered, he was developing an understanding of the events leading up to the explosion and the death of his friend.

The MacKenzies had posted high-resolution photos of the renovations plus videos and blueprints of the house, so Lachlan had a vivid mental picture of it. He concluded, based on the construction techniques—the hand-hewn oak beams, wattle-and-daub wall construction, and many other details—that the house had been transported from England to Wisconsin at some point. And, based on the known facts and a keen sense of intuition, he decided the house in the book and the MacKenzie house were one in the same. He felt certain Kenric had realized the connection and understood that the MacKenzie house and invocation were intimately entwined.

How it had been moved wasn't important.

Why? That was the question.

The story? Five hundred years ago in the north of England, there had been a woman who practiced a particularly malignant form of witchcraft. Her husband had retained Kenric to permanently bind her spirit after her death. For the life of him, Lachlan couldn't remember the family name, but believed the book Kenric had translated was hers and told the story of her death in those final three pages. Her husband had buried her alive, sealed her in a brick tomb. In retribution, she had cast a virulent incantation on her husband and his family. Her name was Anna something-or-other.

From there, the story grew foggy. Had she somehow survived five hundred years, entombed in the house? Had she somehow killed Kenric and stolen his power? It didn't seem likely. That the MacKenzie woman had some powers of her own further confused the picture. Regardless, in the end, Kenric must have decided to destroy the house to end the invocation and eliminate any remnants of evil. But if he understood Dana properly, Kenric was already dead by the time she'd left the house. If so, had Laura MacKenzie blown the house up? Why had she stayed? What had compelled her to destroy the house and kill herself in the process?

He had to go back and try to divine those last minutes from the energies that remained. He packed a small bag with medicaments, amulets, and a small glass vial containing *Psilocybe semilanceata,* better known as magic mushrooms. The psilocybin enhanced his perception when trying to read a space or relive an old event.

Every member of the Aeldo had specialties. His was the ability to read spaces, locations, and structures and compose a story about those places, and that's what he would do.

Hopefully, he would resolve the mystery surrounding the events at the MacKenzie house and use that information to end this business once and for all.

★ ★ ★

Lachlan parked off the road on an old logging trail and walked to the grassy knoll where the house once stood. Though the lot had been bulldozed and landscaped, the fabric and foundation of the house remained, buried beneath. Its presence would be invaluable in revealing more of the story.

He sat in the long grass and lit a tapered incense stick that would repulse the hardiest of bugs yet smelled fragrant, like lavender. After pouring a small glass of red wine, a port, he sprinkled a small amount of mushroom dust into his left palm. He licked up the dust, drank the wine in a single swallow, then laid his head on a small bamboo mat and cleared his mind.

Twenty minutes later, the colors of the trees, grasses, and sky grew more vivid. His mind, now a blank slate, opened to the minute energies vibrating up from the ground. He saw the house as it once was, an authentic Tudor house. A grand structure of dark beams and white plaster, gables and leaded glass windows. Then the MacKenzie woman, and Kenric, at first obscured by a veil of fog, grew clearer and more vivid as he relaxed further into the trippy feeling. A great darkness surrounded the house and those within. A snowstorm raged, the sense of danger and evil in the air oppressive.

Inside the house, a man and the MacKenzie woman fought. She killed the man and then faced off against a someone or something that had assumed the shape of a young woman. After a battle, a different specter appeared and impaled the woman with a pitchfork in a gory drama.

Good Lord! It was scarcely believable!

Kenric arrived. He fought hard against the darkness with every trick in his substantial repertoire. Ultimately, the darkness prevailed. Then Lachlan saw something amazing. With his dying breath, Kenric passed his solution to the MacKenzie woman telepathically. And she carried it out, to the letter, crashing a Range Rover loaded with gas and TNT through the wall of the house. Even though she was trapped inside the vehicle, the woman pushed the button on the detonator and destroyed the house. It was a stunning act of bravery to save her family. The vision moved Lachlan to tears for the second time in weeks. Not normally this sentimental, he knew the psilocybin was apt to toy with his emotions.

When the dust had settled, something remained. A residue. The thing Kenric sought to destroy had suffered a grievous blow, but it had survived.

The darkness.

He didn't understand what this darkness was.

He had encountered all manner of creatures, beasts, lost souls, spirits, ghosts, and manifestations and this fit none of those categories. He truly believed there was nothing new under the sun, but this thing, this darkness, baffled him.

Anna Flecher! The woman's name was Anna Flecher. But she was dead, the house destroyed, and yet, her curse had somehow transmuted into something new and different, and it appeared to be nearly indestructible.

Kenric clearly felt the problem was the house itself—thought destroying the house would be enough—and didn't realize or had no time to deduce that something different was at work. Was it Anna

Flecher? He didn't think so. It had arisen from her invocation, but became something else.

Knowing this was little help in deciding on a course of action. Kenric hadn't been able to destroy it.

Lachlan sensed the darkness from the MacKenzie house had percolated down into the limestone bedrock beneath the foundation. Had it gone off to hide? To plot a return? At first, he worried it had escaped into the rock and disappeared. Lost to him and with it, any chance at retribution. That might be the best outcome but it didn't feel right. As the psilocybin faded, he stood and walked to his car. It was then he noticed a faint disruption in the energies. It was a trail, like a snail might leave, a trail—he was certain—that led to the darkness.

Leah MacKenzie was right.

How she knew he couldn't imagine—considering the distance to her house—but she was right.

It was still out there.

* * *

Rachel Nash sat in the grass in the late afternoon shade of an oak, sweating, sticky, and bored. It had to be a hundred degrees and her Mountain Dew was piss warm. It had been a long two weeks since she found the arrowhead with the inset gem. Stuffed in her front pocket, she took it everywhere, fascinated by the blue crystal that seemed to swirl like a living, breathing thing. At times, as she moved around the field, raking the soil, looking for artifacts, it seemed to grow warmer in her pocket. At dusk, it glowed slightly, especially near the old barn.

Dumping her warm soda, Rachel stood and walked a slow straight line from the corner fence post to the group of boulders, some almost three feet in diameter, at the edge of the field nearest the road. The road was still almost sixty feet off and hidden by dense brush. The old farmhouse stood thirty feet due south and the barn just twenty feet on the other side of her. It had been a slow day in a slow week. She had found a single arrowhead and a few old pennies, including ironically, an Indian head penny from 1877. The lack of success and heat were taking a toll on her enthusiasm.

She had never explored in the barn, though *barn* was a generous title now. The roof had collapsed, taking the entrance and east wall with it. Since it had been pushed in one direction into a disorganized pile, she assumed it went down in a windstorm. Two walls remained and the inside area, mostly clear of debris, was filled with prairie grass and random bushes and saplings. It didn't look safe and that was the only reason she hadn't gone there before. That and a promise to her father. Her dad had been emphatic that she stay out. It was likely dangerous and might have hidden pits and other hazards she could stumble into. He saw no harm in her wandering around a fallow field but made her promise to stay out of the house and the barn.

Having completed a full circuit of the field this summer, feeling she might have depleted it of arrowheads and tools, she decided to risk a walk around in the barn—if one could be *in* a building that had fallen apart. Her first steps were tentative and cut short when she tripped in a runnel hidden in the grass. Still damp from the overnight rain, she fell and landed in mud.

Great. Just great.

Already dirty, she gave in and sat there, trying to wipe the mud from her hands and right knee.

She spotted a chunk of corroded metal poking from the soil. It wasn't Native American. They didn't work with metals. Curious nevertheless, she tried to work it loose. It might be a piece of old machinery, but it could be a knife from the French-Indian wars. She had found one once before, but it was too corroded to save.

The arrowhead in her pocket grew warm and seemed to be vibrating. She pulled it out. It wasn't really vibrating but tingled in her hand, feeling warmer than her body temperature. On a hunch, she moved it closer to the blade protruding from the ground and it glowed slightly as well.

Holy shit!

Excited, she dug deeper using a gardening trowel, uncovering the blade in small increments. The clay soil made for tough digging and progress was slow. It was a knife of some sort, though the blade seemed very long, much of it still buried, tipping down at an angle toward the hilt. Rachel was sweating with the effort, oblivious to the failing light.

Her phone pinged. Her dad: *Home! Now!*

No! Not now. She couldn't leave now! As if reading her mind, he sent a second text: *Now!*

Crap.

After a moment of silent cursing, Rachel covered the exposed segment of metal with branches. She shoved the arrowhead in her pocket, fetched her bike, and pedaled home in a pissy mood.

Twenty-Two

Kiera ran home to change and grab some gear to go exploring, or in this case, spelunking. From her gear closet, she pulled two hardhats with headlights and GoPros, two Maglites, a camera in a shock-resistant case, and two pieces of chalk to mark their way. She changed into jeans and hiking boots and donned a flannel shirt. It was often cold underground. She called Josh, but he was lukewarm to the idea of going into the tunnel. He seemed relieved that she wasn't insisting he come too.

Twenty minutes later, she pulled into the parking lot. Willow was sitting on the bench in front of the bar.

Kiera said, "You freaking out about this yet?"

Looking flustered, she said, "No, yes, maybe. I don't know. I have to, simple as that."

Kiera handed her a hardhat and a Maglite. Willow looked askance at the hat. "You serious?"

"Deadly. Proper gear at all times. Put it on."

Willow reluctantly complied. Kiera said, "Hey, you look hot in it anyway."

"Yeah, right," Willow said doubtfully.

Kiera clipped the camera and phone to her belt and led the way into the basement. With the lights off, she could see a faint glow emanating from the square opening. Even though she knew there was a perfectly rational, scientific explanation for the light, it still sent a small shiver down her spine—her unease perhaps the remnant of some prehistoric fear hidden in the furthest reaches of her brain.

She climbed down the vertical rock stairs and waited for Willow to drop down next to her. The momentary apprehension was gone, replaced by the steely intent of a scientist. If Willow was even remotely right, the possibilities were mind-boggling.

"Ready?" Kiera asked.

"Yep."

Kiera clicked her GoPro on and started down the tunnel, observing more critically this time.

The dolomite walls looked mostly natural, carved by water running and percolating through the limestone. The old tool marks presented an enigma. Was it a mineshaft? A natural cave exploited by cavers? She didn't know. The connection to the tavern sparked a thought: old boot-legging tunnels? An interesting angle to research. It was part of the Niagara Escarpment, a tidbit of interest only to a geologist.

"Where's the light coming from?" Willow asked.

"I don't know. It's a mystery. Bioluminescent bacteria or something."

Featureless, and nearly straight for the first fifty feet, the tunnel then curved to the left and sloped gently downward. The light remained constant. They had now walked farther than she and Josh had. Again, Kiera was struck by the lack of vermin, insects, or any of the other creepy life forms that normally inhabited old caves and mines.

Kiera was thinking they were wasting their time when Willow grabbed her arm and said, "Up ahead. I feel some energy."

"Feels like a wild-goose chase to me."

"Oh ye of little faith. Just you wait."

They both saw the archway at the same moment. The size of a large door, it was cut into the right side of the tunnel wall and seemed more brightly lit—almost glowing—casting a swath of light across their path. Beyond the arch, the tunnel curved to the left, out of view.

They glanced at each other and stopped, Kiera suddenly nervous about what might occupy the room inside the archway.

Willow solemnly said, "I told you."

They moved in step, close together, looking to each other with questioning eyes, Kiera struck by the expression of awe and rapture evident on Willow's face. What did she think she'd find in there? They crept the last ten feet to the arch and peered cautiously around the corner.

The archway framed a large, circular cavern. The space was huge, rising to a dome-shaped ceiling at least forty feet tall. Perhaps part of a natural cavern, someone had carved and chiseled the rock chamber to perfection. A bench, carved from the native rock, ran around the outer edge of the cave.

Kiera stood stunned, speechless and awed, but it wasn't the room that captivated her.

In the center, on a limestone plinth, stood a Viking longship of a type common in the 8th through the 11th centuries. At least fifty feet long, it was fairly narrow, of wood lapstrake construction, the prow rising high and capped by menacing figurehead—a dragon perhaps—and the stern rising to a carved scroll. A mast and square sail sat midships.

"Holy shit." Kiera said in a reverent whisper.

"Wow, it's true," Willow said, her voice filled with wonder.

It was magnificent! And inexplicable. No rational or reasonable explanation existed for the presence of a Viking longship in this cave.

How did it get to the Great Lakes? Someone might have shipped it from Europe during the later European settlement of the area, but how did they get it into the cave? She walked closer and examined the boat carefully, so captivated that she was aware of nothing else, not even Willow.

The detailing was exquisite, with hand-hewn planks fastened with iron rivets, and sealed with pine tar and animal hair. This was no replica. It was the real deal. A genuine piece of history, perhaps the best preserved longship that she had ever seen.

It would require testing and authentication. First, she needed a sense of reference, a look at the bigger picture. The ship was part of something—a display, a shrine, or a collection—and by studying that, perhaps she could determine how the boat had gotten there. And more importantly, why it was here.

She turned from the boat and scanned the room.

As in the tunnel, there was no visible lighting, but the room glowed with a soft luminescence brighter than the tunnel. The walls were adorned with crude drawings: hunting scenes and strange rituals known only to the artists. Some of the drawings were Native American and they looked genuine. Others showed Viking longships and raiders.

At the back of the room, an incredible drawing covered the wall: a group of Vikings and Native Americans meeting in a wooded clearing. A huge banquet, an exchange of gifts, peace pipes, and goblets of wine or mead. If authentic, it would completely rewrite many hypotheses about the peopling of North America and the extent of Viking exploration in the New World.

If it was real.

It seemed too fantastic, too improbable to be authentic.

Beneath the art and drawings, a line of runic symbols wrapped around most of the room. Kiera felt fairly certain it was Old Norse:

ᚷᚨᛏᛏᛁᚱ ᚠᛁᛁᚠᚱ ᚠ ᚱ ᚷᚨᚦᛉᛁ ᛁᚱ ᚠᛗ ᛈ ᛗᚦᛉ ᚠᚤ

"This is awesome—and creepy as shit," Willow said.

"It's all that and more. This could be the archaeological find of the century." Kiera kept spinning and circling, trying to absorb the scope and import of the room, the drawings and art, and the longship. She couldn't get her head around it.

It felt surreal, like suddenly discovering the bland old painting in grandma's parlor was actually a Renoir. She unclipped the camera from her belt and snapped dozens of photos: close-ups and wider angles of the boat and the walls, trying to paint a coherent image of the room. She was also thinking ahead, trying to explain this to former colleagues and professors. They would certainly doubt her and assume an elaborate hoax of some sort.

"Willow!"

Willow lay on the floor, unconscious, arms and legs twitching, her back arched. Kiera ran to her and knelt. It looked like she was having a seizure. Good thing she had been wearing the helmet. It likely protected her head. A moment later, the tremors ceased.

Willow opened her eyes, looking dazed and confused. "What happened?"

"I think you had a seizure."

Willow considered for a moment and slowly sat up, shook her head, and said, "No way. I've never had a seizure."

"Well, you just did. We have to get you to the ER." Kiera took one last look around the room, helped Willow to her feet, and walked toward the access hatch, hanging on to Willow's arm lest she fall again. Kiera felt slammed: by the discovery of the cavern, the longship, all of it inexplicable. She had no time to process it before her best friend had a seizure out of the blue. It left her off guard when, halfway back, Willow shoved her arm away. "I'm fine, back off a bit."

She didn't look fine. She looked angry.

Oh well. They were going to the ER anyway.

They arrived ten minutes later. Willow was reluctant to be seen and tried to talk Kiera out of it. As soon as Kiera said the word *seizure*, the nursing staff grew concerned and a doctor appeared, emphasizing the importance of an exam. Willow grew more cantankerous.

After listening to Kiera's description of the event and performing a brief workup in an exam room, they took Willow for an MRI.

Kiera waited in the room and fretted about the cavern and about Willow. This day couldn't possibly be more screwed up. She was trying to be a concerned friend and Willow was treating her like a meddling bitch. All Kiera really wanted was to go back into the cavern and gawk at the longship, and then spend hours examining every inch of it. She sent a text to Josh that she might be late.

When Willow returned, almost three hours later, Kiera managed one word after the nurse left. "Hey—"

"Get out!" Willow pointed at the door. "Now!"

"Sweetie?"

"Kiera! Go!"

"Won't you need a ride when—?"

"Get out! Now!"

Kiera didn't have to be told again. Screw this! She turned on her heels and stormed out, fuming. After trying to look out for Willow, the woman freaked out. Why? Over what? Kiera had no idea what the problem was. What an ungrateful bitch!

After a quick change of clothes at home, Kiera walked into the tavern just after 6 pm. She waved and greeted the customers she knew and stepped behind the bar.

Josh slid over, looking concerned. "How'd it go? She okay?"

"I think she's okay but she's pissed at me." She looked at Josh indignantly. "She threw me out."

"Un huh. You'll be BFFs again in a week."

"I'm not so sure. This feels like more than a spat."

"Yeah, yeah." Josh waved a dismissive hand. "So what were you all excited about? Your text made it sound like you found the Ark of the Covenant."

"Can you take a short break?"

"Sure. I called Caleb in to help." He yelled, "Hey, Caleb. Watch the bar, please."

"Yes, boss man." He bowed. Caleb was six-two with scruffy dark hair and a short beard. He was quite popular with the ladies.

Kiera dragged him up the stairs to the apartment, grabbed her laptop, and quickly downloaded the pics from the camera. She opened the photo file and turned the laptop so Josh could see clearly.

He did a double-take. "What the hell is that?"

"A Viking longship."

He looked at her, puzzled. "Vikings? The guys with the beards and swords who drank mead all the time?"

"Yep." She put two fingers to his lips and continued paging slowly through the photos, while Josh muttered and said, "Holy shit!" repeatedly. She stopped at the drawing of the ceremony between the Native Americans and the Vikings.

"No way." Staring wide-eyed, he ran a hand through his hair. "That's down in the tunnel? No fucking way!"

"Way, baby."

"No. This has to be a reproduction, or some sort of joke," Josh said. "I'm no expert, but even I know the Vikings never came this far west. They landed somewhere in Canada and booted Chris Columbus off the 'first to discover the Americas' short list."

"Yes, right behind the Native Americans who were already here," Kiera said dryly. "I think it's real. But everyone is going to think it's a fraud."

Josh nodded. Kiera rambled on, thinking out loud. "This simply can't be. Unless the Solutrean hypothesis is valid—no, a hoax is the reasonable explanation, like the Kensington Runestone—"

"I don't know what any of that means."

"The Solutrean hypothesis suggests that some of the people who settled the Americas came across the North Atlantic from Europe. The Kensington Runestone was found in Minnesota and purported to be Scandinavian from 1362. It's widely considered to be a fraud."

"So now what?" Josh seemed to be scheming possibilities.

"I don't know," Kiera said. "There are so many ramifications. First I have to convince someone to come and look at the longship. If they confirm it's genuine, then someone has to decide whether the Vikings put it here, or if the longship was carried here by Native Americans and turned into some kind of shrine. Then there's the whole issue of access, though it's likely they would want to dig directly into the cavern."

"That does sound better," he said, though he sounded doubtful. "Less interference to tavern operations."

"Don't count on it. If this is legit, we'll be swamped by curiosity hounds, creeps, doubters, the tinfoil-hat people, the whole gamut."

He grinned. "More business then."

"Careful what you wish for," Kiera said. "In the meantime, don't tell *anyone*, not even your dad."

Twenty-Three

Scott Robbins, bon vivant and the most successful car dealer in Miller's Crossing, scanned the bottles of wine, looking for the right vintage, the perfect bottle for the perfect evening. Clare, his lovely wife of twenty years, whispered she was a bit horny tonight, an event that occurred roughly once every other full moon. He knew how to play his cards when this moment arose: a glass or two of wine, a subtle romantic approach, and patience. Especially patience.

Although he was a womanizer, he loved his wife and looked forward to these evenings. Ironically, they were also the rationale for his affairs. Because these nights were so rare and because he was a healthy middle-aged male, he had appetites to fill. It was a matter of taking care of himself, maintaining his reproductive health, nothing more.

He decided on an Australian Shiraz, a favorite with Clare. As he turned to leave, the cellar door slammed shut as if shoved by a strong wind. He wrenched on the handle, but it wouldn't budge. Had Clare been teasing him tonight? Had she discovered something and decided to get even by locking him in the wine cellar? Oh, the perils of a guilty conscience.

The ground shuddered slightly, like the passing of a heavy truck. It had happened a few times while they were remodeling the tavern around the corner. Seconds later, the floor trembled again, followed by a brief grating sound—like a heavy stone on concrete. With the sudden feeling that he wasn't alone, Scott looked around warily, fearing a looming presence behind him.

Man, he had to get out of here!

His feet wouldn't move.

Looking down, his gut clenched tight with fear.

Oh my God!

He was sinking into the floor! Sinking into wet, gooey concrete—fresh, as if it had been poured minutes before. How was this happening? But the question was lost to his rising panic. He fought to pry his feet loose, then struggled to break free with a labored running motion that only accelerated his descent into the floor.

He grabbed at the wine racks, which pulled loose. Bottles fell and broke on the floor, splattering wine everywhere. The suction was too great and still he sank, in the thrall of a gripping dread that he would slip beneath the surface of this awful quicksand, his mouth filling with wet choking muck, dying as his lungs struggled to draw in oxygen when none remained.

No, no, no, no, no!

He heard Clare calling, far in the distance. "Scott, come on. What're you doing down there? Jerking off?"

Suddenly released from the paralyzing fear of his fatal vision, he screamed and yelled, "Clare, help me! Please God help me!"

"Scott?" Her voice sounded closer, no longer miles away.

"Help! Help!" Writhing in terror, he realized he was crying and had wet himself. He didn't want to die, especially like this, when he couldn't even comprehend what *this* was. He had always imagined death in the abstract: him a doddering old lump who no longer cared about life, who could barely discern that he still existed. Instead, he had only seconds before he disappeared into the floor. How was this even possible? It had to be a nightmare—

Wake up! Wake up!

"Scott? What's the matter?" Clare was outside the door. Why wasn't she opening the door? His only thought was survival, getting that door open, escaping this awful goo. As he struggled, he sank faster, and was now chest deep, out of reach of anything to grab and pull himself to safety.

"Open the door! Help me!"

He saw the handle wiggle.

"It's stuck!"

"Try harder! I'm sinking!"

"What?"

"Push harder! Hurry!"

He could hear her wrenching on the handle and kicking at the door. The handle moved slowly downward and he heard a *click* as it broke free. He saw the door move, so slowly, but moving, saw salvation—

Scott felt a hand or something grasp his ankle. It jerked him beneath the surface into the wet darkness below, wet concrete filling his mouth with his final stifled scream. Distantly, he heard a voice, plaintive and scared, muffled by the cement filling his ears like a thousand gallons of water.

"Scott? Where are you? Where'd you go?"

Twenty-Four

Willow kicked her flip-flops into the closet and climbed into bed, exhausted after a multitude of tests. One of them, a sleep-deprived EEG, had been performed early this morning after they had forced her to stay awake all night. Tests in hand, the neurologist concluded she had probably just fainted. Syncope, they called it. There was no evidence of abnormal brain activity suggestive of a seizure disorder.

As she lay there, her burning anger wouldn't let her sleep. The whole miserable experience was Kiera's fault—and that bitch had probably slept like a baby in her own bed. Fine friend she turned out to be. Willow knew she had just fainted, but no, Kiera insisted they go to the ER anyway and thus began her long night of misery. She couldn't wait to see the medical bills, even with her insurance. Maybe she'd shove them in Kiera's mailbox.

God, she wanted to sleep, but she couldn't let it go. They had been friends since third grade but now, it didn't feel like they were friends at all. As the anger slowly ebbed, she relived the walk into the tunnel and discovery of the enormous boat. A Viking longship, Kiera called it. The boat, the drawings, the art? It felt like a temple to her, her visit there a spiritual experience. She had searched her whole life for a philosophy that would explain the meaning of life—her life—in the grand scheme of things. She had studied the Judaic religions, the Eastern philosophies, Wicca and other pagan religions. All of her interests—Tarot, numerology, astrology—were an attempt to understand the universe and her place in it.

Then she walked into that cavern and saw the ship. It felt like coming home. She finally understood *everything*. How strange it should be right here where she lived. She needed to go again, to absorb the energies of the place, the wisdoms, the peace. That room was the thin place. A direct portal to the center of the universe. More than that, some sort of tipping point between the good and bad in the world.

Only one problem: it felt like she and Kiera were over. She might even hate the woman a little. Willow couldn't explain it nor did she fully understand it. Normally she'd be mad, but also eager to make up. They had been friends forever. Right now, they just felt broken and Willow felt no desire to fix it.

Kiera mustn't know that. Willow had to hide her feelings and pretend they were still friends. Whatever it took to revisit the thin place and to discover the answers to the big life questions she knew were there.

★   ★   ★

Kiera printed the cavern and longship photos and arranged them into a professional album with a custom cover. She had an appointment with the head of archeology at Milwaukee University. They were casual friends and he sounded curious, even though Kiera had refused to answer his questions until he agreed to a meeting. He had pushed for a dinner meeting, but she felt this was best handled in a professional setting. Besides, the professor had a tendency to get handsy when he drank.

She hated to share this with anyone, but she didn't have the credentials or the standing to present the information and findings to the archeological community. To establish the site as authentic, she would need a second opinion on her work as the project went forward. Most of all, it was doubtful journals would publish any of her findings without the name of a well-known archeologist attached.

An hour later, she parked and walked up to the second floor of the anthropology department and knocked on his office door.

"Come in, Kiera," he said in a pleasant baritone.

"Hi Professor Marshall."

He was a tall man in his mid-fifties, a professional-looking man with shaggy salt and pepper hair, dressed casually in jeans and a blue linen shirt. He stood and shook her hand gently, motioning to a chair. "Please, call me Rustin."

The office was paneled with dark wood and filled with bookcases. The books were mostly scientific, some of them collectibles over a hundred years old. His desk, a very masculine chunk of dark mahogany, was enormous. Mostly neat, there was a laptop and a stack of papers waiting on grades.

Kiera set the album down, but kept her fingers on the cover so he couldn't snatch it away.

"I don't think you're going to believe this, but I think you should try."

Ooh, that sounded dumb.

He smiled a bit gratuitously, "Are you going to tell me what it is, Kiera?"

Kiera sat, crossing her legs, trying to relax. "Some backstory first." She explained about Josh, the tavern, the iron hatch and the tunnel they had found in the basement.

"Anyway, a friend and I went in exploring. I was unable to determine the tunnel's purpose until we found a cavern about seventy-five yards in." She paused for effect, and to collect her thoughts. "We found something absolutely unbelievable in that chamber—"

"What? You're killing me. I get it. A bar, the tunnel, some amazing artifact, I imagine?" He had a tendency to be smug and superior, especially around women. She worried he might be too full of himself to approach this with an open mind. She slid the album across the desk without a word. He spent five minutes paging back and forth through the photos with an amusing assortment of raised eyebrows, forehead furrows, and squints.

Finally, he said, "What's your hypothesis? Since you're here, I assume you have one."

She considered. It was a reasonable question, but also a test and a trap. He wanted to know if *she* had approached this with an open mind, without jumping to conclusions.

"Nothing firm. A hypothesis isn't possible at this time. I believe the longship is genuine. I'm well versed on the Vikings, their culture, travels, boat building techniques and this looks authentic. I assumed the longship had been disassembled, then reassembled in the cave but I could find no evidence that was the case. How it got there? Who put it there? Those are the questions I would start with."

"Indeed. *If* it's genuine," he said. He looked intrigued, not dismissive. "And the rest of it?"

"No idea. A complete mystery." Kiera said. "The paintings and drawings are mostly Native American. That isn't my area of expertise.

We should try to date everything first."

"I agree." He adopted a furtive expression. "We should also keep it very hush-hush."

Kiera could see his wheels turning. "Agreed. For now, the fewer who know about this, the better."

She slid the book away from him and eyed him directly. "One more thing. Joint authorship on all papers and findings. Joint authority on the initial studies and dating. I want it in writing. We both know this could be huge, no matter what theories win out. Even as a hoax, it's unprecedented in scope."

"Fair enough. I've always known you're smart. I must add savvy to that list."

"Have it drawn up and I'll sign it." Kiera stood and pointed to the row of letters that encircled the room on one photo. "So what do you make of the long line of runic script on the wall?"

He rested his chin on his forefinger and squinted. "Looks like Old Norse."

"I thought so. It certainly suggests the Vikings might've been here. I suppose Native Americans could have copied the script—I don't know—but a translation might explain some of it."

"Indeed. We'll need help with a translation—"

"I know someone who can handle the translation," Kiera said, not wanting to give Marshall too much control over the site or the associated information. She simply didn't trust him. She picked up the photo album and tucked it under her arm.

"But you'll share your findings?" He didn't trust her either, evidently.

"Absolutely."

As she left the building, a nagging inner voice suggested this meeting may have been a mistake.

* * *

Josh sat on the floor behind the bar, poking through the coolers, checking the beer and soda levels, making a list of the bottles and cans he would need to open at four. As he closed the last cooler door— polished chrome with a glass window—he saw the reflection of a face. Startled, he jumped and spun around.

No one was there.

He stood up and looked around the bar, but it was empty, as it should be. He was the only person here.

That face. What was it? An odd reflection that looked like a face at a glance? Sitting, he opened the door slowly but saw nothing resembling a face. A fluke then. As he shut the door, the face briefly reappeared.

Jesus! What was happening here?

He opened the door again—nothing.

As he closed the door, the face appeared at a specific point. Josh looked in that direction at the back bar but saw nothing even suggestive of a face. Open and close, same result every time, regardless of where he positioned himself. He snapped a pic with his phone, but the result was murky and indeterminate.

There was only one reasonable explanation: someone was messing with him. But the idea was wearing thin. He couldn't imagine how they were doing this. The door looked like all the others: no wires, cameras, or other devices in evidence. Besides, the hatch and tunnel weren't a prank, as it turned out. He didn't even want to think about that.

The only other explanation was dumb. A ghost.

Nope, he wasn't going there.

A reasonable explanation existed. He just didn't know what it was yet.

Josh slammed the door, shook off his aggravation, and bounded down the stairs to the basement to grab the needed bottles and cans.

Twenty-Five

Lachlan sat in the first-floor study of Kenric's house. He still thought of it that way, even though Kenric had given it to him. It would always be Kenric's house. His energy remained vivid within, ever present and reassuring.

Reclined in an exquisitely comfortable Edwardian armchair, his feet rested on a matching ottoman. On a side table sat a glass and a bottle of rare, fine Port, barrel-aged for forty years. An oak and cherrywood fire lent a fine aromatic flavor to the room. His friend had had impeccable taste: medieval art hung on the walls along with small displays of art from some of the prehistoric peoples of Europe, including the Hallstatt and La Tène cultures.

Lachlan, recognizing the dangers he faced, tried to convene a meeting of the Aeldo. None had replied except Fynn Alden, who was bogged down with a situation in Mongolia. Lachlan shuddered. He had been to Ulan Bator once and found it insanely cold, the air polluted, and the city unbearably grim.

For now, he was on his own.

He knew this: the darkness had gone to ground, literally had seeped through the crevices of the bedrock below, a porous ridge of dolomite, part of an extensive limestone formation that arced from New York state westward and down through eastern Wisconsin. The darkness could re-emerge anywhere with access to the upper world: a cave, a tunnel, an outcropping of the rock.

When it reappeared, he should sense its presence—if he was close enough. A needle in a haystack was an inadequate description of the task. Searching for a grain of black onyx on a beach was more accurate. The darkness should be weak yet. If he could find it before it had time to recover and recharge, he *might* be able to destroy it with the proper incantations and talismans.

Might.

In one sense, the word signified strength and power, in another, it meant uncertainty—as it did now. Modern English was such a strange and wonderful language. Context was everything.

The uncertainty was clear, his target an unknown, with unknown abilities and unknown weaknesses. Trial and error wasn't an option. There were no books on the subject. The subject didn't even have a name. He would need considerable luck and he wasn't a gambling man.

A roll of the dice wouldn't do.

He wasn't deterred either. Though reluctant to admit it, he wanted revenge for his friend. Regardless of the dangers, he would track this thing, this darkness, like a bloodhound. Find it and destroy it once and for all.

He meditated, communing with the spirits, seeking answers and guidance, but none were forthcoming.

It was late. Tired and comfortable, the gentle warmth of the fire lulled him to sleep. Perhaps the answer lay there. In his many years, the most enlightened answers often came to him during sleep. He felt more receptive then.

He dozed, reliving the hours he had spent under the influence of psilocybin in the Kettle Moraine, watching the last night at the MacKenzie house play out. He observed the darkness, grievously wounded, slither down into the bedrock beneath the house. He followed it, sliding into the rock, tracking the darkness, and he wasn't alone. Kenric walked by his side, silent but reassuring in his presence. They traveled for miles through fissures, caves, caverns, like a vapor, ephemeral and gossamer, just like the shadow they were following. The imagery meant something, but he couldn't divine the significance of it. His dreams seldom came with a guidebook.

Mostly, it was dark but his vision was so acute, the places they passed through were dimly visible. In some of the caves, luminescence lit the way.

Far ahead, Lachlan saw an area of concentrated brightness. It looked like his destination. His problem would be trying to conflate this area underground with the surface terrain. He didn't yet know how he'd do it but had every confidence the answer would come in time.

The dream stalled when he encountered a barrier, a black iron gate, and could travel no further. There was a building above. An old house, devoid of paint and weathered grey. A tree grew through the front porch. And a sign:

NO TRESPASSING NO HUNTING

He would know it when he saw it. And something else. Something he hadn't experienced in years.

A realm called *Caol Áit*. In his mind, he heard *keel awtch*.

A magical place. The darkness would be drawn to it, to its energy. He needed to find this place first.

He opened his eyes.

Tomorrow.

The search was on.

Twenty-Six

Kiera, Willow, and Rustin Marshall met the next morning at the tavern. Willow had finally called and apologized for the freak-out at the hospital, thanked Kiera for her concern, and begged to be included. The meeting felt awkward. The professor kept eyeing Willow with some mixture of lust and irritation. It was clear he felt she didn't belong. In turn, Willow kept shooting furtive glances at Kiera. There was something weird about her, Kiera decided. Veiled ire maybe, even though Willow denied being angry. They had been friends for so long, Kiera knew something was amiss. Willow had never denied her feelings in the past, but Kiera was too concerned with gaining Marshall's endorsement to worry about it.

Kiera opted to skip safety gear today, earning a glare from Willow. They descended into the tunnel and Kiera led them along the gently curving passage to the cavern.

The Professor was almost beside himself with excitement. "Bioluminescence lighting the way? Amazing!"

"That's my guess, but I can't find any reference to this type of bioluminescence in the literature," Kiera said. "Wait until you see the cavern,"

As they turned the corner through the archway, Marshall's mouth dropped open as he scanned the room.

"My Lord! The photos did no justice to this. None at all!" He walked over and touched the longship for a minute, then slowly walked the length of it.

Willow walked to the longship, placing both hands on it, and stood with her eyes closed, a thin smile on her face. An expression of utter peace. Kiera just hoped she didn't have another seizure.

Fainted my ass! She'd had a seizure, Kiera was sure of it.

The professor walked along the wall and stopped by the large drawing behind the longship and muttered, "Unbelievable!" for the umpteenth time. "Kiera! Come here!"

When she stepped next to him, he said, enthralled, "Do you know what this is?"

"Not sure. It looks like a pow-wow of some sort between a Native American tribe and a group of Vikings. As far as we know, such an event never took place."

"I'm reasonably certain the tribe is Ho-Chunk. This is a Medicine Dance and they're hosting Viking travelers."

"Ho-Chunk would make sense in this area."

He ran a hand over his hair. "This is literally the find of the century. Damn, look at this!" He pointed to a series of carved symbols beneath the image of the ceremony:

ᚠ ᚨᛏᚺ ᛏᛏᛈ ᚨᛏᚺ ᛏᛏᛈ ᚨᛏᚺ ᛏᛏ

"I believe that spells out *Valhalla* in runes."

"This can't be real," Kiera said. Valhalla was the hall of the fallen in Norse mythology. The place where the god Odin housed the dead warriors whom he deemed worthy of dwelling with him. "This implies they believed this to be Asgard."

"That's what we have to determine." Marshall said. "This is too elaborate for a fake. The question is, did Vikings travel this far west? Or did Native Americans haul the longship from Vinland and build this as some type of homage to the Vikings or as a memorial of their meeting?"

Kiera looked around, checking on Willow, but she remained in front of the longship, eyes closed, hands touching the boat in apparent supplication.

Kiera found some loose slivers of wood on the keel, scraped them into a glass vial and sealed it. Radiocarbon dating was the first thing they needed to do to establish an age for the longship. Though the dating would only tell them how old the wood was, Viking shipbuilders usually built their ships with green wood.

They needed something else. While the professor continued looking over the longship, Kiera climbed into the boat and looked along the edge under the gunwale. Longships were usually sealed with pine pitch and animal hair. She found a sample, a congealed mass of tar and animal hair that had fallen from a seam, scooped it up and sealed the vial. It should be enough for now.

The natural bioluminescent light suddenly dimmed to near darkness and slowly returned to the original intensity as if controlled by a dimmer switch. At that moment, the ground shuddered ever so slightly. Kiera wasn't certain it was real. "You feel that?"

"I did."

Kiera scanned the room and Marshall stood in evident shock. Kiera said, "What the hell was that? Bioluminescence doesn't switch on and off—though I don't know if that's actually the source of the light."

"I have no idea. It's inexplicable. We'll need a chemist, or a biologist, I'm not sure which," Marshall said. "There is no reasonable, rational explanation for any of this. Though that shudder may just have been a truck overhead."

"True." It didn't feel like that, but she had nothing better. It reminded her that she had no idea what lay above them. She worried that he wanted to know, to cut her out of the deal if possible. Besides her professional concerns, she was baffled by the find: the longship, the wall art, the Old Norse runes on the wall, the lighting, by the manner it had been hidden underground. It didn't seem natural.

Nope. It felt eerie. Creepy.

Unearthly.

Twenty-Seven

Josh's friend, Caleb Grenier, unlocked the front door of the tavern, leaving it open for the kitchen staff, then went to the control panel and powered up the lights, the flat screens, and the sound system. He inventoried the coolers under the bar and walked down to the basement cooler to restock for the night. Josh had an appointment with his accountant, so Caleb had offered to open.

He noticed the open hatch in the far corner of the basement and wandered over to look. It had never been open before. Probably nothing of interest down there. He wouldn't have given it much thought if Kiera hadn't made a big deal about staying away from it.

Kiera was a little aggressive for his liking. Hot enough for a woman her age, but too controlling. It seemed like Josh checked his nuts at the door when she was around, though Josh evidently resented the implication. Another good man soon lost to matrimony. Wasn't happening to him.

With the tavern to himself, Caleb decided to hazard a look. He grabbed a Maglite and descended, crablike, on the carved steps into the room below. When he turned and looked along the tunnel, he spoke in one long, drawn-out word. "What-the-fuck?"

He had expected a room, a cellar maybe, but not a tunnel, a long one at that. An old mine perhaps?

Caleb vacillated for a moment. He should stock the coolers. If Kiera caught him, she'd be pissed. Oh well.

Why hadn't Josh told him about this? What kind of friend was he? While Josh might be pissed he was snooping down here, it was wide open so he rationalized that a little snooping was acceptable. Still, he saw little of interest in the tunnel, but then he thought: *maybe the tunnel itself wasn't the attraction.*

Where did it go? And why did it look so clean?

He checked his phone and allotted five minutes to explore further. He walked-ran, looking for the end of the tunnel until it seemed like he had traveled quite a distance. Other than a slight slope downward and pitch to the left, the tunnel remained a narrow, craggy burrow, lit by some weird invisible phosphorescent lighting, uninteresting in every respect. An abandoned mine seemed the most likely explanation, and yet the farther he walked, the more uneasy he felt. The skin at the nape of his neck grew taut, the hair on end, a twist of anxiety tight in his stomach.

Not easily spooked, Caleb felt claustrophobic. The walls of the tunnel seemed to be closing in—though perhaps the passage had just narrowed. He was thinking about turning back when he noticed an archway ahead, more brightly lit than the tunnel. His five minutes were up, but he had to take a peek. Had to hurry. He rushed and turned the corner, stopping in stunned disbelief, dropping his phone in the process.

A ship! The most amazing ship he had ever seen. He had no idea what it was, but he knew it was important. His eyes darted back and forth over the walls and the paintings, which he recognized as cave art, possibly prehistoric cave art.

What the hell was this place?

Why hadn't Josh told him about this? Yet, he intuitively understood the secrecy. This was huge. Unbelievable.

Indiana, this...this IS history.

A line from one of his favorite movies, it described perfectly what he saw.

He could keep a secret if that's what they wanted, but he was pissed Josh hadn't told him. Kiera had something to do with that, he was certain. Bitch. He held his phone sideways and quickly snapped a dozen pics to examine later.

He then noticed the room and tunnel had grown cold. He could see his breath. It wasn't this cold a few minutes ago, was it? His unease returned and the room seemed to be leaking light, growing darker. His anxiety and claustrophobia rose to a finely honed point.

Shivering, he turned and ran and didn't stop running until he reached the end of the tunnel—sensing something behind him. Afraid to look, he clambered up the vertical stairs two at a time and threw himself out of the opening to a hard landing on the concrete floor. He lay for a minute, trying to get a fix on his feelings before bursting out laughing.

Oh Jesus, what a weenie!

He had just scared the crap out of himself for no discernible reason.

When a contrary voice whispered, *There was something down there*—

He quickly muttered, "Shut up, dumbass."

★　★　★

Josh walked into the tavern at five. The bar was crowded and Caleb was still stocking coolers. Josh rushed behind the bar and jumped in, mixing drinks and pouring tappers. He slid over to Caleb and whispered, "Dude, why the hell are you so far behind?"

"Got slammed as soon as we opened, bro." Caleb glanced away from his stare.

He was full of shit, Josh thought. Oh well, he'd get them caught up. No big deal.

Once they had handled the bar orders, Josh helped stock the rest of the coolers under the bar. When he shut the ghost door, the face appeared again.

Whoa! It was much more vivid, almost three-dimensional this time. An old guy, like a salty sea dog.

Josh looked away and slammed the door, trying to shake off the cold thrill running down his spine. Shaking his head, he felt an inexplicable disquiet. He didn't believe in ghosts—but then realized it wasn't entirely true. He had never considered the question.

Do ghosts exist?

His default answer was no, but he had no reasoned justification for thinking that. Being an agnostic, he was open to any possibility—in theory. Maybe he should be receptive to this idea.

He wondered what Kiera thought. They'd never had that conversation. He had no idea what her beliefs were. They hadn't discussed religion and he assumed it wasn't important to her. They lived together and would probably marry; maybe it was time to have that discussion. After they closed tonight, he'd show the door to Kiera, curious whether she would see anything. Perhaps it *was* a bizarre trick of the light. After that, thoughts of ghosts were buried beneath a deluge of drink orders as the tavern filled up.

Just after nine o'clock, Kiera walked downstairs and sat at the bar. Josh said, "Hey, baby. Usual?"

She nodded. "Small order of wings as well, sexy man," Kiera said, acting flirty. "Sounds like it's been nuts tonight."

"And some." He set a glass of Rombauer chardonnay in front of Kiera. It wasn't on the wine list, but poured from her private stock.

They had been so busy, they'd had little time for each other and she looked hot tonight. In the next couple of days, they needed to set time aside for the obvious, and some downtime, maybe dinner out. Soon after, he was buried in drink orders again and loving it. Why had he wasted so much time being an attorney? Though if he hadn't, he never would have been able to afford the tavern.

During a brief lull, Josh leaned over and said, "Did you hear about Scott Robbins?"

Kiera was gnawing on a wing. "No. What about him?"

"Apparently, he disappeared. Wife said he went into the wine cellar and never came out."

"Likely story," Kiera said, shaking her head. "He fancied himself a ladies' man. Maybe the wife offed him and buried him under the wine cellar."

Josh looked at her oddly, "The customer who told me? That's exactly what he said."

Shortly after ten, the crowd thinned. It was a weeknight and they usually closed between eleven and midnight. The bar itself was empty, the remaining customers sitting in booths.

"Want some help closing?" Kiera asked.

"Heck yeah. You want to do glasses or wipe down the bar?"

She slid her glass across the bar and walked around to join him. "I'll do the bar."

As he washed glasses, Kiera wiped around him, discreetly groping him as she worked.

"Settle down, girl," Josh said, then leaned in. "I don't think I've ever asked you this but, do you believe in ghosts?"

"So, I'm horny and you want to talk about ghosts?" Seeing he was serious, she said, "What? You see something?"

"Maybe." He looked defensive. "You didn't answer the question."

"I've never given it much thought, but—no, not really." She stopped wiping and leaned on the bar. "What'd you see?"

"Come here." He gestured and knelt by the door. "Crouch next to me and watch the door."

She knelt. He opened the door quickly, then eased it closed. About the halfway point, Kiera jumped. "What the hell was that?"

"You saw it, didn't you?" He felt vindicated.

She nodded, then examined the door as he had, opening and closing the door, looking for possible reflections. "Holy crap! That's freaky."

He looked at her. "Ghost?"

Kiera shook her head. "Maybe? I don't know..."

"Who do you think that is? Old man Quinlan? Did you find any pics in your research?"

"No. Nothing."

Kiera grabbed her phone and said, "Hold the door right there. Yep, there?" She snapped three photos and paged through them. The first two were murky, but the third caught the faint image of an old guy with a beard in the glass.

"Holy shit! You nailed it! A picture of a ghost!"

"Think anyone will believe it?"

His enthusiasm deflated. "No."

Half an hour later, Kiera locked the front door while Josh killed the lights and the TVs. They met at the stairs, Josh slid his arm around Kiera and they meandered up the stairs, enjoying the moment.

"Wanna mess around?"

She smiled. "Thought you'd never ask."

As he turned and looked up the stairs, someone or something walked across his field of vision in the dark apartment.

Kiera froze. "You see that?"

He spoke in a whisper. "Yeah, I did. Wait here."

He crept up the remaining stairs and flicked the lights on, then said, "Hey!"

Kiera whispered, "Careful."

Josh eased around the corner—with a good view of the kitchen—and scanned toward the front of the apartment.

Nothing.

He peeked around the island, into the bedroom, and then walked to the living room—all were empty.

Kiera tentatively turned the corner a moment later. "So?"

"All clear. Another fricking ghost, I guess."

"That's it? A fricking ghost? Two in one day?"

"They seem harmless." Josh slipped an arm around her and moved in for a kiss.

Kiera put her hand up. "Sorry sweetie, Casper spoiled my mood."

"Seriously?"

"Sorry."

★   ★   ★

Kiera had lost the mood and didn't think she'd sleep either. The little things were stacking up. The ghost in the door, the disturbance in their apartment, and a dozen other weird moments—she swore she'd heard children giggling one day when she was cleaning the bar. Faint, it might have been kids outdoors, but she thought not. The Quinlan children? A crazy idea. Only she was no longer sure it *wasn't* true.

Kiera went to the bathroom to brush her teeth. Looking into the mirror, she almost expected to see a disembodied head behind her. The unease she felt earlier had returned. Kiera knew that everything she thought and felt was filtered by her beliefs. Those beliefs were rational and scientific, grounded in observation, experiment, and discovery. The thin place, the ghosts and hauntings—those things fell outside her beliefs, were not easily embraced, and left her feeling profoundly disturbed.

Twenty-Eight

Willow sat at the table in her study where she dealt tarot cards, prepared her daily horoscope, and studied the numbers in her life. The table was oak and ornately inlaid with symbols for the planets and the twelve constellations of the zodiac, the centerpiece a six-inch crystal ball. She never used the glass, wasn't practiced in the art of scrying, but it looked perfect on the table.

Painted dark red, almost burgundy, the room was shadowy, the windows mostly covered by thick velvet drapes. A contractor had removed all the electrical wiring from the room and she allowed no electronic devices within, not even her phone. Situated at the rear of the house, it was near silent, the only noise her heartbeat and light breath sounds.

This was where her clients sat for readings: tarot, palmistry, and horoscopes. She had a small but loyal clientele and also made money from her weekly blog posts on a variety of paranormal topics. And she had landed well after her divorce from Mike the dermatologist. She had managed to keep the house and they'd had a wonderful daughter who now lived in Cali. Sadly, Willow only saw Gina twice a year at best, the girl on a fast track to the top of a tech startup.

Willow spent a moment shuffling her tarot deck and spread the cards, face down, across the table in a line. She took a few deep breaths and cleared her mind. Focused and looked at the cards, mindfully selecting six and laying them in a descending line—a universal six-card spread of the major arcana.

Judgement. The first card represented how she felt about herself, and in that, the card pointed to the end to an era. It seemed perfect. Time to take stock and chart a new course from here. A time for rejoicing. Soon, she would enjoy the rewards of her efforts.

The second card, *The Emperor,* spoke to what she wanted right now. What she wanted most was success and *The Emperor* was a strong card. Excellent.

The third card represented her fears and was worrisome: *Strength.* She feared she lacked the willpower and strength to deal with something—or someone, and that was Kiera. She couldn't give into the fear, couldn't be negative. She had to be brave.

Justice. The fourth card, an excellent omen representing the things in her favor. Karmic, a reward for good deeds, it pointed to a period of good luck.

Perfect.

Now the card about what stood in her way: *The Hermit.* It wasn't a time for irrational and impulsive behavior. A warning not to make hasty decisions.

The last card? The likely outcome of her endeavors.

The Magician.

Perfect!

A period of positive action with great potential ahead, an excellent omen for success!

The Hermit and *The Magician* were in conflict, but she trusted *The Magician*. The outcome would resolve in her favor.

The cards and her horoscope seemed to imply the same thing, that her life was about to be taken over by momentous events and she needed to be ready. Willow knew this destiny was fully entwined in the thin place beneath the tavern.

She now realized that *thin place* might not be an accurate descriptor, that the space in the cavern might represent some point of Yin and Yang, a place where opposing or contrary forces became complementary and interdependent in the world. Yin was the receptive and Yang the active principle, seen in all forms of change and difference like winter and summer, north-facing shade and south-facing brightness, female and male, and at the most basic, disorder and order, evil and good.

Perhaps it represented a warping of space and time. Although she subscribed to weird science at the far edge of accepted thought, she also firmly believed in practical science: cosmology, astronomy, gravitational theory. It made sense. Those were the core disciplines and her other learnings then probed more deeply into the mysteries of life. It was the narrow-minded charlatans in the universities who refused to give numerology, tarotology, and parapsychology their proper due.

The cards told her one other thing. Her relationship with Kiera, already strained, would become more troubled with time. Willow couldn't allow that to happen. Regardless of how she felt about Kiera— which was surprisingly antagonistic at the moment—she couldn't allow those feelings to interfere with her access to the cavern.

She couldn't even pinpoint why she was so angry with Kiera. Yes, she was upset about the fainting episode and the hassle that followed. But there was something else. The feeling sat and festered and Willow could identify no reason she felt this way, though clearly, Kiera thought she was better than Willow. Always had. The great Kiera, who went to college, got a fancy degree, and chased tornadoes. So what? Willow had gone chasing once and found it boring as hell. It was a matter of respect. Kiera didn't respect her skills because she didn't have a degree. Well, fuck Kiera.

She could pretend and play nice as long as necessary to stay in Kiera's good graces and maintain access to the cavern. Besides, woe to Kiera if she tried to block her access.

There would be hell to pay.

Twenty-Nine

It had been three days since Rachel last visited the farm.

She had been grounded for a week after yelling at her mother. After begging and pleading, her father had reduced her sentence to three days. Still, she had to clear a long list of chores before Mom relented and let her leave the house.

Finally free, Rachel biked hard to the farm and ran to the barn. The late afternoon was hot and languid, the sky cloudless, the air thick and still. The buzz and activity of insects, bees, flies, and such filled the air amid smells of rich loamy soil brought out by an overnight shower.

Using a gardening trowel, she dug deeper through the tough, sticky clay and slowly uncovered almost eighteen inches of the blade. Rachel still couldn't see the haft. Not a knife, it looked like a sword of some sort. After another twenty minutes of work, digging another foot, Rachel uncovered the hilt. It was cross-shaped and covered in mud. She rubbed it back and forth through a nearby patch of grass, then stopped in shock, staring at the exposed metal.

"Holy shit!"

Gold! The real deal.

It gleamed even in the deep shadows of the barn, the sun now low in the west.

No other metal—no yellow metal anyway—could be buried for years and remain untarnished. The blade wasn't tarnished either, just covered with muck that resembled corrosion. There wasn't a mark on the haft or the blade. She assumed the sword was a relic left by the French, but planned to google it when she got home.

There were markings in the gold that looked like hieroglyphs or runes—she wasn't sure which, but the sword was old and clearly valuable. Probably priceless. If she showed it to anyone, they would take it away and put it in a museum. Of that, she was certain.

Nope. She found it. It was hers. End of story. She would show it to no one. For now, she would hide it in her room until she found a safer place.

She turned to check the hole for any other artifacts, stopped and dropped the sword.

At the bottom of the dark, ragged hole in the mud, light shone through a hole the size of a dime. It was fascinating and she couldn't imagine what it meant. As she knelt for a closer look, her phone buzzed. A text from Dad: *Home now!*

Jesus. His timing, as usual, sucked.

She stuck her finger into the hole. It felt like stone around the edges. A cave? She couldn't imagine.

No time to investigate further. It would have to wait. She didn't need another grounding.

After covering the hole with branches and loose grass, Rachel concealed the sword in her backpack as best she could and pedaled home. It was almost dark, so she hoped the sword would attract no attention. She slipped into the yard along the fence line and walked her bike to the house, careful to avoid lights and windows, slipped the sword out of her backpack and shoved it under a bush. Then walked around to the garage and noisily parked her bike.

Dad sat in the living room, in his recliner, watching TV when she walked in.

"About time, young lady." He gave her a mild stink-eye.

"Sorry. Didn't realize it was so late." She plopped down on the arm of his chair. "Where's Mom?"

"Sleeping. She had a migraine."

Sure she did, Rachel thought. Or she was drunk. More likely drunk.

"Out at the farm again?"

"Yep. Found a couple of arrowheads." She kissed him on the cheek. "G'night, Dad."

"Good night, sweetheart."

Rachel ran to her room and closed the door. She grabbed her MacBook and typed *French swords* into the search bar and clicked on *Images.* None of them looked similar, other than an 1831 artillery sword that wasn't really close. She broadened her search to *sword* and found closer matches under the general category of Carolingian swords, though oddly, the pages suggested the sword could be a thousand years old. Not possible. No way. She couldn't wait to examine it but had to wait until Dad was asleep lest he stopped in to say goodnight and inadvertently saw the sword.

He went to bed just after eleven. Rachel waited another full hour before sneaking out the back door and around the house to recover her booty. She slipped back in silently, grabbed a roll of paper towel, a bunch of garbage bags, and returned to her room.

Rachel laid the sword on a garbage bag and wiped grime, mud, and grit away with paper towel after paper towel. A magnificent weapon slowly emerged, stunning in detail and splendor. The blade of steel was inlaid with a strip of gold from tip to hilt. Even though the steel had darkened in spots, it wasn't rusty and Rachel suspected the right cleaner would restore it to perfection. The hilt was incredible. Cast or forged from gold, it was intricately detailed and inlaid with red gems. Someone had engraved small symbols along the hand grip. Rachel knew it was worth a fortune and possibly priceless. She should show it to someone, but she wouldn't.

No, her feelings of guilt were overridden by the desire to keep and own this magnificent weapon.

She admired it, then made a few clumsy parries, her hand barely able to control the heavy blade. Rachel thought about hiding it in the closet but feared her father might find it and take it.

Wrapping the sword in garbage bags, she slid it between the mattress and box-spring of her bed. Her parents rarely ventured into her room, and they never touched her bed. Making her bed and washing the bedding was her job.

Rachel peeked at her phone. Two am. She stripped down to her underwear, slipped into a nightshirt and fell onto her bed.

With the light off, the gem in the arrowhead sitting on her nightstand glowed slightly. Enough so that when she held her hand over it, it lightly illuminated her palm.

She stared at it, awestruck. It was like magic. On a hunch, she slipped out of bed and lifted the mattress enough to see the sword. The jewels in the hilt glowed with the same soft light.

What had she stumbled upon?

Thirty

After dropping a hundred bucks on extension cords, Kiera set up construction lights and spent the morning in the cavern, examining the longship with an LED work light, searching for evidence the vessel had ever been taken apart and reassembled.

She found nothing. Only evidence of tool marks from the original construction plus the wear and tear normal to a boat that had been at sea. And curiously, no evidence of biologics like barnacles on the hull. She had worn a sweatshirt because the cavern had been cold the last time. Now it was sweltering. The lights? Not enough heat to make a difference. She slipped out of the sweatshirt, wiped her brow, and tossed it on the floor.

Her fruitless search had only deepened the mystery surrounding the boat. Frustrated, she scanned the walls of the cavern looking for lines or joints, any evidence of an opening sealed over after they placed the boat in the cavern. That search also yielded nothing.

The purpose of the room remained a mystery. Kiera found no evidence of ceremonial burials, but then realized she wasn't certain of that fact. She hadn't yet explored the full tunnel system. She hoped there weren't any; she'd have to report any remains buried on site. The state would then swoop in to regulate the dig—or stop it completely.

That raised the thorniest issue of all. The entrance to the tunnel lay beneath the bar, on property Josh owned, so for now, they could control access. But if the cavern lay under public, private, or state land, they could lose control of the relics and she couldn't let that happen. How could she determine that?

Ground penetrating radar was the obvious answer. But she had no access to a unit, and a radar device sufficient for her needs was twenty thousand dollars. Maybe she could find something on eBay. Had she made a mistake bringing Professor Marshall in so early? He'd be considering this angle too.

She needed to finish exploring the tunnel. She had been so obsessed with the cavern she hadn't given the rest of the tunnel a thought.

Kiera stood and hugged herself. Without the sweatshirt, she was freezing. How in the hell had it become so cold so quickly? She grabbed the sweatshirt, a hardhat, and a Maglite and turned right into the tunnel. Switching her GoPro on, she ambled, observing, looking for clues that would shed light on this mysterious formation.

The tunnel sloped down and curved to the left for a while, then curved right and rose at a ten-degree pitch. The air grew warmer again. Sweating profusely, Kiera stopped to remove her sweatshirt and tied it around her waist. The erratic temperature changes within the tunnel were baffling and illogical.

She thought briefly of the 'ghosts' in the bar. Did they venture down here too? Had they come from the tunnel?

Yikes! Why was she thinking this way? She had never been superstitious. A woman of science, she wasn't a fruitcake like Willow.

Not fair, she decided, with a stab of guilt. Willow *was* different; it was one of the things she loved about her. The friendship had been rocky lately, though. A couple of silly tiffs, and now, she felt a greater rift had opened between them. Willow still called two to three times a day, pleading for access to the cavern. Now she was calling it a sacred site. Good grief!

She couldn't babysit Willow and couldn't give her a free pass, either. If she inadvertently damaged anything, it would compromise the site. But every time she said *no*, she felt pressure emanating from the phone as Willow grew terse and more angry. Kiera imagined her thinking: *What right do you have keeping me away from this place?* After some back-and-forth, she'd agreed to let Willow visit the longship for an hour today before the bar opened. She also planned to talk with her about her demands and pushy attitude.

The tunnel continued on, featureless and unchanging, walls of limestone chiseled in places to open a passage through the rock. It was fascinating and boring at the same time. She then saw a narrow shaft of light emanating from the ceiling of the tunnel. Diffuse and weak, it looked like sunlight. Kiera looked up. There was a small gap in the rock in that part of the ceiling, the light filtering through a small hole partially covered with branches.

Kiera couldn't decide if it was natural or not, though it looked recent. There was a small amount of dirt on the floor beneath it, but no evidence water had flowed through the opening. There would be dark rivulets from soil carried through the opening by water, patterns on the floor where water had flowed down the slope of the tunnel floor. *Damn it!*

She had to find that opening on the surface before anyone else did. The risk to the tunnel and cavern was unimaginable. If someone dug their way through and gained access here, there would be no controlling the mobs of people who would want in.

Looking forward, she saw the tunnel ran only another thirty feet. Kiera edged slowly to the end, carefully examining the walls and ceiling for any breaches or openings. Beyond the hole behind her, the tunnel remained uninteresting until the end. There, vertical stone steps carved into the rock led to a wooden trapdoor overhead.

Kiera climbed up and shoved hard against the door, but it refused to budge. It looked thick and solid, built with heavy oak planks. Banging her fist against it was equally unproductive. She imagined the door hidden in the floor of a basement somewhere but saw no evidence anyone had been down here in years. A fine layer of dust lay undisturbed on the floor and steps.

She needed to determine where the door opened to and who had access. The threat was real: if the secret got out, thrill seekers would invade the cavern and ruin a priceless, peerless archeological site. Further—now in complete panic mode—Kiera worried she had confided in Marshall too soon. She feared he would cut her out of the dig if he found a separate entrance to the tunnel.

Thirty-One

Rustin Marshall sat at his desk, poring over the cavern photos Kiera had emailed to him. In two weeks, they would have the results of the radiocarbon dating, but he didn't need them because he knew what testing would reveal.

The longship and drawings in the cavern weren't a fraud. They were as authentic as any site he had ever seen—the setting too elaborate, too perfect to have been faked. And whether the Vikings sailed this far west through the Great Lakes, or Native Americans dragged the longship here and had assembled and painted the cavern as a temple to the Gods—and perhaps they believed the Vikings *were* Gods—it didn't matter.

The result was magnificent, breathtaking.

The cavern and longship represented the most significant archaeological find in a century, perhaps as historic as the discovery of Tutankhamun's Tomb or Sutton Hoo, the Anglo-Saxon cemetery and ship burial. Bringing this dig and story to the archaeological community promised to be monumental on so many levels. From professional acclaim and the ability to write his own ticket thereafter, the discovery might elevate his name to mythic level for posterity, along with the greats like Howard Carter and Lord Carnarvon.

Kiera O'Donnell didn't fit into this vision. Instead, she'd be a distraction, diluting the glory of the find and the publicity that would follow. She was unemployed, for God's sake. She had no credentials beyond her degree. No position, no tenure, and no clout. Clearly why she had sought his help.

He needed to write Kiera out of the equation.

Unfortunately, he couldn't just tell her to get lost. She and her boyfriend owned the building that provided the only access to the cavern. Still, based on the tunnel length and morphology, he believed the cavern lay outside the footprint of their property and might be detectable with ground penetrating radar. If so, he would make a case for digging a separate, official entrance for research. Kiera would be out of the loop. Sure, she could claim she found it, for what that was worth. He would lead the official excavation and write the papers describing their findings as they went. Her name would be trampled in the dust of his glory.

He had to think of a reason to use the University's ground penetrating radar without raising eyebrows or undo curiosity. Then he would need to find a discreet way to utilize the device without alerting Kiera to his plans to take control of the site and push her out.

A second possibility existed. Was there another entrance to the tunnel? It extended some distance beyond the cavern. Logic said there must be.

Marshall spent the remainder of the morning poring over county histories, plat maps, and geological surveys, searching for some evidence of the tunnel from the past. It seemed odd that no one knew of its existence until Kiera inadvertently stumbled upon it. Apparently, the entrance had been hidden under decades of junk in the basement of the old bar. Maybe it was a secret, perhaps part of an old mine or more likely, an old bootlegger's cave. There was no official documentation of the tunnel or the cavern or its contents. Of course there wasn't. Even a hundred years ago, such a find would have been sensational.

Unless someone had been hiding it. To what end? It made no sense. They would have tried to capitalize on the discovery. It was simple human nature.

He would never know. That answer had been lost to history.

Almost ready to quit this line of inquiry, he found a curious co-incidence on the plat map from 1880. Joshua Quinlan, who owned the tavern property, also owned an eighty-acre plat of farmland one mile south of the tavern, along the same bearing as the tunnel. That couldn't be a coincidence.

Had Joshua Quinlan known of the tunnel and hidden the evidence of it?

Why?

That someone would hide this was incomprehensible.

Quinlan must have some descendants. Had they heard stories of the longship and cavern? Another angle to pursue.

With no firm proof, acting on a hunch, he felt certain the tunnel led to the farmhouse. Had Kiera explored the entire tunnel? Maybe she hadn't, but more likely, she had and was hiding the second entrance from him. He needed to find out who owned the property now. He vaguely remembered driving by the place, a dilapidated farmhouse and a fallen-down barn. If Kiera hadn't explored the entire tunnel, he wanted to establish a *first right* to that access. Then he would find the current owner of the property and cut a deal with them. A quick look at Google maps confirmed what he suspected, the farm was little more than a ruin at this point.

He grabbed his phone and bounded out the door, convinced the tunnel from the tavern led to Quinlan's farm.

Thirty-Two

Lachlan walked along a country highway, a road lined by tall trees that shrouded the asphalt in a tunnel of green. The trees mostly protected him from the hot sun but he wore an Aussie safari hat to keep the sun off his face where it filtered through. Here and there, patches of prairie grass fought for light. He stopped occasionally, closing his eyes, raising his head as if smelling the warm Wisconsin air. The air was fresh, redolent with smells of rich soil and decaying plant life. The cycle of life at work, renewing the forest and the ecosystem, but he wasn't here to commune with nature.

He was following a dip in the terrain that suggested a rift in the limestone bedrock beneath, walking to the north over the Niagara Escarpment. Pursuing a presence that once inhabited an old Tudor house, killed his friend, and had migrated in this direction, using cracks and fissures in the rock to facilitate its travels.

On the surface, the task sounded like a fool's errand. The hint of the darkness beneath was ephemeral at best. At times, he worried that he imagined its presence. He was very perceptive; perhaps only Kenric had been more perceptive. That didn't automatically make him a bloodhound for all things in the spirit world. As perceptive as Kenric was, it hadn't saved him, a fact that disturbed Lachlan deeply. What had Kenric missed?

Lachlan averaged three to four miles a day. Meandering, he often backtracked if he felt he'd lost the trail. As much as he disdained technology—a disdain arising from his standing as a crusty old codger—he found his mobile phone indispensable now. It provided updated weather information and maps as he followed the trail. An app recorded every step so he had a complete log of his journey.

Something had changed in the last mile. He stopped and closed his eyes. Perhaps imagined, perhaps real, the vibrations seemed a little stronger, clearer. He looked at his phone. The nearest town, Miller's Crossing, was five miles up the road. He decided to quit for the day, marking the location in his app, and walking the three miles back to his car in under an hour. Tomorrow, he would park this side of Miller's Crossing and continue the search.

As he drove back to Milwaukee, Lachlan realized he still had no clear understanding of this thing he was pursuing, the darkness. It felt like a shadow. Could one chase a shadow? Further, he had no plan at the ready once he found it. He hoped the encounter with Kenric had crippled it sufficiently to tilt the coming inevitable battle in his favor, though it wasn't something he could know with any certainty or any quantitative way.

To some degree, one needed to improvise in these situations. A plan wasn't always possible. In life, there were known *unknowns* which he could plan for, at least loosely. But the *unknown* unknowns? By definition, they would remain invisible until they weren't. It would be those unknowns that could be his undoing and he remained acutely aware of it.

All this fretting was pointless and dangerous, distracting from the task at hand and weakening his resolve. He tried to still his mind to no avail. He worried his motives were a problem. The only emotion he clearly felt was anger and hence, his motive was revenge, retaliation. A base passion and one best avoided, but he felt obsessed with avenging an old friend's death. He tried to sugarcoat the truth with altruism: by interceding, he would protect others from the darkness hidden in the rock below. While the Aeldo had no written laws, rules, or tenets, they endeavored to confront and sabotage the dark forces loose in the world—though Lachlan mostly believed that their time had come and gone. Modern warfare and weapons of mass destruction—technology—had rendered them obsolete.

Kenric had gotten that one thing right. He had understood their era was ending and had attempted to reinvent himself in a modern technological world. Now wizards wrote software and confronted new types of evil in the worldwide network of the internet. Lachlan only vaguely understood hacking and the things Kenric did and had no desire to learn.

Perhaps an inventive rewording was all he needed. Not revenge, but retribution—which suggested a just or deserved punishment, often without personal motives—for some past evil or wickedness. Retribution sounded noble, revenge just petty.

Retribution it was.

The thought left him weary. Until Kenric's death, he had considered himself mostly retired and had been content to while away his remaining years in quiet enjoyment of life. Twenty acres of land and a comfortable house in the Lake District, a few familiar faces at the pub, darts every fortnight. Perhaps he was foolish to think he could just fade away into a metaphorical sunset.

Can't always get what you want. Some annoying pop singer had written that, but it was true and there was no turning back.

This cause was the antithesis of that other life, and Lachlan realized nothing would stand in the way of him seeing it through.

Nothing.

Thirty-Three

Kiera grabbed her Fitbit and reset it so she could count her steps to the tavern end of the tunnel. Rushing back through the tunnel, she pulled the plug on the lights in the cavern, and continued to the basement. As she emerged from the floor, Caleb walked out of the cooler.

"Hey Kiera, what're you doing?"

Shit! She didn't want to draw any attention to the tunnel

"Just checking something out." On a hunch, she asked, "Have you looked down here at all?"

He shook his head. "Nope. Why would I?"

Why, indeed. He was lying. It was written all over his face. Was she being paranoid? She thought not. They had to close this up—or keep everyone out of the basement. She followed Caleb up the stairs and went to the office.

The Fitbit had recorded 1845 steps, just shy of a mile. She grabbed her laptop and pulled up Google maps, finding the tavern and drawing a line to the south. Then she clicked to the satellite image, her mouse pointer landing on a plot of land that looked like an abandoned farm. The fields were overgrown with trees and prairie grass. A collapsed barn was visible, as was an abandoned farmhouse in disrepair. She was willing to bet the trap door opened into the basement of that old farmhouse.

Kiera grabbed her phone, a Maglite, the laptop, and, imagining the worst, her Kimber Micro 9. A girl could never be too careful. She yelled to Caleb that she was leaving, ran to her car, and turned onto Martin Road toward the farmhouse.

★   ★   ★

Caleb watched Kiera run out the door and decided to risk another peek at the boat in the basement. He had searched on Google and discovered that it was a Viking longship. Even a small piece of it might be worth a fortune. He weighed his friendship and loyalty to Josh against nabbing a small piece of history. Stealing a souvenir won out. The tavern didn't open for another thirty minutes and he'd come in early to stock the bar—he had the time.

He climbed down into the tunnel and trotted down to the cavern, anxious to get in and out before Josh or Kiera returned. He wasn't certain Josh would mind but Kiera's tone made it clear the tunnel was off limits.

The cavern seemed dimmer and colder than it had yesterday. Caleb shivered and wished he had brought a coat or sweatshirt. No matter, he wasn't staying long. He quickly walked the perimeter of the vessel and, finding nothing of interest, climbed up on the stone plinth to look inside.

A series of small, round carved plaques of animals—foxes, wolves, oxen, and sheep—were mounted next to some of the seats inside the ship. Several had fallen into the crevice between the wall and floor of the boat. There was no real evidence of where they had fallen from.

Perfect. No one would miss one. He nabbed a wolf plaque from the crevice and climbed over the gunwale, satisfied with his souvenir.

He set his foot down, but the rocky floor felt mushy, like stepping on a dog turd.

He tried to pull his foot back to look, but the foot stuck and wouldn't budge.

Shit! He couldn't be found in here.

In a panic, he jerked harder—to no avail—and lost his balance in an awkward flailing of arms, falling backward into a soft squishy mass that stuck like glue. The plaque hit the stone floor and rolled away, clattering as it wobbled and fell flat. Lying on his back, he couldn't pull free, couldn't roll, couldn't even lift his hand. The floor was warm, uncomfortably so. Worse, he was sinking! No amount of squirming broke the grip of this awful stuff.

The more he struggled, the quicker he settled into the goo. He flipped his head side-to-side, desperate and frightened. The floor looked like rock, indistinguishable from the surrounding limestone, except that it was gooey and growing hotter.

Desperate, he yelled out, "Help! Jesus, help me! Kiera!"

There was no one to hear him. No one coming to save him. He was too far from the kitchen for anyone to hear his scream and he knew it.

As he sank and the wet mucky floor oozed around his face, the heat began to burn like someone had flipped a gas burner on.

The heat! *Oh God!*

He was burning up!

Smoke and vapor rose as the heat beneath him became unbearable. In the last microseconds of consciousness as his skin flayed and his blood boiled, he watched the gout of steam and soot that was once part of him blast to the roof of the cavern in a volcanic fit.

Thirty-Four

Kiera saw the farmhouse, surrounded by a sea of weeds, prairie grass, and wild brush, just up the road. A car was parked in front, off the road, and someone was walking to the house. As she approached, she realized it was the professor. Anger rose in her like flaming gasoline.

Bastard! Clearly, he had plans to grab the longship for himself. She pulled in next to his car and jumped out, leaving the door agape.

"Hey! What are you doing?" Kiera yelled as she tromped toward him.

He stopped and turned on her approach. Raising an eyebrow, he said, "Following a hunch. And you?"

"The same. But I brought the information to you and we agreed to work together." Kiera spoke fast and angrily, with a pointed finger. "We had a deal! You were to do nothing until we have a signed agreement. Yet here you are, snooping around! Planning on cutting me out of the dig?"

"Maybe. You have no credentials at this point. What are you bringing to the table?"

"My expertise. Access. Most of all, I found it! I think you should leave." Kiera was glad she'd left the Kimber in the RAV4. She might've been tempted to use it on this smug bastard.

"I don't think so," he said casually, like they were discussing the weather. "You're here for the same reason I am. Somewhere on this property is another entrance to the tunnel and I think you know it."

"What's your point?"

"I probably don't need you."

"You think you can screw me out of the equation?"

"In my position, you'd be doing the same thing." He turned and took a step toward the house.

"Stop, or I'll call the cops!"

"No you won't." He continued walking toward the rear, waving a dismissive hand.

She couldn't shoot him but she wanted to. Kiera grabbed her phone, dialed 911, and told the dispatcher someone was trespassing on the farm just out of town on Martin Road. Marshall disappeared around the back.

Kiera cupped her hands and yelled, "They're on their way."

He reappeared at the corner, looking flustered. "Really? Are you nuts? Do you want everyone to know about this?"

"No, but I'm not letting you keep it to yourself either, jackass." Kiera stood, hands on hips, feeling in control again.

A moment later, a siren sounded in the distance and grew louder. As he looked into the distance toward the sound, she set her phone to record and held it discreetly at her side.

Marshall walked toward her. "Okay. So maybe I'm being a little hasty."

"A little hasty?" She laughed. "Do you think I'll trust you after this?"

A moment later, a county squad pulled into the drive. The tall thin sheriff stepped out of the car, slid his hat on, and walked over to

Kiera and Marshall. "What's going on, folks? We received a report of trespassing here. Are you the owners?"

Kiera shook her head. Marshall looked like he might say *yes*, but evidently thought better of it. "No."

"Then you both need to leave. You're trespassing." As if sensing the tension between them, he added, "I don't know what's going on here but you two stay off this property or I'll arrest you both."

Kiera put her hands up in a gesture of acquiescence and started walking to her car. Marshall, catching up, said, "So when were you planning to tell me about the farmhouse?"

"I just discovered it!" Kiera said, exasperated. "As soon as I established that an actual connection existed."

"Why should I believe you?"

"Seriously?" Kiera stopped and turned on him with a pointed finger. "Why should I trust *you*? I brought the information to you, if you remember—"

The sheriff called out, "Keep moving, you two."

"Yes, you did." He sidestepped her finger.

"Don't you forget it!" Kiera leaned on her car door. "Get me the paperwork in the next two days or all bets are off. And if you try to screw me again, I'll make sure you regret it."

"Understood. I'll get started on the paperwork tonight."

"Hell hath no fury, Professor. Don't forget it!"

Thirty-Five

As Kiera sat in her car, her phone rang.

Willow.

"Hey Willow, what's up?"

"Where are you?" She said, curtly. "You were supposed to meet me at three-thirty. And where's Caleb?"

Damn! She had forgotten about Willow. And where the hell was Caleb? "Isn't he there?"

"No. The kitchen people said he disappeared about thirty minutes ago. Angela's running the bar until you or Josh get here."

"I'll be right there." *Jesus!* Josh's friend or not, Caleb better have a damned good reason for leaving the bar unattended. Bad enough she'd been right about the professor being a jerk. And Willow had sounded positively snotty. *Enough already!*

She parked behind the bar and ran in. "Hi Angela, I've got it. Where's Willow?"

"She's in the basement."

Shit!

Willow had no right to let herself in.

Where the hell was Caleb? She caught up on the drink orders and called Josh. When he answered, she took a deep breath, trying to relax. "Hey sweetie, where are you?"

"On my way. What's up, babe? You sound frazzled."

"A lot, but most critically, Caleb took off and left the bar unmanned."

"What? I'm almost there."

Josh walked in a minute later, phone in hand, looking worried. "He's not answering his phone. That's not like him to just take off. I hope it's nothing serious."

"Yeah, I know. Me too." At the moment, she felt much less forgiving. Caleb should have told someone he was leaving.

Josh laid a hand on her shoulder and said softly, "What's going on with you?"

The words tumbled out of her mouth in a rush. "Willow let herself into the tunnel and I caught Professor Marshall trying to screw me out of the longship discovery."

Josh looked confused. "What?"

"Long story. I'll fill you in later. I have to deal with Willow."

Kiera turned on her heel and sprinted down the stairs in a very unmindful mood. She seldom let anger get the better of her, but she was doing a lousy job of managing it now. People and events were conspiring against her. Caleb. Marshall. Willow. She was the worst, and it was wearing thin: being demanding, taking advantage of their friendship, acting insincere and phony. They needed to talk and they were going to talk right now.

Her nose wrinkled. There was an odd smell in the tunnel, some weird combination of pork ribs and flowers. It was cloying and unpleasant. As she walked into the cavern, she found Willow kneeling, fiddling with something in her purse. She had lit and arranged an assortment of candles on the floor.

Fighting the urge to scream, Kiera hissed, "Well, make yourself right at home."

"Oh, hey, sweetie." Willow said with insincere affection.

Kiera saw something peeking out of her purse: an old piece of wood. "What do you have in your purse, Willow?"

"Nothing."

For a mystic or psychic or whatever, she was a lousy liar. As Willow turned, Kiera caught a better glimpse of the wooden disk within—something from the longship. She was stealing it!

Kiera shoved her hand out. "Give it to me!"

"What?"

"You *know* what, Willow!" Kiera accused. She could barely contain her anger. "This is an important archeological site. You can't take *anything.*"

Willow threw her an angry, defiant look, but reluctantly withdrew the plaque. "Why are you such a bitch?"

Kiera felt primed to explode. She grabbed the wooden carving and pointed to the arch. "Get out of here!"

Willow gathered her candles and stormed out, yelling, "Fuck you, you barren bitch!"

Kiera stood, mouth agape, too stunned to move or speak. Willow knew how sensitive the subject of her infertility was. To use it against her—even in anger—was unforgivable. Kiera didn't know if she could ever look at her again.

Caught somewhere between tears and anger, Kiera closed her eyes and tried to achieve some level of mindfulness. Focus. Breathe. Clear her mind.

She couldn't. Her hurt and anger were deep and now, something felt wrong in the room. Neither a psychic nor a medium, she sensed an unpleasant vibe, the air cold, unusually so in contrast to earlier when it had been sweltering.

Kiera no longer felt safe here. She took a last look around, pulled the plug on the lights, and hurried down the tunnel and up the steps into the basement. Though warmer here, she couldn't shake the dark feeling and sense of unease that gripped her in the cavern. She had come to see the ghosts as some benign presence in the tavern, but something in the cavern had felt malignant. Only when she stepped back into the tavern and closed the basement door did the sense of disquiet fade.

Josh looked up. "What's with you? You look like you've seen a ghost."

Her emotions welled up and she felt the burn of tears under her eyelids. She turned and ran upstairs, crying and hating Willow and wishing she could run far away and hide.

The apartment would have to do.

Thirty-Six

Rachel biked to the farmhouse at six-thirty after a full day of chores, Mom too busy drinking to do anything herself. Rachel had also prepared dinner and the atmosphere at the table had been worse than usual. Mom spilled a glass of red wine on the tablecloth and Dad did his best to ignore her and made mindless small-talk with Rachel. When she left, they were yelling at each other. The ride helped dissipate her anger but not her resolve to stay single forever.

The evening was warm and she was sweating as she hid her bike in the tall grass at the fence line. She climbed through the barbed wire fence and walked to the crumbling barn where a pile of leaves and branches concealed the hole where she'd found the sword.

Equipped with a trowel, a small spade, and a flashlight, she widened the base of the hole and knelt, peering into the dime-sized opening. There was a lit room of some sort beneath, but as she widened the work area, Rachel realized she had run into a solid layer of rock. The hole was merely a narrow crevice in the stone. She tried widening the hole further but only ran into more rock. No way in from here, that was clear.

Shit!

Frustrated, she kicked a rock and succeeded only in stubbing her toe.

Rachel inched around the full footprint of the barn, looking for a door or passage into the space below, but found nothing. Then her eyes settled on the broken-down farmhouse. Could the light be coming from an old cellar, maybe a storm cellar? There wasn't an entrance of any sort in the yard, but the basement seemed a likely possibility.

The porch looked dangerous. She gingerly tested each step before shifting her weight, stepping toward the doorway. That opened to a mudroom with a bare wood floor. The walls cracked and crumbling, a dirty flower print hung crookedly on the wall as if the owner had decided it was too ugly to bother with.

The basement staircase descended ahead; the kitchen, identifiable only by a rusting sink, lay beyond a doorway to the left, the floor littered with missing boards and gaps. The stairwell, festooned with cobwebs, looked rickety and precarious. Clearly, no one had been here in ages. Rachel grabbed a loose floorboard from the kitchen and swept a path through the webs. Noting cracks in several stair treads, Rachel stepped warily along the edge of the staircase, reasoning her weight was better supported near the wall.

Her apprehension rose as the basement came into view. Dark and damp, draped with spiderwebs, the floor was littered with old broken chairs, assorted junk, and smelled of mold and dust. She scanned the walls, but saw solid stone walls in every direction, no hint of a doorway. More and more, this felt like a bad idea.

When she stepped onto the floor, Rachel realized it was dirt, not just covered in dirt. Boulders poked through the uneven earth here and there. A dirt floor? Why?

Stepping slowly, sweeping webs from her path with the board, she kicked junk crates and old cans aside as she walked around the staircase in a circle. She cringed when she brushed into webbing, feeling nervous and jumpy, watching the darker corners for movement. The basement was damp and airless. Sweat trickled down her neck from her hairline. On her second pass around the basement, her foot bumped into an immovable object. Kneeling for a closer look, she felt a wood corner, a door perhaps, jutting from a pile of scrap wood and fruit crates. As she shoved the junk out of the way, she uncovered a group of rocks resting atop a wood panel or trapdoor of some sort.

Conflicted between her rising anxiety and insatiable curiosity, Rachel moved the boulders, grunting as she dragged each rock off the panel. She grew sweatier and grimier and became obsessive in her need to look beneath the wooden trap door emerging from beneath the stones.

The panel clear, Rachel stood and wiped the dirt from her hands. The moment of truth.

She eyed the door apprehensively. It didn't look like a grave but if she found a dead body underneath, she was freaking out and running home screaming. That was the plan. She tried to lift it by an edge but it wouldn't budge. Grabbing the trowel from her backpack and, using a board as a fulcrum, she stepped on the handle.

The door moved a little. She worked the edges, using boards to pivot the trowel against the trapdoor. After five minutes, moving the trowel around the edges, stepping and resetting the tool, the plank door popped free.

Rachel stopped to catch her breath, then reached down, lifted the door and leaned it against the staircase—

A strange roar rose from within. Rachel stepped back and ducked as an arctic gale blasted out of the ground. Fearing ghosts or monsters would fly out next, Rachel lay, paralyzed with fright, arms clenched to her chest. Instead, a great gout of dust and two dead mice blew from the hole.

Holy shit!

If she got out of this alive, no way was she going down there!

The wind stopped abruptly. Rachel waited a moment, then flipped the board down, stomped on it and ran up the stairs, two at a time, heedless of the risk. When she burst through the back doorway, it was almost dark. She ran for her bike but stopped sharp at the fence line.

A cop car sat just down the road and the cop seemed to be watching the house. Maybe he wasn't, but she would need to be more careful coming and going—if she came back at all. Rachel walked south and stepped onto the road beyond a slight rise, out of view. She hopped on her bike and pedaled toward home.

Passing the farm, she stopped in shock and planted her feet on the asphalt.

The house was lit up! Eerie white light streamed through the windows. Her mouth gaped open until a moment later, she realized why.

The full moon was rising directly behind the house.

Natural enough...

And creepier than shit.

Thirty-Seven

Kiera, distracted by the fight with Willow, struggled to stay on task. They were busy and she had bungled several drink orders. During a brief lull, Josh stepped over, handed her a glass of chardonnay, and said, "Take a break, down at the quiet end of the bar. Angela will cover for a bit. Talk to me."

Giving him a peck on the cheek for reading her so well, she complied, sitting by the kitchen and wait station. She tried to relax, feeling the tension from her neck down to her toes. Josh set a Spotted Cow on the bar and plopped down across from her.

After a swig of beer, he said, "Tell me what happened between you and Willow."

Kiera described Willow's increasingly imperious attitude and her attempt to steal a piece of the longship. She sipped her wine and concluded, saying, "...and she stomped out after calling me a barren bitch."

"Jesus!" He looked at her, concerned. "Sorry that happened, babe. What's her problem?"

"I don't know, but I don't think I can talk to her, not for a while anyway." Even now, Kiera struggled with her emotions; felt betrayed by her best friend.

Josh, silent for a moment, said, "So what did Marshall do?"

Kiera described her discovery of the trapdoor in the tunnel and her conclusion that it opened into the basement of an abandoned farmhouse on Martin Road, then driving there and finding Marshall trying to sneak in.

"Sounds like the tunnel and the boat might be more trouble than they're worth."

"Are you nuts? This could be the biggest archeological find since Tutankhamun's tomb. I don't want people getting in and damaging something before we can properly manage and protect the site."

"You're the expert."

Did he just roll his eyes a bit? Kiera was in no mood for mockery. "So where's Caleb?"

"I don't know. He isn't answering calls or texts. His phone goes right to voicemail."

"That's not like him." But actually, it was.

"I know. I'm a little worried. I think I'll call his sister."

Kiera downed the rest of her wine and said, "I better get back to it, Angela's getting backed up."

"Yep, me too."

Bar orders were heavy for the next hour and Kiera mostly forgot about Willow and her ugly comment. She did wonder how she would handle a call or text from her, trying to make up. Still hurt, Kiera realized she didn't want an apology, just the opportunity to bitch at Willow. Petty? Yes. She didn't care.

Near ten o'clock, two thirty-something guys walked in and sat at the bar, one wearing a Milwaukee Brewers tee, the other wearing

Packers colors. They both ordered Miller Lite on tap. As Kiera set their glasses down, the Packers guy said, "So, where's that boat that's supposed to be here?"

Kiera felt a cold flush of apprehension run down her spine. "Boat? I don't know what you're talking about."

Dismissing her, looking around, he said, "The owner here then? He'd know."

"I am one of the owners and there's no boat here," Kiera said firmly.

"Seriously? I saw a pic. It was so cool! A Viking something or other." The guy was enthusiastic, like talking about a new theme park—her worst nightmare.

"Someone's messing with you. There's no Viking boat here."

"Damn it!" the Packers guy said. He seemed satisfied with the denial, for now.

Kiera was afraid the lid would blow off this story, a feeling approaching panic. "So where'd you see this picture?"

"A friend's Snapchat. It's gone now."

"What's your friend's name?"

"Caleb Grenier."

Her anger rose so quickly, Kiera thought she might have a stroke. Caleb? That asshole! When Josh found out, he would be furious.

She turned and strode over to Josh and said, pointing discreetly, "Those two guys over there? They came in to see the Viking longship."

Josh froze, mouth open. "What? Are you kidding?"

"They saw a pic of it on Caleb's Snapchat."

"That fucker!" Josh muttered forcefully as though his head might explode. "No wonder he's not returning my calls. Now what?"

"Deny, deny, deny. It's all we can do, but I think we need to beef up security."

His shoulders slumped. "Shit. I'll work on it tomorrow."

"We need a security gate or something."

"Don't worry." He looked upward, thinking. "I have something in mind."

"Will it keep Marshall out as well?"

"Yep. Cast-iron fence gate should do the trick—"

A loud thump overhead startled Kiera, temporarily quieting the people at the bar as they looked up. Josh and Kiera looked at each other with expressions of *what now?*

Her first thought was Willow. Kiera said, "I'll go. I could use a short break."

Josh nodded. Kiera ran part way up the stairs, stopped and peered at floor level in the general direction of the noise. A half-shelf in the kitchen filled with cookbooks had toppled over, dumping everything on the floor.

"Shit!"

She climbed to the landing. "Willow? Are you in here?"

Kiera walked a circuit through the apartment. There were few places to hide and it was soon obvious no one was there.

Fabulous!

Even the ghosts had it out for her.

Thirty-Eight

Lachlan parked his car halfway between Miller's Crossing and the spot where he'd quit yesterday. The day was warm but cloudy, more comfortable for walking on this unshaded road. A single hawk circled overhead. He walked half-a-mile south before realizing the trail was growing colder—that the darkness lay somewhere to the north. Turning back, he sensed a slow but steady increase in energy as he passed his car, walking another mile before he reached an abandoned farmstead on the right side of the road. A sign marked the property, a sign he recognized at once:

NO TRESPASSING NO HUNTING

It was the farm in his dream, though he would have recognized it, regardless. The place was literally glowing with energy, a very faint blue like St Elmo's Fire.

He looked both ways. The road was deserted. He walked across and up a gravel drive overgrown with grass. The building had been abandoned for decades, the paint peeled away, the siding grey, the yard reclaimed by nature—though a couple of vehicles had recently trampled the grass underfoot. Curiously, most of the energy emanated from the ground and not the building.

Walking a circuit of the house, he noted a tree growing through the front porch. The steps looked too frail to support his weight anyway. He saw things moving within through the broken windows—spirits, he was certain, the usual assortment of lost souls and unhappy former tenants who had the fortune or misfortune of dying at home. Lachlan decided to go through the back doorway. The door itself was nowhere in sight.

He heard a siren from the road but gave it little thought until a squad car swung into the driveway. A young cop jumped out and yelled, "Step away from the house, old man, and get over here right now."

Old man? The little tosser. But with little reason to argue, Lachlan walked over, eyed the name tag, and said, "Problem...Officer Taylor is it?"

"You didn't happen to notice the 'no trespassing' signs while you were trespassing, did you?"

Oh, clever fellow.

Lachlan said, "Do you know who owns this property?"

Taylor hesitated a moment. "Um...no."

"Then how do you know I don't own it?"

With an unwavering eye and a soft, firm voice, he said, "Unless you have the property deed in your pocket, you're under arrest."

Checkmate. Lachlan smiled and held his wrists out. "Take me away, sir."

Taylor waved him off. "That won't be necessary. Where's your car?"

"Just up the road." Lachlan pointed south.

"Okay. I'll drop you at your car and you can follow me in."

Ten minutes later, he turned into the municipal car park and followed Officer Taylor into the building: two stories of glass and clay-colored brick. Then down a hallway to a room littered with desks but devoid of people. Certainly one of his more pleasant arrests. Taylor directed him to a desk and sat across from him. "Let's start with some ID."

Lachlan handed him his passport.

"A Brit, huh? Explains the accent."

Lachlan nodded. Things would get difficult from here. He had no reasonable explanation for trespassing on the property. He had to think creatively.

"So, what were you doing there, Mr. Hayward?" Taylor asked, paging through the passport.

"I'm a paranormal investigator."

The cop stopped and looked up. "Seriously?"

Lachlan held his gaze. "Assuredly, yes."

"And why were you at that house?" He closed the passport and casually dropped it on the desk.

Lachlan decided the truth was just ridiculous enough to end this conversation. With Shakespearean sincerity, he said, "I've been following a malignant spirit from the heart of the Kettle Moraine to that house."

The cop stared for a moment—no hint of disbelief or ridicule—then picked up and handed the passport to him. "I'm going to let it slide this time. But get permission in writing next time or stay away. We're keeping an eye on that property. There's been some trouble lately."

"Thank you, Officer Taylor. How would I locate the owner of the property?"

He gestured with a thumb. "Next building over, check with the county tax assessor."

Lachlan spent an hour at the assessor's office, trying to resolve the question of ownership. The taxes were paid from a trust drawn on a Chicago bank. Beyond that, the clerk knew nothing about the account or the owner of record, Mr. Somerset Quinlan of Denver, Colorado. His given address was a post office box.

He could write to the postal box but it felt like a wasted effort. Frustrated, he concluded it was best to sneak in at night, to search the house and determine the source of the energy he felt. Tonight, at home, he would plot a course to the house that wouldn't result in arrest. Sliding into the Honda Civic, he realized he was famished and didn't care to wait another hour for food. A Guinness would be nice as well.

A half mile up the road, he passed Quinlan's Tavern, a lovely old pub advertising food. Lachlan swung around and turned into the car park behind the building.

Stepping out of the Honda, the energy levels he felt from the building were intense.

Oh my!

The tavern was radiating the same vivid energy and faint blue aura as the farmhouse. Perhaps he needn't to go back to the old farmhouse after all.

★   ★   ★

Rustin Marshall spent an hour at the county tax assessor's office, trying to discover the name of the person who owned the farm, hoping to cut a deal with them that would grant him unfettered access to the tunnel and the Viking longship.

The tunnel was only half of the dilemma. Who owned the property lying directly over the cavern? That was the real issue, but perhaps he could obfuscate the problem by gaining quick legal access through the farmhouse and establishing a claim to the site. It may have been a mistake trying to cut Kiera out, alienating her in the process.

Hell hath no fury like a woman scorned—or betrayed!

Might be too late to properly mend things now. He was further discouraged to learn his was the second inquiry about the property today.

The owner of record was Somerset Quinlan with a PO box in Denver, Colorado. He returned to his office and performed a name search, starting in Denver and expanding across the country. He couldn't find a single entry matching that name. Mr. Somerset Quinlan evidently lived off the grid. Marshall fired off a letter with a promise of money to the PO box, sending it Express Mail, guaranteeing an overnight delivery. He suspected without basis that he would hear nothing from Mr. Quinlan.

If so, that left two options. Enter through the farmhouse late at night or keep the deal with Kiera who, he suspected, would have little interest in any stalling tactics. If he didn't hear from Mr. Quinlan in a day or two, and couldn't get into the farmhouse, he would have to swallow his pride and sign the contract with Kiera.

Thirty-Nine

Rachel spent an hour in her father's workshop, lovingly cleaning the sword. Having the house to herself was a rare treat, the silence heavenly. Mom and Dad had gone furniture shopping followed by dinner. They wouldn't be home until eight or nine.

So chill.

Using a stainless steel cleaner, she removed the final layers of grime from the blade. The hilt was trickier, and she used a small brush and Q-Tips to clean the fine detailing. It was almost certainly gold inlaid with gems. Remarkably, any remaining discoloration or corrosion on the blade and handle disappeared once she brought heavier cleanser to bear. While she worked, she debated a return to the farmhouse. She was annoyed with herself for being so easily scared away.

Yes, it was creepy, but other than the wind, nothing had *actually* happened. While she didn't know whether the old house was haunted, she knew there were many rational explanations for supposed ghostly phenomena that didn't include ghosts. Besides, it was near dark last time and the suggestive shadows in the half-light might have looked eerie but they weren't necessarily supernatural. Now, her more rational brain decided the wind had been a random wind tunnel effect caused by opening the door.

At the core of her struggle was pure, insatiable curiosity. She had to explore the space under the trapdoor. Needed to do it. Thus, somewhere in her sub-conscious, the decision was made. She was going back.

Now. The day bright and sunny, there would be fewer creepy shadows. Possibly some weird wind-tunnel effect again, but probably no ghosts.

Wiping the blade a final time, Rachel cleaned and erased any evidence of her work in the shop and returned the sword to the hiding place beneath her mattress. Cleaned, it was a stunning, one-of-a-kind relic that had to be priceless. She still couldn't bring herself to consider giving it up, even knowing—as a future archeologist—it was the right thing to do. It would remain a secret until she died. Unless she married, and then she *might* show her husband—*if* she married. She just didn't find boys very interesting.

Rachel filled her backpack with a flashlight, snacks, and a soda. Grabbing her lucky arrowhead from the nightstand, she shoved it into her front pocket. It went everywhere with her and though she didn't necessarily believe in ghosts, she felt the arrowhead might somehow repel evil spirits—just in case they *did* exist.

The day warm, the sky a mix of clouds and clear hazy blue, Rachel was sweating when she approached the field entrance she used to sneak up to the house. Further up the road, she glimpsed a county cop car hiding in the weeds again. He probably had a good view of the farmhouse. What was he watching for?

Rachel followed her circuitous route through the field and crouched low through the grass the last fifty feet to the back porch, then sidled carefully down the edge of the steps to the dirt floor. Sunlight filtering through dirty windows cast wan light across the basement, shadowy but not as forbidding as last night. The door wasn't fully seated in the floor so she was able to pry it free with a couple of stomps on the trowel. Pulling the door open, she leaned it against the staircase and hid behind it. Waited for the blast of wind.

And waited.

Nothing happened. Not so much as a puff of wind.

After a few minutes, she crawled to the hole and found she didn't need a light. The space below the floor was lit.

She called out, "Hello? Anybody down there?"

It seemed unlikely but she was taking no chances. She tested the steps, climbed down to the floor, and turned around, her mouth falling open in awe.

In a hushed voice, she said, "H-o-l-y shit!"

A tunnel! Going as far as her eye could see.

What was this? She called again but received no answer, not even the echo of her voice. She walked slowly, nervous, anxious, but compelled forward by her insatiable need to explore and examine this passage, whatever it was.

She had stumbled on something amazing and wondrous, the nature of which she couldn't comprehend. The tunnel and walls themselves lit the way. It was like a movie, CGI even. Pretend, not real—except she was in it, seeing it, smelling it, touching it. She had to know where it went. Unlike the basement, the tunnel was spotless: no spiderwebs, no dirt, nothing. She stopped, a sudden, weird thought popping into her head. Maybe the tunnel was self-cleaning? That would explain the wind.

Nope! She shook her head. *Not likely.*

Thirty feet up, she found a small spot of dirt and looked up. Daylight peeked through a small crevice, probably the spot where she'd found the sword.

Her pocket felt warm. *That's weird.*

She fished the arrowhead out. Warm to her touch, the inset gem seemed to swirl like clouds in a snow globe. While there appeared to be no rational reason for it, something in the tunnel seemed to excite the gem, and as she continued forward, the glow grew more vivid.

Whatever this place was, she felt no fear of it and couldn't explain why, beyond a feeling that the lucky arrowhead protected her. It sounded irrational but something emanated from the gem, a pleasant feeling, warm like the stone itself. She walked, phone in one hand and arrowhead in the other, on and on for what seemed like a mile, until she saw light washing across the floor of the tunnel from a side room on the left.

"Hello? Hello?"

She inched to the opening. A black gate blocked access to the room. Wrought iron, bolted to the wall on the hinge side and locked with a large Master padlock on the other. Rachel edged forward to the corner, turned and looked through the gate, then gasped, her eyes darting back and forth, trying to comprehend the incomprehensible.

She spoke quietly, almost reverently. "Holy shit!"

Stunned by the scope and size of the cavern, by the drawings, and by the ship—the centerpiece of the amazing scene before her—Rachel only then noticed the arrowhead vibrating subtly in her hand. When she held it up, the gem and the ship appeared to resonate as one, both of them faintly aglow.

She stood, transfixed, mouth agape, awed by the Viking ship preserved here underground, a ship that had no earthly reason to be here, a ship that also seemed to exist in strange harmony with the Native American arrowhead in her hand.

She couldn't imagine why—what it meant, nothing. It seemed like magic. Not the sleight of hand nonsense but fantastical magic: paranormal stuff, a world where wizards, unicorns, and spirits existed. Having written off ghosts ten minutes ago, this was a stunning surprise. Maybe she was full of shit and needed to be more open-minded. Actually, what choice did she have? This was real. Not a dream, nor a nightmare. She didn't mess with drugs and didn't drink. Nope, it was entirely real.

The gate meant there was a caretaker or guard. The clean, modern lock meant they still looked after it. Was this a known relic being quietly maintained in secret? Or was someone hiding it like she was hiding the sword?

Again she wondered: what the hell had she stumbled upon?

So many questions without answers.

Rachel snapped a bunch of pics of the ship and the cavern and decided to leave—for now. She was going to research the hell out of this and find those answers.

Then she was coming back—with a hacksaw.

Forty

Lachlan stepped into Quinlan's Tavern. He loved the decor, an early twentieth century American tavern with a hand-carved oak back bar, large mirrors, period decor—but also a child of the twenty-first century, with wide screen TVs discretely placed around the bar, comfy booths, and tasteful LED lighting.

The aura of the place was deeply troubled though, and it was more than the errant presence he'd been trailing. The place was alive with psychic energy, some benign and some downright frightening. It was a blessing and a curse of his life that every building, every grove of trees, every field held some energy, energy he was receptive to whether he wanted it or not. In some places, the energy was warm and pleasing. Good things had happened there. People had lived, loved and died in a positive way. That happened rarely. More often, he encountered unhappiness, anger, jealousy, greed, spite. Such was the human condition: life much too short, most of it wasted on negativity. A lesson he learned eons ago. The current generation called it mindfulness. He didn't have a title for it. He had simply learned that living in the present, letting go of the past and not worrying about the future was the secret to a reasonably happy life.

He felt something else. Something more subtle. Just an undercurrent, but everything he felt was related to that something else, and the presence of the darkness lurking somewhere nearby. This was the right place. More serendipity. Officer Taylor had done him a favor.

He sat at the bar and studied the decor. They had labeled one wall *The Haunting of Quinlan's Tavern.*

An attractive woman approached. "What can I get you?"

"Guinness, tap please."

He left ten dollars on the bar and walked over to the ghost wall. There were a number of articles and some fuzzy noir photos. Nicely done but thin on substance. Thing was, they were right about the ghosts. The usual cast of wayward spirits and lost souls often found in older buildings were here. Just nothing like the ghost wall.

Beneath that lay something darker, the presence he was following. The darkness wasn't even in the bar. It lay beneath it, about thirty feet down. Was there a cellar beneath the cellar? That seemed illogical. And something else.

Whoa!

He realized what it was with a start. A sensation he first noticed at the farm.

Caol Áit.

Gaelic for what many people called a thin place. An interface between this world and other worlds. No wonder the darkness had been drawn here.

When the woman returned with his change, he said, "So have you seen any of the ghosts that supposedly inhabit this old tavern?"

"Me?" She hesitated. "No, not really."

She had, he was certain.

"My name is Lachlan, Lachlan Hayward. I have an interest in the paranormal."

"Hi Lachlan, I'm Kiera." She leaned in, against the bar. "So, have you ever seen a ghost?"

"Yes. A few." What could he say? He saw them every day.

"Fascinating." Just then, an impatient drinker summoned her to the other end of the bar. She didn't look like a bartender. He felt sure she was college educated. Side job? Fallen on hard times? He couldn't quite get a read on her. He then saw her talking to the other bartender. Judging by the way she leaned into the conversation, they were together. Perhaps that explained it—though *he* didn't look like a bartender, either.

Lachlan sat and absorbed the surrounding energies, feeling uneasy. The darkness sitting below ground somewhere near the tavern felt imposing. Was that what Kenric had faced? There was a lesson here. The darkness had killed his friend, the most gifted sorcerer who ever lived. He could only hope he was better informed, better equipped, and more creative in his preparations. Besides wits, tools, amulets, talismans, he needed help. Help that wasn't available. At the very least, he needed to find a medium. Without another of the Aeldo, a medium was the next best option. Sure, he could wait for Fynn Alden, but he feared the darkness would grow more powerful in the presence of Caol Áit, perhaps too powerful if he waited. No, he had to act sooner rather than later—in the next few days.

He felt some disruption in the energy flow, some balancing force that repelled or attenuated the darkness. What was happening here? Multiple things were distorting the energy flow through the building and he had no idea what they were.

The place smelt heavenly, a mishmash of fried stuff, herbs, and meats. Time for food. He too needed to recharge. He perused the menu and ordered the fish and chips. There was little chance they would get them right, but he was feeling a little homesick and close would do.

At first, he saw no reason to return to the farmhouse, but the more he thought about it and absorbed the energies flowing through the bar, he realized they were all connected: the bar *and* the farmhouse. How he wasn't certain, but he thought about the energy below and the sense that something inhabited the basement of the farmhouse as well.

How could they be connected? He thought about the underlying rock, the Niagara limestone, and the possibility of interconnecting passages, caverns, and crevices. That was the answer. He had to return to the farmhouse and do so without getting arrested.

His fish and chips arrived.

They were excellent.

Perfect.

Forty-One

Kiera tended bar in a distracted mood and fretted about her relationship with Willow. The words had been hurtful, but she would get over them. While Willow was impetuous and prone to ill-considered words and actions, they had never had a serious blowout in their friendship and Kiera already missed her company. Something was different with Willow, and her obsession with the longship seemed malignant. Would she call or stay angry?

At least Josh had gated and locked the cavern. Still, she worried people would find a way in.

Caleb remained MIA but she suspected he was lying low until Josh's anger blew over. Kiera had never seen him so angry. It was strange. Suddenly, both she and Josh were at odds with their best friends.

She had taken a liking to the older British guy at the end of the bar. He ate his fish and chips, complimented the chef in a quaint manner, and ordered another Guinness. When the bar slowed down later, she grabbed a stool, poured a chardonnay, and sat by him. He had a full head of grey hair, professionally trimmed. A matching grey cookie-duster of a moustache. A finely featured, handsome older man with striking blue eyes. There was a Viking ancestor somewhere in his past.

"Tell me about your interest in the paranormal," Kiera said.

"Not much to tell, really. I investigate hauntings. Most turn out to be nothing. A few are more interesting." He looked at her with a raised eyebrow. "You've seen something, haven't you?"

"Yep." Kiera nodded. She pondered for a moment and said, "Come here, around the bar."

Lachlan walked around the bar as she knelt by the cooler. She opened the door and closed it slowly. He jumped back a bit and said, "Blimey!"

"Right?" Kiera was happy he'd seen it. His placid manner suggested it was no big deal.

"Do that again." Lachlan scrutinized the door as she closed it. "Well?"

He smiled and held a finger up. "Wait here, please."

Striding out of the bar, he returned with a satchel and knelt by the door. He pulled a strange orb from his bag and set it on the ground under the door. Silver with short spikes sticking out at angles, the spherical object looked like a miniature satellite.

He spoke a strange German-sounding language while touching the glass door and the orb: *"Gæð ā wyrd swā hīo scel! Áblinnest!"*

She frowned, skeptical. This looked like real tinfoil-hat stuff. Expecting something dramatic, the face simply faded from view.

"That's it? It's gone?"

He swung the door back and forth and said, "I believe so, yes."

Intrigued, Kiera said, "How'd you do that?"

"An old, trusted technique."

A tepid explanation, she thought. "Is there a scientific explanation for that...procedure?"

"None that I know of." He looked thoughtful for a moment. "I had a friend who would've known the answer to that. All that matters to me is that it works."

"That looked easy. Was it?"

"You were expecting fire and brimstone?" He gave her a quizzical look with raised eyebrows.

"A flash, a poof? I don't know." Kiera shrugged her shoulders. "You didn't answer my question. Was that easy?"

"Hardly. I'm very skilled at what I do, and I say that with all modesty." He bowed slightly and returned to his perch at the bar. His calm demeanor was reassuring. Kiera swung the door back and forth, but the ghost was gone.

She sat down thinking: *Holy crap! Who is this guy?*

She said, "You're hired."

He raised his eyebrows. "You have an opening for a paranormal investigator?"

"Maybe. So what do you feel in this place?" As she asked the question, she wasn't sure she wanted an answer.

"A considerable amount," he said. "Some of it good. Some of it bad."

Kiera felt her belly tighten. "What do you mean by *bad?*"

"I suspect you'll need my assistance again." His expression grave, he sipped his beer.

"Oh? When?"

"Soon."

Forty-Two

Willow sat at her kitchen table field-stripping her Kimber Micro 9.

The oak table was an antique, part of her shabby-chic theme, the walls pastel blue, the room decorated with baskets and vintage floral paintings, ruffled curtains, and ceramic canisters on the quartz countertops. A sideboard in distressed wood was adorned with decorative china and glass vases with faux greenery.

As she worked, she stewed over Kiera's treacherous behavior. After everything Willow had put up with over the years, that bitch had the nerve to deny her any access to the cavern and the longship! The idiot was worried about her stupid boat and ignoring the magnificence of the cavern itself and the thin place. Kiera was just an insensitive putz who couldn't possibly understand the beauty and spiritual significance of something so magical. Clearly, the Vikings and Native Americans had understood perfectly. How could Kiera be so blind? How could she have ever been friends with such a shallow person? No matter now. They were done.

Fuck Kiera!

As she slid the recoil spring and guide rod into the slide, Willow

decided she would find a way in, come hell or high water. She wondered where the tunnel went to beyond the cavern. Was there another
entrance? Some way to get in and bypass the meddling bitch?

Damn it! She was going to find out.

Willow positioned the slide stop and seated it, checking to make
sure her weapon operated properly. She loaded two clips with Luger
9mm JHP rounds, sliding one into the pistol, leaving the other on the
table. Her plan was simple. Sneak in at night, explore the cavern, maybe
learn the answers to all her questions. She didn't expect to actually
use the gun. Maybe just wave it at Kiera if she tried to interfere. Kiera
wouldn't engage her in gunfire.

Oh, and she was taking a wooden plaque this time to grace her
study.

Sometime in the next couple of days.

She was going in.

Forty-Three

Kiera lay in bed, tossing and turning, unable to sleep, listening to Josh snore lightly. Her overactive thoughts careened between the fight with Willow, who still hadn't attempted to apologize, the strange old guy in the bar who made a ghost disappear, and her duplicitous friend, Rustin Marshall. She lay on her back, trying a relaxation exercise to no avail. Then Ghost growled, a low, menacing warning. Great, just what she needed. A moment later, the alarm system went off.

She jumped from bed and shook Josh, but he didn't even stir. Shit! The man could sleep through an earthquake. She jumped into her jeans, shimmied a tee on, and grabbed her gun. Quietly she stepped to the stairwell and looked down. They left the lower stairway door open at night and she had a clear view of the outside door—still closed, but it looked ajar. Hopefully, the alarm had scared them away.

Kiera dialed 911 and quickly reeled off her name and address and reported the attempted break-in to the operator.

The door rattled slightly. Kiera yelled, "I'm coming down and I'm armed! Cops are on their way!"

Silence. No sound, no fleeing footsteps.

A minute later, a squad—lights blazing—pulled in. She left the gun on the landing and went down to meet the cop. The back door was still locked but someone had cracked the jamb. Owen Prosser, the city cop who came out the night of the fire, stepped out of the car. Relatively new to the force, Owen looked like a runner. Lean and muscled, he probably did well with the ladies and he was single. Kiera opened the door for him, letting in the warm, muggy night air.

"Hey Kiera. Whoa!" He sized up the door. "Looks like someone tried to break in."

The door was dented and scratched near the handle. A breaker bar lay nearby in the grass.

"Do you have a way to secure the door for the rest of the night?" Owen asked while jotting down notes.

"I can padlock it from the inside."

Resting a hand on his gun, he said, "Do you want me to look around before I leave?"

"No. I'm good. I'm pretty sure no one came through the door." She just wanted to go back to bed.

"We've had a rash of amateur break-ins recently. Probably the same guy or crew. I would love to nail them." He gave her a two-fingered salute. "I'll stop by in the morning for some pics to file a report."

"Sounds good. Goodnight Owen. Thanks."

Would this be the new normal? People trying to break in? Trouble in the bar? Kiera closed the door and jogged downstairs to the basement. Halfway to the workbench, she stopped and started, scanning the room. What if someone *had* gotten in and were down here? It was quiet. Nary a peep from man nor beast. The tunnel perhaps?

Kiera grabbed a heavy Master Lock and secured the side door. She ran up the steps, grabbed her gun, and hurried down into the basement.

Breathless, she stopped at the edge of the hole and listened.

Silence.

A soft breeze wafted up from the tunnel that felt colder than Green Bay in January. She grabbed Josh's sweatshirt hanging by the stairs and clambered down into the tunnel. Gun held at her side, Kiera eased along the tunnel, but saw no evidence anyone was down here. Why was it so frigging cold? She could see her breath. She would go to the cavern to satisfy her anxiety that it remained safe and turn around.

As she approached, the gate appeared to be locked but something was wrong with the light coming through the archway. It was soft, filtered in some way.

Kiera looked into the cavern and froze, stunned, scarcely believing her eyes.

Snow! In the cavern, falling from the ceiling, covering the floor and the longship, about an inch of it in dry itty-bitty flakes. This wasn't possible, was it? Snow inside a cavern? No way. She could think of no atmospheric effect that would cause this.

It looked beautiful—like a life-sized snow globe—and terrifying, all at once.

She ran back upstairs to grab her camera, running every possibility through her head, real or imagined. She thought of Lachlan—the ghost whisperer, as she now thought of him. Had banishing the ghost done this? God, she wished she had his number, to call and ask him about this. She might have to eat crow and call Willow. This was simply light-years beyond anything in her experience.

Kiera tried to wake Josh. "Josh. Josh!

When he stirred, she said, "Josh! It's snowing in the cavern!"

He half-opened an eye, shrugged and rolled over like she was merely a bad dream. How could he sleep like that?

Kiera jogged to the cavern and snapped a dozen photos. She opened the gate, stepped in the snow, and caught some flakes in her hand. It was the real deal. For a moment, she felt like a kid.

Looking up, she noticed the falling snow obscured the ceiling. Or was it a cloud of some sort? She couldn't tell. Perhaps she was documenting some hitherto undiscovered phenomena, though it seemed unlikely.

Had Lachlan caused this? Was it an omen of some sort?

'Some of it good. Some of it bad,' he'd said.

Which was this?

The snow ended abruptly. The ceiling now visible, she could hear water trickling as the snow melted and dripped from the gunwale of the longship. As the snow disappeared, the room grew darker and Kiera felt something else in the room, a presence, something dark and dangerous that sent a wave of cold furrowing down her spine, a sensation unrelated to the snow.

She bolted for the gate, locked it, and ran up the tunnel and both flights of stairs until she stood in the apartment, shivering, believing her life had been in danger. The tame little haunting of Quinlan's Tavern no longer felt so tame.

Some of it good. Some of it bad.

Kiera was certain of one thing.

The presence behind her?

Decidedly bad.

Forty-Four

Lachlan, asleep on the cot in Kenric's office, worked on a puzzle. He had directed his mind to solve this riddle while he slept: why did he sense the darkness at the farmhouse and the tavern in equal measure? His mind imagined how it had traveled here through the rock and thought about the porous limestone underlying the surface. The answer was obvious. A cave or tunnel—or both—and it had to run between the tavern and the farm.

He awoke soon after and considered the idea. He'd sensed a space beneath the basement of the tavern; it made sense. Was Kiera aware of some entryway into the rock?

He really couldn't ask, not at this point, and didn't want to expose her to any untoward danger. He had taken quite a liking to the woman. Strong willed, intelligent, and personable, an uncommon breed of woman in centuries past. He fully approved of the acceptance of women as equals in the modern world. In his mind, they always had been. He had married three women in his long life and they had all been fierce, independent souls: full partners in life, not simply wives.

Regardless, it meant going back to the farmhouse to search for access underground. After poring over satellite images, Lachlan charted a course from a side road and along a tree line to the farmhouse. The wild prairie behind the house would conceal his approach. He found a fire lane a half mile away to conceal the car lest the sheriff also checked the side roads around the house.

⋆   ⋆   ⋆

He might be older than dirt, but he was spry and walked along the tree line and through the prairie grass with little trouble. He was approaching the back door when he saw a young girl—a teenager, wearing a backpack—break from the brush to his left and run to the back door. Her approach was also stealthy. That could mean only one thing: she also knew about the tunnel.

Lachlan crouched and ran to the porch, creeping up just as the girl stepped through the doorway. She turned and froze, evidently thinking she was busted. She eyed him with trepidation spiced with a little anger, but no fear.

"Relax. I think we're after the same thing," Lachlan said quietly.

She stood rigid, mute, expressionless, standing her ground.

"The basement, right?"

She nodded, looking apprehensive. "Am I busted?"

He waved a dismissive hand. "No, no. Let's talk. You found a passage in the basement, didn't you?"

She nodded but remained silent. Not very forthcoming, this one. She was hiding something as well. "My name is Lachlan. I'm interested in seeing what's down there."

Resolute, holding eye contact, she said, "I'm Rachel, and I found it first."

"I understand. I doubt it'll stay a secret for long, I'm afraid. For what it's worth, you can keep the other thing."

"Which one?"

He smiled. "Ah, there's more than one?"

A slight nod. She looked at him suspiciously. "You aren't a creeper, are you?"

"What, an old guy like me?" Lachlan feigned shock, holding an open hand to his chest, amused by her blunt manner.

She humphed. "Creepers usually are old guys like you. I know karate, you know."

"Most impressive." Did she? Her stance looked a little uncertain. A bluff probably, but a good one. "I assure you that you're perfectly safe with me. I'm a paranormal investigator."

"A ghost guy?" A twinkle of interest in her eyes.

"One and the same."

Regarding him warily, she said, "What's with your accent? Where are you from?"

"London."

"England?"

"Indeed. The Queen, Winston Churchill, and all that."

"Who's Winston Churchill?"

Lachlan shook his head with a mental eye-roll. Young people these days. But she seemed to be relaxing. He needed to gain her trust.

"No matter," he said; then asked, "Do you mind if I take a look?"

She regarded him with suspicion, but nodded, saying, "I suppose, I've already been down there. I'm coming too."

They descended into the tunnel, Lachlan admiring the hand-crafted stairs as he climbed down, astounded by the tunnel itself. Rachel led the way while Lachlan pondered the lighting. It was quite a trick to make limestone fluoresce and required a great amount of energy. Where did the energy come from? The tunnel, following a natural rift in the rock, must have required tens of thousands of man-hours to carve out. Who had done this? Why?

"How old are you?" Lachlan asked.

"None of your business," she said without turning. Quite the little warrior. He liked her, but apparently, the feeling was not yet mutual. He asked a few more questions, then gave up trying. It was clear she intended to share nothing. Part of his brain remained attuned to the energies flowing through the tunnel. They were growing more intense and were clearer underground.

He identified three elements: the darkness, the Caol Áit or thin place, and another element he hadn't encountered in many years, centuries perhaps. It had several names. The site in Turkey was called Pluto's Gate, in Ireland on Lough Derg it was St. Patrick's Purgatory. Lachlan preferred the Gaelic name: *Geata de Ifreann* or Gate of Hell. These places were physical entrances to the underworld, the meaning of which varied by faith. While purgatory suggested the possibility of redemption, hell did not, and Lachlan had never heard of or witnessed anything good happening in proximity to one of these portals. For him, hell seemed the best definition.

They walked a while, almost three-quarter miles, Lachlan deduced. The entire limestone structure now vibrated subtly with the energies as an archway came into view. Rachel ran ahead and looked first, wonder in her expression. When he caught up and looked, it felt like the world shifted sideways. No words could describe it. Stunning, spectacular, remarkable—all were woefully inadequate.

He stood, transfixed by the Viking longship, perfectly preserved, the centerpiece of a shrine or temple. In its own right, such a ship was a thing of beauty, but set on a plinth in this cavern it seemed like a vision from the Gods.

Like the house and tavern, the boat glowed with a faint, ephemeral blue aura likely invisible to Rachel.

It raised a thousand questions.

Who built this? Why? He had to believe it depicted an old, unknown peace ritual or gathering. The writing on the wall was Old Norse but the art and pictographs were Native American. There wasn't a single historical event or record that supported the idea that Native Americans and Vikings cooperated on building this or any other structure. How had this remained a secret for so long? He understood what had drawn them here. Perhaps the site honored the sacred interface, the thin place that existed in this cavern, or as he preferred, Caol Áit, the older Gaelic name.

Here, alternate dimensions met in inexplicable ways. Christians believed they were nearer heaven, but it wasn't that simple. That's what Christians felt. The Vikings evidently felt they had found Valhalla. Lachlan felt a pivot point between light and dark and it was the light that people perceived as spiritual warmth. It was all things to all people. To Lachlan, old pagan spirits lurked just beyond. Remarkably, the Caol Áit somehow existed in equilibrium with the dark side, the Geata de Ifreann.

Now things had changed. People had uncovered it and he feared the darkness would upset the balance that had existed here, perhaps for hundreds or thousands of years.

Rachel held something in her hand, and he had a sudden flash of insight. "Were you down here yesterday?"

She nodded.

"What's that in your hand?"

She gave him a brief glimpse of an arrowhead and clamped her hand shut. "It's mine."

"Absolutely." He jiggled the padlock, mumbled a brief incantation, blew on it, and the lock fell open.

"Awesome! How'd you do that?" Mouth agape, eyes bright with wonder, she seemed to be warming to him, finally.

"Shh, that's *my* secret," he said good-naturedly.

They stepped through the arch. He noticed the floor was damp, the room cold. They weren't alone. The darkness was nearby.

He pulled an amulet from his pocket, a small teak disk bearing the face of the god *Thunor* and a lightning bolt, and handed it to Rachel. "Put this in your pocket."

"Why?"

"It will protect you."

She studied it skeptically. "From ghosts?"

"And worse."

He caught her quizzical look but decided the less she knew about the darkness the better. As they approached the boat, he sensed the energies flowing through the wood, but they also curved and flowed through Rachel. Lachlan noticed a faint glow from the arrowhead in the girl's hand.

Oh my.

The arrowhead and longship were connected and he realized it was a key, or a control of some sort. Suddenly, he knew the girl was in grave danger. The darkness would want the arrowhead and do most anything to get it.

"This is so dope," she said, touching the longship with reverence.

He assumed she meant cool. "Indeed. But we need to leave."

"What? We just got here."

"You are in serious danger here." He tried to hide the alarm he felt. "We need to talk, but not here."

Fists on hip, feet planted, she said, "Listen, dude. I agreed to come with you, but I'll leave when I'm ready."

The girl was no shrinking violet. "Listen to me. I'm the ghost guy, as you put it. There are things in this cavern you can neither see nor feel—dangerous things, and they will want that arrowhead. Haven't you wondered why it's glowing?

"You can't have it." She gripped it in a tight fist. "I'm serious!"

"I don't want it." That wasn't entirely true, but he needed to make her understand the dangers here. "We need to talk but it will take too long to explain here. I'll explain when we're safe above ground. Just talk, that's all I want to do."

She grumbled a bit but turned and walked through the arch. Lachlan followed and locked the gate behind him.

Powers were converging, the energy levels intense—a harbinger of a fearsome reckoning ahead.

He had very little time to figure this out.

A day or two at best.

Forty-Five

After leaving the tunnel and running upstairs, Kiera decided she would only sleep if she went to her house.

She left a detailed note of the night's events for Josh, summoned Ghost, and drove home. Pouring a splash of chardonnay, she took it to her bedroom, stripped to her panties, and slid into bed. She sipped wine and read a book, waiting for fatigue to catch up. Fifteen minutes later, Kiera silenced her phone, turned the bedside lamp off, and passed out.

She woke at noon to Ghost sniffing at her face. Poor guy was probably starving. She felt well-rested despite the long troublesome night. Kiera checked her phone—Josh had called a half dozen times. He could wait. She prepared food for Ghost and threw a cup in the Keurig.

After Ghost had eaten, they went out and she sat on the patio with her coffee. It was a beautiful day, sunny and breezy. The sense that she had encountered something dark and dangerous in the tunnel receded in the bright sunshine, as such feelings often did. They did need to consider more serious security in the short term. Caleb was still missing, and she felt the break-in attempt was related to the longship rather than amateur burglars. If anything gave her pause, it was the snowfall in the cavern. She grabbed her laptop and googled *snow falling in caves* but found only links about building snow caves, an entirely different animal.

Kiera needed to know more about the tavern. Maybe something in the history of the place would explain some of this, but she had no time and little inclination to chase it down herself. She had a friend, Ari Thomas, who worked as a quasi-historian/researcher/private investigator. He might be willing to help. Mostly, he traced family histories, lost siblings, runaways, and errant spouses. He worked from home and knew all the best internet resources for that kind of search. Kiera fired off a quick email with her request and a promise to pay him for his time.

After a short walk with Ghost and a long hot shower, Kiera pulled up to the tavern at three. Josh was opening for the day, stocking the snacks.

He turned with a quizzical expression. "Hey babe, not taking my calls?"

"No, you deadbeat." She dropped her purse on the bar. "You slept through a shit storm last night."

"So I gathered. Sorry. Want to tell me about it?"

They sat at the bar after Josh poured two half-glasses of wine. Kiera described the events: starting with the attempted break-in, ending with the snow in the cavern.

"Snow? In the cavern? Is that even possible?"

"I don't know, but it happened," Kiera said. "I'm worried that Caleb spilled the story and now, people will try to break in, maybe even steal artifacts. Have you heard from him?"

"Nope. Not a peep. Neither has his sister. She's seriously worried," Josh said, shaking his head. "He hasn't been home and he hasn't been to work."

"Shit, I may be mad at him but that doesn't sound good," Kiera said.

"I know. It's been over forty-eight hours. She filed a missing person's report today."

She had a sudden unwelcome thought. What if he'd ventured in the tunnel and hadn't come out? A few weeks back, a customer who lived nearby, Scott Robbins, had disappeared from his basement and hadn't been seen since. It was a deeply disturbing possibility. She was no longer sure her bad feeling last night was just nerves and a lack of sleep. She hated to think that way, but a number of her beliefs had been severely challenged in the past few days.

Staff filtered in. They could finish the conversation later. She wiped down the bar and back bar while Josh made a list to restock the coolers. Soon after, the customers followed and the place grew busy. At least six people had come in asking about the Viking boat. It was good for business in a perverse way—they all stayed for drinks or dinner—but how long before the media came snooping around? How much longer could they keep it a secret?

Professor Marshall walked in at five with a handful of papers and an insincere smile. "Hello, Kiera. Here's the paperwork you requested, everything above board."

"Right." She gave him a skeptical eye. "Something to drink while I read?"

"Please. Glenlivet, on the rocks."

Kiera poured the scotch and signaled to Angela to cover the bar. She sat down and read through the contract, looking for any hint of double-dealing.

"It looks okay to me. I'm going to have Josh look as well," Kiera said. "He's an attorney."

"By all means. Like I said, it's completely equitable."

"Uh huh." She side-glanced him, walked back to the office and handed the contract to Josh. "Can you read this quickly, just to make sure Marshall hasn't tried to screw me on anything?"

He wrinkled his nose. "You're going to trust him after what he pulled?"

"I don't trust him, but I need his name."

A few minutes later, Josh said, "Looks fine. Standard boilerplate. Have him come in and sign in front of me."

Kiera waved him into the office. She then signed and handed the papers to Marshall to sign. Josh notarized both copies, then handed one to the professor and slid the other into the safe. "There you go, kids. You are now partners in crime."

After Marshall walked out, Kiera said, "Still don't trust him."

"You shouldn't."

★   ★   ★

Around seven, Lachlan wandered in and sat at his seat from the night before at the street end of the bar.

Kiera walked over. "Guinness?"

He nodded and said, "Yes ma'am," with his lovely accent.

As she set the glass down, he said, mirth in his eyes, "Any more ghosts needing my attention?"

"Maybe. You going to be around for a while?"

"Absolutely. I'll need another order of the fish and chips in a bit as well."

The bar was busy and Kiera worried that she and Lachlan might not have an opportunity to talk before he left, but he ordered another Guinness and seemed content to wait. At nine, she poured a chardonnay and sat across from him, behind the bar.

"So Lachlan, tell me a bit about yourself." She rested her chin on her hand.

"Not much to tell, really." He shrugged.

"Nonsense. I suspect you've led a very interesting life. That little trick with the ghost was amazing."

Fiddling with his glass, he said, "Retired professor of European History. Widowed. Bit of a hermit. Here in the States to handle the estate of an old and dear friend."

"I'm sorry to hear that."

"Thank you." He cocked his head. "So tell me about this other ghost of yours."

She debated revealing the details but thought, why not? He seemed trustworthy and she welcomed his expertise. "Can you keep a secret, Lachlan?"

"Absolutely. I know few people in this country and I'm a firm believer in the adage *loose lips sink ships* and all that."

"Until yesterday, I believed the paranormal was fringe science at best. I might have considered you a crackpot. Now, I suddenly find myself in a situation where I might need a paranormal investigator."

Lachlan raised an eyebrow. "Fascinating. Do tell."

"Just a sec." She ran to handle two drink orders and waved Angela over to cover the bar.

She sat down. "You're a historian?"

"European history in particular, yes."

"Then you must know a good deal about the Vikings?"

"Yes. A specialty of mine. Even speak a little Old Norse." He smiled a knowing smile. "And your interest?"

She struggled with her aversion to discussing the ship, but he *was* an expert. "What if I told you there's a Viking longship in a cavern underneath this tavern?"

He held eye contact, seemed to weigh a response, and then said, "I'd believe you. I've seen it."

"What?" At first, his answer didn't compute. When she realized he was serious, she said, "When? How?"

He sipped his beer, leaving a thin foam mustache on his lip. "There's an access panel to a tunnel in an old farmhouse about a mile south of here. A teenage girl discovered the tunnel about the same time as I did. I doubt it will remain a secret much longer."

Kiera sighed. "I was afraid of that."

"Placing the iron gate was a wise choice, but I fear you'll need to bring in the authorities to protect it. The site is stunning. It may upend large parts of New World history."

"So what is it? A shrine?" Kiera asked.

"I have no idea. I've never seen anything like it, and I've seen hundreds of medieval ceremonial sites."

It was disturbing that he had no idea. "Your best guess?"

"It's possible the people or peoples who created the cave art and placed the longship there recognized the cavern as a special place."

A light bulb lit up in her head. "A thin place?"

"Yes, quite right." He looked at her curiously. 'How do you know that?"

"A friend of mine—Willow—she's sensitive to stuff like that."

"I should like to meet this Willow. I might need her help."

"For what?"

"To deal with your problem in the cavern."

"My problem?" She put a hand on her chest.

He put his hand on hers resting on the bar. "I don't wish to alarm you. Your friend in the door? A minor haunting. The cavern is haunted by something darker and more dangerous. I feel you've sensed that."

She did. Her stomach fluttered with anxiety. "Why are you really here?"

"A good question. I'm searching for something and I think it currently resides in the cavern."

"What is it?"

"A darkness. Perhaps the devil himself."

"That's rather dramatic." Regardless, the comment sent a deep shiver through her.

"It is. I'm sorry, I wish it wasn't." His expression—furrowed brow, eyebrows drawn together—was disconcerting.

"There was snow in the cavern this morning. What does that mean?"

Lachlan closed his eyes for a moment as if pondering an unpleasant truth. He looked at Kiera and said, "I suspect the snowfall means it—the darkness, for want of a better word—is here."

"Oh shit." Darkness. The perfect word to describe what she felt down there.

"Indeed."

Forty-Six

Kiera felt like she was trapped in the movie *Groundhog Day*.

For the second night in a row, she lay in bed, tossing and turning, not sleeping, listening to Josh snore lightly. Her overactive thoughts spun between the fight with Willow, who still hadn't called to apologize, Lachlan the ghost whisperer, and her dishonest friend, the professor. She lay on her back, trying a relaxation exercise to no avail. Then Ghost uttered a low, sustained growl. Great, just what she needed. She waited for the alarm system to sound.

The alarm remained silent, but Kiera thought she heard a faint footfall in the bar. Was she imagining it? Power of suggestion? Fatigue?

Damn!

She wouldn't sleep unless she checked. Kiera dressed quietly, grabbed her gun, and whispered to Ghost, "Stay here, buddy."

Poised on the landing, she checked the lower outside door. It appeared closed and locked. She eased down the stairs, drew tight to the corner, and scanned the bar. The room was dark but for the light from the electronics. She flipped the lights on—the room was empty. Maybe she imagined the noise but she decided to walk a circuit of the room anyway.

Kiera caught a scent. Something familiar. Something feminine. Willow.

Damn it! She knew the code for the alarm system. The scent smelled fresh—she was somewhere in the bar or the tunnel. Now she was breaking in at night? She truly *had* lost her frigging mind.

Kiera went to the basement steps, hit the lights and walked down.

"Willow? Willow!" She was livid; she couldn't believe her friend was acting this way. Well, Willow had a surprise coming when she reached the gate and couldn't get in.

Ha!

Kiera dropped into the tunnel. "Willow?"

She heard a clattering noise, perhaps Willow kicking the metal gate.

"Kiera? Open this fucking gate!"

The bitch breaks in and is now issuing orders? Screw her!

Willow kicked the gate again. "I'm serious, Kiera. I will fucking shoot you if you don't open this gate."

As Kiera eased along the curved wall of the tunnel, she caught sight of Willow as she turned and glared. She saw the gun in Willow's hand—a small gun, a Kimber maybe—and saw the barrel rising.

The woman's gone crazy!

Kiera ducked back. "Willow? What the hell is wrong with you?"

"I'm serious, Kiera! Open this fucking gate!"

"No! You can't go in there!"

Willow fired two quick shots that ricocheted off the opposite wall.

Jesus!

"Willow. I've got a gun too. Back off!"

Willow fired again. "Bring it, bitch!"

She hazarded a look and saw an angry, crazed Willow walking toward her, gun raised and ready. "Give me the fucking key, Kiera!"

Kiera aimed past Willow and fired, then turned and ran. This was nuts! The woman had lost her mind! She had no intention of having a shootout with her. Kiera looked over her shoulder. Willow, still charging, fired another shot.

Christ! She might not make it to the ladder in time and Willow was no slouch with a pistol.

Fueled by a confusing mixture of fear and adrenaline, her heartbeat thumping in her ears, she ran a serpentine line the last twenty feet and leapt halfway up the wall, catching the handhold on the stairs and launching herself up into the basement, losing her grip on her gun.

The gun skittered across the floor.

Kiera scrambled after it, grabbed it, and rolled toward the stairs and to her feet, clambering up as Willow's head appeared, followed a second later by her gun, which swung toward Kiera and barked as Willow fired again.

Hyper-aware, hyper-focused, she'd never been in combat, but it must feel like this, she decided. It was scarier than she could possibly imagine. Her legs and her lungs burned with the effort. Kiera slammed and locked the door, knowing it might not stop the crazy woman behind her. A worry confirmed a moment later when a bullet splintered the wood by the door handle.

Tearing up the second flight of stairs, she heard Willow burst through the door. As Willow turned the corner, Kiera fired down the stairs into the floor and yelled, "Willow, I'll kill you if I have to."

"You might have to."

As Willow turned to fire, Kiera lobbed off another shot and ducked sideways but heard nothing.

Was Willow's clip empty?

How many had she fired? She counted...yep, six. Willow's concealed carry was a Kimber Micro 9 just like hers. The clip held six bullets. Had Willow brought a second clip? There was no sound from the landing except for Willow's breathing.

"Kiera!" Josh yelled. "What the hell's going on?"

Now he wakes up. *Jesus!* Kiera yelled, "Stay there. Willow's lost her mind."

"Willow?"

Kiera yelled down the stairs. "Ha! Didn't bring another clip, did you?"

Silence.

Forty-Seven

She heard Willow run out the front door.

Thank God!

"Josh, call 911. Intruder in the bar." Kiera laid on her back on the landing, panting, heart pounding, bathed in cold sweat. As her heart and breathing settled, she had second thoughts about the 911 call.

She yelled to Josh. "Hang up. I don't want the cops here but we're gonna have to beef up security."

He appeared in the doorway, sleep disheveled. "You want to tell me what the hell is going on? Was that gunfire?"

Kiera sat up and nodded. "Give me a sec. I'm going to lock up."

He yelled down the stairs, "Careful!"

She walked down the steps, scanned the bar from the doorway: empty. Kiera ran to the front door, locked it, changed the alarm code, and reset the alarm.

Things were getting out of hand, running away from her. She should call the cops and have Willow arrested but didn't want to draw attention to the longship. She wasn't being rational and knew it. Willow had lost her mind. Caleb was missing. As much as she liked

Lachlan, his answer to the question about what he was searching for remained vivid and bothered her the most: *The devil himself*.

Josh would wig out when he heard the whole story. This tavern was his dream and it was rapidly turning into a shit show.

As she climbed the stairs, Josh stood waiting, leaning against the wall, looking tired, confused, and angry.

"What's going on Kiera? Was that Willow? Shooting a gun in my bar?"

"Yes. She's lost it." She could hardly look at him. Indirectly, this was her fault.

He punched 911 into his phone.

"Wait!"

"What Kiera?" He was livid, gesticulating angrily. "You're worried about that fucking boat? Really? What if she'd killed you? Or me? What if she comes back and kills someone in the bar?"

"You're right." She sat at the kitchen table and put her head in her hands. "I'm sorry. You're right."

Ten minutes later, someone knocked at the side door. Kiera walked down and peeked out. Two cops, Owen Prosser and Noah Weber, stood waiting. Kiera let them in and re-locked it. Josh was standing on the bottom step.

"Josh, Kiera, what's going on. Something about gunfire?"

Kiera explained the situation with Willow: the shootout in the tunnel and in the bar before Willow ran off. She then pointed out the bullet hole in the door by the lock and the two she'd put into the floor.

Owen looked to Josh. "Did you witness any of this?"

"Not really. I'm a pretty sound sleeper. I just heard the last couple of shots."

"You slept through gunfire?" Owen shook his head with a bemused expression. "Can you show us the tunnel?"

Kiera led them down the stairs and into the tunnel. She pointed to the bullet marks on the wall and finally, showed them the cavern with the longship.

"Oh my God," Noah said. "What is that?"

Kiera gave them the short version about the cavern, the tunnel, and the farmhouse.

"That explains all the activity around that old farmhouse on Martin Road," Owen said.

Noah nodded and said, "Who has the key to this gate?

"I do," Josh said. "Do you need it?"

"No, not really."

Owen photographed the cavern, the ricochet marks, and collected the brass Willow left behind. They took Kiera's gun as well.

As they walked out the side door, Owen turned and said, "I'll let you know when we have Miss Monroe in custody. Until then, keep your doors locked and your system armed."

Kiera locked the door and said, "Shit. This thing is getting out of hand."

He gave her a snarky face and said, "You think?"

Yep, still mad.

"I'm going back to bed. Wake me when Willow's in jail."

Forty-Eight

Late at night, Lachlan walked the dark, quiet streets around Kenric's house. Unable to sleep, he hoped walking would help him divine a course of action to end the darkness that had killed Kenric and most of the MacKenzie family.

There were so many unknowns and he couldn't fully separate the disparate elements in the cavern from each other. Thin places were refuges, areas of peace and tranquility; the Geata de Ifreann was the polar opposite, and yet, even in close proximity, they had achieved an equilibrium he wouldn't have believed possible.

Someone—the Vikings, the Native Americans, or both—had wisely hidden this interface underground where it couldn't be easily accessed. Old man Quinlan must have recognized the importance of the site and carefully hid the access between his house and the tavern to maintain the secret. Now it was open, exposed to the world. Scientific examination of the site would disrupt the delicate balance the Vikings, Native Americans, and even old man Quinlan had somehow achieved. Mix in the darkness that had migrated there and he was no longer certain what he was dealing with. Its presence had upset the energy equation, creating a disturbance, the nature of which wasn't easily understood nor readily anticipated.

Mainly, he hoped to visualize how these three things would interact and potentially play out. Factor in the people intricately woven into the equation: Kiera and her partner. Willow, a woman he'd never met, yet a woman he sensed would be integral to his quest to eliminate the darkness. And Rachel—who held an important piece, the arrowhead. It was a troublesome issue. He could simply steal the arrowhead with a spell and keep her out of this. A nervous foreboding held him back. She felt integral to the solution and he didn't want to lose her trust. She was the key-holder, but it wasn't just that. She possessed another object critical to finishing this. As yet, he had no idea what the object was nor where it was hidden.

He preferred working alone or with one of the Aeldo, or with a medium or other intermediary, someone he had worked with previously. None were an option. Willow might be acceptable but probably knew little of Caol Áit or the other realms they would encounter. She knew nothing of the darkness.

Lachlan prepared a mental list of tools, devices, and sundry items to take: amulets, talismans, Celtic crosses, herbs and powders. And critically, a *cargástriftr*—literally *ghost-scythe*—an athamé to assist in dealing with the confluence of forces in the cavern. He'd seen one in Kenric's basement. It was essential he remembered to bring it along.

He planned to meet with Rachel at four o'clock at the tavern. Now that Kiera was willing to accept his help, there was no reason to risk arrest at the farmhouse, and time was rapidly running out.

Despite his reservations and anxieties, Lachlan felt as prepared as he could be.

Just as well. Today was the day this story would play out.

Of that, he was certain.

⋆   ⋆   ⋆

At dawn, unable to sleep at the apartment, Kiera went home, planning to sleep until noon. It had worked well the night before. She could also grab her Sig Sauer from the safe just in case Willow was still running loose.

The day promised to be hot and humid—oppressively so. A strong southerly wind, backing to the southeast, helped temper the rising heat. She made a mental note to check the weather when she reawakened. It felt like a severe weather day.

Grabbing the mail, she fed Ghost and let him out. She set her alarm, switched her phone to silent and fell into bed. Ghost jumped up and snuggled against her back, happy she was certain, to have Kiera to himself again.

Somewhat later, she was deep in the tunnel being pursued by Willow when she heard Ghost growl. She called his name and then awoke when he barked. Kiera jumped out of bed and searched the semi-dark room for her Sig, then heard children playing outside.

She sighed and relaxed.

Fell back to sleep.

⋆   ⋆   ⋆

Kiera watched Josh stock the coolers with angry, jerky motions, just so she would know exactly how unhappy he was—angry about the gunfire in his tavern, angry about cops hanging around the bar, angry her best friend was now considered armed and dangerous and still on the loose. Angry because the cops insisted he provide his own security, unwilling to provide what amounted to unpaid protection for his business.

She understood his feelings. This tavern was his dream, it was turning into a nightmare, and it was mostly her fault.

At four, opening time, Lachlan walked into the bar with a teenage girl. They sat at the street end of the bar. Kiera walked over. "Hi Lachlan. Who's your friend?"

"Hello, Kiera. This is Rachel. I met her at the farmhouse. Is it okay that she's here with me?"

"As long as you're not buying her alcohol."

He shook his head dismissively.

Kiera shook her hand. An attractive girl with long, dark hair pulled into a ponytail, she looked about seventeen with a steely, sassy demeanor. She wished they could sit and talk but the bar was filling fast. Somehow, she would find the time.

"I'll be right back," Kiera said.

Josh was busy talking to the security guy, Charlie Oliva, who had just arrived. Tall and muscular, he had a buzz cut and a snake tat on his arm and looked ex-military. She knew he was armed but the gun was well concealed. He took up a discreet position by the back hallway.

Owen Prosser swept in the front door, looking serious and angry, and walked toward Josh.

A lot of anger around here. Curious, Kiera slid over by Josh. "What's going on?"

"Someone started a grass fire across the road from the farmhouse," Owen said. "While the county sheriff dealt with that, one or two people ran into the farmhouse. We assume they're in the tunnel."

"You want my guy to nab them?" Josh asked.

"No, just wanted you to be aware what some of these people are up to. I'll go down from this end. The sheriff is watching the farmhouse. They should be stuck down there, right?"

"Yep. There's no other way out." Kiera then asked, "Have you caught Willow, yet?"

Owen shook his head. "We're thinking she's one of the people down there." He disappeared down the basement staircase.

Mixing a round of old fashioneds, Kiera's eyes strayed to the TV set on the wall. A weather bug ran along the bottom of the screen:

...a PDS Tornado Watch is in effect until 11pm for the following counties in eastern Wisconsin...

The PDS stood for Particularly Dangerous Situation, enhanced wording used when a higher than normal risk of strong to violent tornadoes existed.

Shit! How had she missed that?

She had forgotten to check the weather when she woke up! Then Kiera remembered her day had started with gunfire in the basement. Screw Willow anyway. This whole day was going to hell and it was entirely her fault. After gesturing for Angela to handle the bar, she ran back to the office, sat at the desk, and flipped her laptop open. Then she brought up the Storm Prediction Center page.

Crap! Most of Wisconsin was under a Moderate Risk for severe weather. A smaller High Risk area was outlined over eastern Wisconsin.

Shit, shit, shit!

She was sitting in the dead center of the High Risk area. Between Willow, her hours at the bar, and the longship, she had let everything else in her life slide. There were dozens of emails and texts on her phone: fellow chasers, a couple of TV stations, and friends wanting to know where she was heading to and when.

She clicked through the forecast sites and weather models, and quickly decided that ground-zero was nearby, in Auburn and the surrounding counties. Cells were already popping up and going severe across the central part of the state.

When she returned to the bar, Angela was buried in orders. Lachlan gestured for her to step over. Kiera wanted to scream. She was half-tempted to run out the door with a big *screw you all!* but she was far too responsible to do anything of the sort.

She held a finger up to Lachlan, mixed a half dozen drinks for Angela, and sidled over to Josh.

"Dude. I know it's not the best timing but it's High Risk—*right here*." Pleading, hands clasped together. "Please...can I sneak out?"

"Seriously?" He stared at her with a mixture of annoyance and disbelief. "How good?"

"PDS box. CAPE and helicity are off the charts." She could barely contain her excitement.

His forehead furrowed with concern. "Do I have to worry about the bar?"

"Possibly." The actual likelihood was small, but she hoped her ability to keep him informed would work in her favor.

"Christ, that's all we need." He ran a hand through his hair. "Can you keep me updated?"

"Yes, absolutely."

"Okay, I'll keep Angela behind the bar for now. You owe me."

"Absolutely." She smooched his cheek. "Thanks, babe."

Yes!

That could have gone badly in several ways, given Josh's anger, but he knew how important a chance like this was to her. He was a good guy—she needed to remember that.

Kiera walked over to Lachlan, "Sorry, but I have to leave."

"Oh dear." A worried looked washed over his face. "Problem?"

"There's significant severe weather developing nearby. I chase storms so I have to go out. I'll be back later but I'm not sure when. Can we get together tomorrow?"

"Of course. But unless you're very late, I'll be waiting here."

"All right. Stay alert to the weather here." Something in Lachlan's manner gave her pause, but she was too absorbed with the impending chase to question it.

At that moment, Abbie Illingworth burst through the front door. A former co-worker and casual friend, Abbie was five-eight and lanky with a short dark bob-cut and fine features. A weather nut, she had bugged Kiera incessantly to go out on a chase.

Abbie looked around until she saw Kiera and waved. "Are we going? You promised!"

Amped by the promise of a chase, relieved to have a diversion from Willow and the bar, Kiera said, "Yes, we're going. Now!"

Forty-Nine

"So now what?" Rachel asked.

Lachlan sensed that the storm was central to the story unfolding and that he needed to stay.

"We need to stay here, I feel that strongly. I'm not sure why. What about your parents? Are you supposed to be home?"

"Not really. My dad works a lot and mom's a drunk." A brief dark cloud crossed her brow. "They don't usually miss me."

Lachlan marveled at the level of dysfunction in modern families. He and his first wife had had three children and had committed twenty years to raising them to the exclusion of everything else, other than growing crops and tending to their animals. Sadly, only one, Giles, was gifted and remained alive to this day. A former member of the Aeldo, he was living with a woman in New Zealand and had sworn off magic. Lachlan decided he needed to visit them—if he survived this muddle.

"You know, if your parents find you here, with me, they're liable to think I'm a—what'd you call it?—a creeper?" He hadn't considered that angle himself. These days, a man his age befriending a young girl could easily land himself in trouble, regardless of intentions.

"But you're not." She was more relaxed today. Definitely warming to him. Her expression bordered on affection, likely due to a lack of it at home.

"Quite right, but they still might get the wrong idea. Meanwhile, we should probably eat something. Something to drink?"

She smirked. "A glass of malbec would be great."

Lachlan admired her chutzpah. "I don't think so, young lady."

"Fine. Mountain Dew."

Lachlan crinkled his nose. "Hmm. The malbec is probably better for you."

"Now you sound like my mom."

"Do you have the arrowhead with you?" Lachlan asked.

"Yep. Always. It's mine." She had a guarded look again.

"I know it's yours. May I just look at it?"

"I suppose." Rachel dug into her front jean pocket and handed it to him. As she did so, the faint glow of the flint faded. Was that the issue? Only her touch would activate the piece?

It was extraordinary: a ceremonial piece, an exquisitely shaped flint with a gem inclusion. The gem seemed to scintillate even without light falling on it. Someone had carved a small runic inscription on the other side:

ᛊᛁ ᚲᛚᛁᛊ ᚾ ᚨ ᚺ ᛚᛁ

Rachel, watching him, said, "What is that?"

Lachlan searched his memory for the Old Norse phrase. A moment later he said, "It's a runic inscription. It's odd because Native Americans didn't use written languages."

"I know that. But what does it say?"

"Roughly, it says: *jewel is dead person protection*."

"What?"

"It's a talisman. It protects the holder from ghosts." He suspected it actually protected one from the Geata de Ifreann, acted to suppress it. It disturbed him that it only glowed when Rachel held it. She had a special connection with it he didn't understand.

"No way!"

"*Way*, as you kids say," Lachlan said. "I think that's exactly what it does."

"We don't say that."

He handed it back and she shoved it in her pocket.

Sliding off her stool, with evident regret Rachel said, "Actually, I think I better get home and check on Mom. I'll come back after the storm."

"Please do. I may need your help."

She raised an eyebrow, smiled, and ran out the door.

Lachlan ordered a Guinness and settled in to wait for Kiera's return.

★   ★   ★

Owen Prosser climbed down into the tunnel and slid along the wall, hugging it, looking ahead, his gun at his side, his left arm leading, ready to lock aim with his gun hand and fire. He had never been in a situation remotely like this. He had pulled his gun in a few domestic situations, but he had never fired it outside the range. He had no illusions or aspirations about being a hero. He chose to be a small-town cop because he never expected any serious danger or gunfire in Miller's Crossing.

He suspected gunfire was unlikely but one couldn't be too careful. He had known Willow Monroe for years and she didn't seem to have a violent bone in her body. Still, she was a crack shot and no one to mess with in a shoot-out.

It was quiet in the tunnel but cold. He thought he could see his breath. And where was the creepy lighting coming from? No lights, no bulbs, it seemed the walls themselves were aglow. Owen walked to the cavern but the gate remained locked. He looked the boat over again. Some sort of giant Indian canoe. Didn't Kiera say it was Viking? Whatever. He didn't know what Viking meant. Probably some Indian tribe from Minnesota. The real question? Why the hell was it here, underground? How did they get it down there?

With no sign of trouble, no sounds of activity, he decided this was a wild goose chase. With the coming bad weather, he needed to be out on the streets. As he made the executive decision to turn and leave, he heard soft footsteps approaching.

Willow walked toward him from farther down the tunnel, holding a gun at her side, a determined expression on her face.

"Willow!" He pointed a finger down the tunnel. "Stop and go back. I don't want any trouble with you."

"Owen?" She didn't falter, just kept walking toward him.

"Yes, Willow, it's me."

"If you don't want any trouble, get out of here!"

Jesus! She looked angry, dangerous—unhinged. "Sorry. Can't do that, honey."

She fired a shot over his head and ducked aside. "Get out, Owen, or else!"

Holy shit! Had she lost her goddamn mind? Shooting at a cop?

He tucked in tight and slid back. He had no intention of firing at Willow. They could fire him. Clearly, she'd lost it.

"Come on, Willow. Give me a break! I'm not going to shoot."

"I am, Owen!"

Two rapid shots echoed and ricocheted off the opposite wall.

Fuck!

He threw himself backwards against the wall. The slight curvature of the tunnel should afford him some cover. He expected to slam into hard rock. Instead, he fell through a crevice in the wall and plummeted for what seemed like forever.

Fifty

Kiera grabbed her camera, the laptop, the chase bag filled with snacks and weather gadgets, and ran out to the RAV4. The afternoon was hot and muggy with a stiff south wind swirling litter about in gusts. Towers of cumulus exploding to the west triggered a rush of adrenaline. She laid her camera and gadgets across the back seat and jumped in, fastening her seatbelt, insisting Abbie do the same. Kiera bolted the laptop to a swivel mount between the seats.

"I hope you don't mind that I just came," Abbie said. "You weren't answering your phone."

"No. It's fine," Kiera said, thinking precisely the opposite. She would likely be a distraction.

"Where are we going?"

"Southwest, forty or fifty miles," Kiera said. She pointed to a red splotch on the radar. "That cell looks promising. Good old tail-end Charlie."

"Tail-end Charlie?"

"The last storm in a line, the southernmost cell, is often stronger because of less interference from other storms." She quick paged through multiple windows showing warnings issued, current weather models and surface charts, and a satellite view. "Yep, that's where we're going."

Kiera rolled out of the driveway and drove west, referring occasionally to the radar. She paid little attention to her speed. Things were developing quickly and she didn't want to miss a minute of it.

Abbie, looking dismayed, said, "Don't you worry about speeding tickets?"

"Not much. The cops are usually busy during severe weather events and this baby watches my back." Kiera pointed to a high-end Escort radar detector mounted on the dash.

"Is that even legal?"

"Of course. You don't have one?"

Abbie shook her head, looking mystified. "I guess I don't speed."

Keeping an eye on the radar, Kiera drove on autopilot, watching the sky as cumulus clouds exploded skyward and mushroomed into elongated anvils surging to the northeast. The cell she targeted looked particularly promising, a robust tower of crisp cumulus that was visibly rotating in slow motion. Kiera pointed out various features for Abbie's benefit as they drove.

About forty miles out of town, Kiera pulled over and grabbed her camera, the Sony Alpha A7.

"Get your camera ready," Kiera said.

Abbie held up her phone. "What's going on?"

Kiera pointed at a dark circular base of cloud several miles to the west. "That's the rain-free base. The updraft base of the storm. If we get a tornado, it will happen right there."

The base was low, which was good, and the bit of the updraft still visible was clearly rotating. She pointed to dark pendulous clouds hanging beneath the anvil overhead. "Up there, amazing mammatus."

"Cool," Abbie said, looking confused. "What's that mean?"

"The storm updraft is strong and vigorous. That's a good thing."

A dark nub developed beneath the rain-free base and drew a thread of cloud from the darker rain core to the north.

"What's that," Abbie pointed, her voice rising. "Is that a tornado?"

"No. Relax. Inflow and scud—scud are the raggedy-looking clouds. It looks promising, though."

It was good to be out, chasing. The tensions of the day melted away as she became fully engaged in the moment: processing the weather data in her head, watching the reality, the drama, unfold in glorious detail across the sky. There was no greater thrill, not even sex. Just then, the light abruptly modulated darker, as if someone had switched a light off.

Abbie said, "That was weird."

"The light?" Kiera was still trying to process it herself. It was very odd.

"Yeah. Is that normal?"

"Uh, no and yes. In these situations, normal is relative." But she didn't quite believe that either. She had never seen anything like it.

The storm continued to draw a swirling band of dark ragged cloud into the base, creating a lowering that looked like a black UFO attached to the center of the rain-free base, a striking wall cloud that swirled and rotated with chaotic motion.

A tornado was imminent.

Behind the wall cloud, a lighter, V-shaped notch began slicing through the rain-free base, coursing to the left, with a sharp contrast between light and dark. Vivid enough that Abbie said, voice rising in pitch, "What's that lighter area? What's happening?"

"That's the clear slot. The rear-flank downdraft—a descending column of wind that's eroding the rain-free base. This storm is about to tornado."

"Holy moly!" Her voice rose at least two more pitches. "Are we safe?"

"Yes. Yes we are. Don't get cold feet now, sweetie." Kiera knew it. Abbie was losing it. She always gave people who rode along the same warning. Once they started a chase, she wouldn't break off for any reason. Can't handle that? Don't come.

A tornado alert started beeping in the car and seconds later, tornado sirens went off somewhere nearby. Kiera had been doing this for years and the sound still sent shivers down her spine.

Kiera snapped dozens of photos while Abbie clicked away on her phone. A minute later, a swirl of dust kicked up beneath the wall cloud.

"Touchdown!" Kiera whooped with a fist in the air. She tapped her National Weather Service phone contact and quickly reported the tornado and her location.

Abbie stood rigid, anxious, eyes fluttering. "Shouldn't we be going?"

"Not yet. I told you, we're here for the whole show. Don't worry, we're safe."

Despite the imminent violent weather, birds chirped nearby and the air was still. Kiera always marveled at the incongruous contrasts around tornadic storms.

At first, the dust swirl at ground level and a thin funnel above were the only visible elements of the tornado, but a minute later, the condensation funnel reached toward the ground, connecting with the whirling debris cloud. The tornado grew in diameter and kicked out larger and larger clots of debris. Instead of the normal ebb and flow of the inflow winds and funnel common in the first moments of tornadogenesis, the tornado intensified rapidly. About a mile away, it now resembled a stout stovepipe.

"Okay, we gotta move." Her friend seemed frozen. Kiera yelled, "Abbie! Move it!"

Kiera hustled Abbie into the car, jumped in herself and backed up a hundred feet to a driveway, pulled a quick Y-turn and floored it. She wanted about three miles between her and the storm. At the same time, Kiera did a quick calculation of storm speed and direction and realized it was heading toward Miller's Crossing—if it held together. Right now, it showed every indication it would.

The base of the tornado continued to widen in her rearview mirror and she could tell Abbie was verging on hysteria. The girl would have a hell of a story to tell if she didn't lose her shit. This thing was nuts!

She stopped in the middle of the road, jumped out, snapped another dozen pics, and called Josh. "Batten down the hatches. I'm twelve miles out of town and it's coming right at you."

Josh sounding frazzled, said, "Damn it! How big?

"Big. Huge. Well on its way to wedge status."

Behind her, Abbie said, "Holy crap, that's—that's huge, Kiera. We should move."

Kiera snapped another dozen pics and collected a minute of video. "Okay, let's go!"

The highway ahead was empty. It was then she realized: *they were the only people out here!*

It was the weirdest thing she'd ever seen. No spotters, no chasers, no media. What the hell was going on? But there was no time to consider. They had to move fast. The road network was good and Kiera, driving like Danica Patrick, kept ahead of the tornado, stopping frequently to snap more pics and capture video. And as she did, she grew more and more nervous. The tornado appeared to be near a half-mile wide and until now, hadn't caused too much damage, moving mostly over open fields and wooded areas.

It was heading into an area with more people, more houses, and more buildings, schools, and stores, including Miller's Crossing. She was always thrilled to see something like this out on the Plains. People were rarely affected. She was afraid of something this dangerous moving into a populated area. People would be injured and killed. The property damage would be immense.

As she stopped and jumped out of the RAV4, the tornado engulfed and obliterated a farmhouse in a dark, chaotic swirl of debris.

Kiera clasped a hand to her chest. "Holy shit! I hope they were in the basement."

Abbie stood, grasping onto the car door for dear life.

Ahead, Kiera saw a sign:

Miller's Crossing 5

She texted Josh: *Go to the basement now!!!!*

Just then, two intense power-flashes lit the dark underside of the storm as the tornado tore through a major power line.

"Come on Abbie, we have to go!"

Abbie jumped in the car, her face drained of color.

"That was awful!"

"I'm afraid it's about to get much worse."

As they pulled into town, she drove straight to the tavern to make sure everyone got into the basement. She knew how people tended to dismiss warnings and the last thing she wanted was anyone killed in the bar. Josh would take her seriously but would everyone else? She hated to break off such an amazing chase, but it was the right thing to do.

She took another look behind in the rearview mirror. "Jesus!"

The tornado filled the mirror.

No doubt now.

It was headed straight for the tavern.

Fifty-One

Willow stood a hundred feet along the tunnel and listened.

Silence.

Perfect. The ruse with the grass fire had evidently worked. With no one pursuing her, she assumed she had slipped into the farmhouse and tunnel unobserved.

Regardless, she strode along the tunnel, still worried that someone would try to stop her. Willow didn't fully understand her fixation with the longship or the cavern, but she could think of nothing else. A pure unadulterated obsession, she believed she would become fully enlightened once she was in the room. Even here, a half mile away, she could feel it calling to her, drawing her forward. She just had to get there before that bitch Kiera tried to meddle again. If she did, Willow was prepared to shoot her, her dog, her boyfriend, and anybody else who got in her way.

The passage still silent, she ran. The less time exposed in the tunnel, the better. Willow felt she would be invincible once she stood inside the cavern, believing what waited for her would strengthen and protect her. She came fully prepared with a small bag of tools: a hacksaw, a pry bar, her Kimber and the .44 Mag if she needed to blast the lock—or shoot somebody, though she hoped that wasn't necessary. Willow would not be denied. Less noise was better, less likely to summon Kiera who would mess things up, and with the cops involved, the risks had doubled.

She heard footsteps. Stopped and listened.

Silence.

Willow walked, slower, wary. Then she saw someone, a cop. It looked like Owen Prosser.

Damn!

He saw her.

"Willow! Stop and go back. I don't want any trouble with you."

"Owen?"

"Yes, Willow, it's me."

Owen was a pussycat. He wouldn't engage her. "If you don't want any trouble, get out of here!"

"Sorry. Can't do that, honey."

She fired a shot over his head and ducked aside. "Get out, Owen, or else!"

"Come on, Willow." His voice had gone up in pitch. "Give me a break! I'm not going to shoot."

"I am, Owen!" He didn't want to face off with her. She raised her gun and fired two rapid shots to his left.

Silence.

"Owen?"

Perhaps he thought better of challenging her. She called out again. "Owen?"

She breathed a heavy sigh of relief and walked to the gate. Imagined stepping through it, into the room, stepping through the gateway into the thin place and—

She couldn't picture it but knew it would be fabulous.

Life-altering.

⋆   ⋆   ⋆

Rachel stepped outside, stifled a scream, and uttered, "Holy crap!"

The sky was as black as she had ever seen it, and not just dark, but roiled by crazy motion. The clouds appeared to be moving in opposite directions in irrational ways and yet, the air remained still and birds chirped as if unconcerned by the impending danger. It was eerie.

Scary.

The tornado sirens wound up and blared, startling her into action. She jumped on her bike and pedaled furiously, feeling a bit like Almira Gulch. Worried about getting home in time, concerned her mother might underestimate the danger or, worse, be oblivious of the impending severe weather.

She arrived just in time, sliding into the garage and smacking the button on the door closer as she barreled through the back door.

"Mom? Mom!"

"In here, Rachel."

Her mother was in the dining room, pouring a glass of wine when Rachel turned the corner.

Rachel was breathless. "Mom! Don't you hear the sirens?"

"Is that what the racket is?" She looked at Rachel, puzzled, clueless.

"Yes, Mom. Tornado. Basement. Now!" Rachel grabbed her free hand and tugged.

Her mother stood without faltering and motioned to Rachel like a servant. "Bring my bottle, dear."

"Yes, Mom. Just hurry."

"You need a little more conditioner in your hair, Rachel. It looks dry."

★　★　★

Rustin Marshall decided the severe weather was the perfect cover for an end-run at the longship. He knew Kiera chased storms and would be out in this nasty weather. The cops would likewise be occupied. Maybe this Quinlan would get back to him yet, though there had been no phone call nor a letter. Maybe he would discover another access point by exploring this end of the tunnel. He didn't have a fully realized plan, but felt certain that his attorney could devise some legal strategy to nullify the contract if he did find another way in. Regardless, the contract bound Kiera if she found him out and contained no provisions or penalties if he attempted to void the agreement legally.

He realized he wasn't behaving rationally. The longship and the cave drawings were the find of a lifetime. It was like discovering a vein of gold. All reason went out the window, all caution to the wind. A lesser man might be content to share the glory, but he was no lesser man. Kiera had stumbled upon this. She surely didn't deserve it. Besides, she was a woman. He quietly believed men were superior to women. Nature had decreed as much in making men bigger, stronger, smarter, more rational. Such opinions weren't popular at the moment and he fought to hold his tongue and keep those views to himself in this age of female empowerment, political correctness, and the clamor for equal rights.

An intelligent man didn't need empowerment.

And he was an intelligent man.

Fifty-Two

Lachlan sat nursing his Guinness, feeling the energy in the building rising to some peak, a maelstrom of positive and negative energies. He was likely the only one aware of it. He had been watching the weather information on the TV and suddenly concluded this was no normal weather event—that it somehow emanated from the cavern below. Ready or not, with or without help, the time had come. The darkness in the tunnel was the script-master and planned to confront him here and now. Willow was somewhere nearby, perhaps in the tunnel below. He had to find her, needed her to have any hope of successfully challenging the beast in the bedrock beneath him. And he needed the arrowhead.

Jewel is dead person protection.

Precisely what the situation called for. Lachlan lifted his head, attuned to a sudden, strong change in the aura around the tavern. He suddenly feared he was about to become daisy fertilizer like his friend, Kenric. Josh continued to mix drinks while he glanced furtively between the windows and the TV overhead. The customers seemed unconcerned or unaware of the unfolding drama. Josh then stopped to answer his phone. His faced darkened and Lachlan knew trouble was coming.

A moment later, the flat screens began bleating the drone of the Emergency Broadcast System followed by a concerned weather guy with a dire warning of a large tornado on the ground. On cue, the tornado sirens blared outdoors. He'd survived the Blitz on London in World War II and little unnerved him, but the sound of sirens still did all these years later, sending a shiver down Lachlan's spine and through his belly.

He grabbed his satchel and made for the stairwell.

The security guard stepped out and blocked his path. "Where are you going?"

"Basement! Haven't you been listening?" Lachlan pointed to the TV.

"What—?"

"Tornado! You need to get everyone downstairs!"

Lachlan then saw Josh trying to herd people toward the basement door. Josh yelled, "Kiera called. There is a tornado headed this way. Nobody leaves, everyone in the basement, now!"

Heedless of the risk, several people bolted for the front door and ran for their cars.

Fools!

Though perhaps no more foolhardy than he. The sane response to the situation in the cavern? Listen to his boisterous survival instinct, the one yelling in his head:

Run! Run like hell!

★   ★   ★

As Kiera ran in the front door, she saw Josh herding people to the stairs. A few hung back, trying to look out the windows. She gave them a gentle push to the stairs, "Come on! Move it, people! This is the real deal!"

Kiera pushed Abbie ahead of her and, when she reached the stairs, nudged Josh as well, down the stairs, yelling, "Hurry. Hurry! Move it!" She ran to the apartment door and yelled, "Ghost! Come on, buddy. Let's go!"

Ghost came tearing down the stairs and ran ahead of Kiera to the basement. For a moment, she worried about taking people downstairs, so close to the tunnel and the problems there, but the tornado was the greater, more immediate threat.

When she reached the bottom of the stairs and everyone had moved into the basement, she slammed the door and looked around, deciding what furniture and work benches were available for shelter. Time was fast running out.

She counted seven customers. Del Riemann and Mick Herzlinger usually came in together. Del was weaselly, no better word for the man. About five-seven, he had a thin moustache, dirty blond hair swept to the side and a narrow face. Mick was heavy, not the brightest, and seemed content listening to Del most of the time. Katy Oldman and Dani Friesen were thirty-something nurses—Kiera thought they were a couple but played it cool in public. Too bad really. Kiera didn't have a problem with it. She pushed and shoved the four of them under a workbench, not overly concerned with being delicate in the process.

Robby and Jami Braugher, a middle-aged couple who had been coming in two to three nights a week, she pushed under the remaining workbench. Robby, a hulk of a man who had to squeeze into the space, pulled his wife, a small woman, into his arms. The last customer, Matt Luecke, she shoved under a wing of the table saw. Matt wasn't her favorite customer, a hipster know-it-all who was never afraid to offer an opinion.

She opened the cooler door and herded the staff in there. Angela, Doyle the cook, Bella and Kyla. There really wasn't room for more but she squeezed Abbie and Lachlan in there as well. There was a patio table with a granite top next to the cooler that Josh had been meaning to move outdoors behind the bar. She ducked under it with Josh and pulled Ghost in, holding him tightly. She waved Charlie, the security guy, over to join them but he sat against the cooler wall and gave her a thumbs up.

Rain hit in a wave that lasted just a few seconds, followed by three or four rapid lightning blasts and a long rolling volley of thunder.

For a moment, it was deadly silent. She could see fear and disbelief in most of their faces—except for the few skeptics who thought this was all just so much melodrama. Kiera had never ridden out a tornado like this, but found herself unafraid and analytical as the storm approached. She prayed they were out of the path of the tornado but it had been headed directly for the bar when she pulled in. Contrary to a popular myth, tornadoes didn't suddenly veer off course or turn corners—other than a drift to the left as they roped out and dissipated. No, the storm would cause catastrophic damage in and near the funnel as downdrafts and satellite vortices spun into the main tornado, and that would include the tavern. She only hoped everyone would be safe down here.

A couple of bangs and crashes—breaking glass—broke the silence. The wind whistled in a peculiar manner followed by a fierce drumming on the roof for five or ten seconds. Kiera imagined golf-ball-sized hail or larger pummeling the building. More windows broke and crashed to the floor overhead. The lights failed.

The wind ramped up—a couple of wild whistles and odd pressure changes felt in her ears. Then a more sustained assault, a howl that sounded like demons tearing at the building. It intensified quickly and the floor over their heads shuddered multiple times, accompanied by the crash and clatter of random objects breaking on the maple planks. Kiera hoped the brick frame of the building might hold but knew the windows would be deadly. Almost on cue, more glass shattered as wind and airborne debris assailed the remaining panes. The wind—a grinding, rending, tearing monster—was deafening. A sudden pressure fall squeezed painfully on her eardrums.

The tornado had arrived.

Comparing the sound to a freight train was a woefully inadequate description of the cacophony of rabid, swirling, colliding masses of debris overhead. Listening to the wind tear at every loose edge of the building, hearing sounds she couldn't even describe, the gales assailing the floor above with such force that she was certain at least part of the brick structure had failed.

Then came a tremendous explosive crash—it sounded like a brick wall falling. The floor shuddered and Kiera thought the wind would shred the wood planking and tear it right off the joists. Maybe even take the joists, which happened often enough.

The sound of the tornado lessened, but the clatter of debris on the floor above was still quite intense. That eased as well, leaving only the sound of dripping water where it leaked through the wood floor above.

A final fierce gale of wind, a downburst rolling off the rear flank of the storm, was followed by two blasts of thunder. The roar of wind and debris receded into the distance and Kiera fired up her phone for light as many of the others did the same.

It seemed like an eternity and yet, Kiera saw only that fifty-four seconds had elapsed on the timer she set on her phone just as the winds hit.

Kiera yelled, "Everyone okay?"

General murmurs of assent followed.

Whew! Everyone was okay!

Thank God!

Probably the only good thing in an otherwise awful day. The bar was devastated, she was certain. The sounds overhead had been horrendous. That the floor survived was possibly luck, or a testament to the carpenters who had used four-by-twelve joists overlain with a rough oak sub-floor, finished with maple planks. Kiera looked over and saw the cloud of worry on Josh's face. She shook her head; she had no words for him.

Kiera went to a cabinet looking for flashlights, handing out the two Maglites she found while Josh walked to the basement door.

When he opened it, a confusing mass of debris including a mangled car jammed sideways into the staircase confronted them.

"Holy crap!" He shook his head and tugged at some of the twisted metal, but none of it budged. It would be many hours, maybe days before anyone could free them.

Josh looked to Kiera, "How about the tunnel?"

Still reeling from the intensity of the storm, a series of scattered worries added to the noise: the longship, the thin place, her fears about people damaging the cavern. Finally Kiera said, "I don't know."

Lachlan edged over to where she stood. "That may not be a good idea." Quietly he added, "There's trouble in the tunnel."

Kiera looked at him. "What?"

Josh came over, looking unhappy. "Trouble? What trouble? And why are you involved?"

Looking at Kiera, Lachlan said, "Your friend Willow is down there."

"Shit. Are you sure?"

One of the customers, Del Riemann, walked over. "Are you saying there's a way out of here through a tunnel?"

"Maybe," Kiera said. "But there may be some danger as well."

There was no point trying to keep it secret at this point. She briefly laid out the presence of the tunnel and the cavern, and the shooting that had occurred earlier in the day.

"Besides," Kiera said. "We don't know if the other end of the tunnel is open or also blocked with debris."

"Shit." Del said. "You don't know for sure if that woman is even in the tunnel. Maybe someone should go down and check."

There were several murmurs of approval.

Kiera understood it. Stuck here in the dark wasn't what she wanted either. The power might not be restored for hours or days. They had no clue when people would start looking for them. She knew the damage out there was widespread and severe, probably on a level with the devastation caused by tornadoes she had seen in Joplin, Missouri and Moore, Oklahoma.

Lachlan spoke quietly. "Willow isn't the only danger down there."

She looked at him curiously.

Though he hadn't explained in detail why he was here or what he was seeking—other than some nonsense about chasing the devil—she sensed it was dark. It wasn't a conversation they could have here.

As Del Riemann started toward the tunnel, Kiera touched his arm and said, "Wait. Let us go down first and see if Willow is there. If so, we can talk to her—"

"Sure, fine." But he didn't look happy.

As she turned toward the tunnel opening, Josh pointed at Lachlan; his eyes narrowed. "Why him? Suddenly *he's* your best friend?"

Kiera put a hand over his heart. "Josh, trust me, please."

She then turned to the others. "Please, just give us a few minutes to figure this out, okay?"

They murmured in assent, but Kiera suspected they had very little time before the group grew restless and bailed any way they could.

They climbed down. Kiera, then Lachlan, holding his satchel. Josh glared down from above.

Once in the tunnel, Kiera walked twenty feet, stopped, and turned to face Lachlan, jabbing a finger at him. "Okay buddy, spill! Why are you here? And what's the danger?"

Fifty-Three

Rachel rolled her eyes and ran up the basement stairs. Mom had passed out on the sofa, not from excitement but from too much merlot. Dad hadn't called or come home. He was either stuck at work or using the storm as an excuse to avoid the shit show their family life had become.

Looking out the window, she saw numerous tree branches blocking the road. Otherwise, it seemed the neighborhood had escaped major damage. She had to get back to the bar and check on Lachlan. He needed her and she didn't know why, but it was important and she was going to find him, come hell or high water. She also wanted to know what Kiera had seen. A storm chasing girl? So cool!

Grabbing her backpack, Rachel threw snacks and sodas inside, shoved the lucky arrowhead into her pocket, and ran to the garage. She stopped, ran back and grabbed the sword from under her mattress, knowing she needed it even if she didn't know why. In a moment of ingenuity, she grabbed a roll of duct tape, binding the sword to the top truss on the frame so she wouldn't have to carry it. Rachel then hit the garage door switch, hopped on her bike, and rolled down the driveway.

She rode three of the five blocks to the bar, encountering increasingly severe damage and ever more debris blocking her way: fallen trees and branches, wires, chunks of wood fencing, shutters, lawn chairs, grills, outdoor toys, garden sheds, garbage cans, and notably, a blow-up doll.

Suddenly, the path ahead was blocked. Random chunks of building materials—shredded houses and garages—trees, telephone poles, cars, furniture, and other debris were mashed together into an impossible puzzle of splintered wood, wire, metal, plastic, and every manner of yard junk imaginable. In areas, especially along the center of the damage path, the ground had been swept clean but for broken tree stumps and the gaping rectangles of exposed basements.

The devastation was unbelievable, near total. A nuclear bomb couldn't have been much more destructive.

Rachel could now look almost a half mile across town over the crushed and flattened remains of Miller's Crossing, but she couldn't reach the tavern, which was mostly gone anyway. Only two walls of the bar remained, jagged fangs of brick jutting into the sky.

She looked at the destruction in a daze. Then she saw old Pete, a friendly retired guy, lying on top of the rubble, dead as dead could be, a board protruding from his chest. She turned away, unable to look, her stomach turning somersaults.

She thought about Lachlan and couldn't contain her feelings, her heart a lump in her throat, tears running down her face.

Was he okay? What if he hadn't gotten to safety? She had to know, but couldn't reach the bar without risking serious injury from sharp metal edges, dangerous shards and splinters, or death from the live electrical wires scattered everywhere.

The tunnel!

They would have gone into the basement or even the tunnel. She jumped back on the bike, zig-zagged several blocks around the damage and burned south on Martin Road as fast as her legs would carry her. He *had* to be safe. He *had* to be in the tunnel. She was sure of it.

★   ★   ★

Kiera looked at Lachlan, frustrated and impatient.

She could see him weighing options, trying to decide how much to tell her, but she was in no mood for any waffling, dissembling, or lies. Her life had been upended in ways she could only guess at. The bar and apartment were likely gone. Her house might okay but she would love to know for sure. Willow was armed and lurking somewhere just ahead. A crowd of anxious people lay behind her, ready to trample over her in their rush to escape the basement.

Finally, he said, "Simply, I came to avenge the death of my friend. He died almost a year ago not too far from here. His name was Kenric Shepherd."

Kiera gave him a piercing look. "Shepherd? That house that blew up in the Kettle Moraine? This is related?"

Lachlan nodded gravely.

"How?"

Lachlan explained what he knew and what he suspected. Kiera looked at him, mouth agape, feeling varying shades of skepticism, shock, and amazement.

"Assuming I believe you—a huge *if*—what can you do? This thing can command the weather and hide out in the earth—in bedrock? What can you do?"

"Firstly, we need Willow," he said.

"What?" She was incredulous. Willow had gone full-on crazy. Lachlan didn't seem far behind.

"I can't do this alone. I need a medium, psychic support—it's like using an amplifier," he said. "Maybe she and I together can overcome the force, but my friend was unable to defeat it and he was the most gifted sorcerer on the planet."

Kiera regarded him with unbridled suspicion. "Sorcerer? Are you serious? How do I know you're not crazy like Willow? Paranormal investigator, huh? I think you left out a few details, buddy."

"We don't have a lot of time." He turned toward the archway.

Kiera stood squarely in his path. "Oh yeah? We do until you start making sense—"

"Did I get rid of the ghost in the door?"

"Yeah, but—"

"Trust me. I sense you do. This is simply too much to absorb at once. Let's walk slowly and I'll talk."

His calm demeanor was reassuring. Kiera listened as she edged along the wall. It was a fantastic story, literally too fantastic to believe except that the cavern ahead and the longship within were equally fantastic. She held her gun at her side, praying she wasn't forced to use it. Willow was now a threat to everyone in the basement. Still, as angry and frightened as she was, Kiera wasn't certain she could shoot her. Now Lachlan needed her help.

Unbelievably crazy!

She desperately yearned to wake at home, discovering this was only a nightmare, but it refused to quit. Dark forces, sorcerers, witches? Stories from books and movies of a dream world or monster-laden landscape? She had read the books and watched the movies, believing none of it to be true and yet, those stories managed to raise hackles of fear deep in her primitive brain—a primitive brain wisely afraid of the dark, instinctively afraid of the unknown, a primitive brain in which ideas of gods and demons and forces beyond imagining reigned supreme.

A child of science, she embraced the rational, the theories and dogmas of a scientific and modern understanding of the world. She believed in that system and suddenly, it seemed perfectly worthless, a joke, because when you turned the lights out, all that rational stuff disappeared and the primitive reptile brain ruled the dark.

"So how old are you?"

"Quite...old."

Kiera stopped. "In my world, very old is ninety plus. I suspect your world is very different. You said Shepherd was alive five hundred years ago. Older than that?"

"Much. And we're running out of time."

Kiera looked forward again and the archway was now visible, the iron gate wide open. Willow had to be inside. Lachlan stopped.

Inching forward, Kiera called out. "Willow?"

Silence. She slid a little farther along the wall.

"Willow?"

"Back off, Kiera! I mean it!"

Fifty-Four

"Willow? I'm not coming in, but I have someone who needs to talk to you," Kiera said.

"Lachlan? Is that who's out there?"

Lachlan gestured, slid past her, and drifted down the wall. "Yes, Willow, it's Lachlan. We need to talk."

"Kenric says you're here to cause trouble, that you'll dismantle the thin place."

"Kenric Shepherd? Is that who's talking to you?" It wasn't Kenric, of course. The darkness was playing mind-tricks on her.

"Yes."

"Kenric's dead, Willow. He was my friend." Lachlan pulled a small canister from his satchel and sprinkled blue dust about them. He then retrieved two silver amulets that looked like tube lockets covered with miniature pictographs and runes, handing one to Kiera and holding the other tightly in his hand. He closed his eyes and concentrated.

"Willow, I'm going to talk to you, communicate with you and show you what my friend Kenric looked like, what he sounded like." Lachlan said. "Whatever's in the room with you killed Kenric and intends to kill you. You, Kiera, and I."

He felt certain it was true. Had Willow been kept alive to draw him into the tunnel? What strategy was the darkness working? He didn't understand the purpose of conjuring up the storm, though obliterating the bar and entrance made some sense.

Lachlan kept his eyes closed and set his jaw. Sweat beaded on his forehead. For a minute, two minutes, three minutes, he concentrated on the connection between Willow and the darkness. An unwavering laser-fine stream of consciousness, disturbing and disrupting that tenuous bond.

★   ★   ★

Kiera forced herself to stay silent. Something was happening. She could see nothing, but there was a palpable energy in the tunnel that seemed to flow back and forth between Lachlan and the cavern.

Finally, Lachlan spoke in a strange tongue, *"Áblinnest, swa he selfa bæd!"*

Silence.

He spoke again in a menacing, rising tone. *"Áblinnest, swa he selfa bæd!"*

A faint rumbling disturbed the silence. Lachlan held his amulet tightly in his raised hand. It glowed slightly. There was strong tension in the air. Kiera felt the hair at the nape of her neck stand at attention. This was the eeriest moment of her life, bar none.

"Áblinnest, swa he selfa bæd!"

Willow screamed and came running from the cavern, running into Lachlan's arms. He held her and spoke quietly. Kiera only heard, "I'm sorry you had to see that."

Kiera was eternally grateful to have missed whatever Willow had seen. When Willow had calmed down, Lachlan held her at arm's length and drew Kiera in. "We're not done here, not by any means. Kiera, you need to keep people out of the tunnel. It's going to become very dangerous down here."

The ghost in the cooler door was a parlor trick compared to what she had just seen. It was going to get dangerous? Seemed like they were already there. Her mouth went dry. She could only manage a croaky, "Okay."

He led them into the cavern, ambling, his hand on Willow's shoulder in reassurance. He seemed to be steeling himself as well. Kiera had never been more scared in her life. What had she gotten into?

Lachlan whispered, "We need Rachel. She's on her way."

How could he possibly know that?

Just then, Kiera saw two people run past the cavern entrance toward the farmhouse. It looked like Del Riemann and his buddy, Mick.

Damn it!

She yelled, "Hey!" but they kept running. She then texted Josh: *Stay there! Keep everyone there!*

But it failed to send. No signal.

Lachlan held Willow's hands, looking into her eyes. "Are you ready for this? I need your help."

Willow nodded. She then turned and tried to hug Kiera. "I'm so sorry, honey. I don't know what came over me."

Kiera pushed her back, tense, not quite ready to make nice. "You shot at me!"

"I know." Willow hung her head. "I'm sorry. I wasn't myself."

Lachlan said, "Ladies, we need to concentrate on the task at hand."

Kiera nodded and gave Willow a half-hearted hug. "What do you need me to do?"

Taking command, sounding calm and professional, Lachlan looked at Kiera and said, "Stay out of the cavern. It's not safe in here. I'm not sure it's safe out there either, but it's safer than in here. Don't let anyone else through the tunnel."

As Lachlan took Willow by the shoulders and explained what he needed, Kiera set up outside the archway, her back to the wall, with a view of the cavern and the tunnel in both directions.

Kiera realized she was shaking with a sustained adrenaline rush that showed no sign of abating. The chase, the large wedge tornado, the tavern—she feared the tavern and apartment were gone. That had been the strongest tornado she'd ever seen. Now they were trapped in the basement with some ancient guy who communed with ghosts and spirits. A guy embarking on some dangerous fix that she didn't even pretend to understand. He talked about some dark force that had taken up residence in the cavern and thin places like they were real.

Maybe they were, but the experience was surreal.

A lapsed Catholic, she gave little thought to religion, spirits, or ghosts. She thought the stories about the haunted tavern were cute but anecdotal—until actual ghosts started manifesting in the bar and apartment. Then it was Willow and thin places. Now, Lachlan was here and she stood in the middle of something between a dream and a nightmare.

And still, her *biggest* worry was keeping the longship safe.

She heard a commotion down the tunnel, towards the farmhouse. Raised voices at first, muffled and indistinct.

Then a scream, followed by gunfire.

Fifty-Five

Del Riemann and his friend, Mick, edged closer to the tunnel opening while Josh, distracted, went through a cabinet looking for more flashlights and batteries. Del had no intention of hanging out in this dungeon for even a second longer.

Angela yelled, "Yo Josh, some guys are trying to bail!"

Del glared at the nosy bitch and dropped through the opening. Mick followed. Del grappled with the carved stone stairs and missed several of them, falling hard onto the stone floor. His friend proved even less graceful and landed on top of him.

"Jesus! Get off me, fat ass!" Del hissed.

"Sorry, Del. Now what?"

"We walk and hope the other end of the tunnel isn't blocked, dummy." Del brushed himself off and strode down the tunnel, wondering why he hung around with this moron.

Mick struggled to keep up. "What if we run into Kiera and the old guy?"

"What? You scared of them?" Del mocked. "Jesus, Mick. We walk by them. For all we know, they're already out."

"True. Kiera had a gun though—"

"What? You think they're gonna shoot us?"

"I heard the old guy say there was some danger in this tunnel." Mick said, his brow bunched in worry.

"God Mick, I had no idea you were such a pussy." Del taunted in a girly voice: "What, are you scared?"

"No, but I wish I knew what he was talking about."

At that moment, Del spotted the archway and heard voices. Kiera and someone else, off in a side room, talking. Something about a boat.

Perfect.

He yanked on Mick's arm. "Pick up the pace and let's cruise past the doorway."

Del bolted and Mick ambled forward in the manner only a big man can.

Kiera yelled, "Hey!"

Past the archway, Del stopped, huffing for breath and said, "Good, we're in the clear. This tunnel is long enough that we should be away from the damage outside."

"Are you going to let the other people know we got out?"

"No. We'll get help and send them down there. Not our job." Del started walking. "Let's go. I want to go see if my house is still standing."

"Oh yeah, good idea."

The tunnel seemed to go on forever. Del Riemann wondered about the light in the tunnel. If anything creeped him out, it was that light, oozing from the tunnel walls with no wires or light fixtures anywhere in sight. The tunnel seemed to be growing colder too. Wasn't it always warm underground?

He began to worry there was no way out. They had fast-walked forever and now he was freezing to boot. It felt like winter in this part of the tunnel.

Del saw something ahead. Fuzzy at first, he realized two men stood farther down the tunnel, their backs to him. He put a hand out to slow Mick. One of the guys looked like a cop.

Shit! Did they intend to stop them?

As if noticing Del and Mick for the first time, the guys turned and walked toward them. Yep, one was the cop who'd been in the bar earlier, the other a bartender. What the hell was his name? Caleb? That was it, Caleb. Wasn't he missing?

A dark, vibrant thrill ran down Del's back. Something was wrong. He stopped, grabbed his friend's sleeve and backed up. "Dude, something ain't right."

Oblivious to any trouble, Mick called, "Yo guys, can we get out up there?"

They didn't answer. Their expressions didn't change. Something about their gait gave Del the willies. Nope! He was leaving—

The next moments flew by in a confused blur. As he turned to run, grabbing his buddy's arm to yank him along, the cop raised his gun.

Mick yelled "No!" and then screamed as the gun rose level with them. Del took a single running step, unable to take his eyes off the cop, suddenly certain the guy was dead or something.

The cop fired, a deafening blast in the tunnel, and the bullet knocked Mick back, his body toppling with a forced exhalation of air as he crashed to the floor, eyes wide open and perfectly dead.

Del yelped and took another step into something goopy. He looked down, saw his foot sinking into the floor of the cave, bogging him down, his forward momentum tripping him up. He crashed to the floor, then rolled over to face the threat after he jerked his foot free. He had no time to react further.

The cop and the bartender walked onward, stepping onto his chest, crushing the air from his lungs. A rib snapped. Time drifted to a halt, his eyes locked onto the men or creatures that stood on him, expressionless and unconcerned, as if unaware he was there dying in silent horror.

Del couldn't breathe, couldn't inhale, couldn't draw in the slightest bit of air.

Couldn't utter a word, a moan, or a scream.

His view grew dim and starry like a hazy night.

Folded to a dim point of light.

Blackness.

Fifty-Six

Doyle, the chef, said, "We need to find a way out of here."

Josh was trying to hold an increasingly fragile calm over the people trapped in the basement with him. There was no sign that anyone above was looking for them. They heard sirens but they sounded far away. None stopped near the tavern. Maybe the tunnel was the right idea. Far better than being trapped here for days on end. Del and Mick hadn't come back and it seemed possible they had made it out of the tunnel.

Where were Kiera and Lachlan? What were they doing? Something secretive had transpired between them. While he wasn't jealous, he was angry to be cut out of the loop. He was also angry about the tornado, his tavern, and the apartment, both of which had likely been destroyed. Locked somewhere between rage and despair, the last thing he wanted was to be stuck here. The more time that elapsed, the stronger the feeling grew.

He tried to project calm regardless. "Okay, I agree. It looks like it might be awhile before help comes. We might as well try the tunnel."

Everyone agreed except Kyla, who said, "I can't. I'm claustrophobic. I'll freak out."

"Fair enough. Is someone willing to wait here with Kyla?"

Bella, the other waitress spoke. "I'll stay."

A gunshot reverberated through the tunnel, seemed amplified by it and startled them all.

"What the fuck?" Doyle said. "That didn't sound good."

"Nope." Now Josh was worried, angry, *and* afraid. Kiera was down there. Had she fired the gun? Was Willow the shooter? It wasn't safe to look and he saw his emotions reflected in all of their faces. They were trapped and something bad was happening in the tunnel. Where were Del Riemann and his buddy?

A hand reached over the edge of the tunnel and Scott Robbins, the car dealer who had disappeared a week ago, climbed out of tunnel and sat on the floor, seemingly oblivious to the people in the basement staring at him.

He looked pale and confused.

"Hey dude, what's going on down there?" Josh said.

Ghost edged over, crept to within two feet of the guy, tucked his tail and scurried to Josh.

Scott stared into space as if he hadn't heard. Josh walked over and said, "Are you okay?" as he put a hand on his shoulder. Hairs rose on the back of his neck. Scott did not respond and was cold to the touch, a cold that seemed to suck heat out of his hand, which felt like it was exposed to a winter wind. He jerked the hand away and jumped back as the body went limp and fell back into the tunnel with a wet splat.

"What the fuck was that?" Angela said, voice rising, mouth and eyes wide with terror.

"I don't know." Josh yelled, "Kiera? Kiera!"

Silence.

He wanted to slam the hatch down and block the tunnel off but he couldn't, not with Kiera down there.

What the hell was going on? Scott Robbins had been as cold as a block of ice. He was pretty sure he was dead, except that was impossible. Was this some aspect of the tavern haunting? Except this wasn't like the harmless ghosts in the bar. It was disturbing, evil and horrific. The others backed away from the opening.

Doyle spoke. "What's up with that guy, Josh? Are we trapped here?"

Josh held a hand to the back of his neck, seriously shaken. "For now, yes. The tunnel is dangerous in a way I don't understand. That guy that just climbed in here? I think he was dead."

Startled murmurs ran through the group and they broke into frantic conversations.

"Holy shit! Are you serious?" Doyle said. He ran a hand across his bald pate.

Josh was freaking out. It was too much to process. "I don't know what to tell you."

"We need to close that off." Doyle pointed with an anxious scowl.

"I agree but I'm worried about Kiera." Josh rooted around in a pile of scrap by the wall. He found a length of black pipe left over from plumbing gas to the kitchen. If that thing tried climbing up again, he was going to nail it. Josh risked a quick glance down the opening in the floor. He saw the guy, one temple caved in from the fall but zero blood. It was the grossest thing he had ever seen.

"Let's close it most of the way then."

Josh nodded. "Yep, good. I need help. It weighs at least two-fifty."

Charlie Oliva, Doyle, Josh, Robby Braugher and Matt Luecke gathered around the grate and grunted as they lugged it into position. No one looked down as they laid it over the opening, leaving just a small gap so they could hear if Lachlan or Kiera returned and wanted out.

Josh was a mass of conflicting anxieties. He felt he should go down, find Kiera, and haul her back to safety. She might kick his ass if he came down to *save* her, unless she was in immediate jeopardy. Then she'd kick his ass for not coming. Why was he thinking like this? And how would he get past Scott Robbins?

Just then, the floor shuddered and rumbled as debris shifted above. Dust and grit fell from the ceiling. Josh had lived in Cali for a year, had experienced earthquakes and tremors, and he was certain of one frightening, surreal thing.

That was a tremor.

Fifty-Seven

The gunshot was an omen of trouble approaching and Lachlan knew it. Time was short. He could feel forces and circumstances rushing to a conclusion, a climax being orchestrated by the darkness in the tunnel and the cavern. The storm had been a manifestation of the darkness, he decided, and also a mistake. It must have taken immense energy to harness the power of the storm and it had probably weakened the darkness considerably. Lachlan couldn't imagine the purpose or intent. An attempt to keep him away from the cavern by blocking the access? If so, it had failed.

Instead, for better or worse, he was here, trapped with limited resources to mount an attack, a defense, anything. He sensed the darkness gathering energy and momentum, preparing to kill him along with anyone and everyone in the tunnel. He now feared that in making this about settling a score, about retribution, his judgement had been colored, and in his haste to resolve it, he had exposed the others to dangers he could only guess at.

Involving Kiera and Willow felt like a mistake. It was one thing to risk his own life. He had a cause. Yes, Kiera and Willow were adults and came here of their own volition, but did they truly understand what they were getting into? Why was he exposing them to the risk?

The reality? They had no other choice. Willow was already here and Kiera had been forced into the basement by the storm. He hadn't lured them here, and it was no longer possible to leave even if he explained the dangers. The tavern end was blocked. Something bad was approaching from the other end of the tunnel where the gunshot had come from.

With that realization, he recognized that Rachel was also in danger. He didn't know if she would be receptive to his messages but he mentally warned her to be careful regardless, knowing she would be coming through the farm end of the tunnel.

Lastly, he realized these stray thoughts were a non-productive distraction. They weren't helping.

He had to focus.

The gunshot confirmed his fear that the darkness would fight back by any and all means. Whatever approached in the tunnel was just the first wave. He quickly finished preparing his workspace, protecting himself and Willow with amulets and talismans, laid out his powders, crosses, and slid the cargástriftr into his back pocket. Then he positioned Willow in a strategic position to enhance his powers and draw from the energies of the Caol Áit, or the thin place as she called it.

Caol Áit was a place of spiritual bliss. A Christian felt the presence of their God at the gates of Heaven. A Muslim sensed the nearness of Allah, a Buddhist the spirit of Gautama Buddha. The Vikings who visited this cavern must have believed they were in Valhalla, the home of their gods. The Native Americans would have felt the same spiritual miracle. No wonder they had coexisted here and felt the need to build this shrine. The Caol Áit was all of those things. Lachlan had personally experienced the mystery many times in his life.

The presence of a second portal, the Geata de Ifreann, was inexplicable. More than a door, it was an interface between two worlds. Behind that door lay everything people feared: every beast, every monster, every horror people could imagine. The doorway to hell was a fitting title.

Somehow, in this cavern, the two were in balance. The darkness threatened to upend that, would tap into the greater darkness within and could become immensely stronger.

He was missing one vital element: Rachel and the arrowhead. They were integral to any chance he had to defeat this thing and settle the score for Kenric's death. Why? He didn't know and didn't need to. He just knew it was true. The arrowhead was the key to the Geata de Ifreann and Rachel seemed to be the only person who empowered the key. A curious state of affairs that he didn't understand.

Most disturbing, Lachlan couldn't know if Rachel would arrive in time or arrive at all. With the arrowhead in her possession, the darkness would try to stop her. He would try to watch out for her. Maybe Kiera could help bring her in. And maybe her control over the arrowhead would protect her.

They had to hurry. He distantly heard Kiera talking or yelling. Too much was going on in his head to focus on it.

A gunshot rang out and Kiera fired her gun. Twice.

Then the ground shuddered as a tremor shook the earth.

Fifty-Eight

Kiera ducked back, just inside the arch, and kept her gun pointed down the tunnel toward the farm. She thought she heard shuffling feet approaching but couldn't imagine the portent of the sound. Lachlan worked behind her, talking, mumbling, trying to prepare and orient Willow for some rite or ceremony.

Ahead, two shapes resolved into people in the dim light of the tunnel. She was about to say *hello* when she noticed one of them looked like a cop with his gun raised and pointed toward her.

Owen! Why was he aiming a gun at her?

His voice garbled, like he was chewing on something, Owen yelled, "Freeze bitch!"

Kiera could scarcely believe her ears or her eyes. She almost put her hands up, until she noticed the other figure looked like Caleb!

What the hell was happening here?

But Owen wasn't looking at her, and it looked like blood was leaking from his eyes! Caleb was a weird black color, sooty, like a coal miner. Something smelled burnt.

In a sudden flash of insight, Kiera sensed that something terribly wrong was afoot. She yelled, "Stop or I'll shoot. Owen! Caleb! I'm not kidding! Back off!"

Owen fired a wild shot that ricocheted off the ceiling overhead.

Shit!

It was all the provocation she needed. She drew a quick bead and fired—rushed it—pulling up and shooting high. Owen kept firing wild, random shots.

Kiera set a firm stance, aimed, held and released a breath. Fired.

The bullet blew through Owen's forehead and jerked his head back. He kept walking, as if being shot in the head was a minor inconvenience. She emptied the clip into the two of them. Caleb fell and stayed down, but Owen kept coming, his empty revolver clicking as he continued to pull the trigger, then staggering as the ground beneath their feet trembled.

Kiera felt a black oily fear rising, a horror beyond her wildest imagining. Had Caleb been hiding out down here? And what the hell had gotten into Owen? And her brain barely touched on the thought that she had shot a cop, though it was the clearest case of self-defense she could imagine. Everyone, it seemed, went crazy in the presence of the longship and the thin place—or whatever crazy phenomena had been unleashed here. Owen just kept coming, walking like a robot.

Kiera snapped a new clip into the Sig, backed into the cavern and screamed, "Lachlan!"

Fifty-Nine

Rustin Marshall parked in the field across from the Quinlan farm and ran across the road. No cars, no police were visible. He imagined they had their hands full with the storm in town. He had barely escaped Miller's Crossing with his life as it was. He'd never seen a tornado in his life and had been terrified by the black twisting wall of vapor and debris that bore down on him and the town. He had floored the accelerator and raced at over a hundred miles an hour getting away from it. He was still shaking from the experience. He sat in the car for five minutes, waiting until his heart no longer threatened to burst from his chest. Good thing he didn't believe in omens.

Armed with a flashlight, an HD camera, a hacksaw, and a rock hammer, he slipped through the back doorway and duck-walked down the edge of the staircase to the basement. The hatch was open.

"Christ!" He knew the hatch was there. Evidently, someone else did too and had already gone into the tunnel. How many people knew about this? Time was fast running out on this secret.

He eased himself into the opening and down into the tunnel. It was quiet, though he imagined hearing soft voices. Perhaps they were an illusion, like holding a conch shell to your ear. Nevertheless, he inched forward, knowing at least one other person was down here. He was also watchful for any other access points into the tunnel. About thirty feet up, he noted a small hole in the roof. He would flag the spot next time.

The tunnel, partly a natural limestone formation, had been cut in places with hand tools. Old hand tools, possibly stones adzes. If so, it was hundreds of years old. The tunnel itself was the best proof of its antiquity. The air was warm and fetid. He had smelled decomposing flesh before and this faint malodor smelled human. Or maybe he was waxing melodramatic given the wild events of the day thus far. Could be a dead animal. The tunnel seemed dimmer than usual so he flicked the flashlight on and pointed the beam down the tunnel.

There was something on the floor ahead. Indistinct. It looked like a sack. As he stepped closer, he realized it was a large man, laying prone on the floor.

Just beyond lay a second man, flat on his back. His chest looked oddly sunken. What the hell was going on here?

"Hey! You guys okay?"

The bigger man stirred and sat up, looking confused. A dark stain had spread across his chest. As Rustin aimed the beam there, he saw a telltale hole in the shirt. It looked like a bullet hole. How was the guy still alive?

The man focused on Rustin and said, "Yo dude. Give me a hand."

The voice sounded bubbly. A dark feeling passed through the professor, surely the feeling of heavy footsteps on his grave. He stopped and stepped back slowly, trying to conceal his fear and intended retreat. Something was so wrong here.

"Seriously, dude. What's your fucking problem?" The big guy rolled to one side and stood up with an agility that belied his size.

The professor couldn't speak. That bullet hole stared at him like an evil black eye, a juju that meant him harm. He dropped all pretense, turned and ran, certain his life was in mortal danger. Had the Vikings left some sort of malevolent spirit behind to guard the longship? It was absurd, though no more absurd than a big guy with a bullet hole, dead center in his chest, walking and talking.

Footsteps followed him. Big, heavy footsteps closing fast. Rustin hazarded a quick look and almost puked in fear. The guy was only ten feet behind! The professor turned and threw the flashlight with considerable force.

Boom! Nailed the guy right on his big fat forehead!

The guy didn't even falter!

Jesus!

He grabbed the rock hammer and swung it at the guy's temple as if swinging for the fences and sank the sharp end three inches into his brain.

The guy didn't blink.

Instead, he plowed into Rustin and smashed his fist into the professor's face in a dazzling blaze of stars and agony.

The world spun as he struggled to move. He feared he had only moments left to live. "Stop! Stop! Please stop!"

The big hulk stared down for a moment as if in a trance.

He then yanked the rock hammer from his head and swung it down, the professor unable to look away as the spiked end pierced the bone between his eyes.

Sixty

Rachel biked down Martin Road like a maniac. She saw no need to cover her approach to the farm. The cops would be far too busy dealing with the aftermath of the storm to worry about some kid trespassing there.

She wheeled into the drive and plowed through the long grass, dumping the bike behind the house and running for the gaping doorway. The back hall was slick from the rain and Rachel slipped, sliding and tumbling down the broken staircase. She rolled with most of the fall but her head slammed into the dirt floor in a blaze of stars.

Lying for a moment, stunned and winded, she stared at the ceiling. After a quick limb and neck check, she rolled and crawled to the hatchway in the floor. Rachel hung her head down into the tunnel. It smelled funky with the faint whiff of something bad.

"Lachlan?"

Rachel heard a faint sound that might have been gunfire but then decided that couldn't be. Nobody would be shooting down there, would they? Probably not, but she decided to be careful just the same—and as she thought that, she also imagined hearing Lachlan speaking, telling her to be careful, right inside her head!

Holy crap! That was some serious *Stranger Things* type shit! Maybe spookier. She had seen most every episode and could remember nothing as creepy.

It had to be related to the longship in the cavern. The boat had no earthly right to be there a thousand miles from the Atlantic, miles from any water at all.

She touched her pocket. Yep, the arrowhead was still there. It felt like a talisman—even if it was wishful thinking.

The sword!

She walked back up the stairs, carefully this time, and ripped the tape and sword from her bike. Somehow, the sword and the arrowhead were important, part of what Lachlan was trying to do in the cavern.

Rachel climbed down the tunnel wall using the carved steps, keeping an eye over her shoulder, feeling an aura of danger emanating from the tunnel, from something within both dark and soulless. She couldn't explain the sensation but knew it came as a warning from Lachlan. Somehow, he was telling her in feelings, not words, to be very, very careful.

Sixty-One

Lachlan yanked himself out of his trance, trying to read the heart of the beast in the room or somewhere nearby. Whatever confrontation Kiera faced was part of it and he needed to deal with that first.

"Willow, stay exactly where you are. Don't move!"

She nodded, eyes closed, seemingly far away.

He grabbed his satchel, ran to Kiera at the doorway, and risked a peek around the corner of the archway. A cop, his body riddled with bullet holes, walked toward him, firing an empty revolver, looking like a vision straight out of a Bosch painting or a Romero movie.

Behind the cop lay another body and Lachlan recognized the danger. The darkness was animating the dead, using them as diversions and tools of destruction. It was a horrifying thing if you didn't know the truth of the matter. It also suggested to Lachlan that the darkness was weak still and resorting to parlor tricks to avoid confronting him. He fervently hoped that was the case.

He dug through his satchel and pulled out a pair of Celtic crosses. He held one in each hand and muttered the words of an ancient incantation in Old English over them.

Lachlan stepped into the tunnel and strode toward the cop-creature, who seemed undeterred by the Celtic crosses. There was no reason it should be. They were entirely useless as a religious symbol because the darkness honored no god, no devil, nothing but itself. The cross and attached invocation were simply blunt instruments to short circuit the process by which the darkness animated the poor bastards.

He stopped and waited, watching, timing his strike, imagining the move he would make.

Ten feet...five feet...

Lachlan stepped in and swiftly executed the maneuver like a martial artist: shoving the gun hand aside with the cross in his left hand while swinging the other in an arc and jamming the sharpened end into the bullet hole in Owen's forehead.

The body dropped like a sack of potatoes.

Behind him, Kiera screamed. She backed away in horror and yelled, "What the holy hell was that?"

He held up a finger and approached the corpse of Caleb, who had started to roll over. He leaned over and confirmed he was dead by touching the cold burnt skin on Caleb's neck. As the corpse reached to grab his arm, he flipped the cross to his right hand with a deft move and stabbed down sharply, burying the cross in Caleb's chest.

Caleb collapsed. Lachlan turned and ran, pushing Kiera ahead of him into the cavern.

"The darkness is animating the bodies of the dead in an attempt to stop me. A cheap but dangerous ploy." He turned her and sat her on the floor, facing the archway. "You need to protect the cavern."

He grabbed two of the Celtic crosses, spoke a brief incantation, and handed them to her. "Use these. Your gun is worthless here."

Kiera's face contorted somewhere between disbelief and horror. "What? I can't do that."

"You have to. It's a matter of life or death. You're a strong, determined woman. I have every faith you'll do whatever's necessary to protect us."

The ground shuddered again, a bit stronger than before. The longship wobbled on its mount and dust and small rock fragments fell from the ceiling.

Damn! Time was quickly running out. He bellowed, *"Áblinnest!"*

The earth shook again.

Bloody hell!

None of this would be easy.

None of it.

Sixty-Two

Josh sat rigid until the shaking stopped.

What in the hell was going on? He had studied enough geology to know there were no fault lines or seismic zones anywhere near here. Still shaken by the violence of the tornado, being trapped in the basement, the appearance of a guy who had gone missing and now looked dead—this tremor was nearly more than he could stand. The same strong emotions were evident on the faces of the remaining people stuck in the basement with him.

There were no signs that people were searching for them. No one had any cell service—either because they were underground or because the storm had destroyed the towers, but the result was the same. No phones.

He braced himself as the ground trembled again, stronger than before. The debris in the stairwell seemed to settle even more—if that were possible—and dust and grit sifted down from above. A work cabinet tipped over, narrowly missing Jami Braugher. She screamed and her husband, Robby, yelled, "Shit Josh, we have to get out of here!"

Robby was a big dude. He wasn't arguing with Robby, but Josh had no idea how safe they were in the basement. The tunnel could be worse. Who knew?

Just then, a rough-hewn four-by-twelve joist snapped with a huge crack, crashing down onto Charlie Oliva, the security guy, slamming him to the ground, crushing his skull.

Time stood still for a moment of shocked silence, then the basement erupted in screams of horror. Josh recoiled from the awfulness of the sight, something so dreadful that it hardly seemed real. He was horrified by the randomness of Charlie's sudden violent death. By the realization he could be next. Josh thought he might puke. Someone else did, by the wall.

Josh moved closer to the wall of the main cooler and gestured quickly for the others do the same. Ghost, whimpering, tried to push in between Josh's legs and the wall.

Josh said, "We should be a little safer here. This block wall seems solid."

Pacing, Doyle said, "I don't think we're safe here at all, we should try the tunnel—"

"You forget about the dead guy down there?" Josh said, shuddering at the thought himself. As if wishing to voice an opinion of its own, fingers slipped through the thin crack between the grate and the floor, the heavy cover creeping open.

"Oh Jesus, no!" Josh yelled. "Help me, close it quick!"

Robby, Matt, Doyle, and Angela rushed over and helped Josh slide it closed, severing the fingers, which now lay on the concrete like little white sausages. There was no scream, no complaint from below—a silence that was the creepiest thing Josh had ever heard.

Katy Oldman, arms cupped in her hands, said, "What are we gonna do?" She seemed one of the more composed members of the group.

"I don't know but I think Doyle's right. We're not safe here," Josh said, as he looked around, dust still falling from ceiling and settling on the concrete, seeing Charlie again, crushed under the beam. "This whole place could fall on us."

Matt Luecke said, "I'm not going down there with that thing in there."

"You'd rather be crushed like Charlie?" Katy said, looking at him with flat eyes. She didn't like him much, evidently.

"I'm not sure going further underground is the answer," Robby said.

"What then?" Josh said.

They all stared at him blankly. Clearly, the decision was his. He said, "I say we go. Quickly, before any more tremors. Arm ourselves and go past that thing. Beat the shit out of it if we have to. Kiera said the tunnel's about three quarters of a mile long."

"Man, where is Kiera?" Angela asked.

"I don't know. That's another reason I want to go down, to see if she's okay."

"What do you have for weapons?" Robby asked.

"The tools are over there. I have this piece of black pipe. It's heavy."

They all ran to the toolbox and grabbed sharp or heavy tools. Thus armed, they pulled the cast iron cover back and looked down.

Scott Robbins was gone.

Josh didn't know if he was relieved or more nervous knowing that guy—*that thing*—still wandered loose down there somewhere.

"What about the dog?" Doyle asked. "Stay with them?"

"Nope. I have an idea. You guys start down." Josh looked to Bella and Kyla. "Sure you don't want to go with us?"

Kyla shook her head vigorously, Bella less enthusiastically.

Josh looked around. The cooler was the strongest structure, and no longer cold with the power out. "Okay, stay in the cooler. You're probably the safest there. I'll send help as soon as we're out."

Taking a flashlight from Josh, they settled into the cooler with frightened but stoic expressions.

One by one, the others climbed down the vertical stone steps and disappeared into the tunnel. Josh found some strapping and made a makeshift rig to move the dog into the tunnel. Ghost did not look happy but Josh lifted and lowered him to Doyle before he could squirm out of the sling. Josh grabbed his piece of black pipe and followed them into the tunnel.

He had never felt more afraid.

Sixty-Three

Lachlan shut out his fear and closed his eyes, gathering all his resources inward, drawing energy from Willow.

From his bag, he drew a Celtic Cross made of solid gold, an instrument he had cast over a thousand years before. It held no religious significance. The cross was simply the best shape to draw energy from the ether. He and Kenric had experimented with dozens of shapes and this design was far superior to the others. Why, they didn't know. It didn't matter. At least it didn't to Lachlan. Kenric was always obsessive when it came to those kinds of questions, always trying to understand the science behind the magic. To Lachlan, it only mattered that it worked.

A vibration disturbed the silence in the room. So low, it was probably inaudible to the others. He could feel the darkness resisting him, pushing back. It grew in volume and intensity, felt like it was wrapping around his head and infiltrating his brain through his nasal passages. Invasive and unpleasant, he concentrated on pushing it out, trying to create a protective barrier around himself.

Willow was a superb medium, amplifying his efforts. She was a natural, one of the best he'd worked with in years. Hell, had it been a hundred years? But that little question, just extraneous background brain noise, distracted from the task at hand. He tried to shut off the normal low-level brain activity, trying to achieve a meditative level of consciousness. Giving himself over totally to the process, he mumbled incantations in the Mercian dialect of Old English.

Lachlan felt the darkness receding, unable to withstand the combined energies that he and Willow were directing outward. Meanwhile, Rachel, somewhere further down the tunnel, armed with the arrowhead, had effectively blocked access to the Geata de Ifreann, all visible in a vivid image in his mind. His eyes were closed but he could see the room in precise relief, lit by the energies competing and conflicting in the room, powerful forces drawn from the bonds of the atoms in the room, literally a visual display of the Einstein equation in four dimensions.

He was winning, overcoming the darkness, depleting it. He felt deeply empowered.

Two rapid gunshots broke his concentration.

Sixty-Four

Kiera watched Lachlan, captivated by the spectacle unfolding in the cavern. Lachlan stood, mumbling quietly, his eyes closed, a golden cross held in two hands straight out from his chest. He and the cross seemed to glimmer, sending out waves of energy. The room vibrated with the energies flowing through it. Dust filtered down from the ceiling and the longship rocked gently and it too seemed to glow. She had no idea what was happening but she was in awe of it, almost completely entranced by the spectacle.

Almost.

She heard somebody shuffling down the tunnel from the tavern side, the same shuffling gait she'd heard as Owen and Caleb approached her, but maybe only one person, not two.

Damn! Damn! Damn! She thought her head might explode. Dealing with it was her job and she didn't know if she could do it. A man materialized in the dim tunnel light.

Oh Christ! It was Scott Robbins! He had been missing for a week!

Fuck! This was creepy as shit and instinctively, she raised her gun and fired once, twice before she realized she was wasting her time.

Your gun is worthless here.

She laid it down and grabbed one of the crosses. She was supposed to drive a metal cross into his dead body?

Yuck! No way!

But her vivid imagination ran off on its own, picturing those cold meaty hands closing around her throat, breathing some awful dead-man breath on her, falling on her, all that dead meat pinning her to the ground, killing her in the most awful way imaginable.

Kiera grabbed the cross, held it like a knife, steeled herself. She ran and stabbed the dead guy in the chest in a swooping, arcing lunge like a ninja going for the kill.

Dead Scott Robbins stopped and folded up, collapsing like a deflated hot-air balloon.

The wave of horror and nausea that flowed through her in that moment robbed her of all balance. She slumped against the wall of the tunnel and threw up. Then retched again and again as her system rebelled against the grotesque realization of her deed and the cloying smell of death and decomposition from the body next to her.

Kiera wiped her mouth and prayed to God that she never needed to do that again. She stood, steering clear of the body and stumbled back to the cavern.

Lachlan remained standing in the same spot, eyes closed, jaw set, the face of a man fighting demons she couldn't see. It was no longer possible to distinguish between reality and nightmare. Spirits, ghosts, sorcerers, a longship, a secret cavern, Viking and Native American spirits, a thin place and a gate to hell?

Fricking nuts!

What if Lachlan couldn't stop this force or darkness, as he called it? She hardly knew him and yet, it seemed her life hung in the balance and he might be the only person who could save it. Same for Josh, Willow, and everyone else down here.

There was nothing she could do. Her fate was out of her hands. Difficult to swallow when she so prized her independence and ability to be her own person. Where was Josh? Hopefully, they had realized the danger and had closed the hatch. Perhaps they had gotten out some other way, though that seemed unlikely. Eventually, they would grow impatient and try coming through the tunnel, which was a very bad idea. She had no way to warn him off.

Lachlan muttered away in a language she didn't recognize. It sounded Germanic, but even though she knew some German, she didn't understand a single word. The energy waves in the room seemed to modulate with the intensity of his chants. It felt like he was winning, if it was possible to win a conflict like this.

She heard shuffling in the tunnel. From the other side, the farmhouse end. Lachlan must have heard them as well. He broke his chant and yelled, "Kiera! Stop them!"

Them? Oh God, no!

Who else was down here?

Kiera peeked around the corner and saw them coming. Del Riemann and Mick Herzlinger. They must have been the two who slipped by her earlier. She didn't think they were coming to help. Mick had a dark bloodstain on his shirt and Del's chest looked weird and flat. They were like the others.

Damn!

She had only one cross left.

Sixty-Five

Rachel slid along the tunnel wall, growing increasingly nervous as she moved forward, the smell in the tunnel growing stronger. Sickly sweet but gross, it reminded her of dead animals in the woods. She also heard muffled voices and sounds like gunshots. Why would anyone be shooting down here? She also worried because she didn't see anyone. Surely people would've come this way to get out? Kiera and Lachlan both knew the tunnel opened into the basement of the farmhouse. Maybe they were still in the cavern. Why?

All the while, the arrowhead vibrated lightly in her pocket as did the sword in her hand.

Lachlan was one strange dude, she decided. She liked him but he hadn't been totally honest about why he was here. Supposedly a ghost dude, she felt certain he was after something bigger. Rachel couldn't imagine what that might be and wondered if she was safe down here. Even if she wasn't, she felt compelled to find him, to make sure he was okay. She hardly knew him, yet he felt like family already, an attachment she couldn't explain beyond her lack of a real family otherwise.

It seemed lighter ahead, but it was growing colder. She pulled a sweatshirt out of her backpack, slipped it on, took a step, and stopped, startled.

A guy sat on the floor about thirty feet ahead, motionless, oblivious to her approach. Further up, it looked like two guys were walking away from her, toward the cavern. Some of the people from the tavern? Hopefully, it meant everyone was safe. She was about to call out when her shoe scuffed on the stone floor.

The guy on the floor turned, staring at her in a way that sent an ice-water chill down her spine. His expression blank, even in the dim light it looked like he had a dark hole right between his eyes.

"Holy fuck," she whispered. Her insides clenched. It felt like she might pee her pants. She backed up a step as he rocked and stood up, eyeing her, that bloody dark hole in his face freaking her out. There were no words, no thoughts, just blank, flat-out terror and now, the guy was walking toward her!

She yelled, "Lachlan! Kiera!"

The guy walked faster.

Rachel turned and ran. Snapped her head back for a quick peek— no way she'd make it to the steps before he got to her. She suddenly realized she held a sword in her left hand. And though she'd never killed anyone she had the strange feeling the guy was already dead.

Seriously, who could live with a big bloody hole like that, right between the eyes?

She made a split-second decision born of fear, a sturdy survival instinct, and flat-out teenage naiveté: turning and jabbing the sword outward with every bit of strength she possessed.

The dead thing that had been Rustin Marshall plowed right into it, the gold-silver blade sinking six inches into his abdomen before he vaporized in a cloud of dust that rained lightly over Rachel and the floor of the cave. Rachel held her breath and shuddered.

Ugh. Dead guy dust.

Yuck! Yuck! Yuck!

She shook her head vigorously and brushed her hair with her hands.

Just then, she heard Kiera yelling from far down the tunnel.

Sixty-Six

Josh, gripping the black pipe as if his life depended on it, led the way as they inched along the wall of the tunnel. Ghost trailed just behind, head down, uttering a low growl. The ground juddered slightly and they all threw themselves to the wall, their backs flat and tight against it. Small rocks fell from the ceiling along with sprinkles of dust. Josh wondered again if they had done the right thing by coming down here, deeper underground, more at risk from earth tremors.

What the hell was with the tremors? Some consequence of the tornado? He had taken geography electives in college and there were no fault lines in Wisconsin. The tremors only added to the surrealness of their situation. Josh had seen so much footage over the years of people's lives disrupted, displaced, and upended by a disaster. He never imagined living through one.

When the shaking stopped, they continued creeping along the wall.

Where was Kiera? What had become of her and Lachlan? Perhaps they had gotten out and gone for help, but that didn't feel right. Kiera wouldn't have left them behind without some sort of explanation—

though the appearance of Scott Robbins suggested that *normal* was on the bus and gone. Indeed, weird had run riot and things were happening that none of them understood.

Robby said, "This is starting to feel like a bad idea."

"I agree, but I don't know if we have much choice," Josh said. "The bar might collapse on us long before anyone comes looking for—"

Josh saw a body ahead. "Shit!"

"What?" Robby swung out around him and saw it too. "Jesus! What now?"

Josh vacillated before speaking. "Unless you want to go back, we have to go past him."

"Man, I don't know," Robby said, his face wrinkled in disgust.

Josh crept a little closer, saw a cross protruding from his chest. "Jesus Christ!"

He jumped back, his hand swooping through an involuntary sign of the cross.

What the hell was that about?

Looking to Robby he said, "Dude, this is—I don't know if I can pass the guy. There's a cross sticking out of his chest."

The others backed up a step as well, faces locked in uniform expressions of shock. Except for Matt Luecke, who lost it. "We're all gonna die!"

"Shut the fuck up!" Robby yelled. "Things are bad enough without you freaking out like a girl."

"Hey! You shut up too," Angela said angrily. "We have to go past him. Let's just get it over with. I don't plan on dying down here."

She looked to the others who seemed to draw on her resolve. The dead guy wasn't moving and suddenly, it seemed like a good idea to get past as quickly as possible. Angela, brandishing a large crescent wrench, said, "I got it. I'll take the lead."

Josh looked at her with newfound respect. He knew she was tough but this was impressive.

"You heard the lady, let's move!" And he fell in line behind her.

God, if they got out of this alive...

If.

Sixty-Seven

Lachlan struggled to maintain the upper hand over the darkness. The interruptions, the tremors, the conflicting signals in the cavern—from Rachel, Kiera, the darkness, the Geata de Ifreann. All conspired to keep him off balance. His earlier confidence had faded. Even allowing such thoughts worked against everything he was trying to do. There was a time when he could have stood here for days and communed with this cavern, the Caol Áit, the darkness and brought great powers to bear. No doubts, no reservations. He had been a master of the universe—his universe anyway.

Suddenly, he felt old, ill-equipped, and past his prime. Maybe no one should live this long. But for Giles, he had outlived his children, grandchildren, and great-grandchildren many times over. Now angst threatened to steal his thunder. Yet he realized that if he failed, no one else could stop the darkness. It would grow and fester, mutate and metastasize, become too powerful to challenge.

Life was strange. Only because of extraordinary luck was he here to challenge the darkness at all.

The word for it? Serendipity. One of his favorite words. Derived from a fairy tale in which the heroes *were always making discoveries, by accidents and sagacity, of things they were not in quest of.*

He just happened to fly to the States to settle Kenric's estate. He'd found sufficient evidence of his death, murder really, to become incensed and cultivate the desire for retribution. To further stumble across this town and this place, this Caol Áit, seemed like extraordinary good luck. Depending upon one's point of view, some might consider it a curse, but this was what he did. His *raison d'être*. Fighting the good fight.

His mind drifted back to the time he and Kenric challenged Reynard Alington, a powerful baron whose lands lay just outside the city of Northampton. A miserable tyrant who levied onerous taxes on his subjects, Alington also charged travelers heavy tolls and often robbed them even after they had paid him. A group formed to challenge the baron. They in turn enlisted Lachlan and Kenric to their cause.

Alington, deeply corrupt and amoral, had in his employ scores of mercenaries, sorcerers, witches, and villainous spirits, and he used every deceit available to this dark army to gain the upper hand in any dealing, dispute, or battle. Even as revered founders of the Aeldo, Kenric and Lachlan faced impossible odds and the cause seemed hopeless. Then Kenric conceived of a plan both daring and bold, a scheme doomed to failure if only for its audacity. He created a phantom army of ruffians out of hay bales, cornstalks, and thin air. The most wretched looking phalanx ever imagined—literally—and marched them toward Alington's estate.

They laid a trap and used that army to draw their opponents to the center. When Alington's forces surrounded and set upon the army, the phantoms disappeared into clouds of dust and hay. Kenric then blew Alington's people to bits with a massive brew of saltpeter, brimstone, and charcoal—Kenric had a penchant for blowing things up. Their compatriots swooped in from opposing quadrants and quickly destroyed the remaining stragglers. It was a total rout of Alington's dark army and he was forever weakened and ultimately deposed.

When Lachlan asked Kenric from where he drew inspiration, he had uttered one word, *Cannae,* the famous battle in which Hannibal defeated a much larger Roman army with a somewhat similar feint.

He smiled, then returned to the present. That brief journey had been another distraction, but it focused Lachlan on his value and purpose here.

He had once been a star. Perhaps, even now, he was that good, still that gifted. Maybe he didn't fully appreciate his powers after all these years. Still, he had been alive for over a thousand years and this was the most extraordinary situation he had ever encountered.

No matter.

He couldn't fail. Who else could stop this? Who would?

Lachlan redoubled his efforts to attain a hyper-focused state, growing mindful to an extraordinary degree. He closed his ears to the world; there was nothing he needed to hear. Then closed his eyes; there was nothing he needed to see.

The darkness was palpable through his skin—but also visible to a sixth sense he had developed to a highly tuned state over the years.

He focused his energies and those of his friends into a psychic laser beam and brought it to bear on the darkness.

Sixty-Eight

Kiera slipped the Celtic cross from her pocket and gripped it tightly as she slid along the wall towards the two men shuffling toward her. They didn't appear to be armed—meager consolation since Del and Mick were probably dead.

Your gun is worthless here.

Mick put a hand up and summoned her with his fingers. "Bring it, bitch!"

The voice threw her off balance. Was he alive? She focused on his chest, confused by the bullet hole and the big red stain. He couldn't be alive, but he was walking and talking just fine. Nausea rose in her throat in an acidic wave though she felt certain nothing remained in her stomach. Her mouth and tongue felt dry and pasty, her skin crawling at the thought of another confrontation, the vision and smell of dead Scott Robbins fresh in her memory.

This was worse than a fool's errand. She was as good as dead. Either they killed her and moved on or, if she somehow survived the confrontation, they would just kill Lachlan. Then, whatever beast Lachlan hoped to banish from the cavern would kill her instead. It seemed hopeless.

One cross. Two guys.

What were the rules? Could she stab one and then the other? Did the cross have to stay in place? Any miscalculation would be fatal. She didn't want to interrupt Lachlan again. He'd made it clear *any* interruption was dangerous.

Kiera stopped and waited.

An idea germinated. She would let them approach her, ready herself, lock into a rock-solid defensive stance—she had one shot at this.

The men shuffled toward her. Forty feet, thirty feet, twenty feet... Just one shot.

Then she heard Rachel yell, "Lachlan! Kiera!" Her voice sounded far away.

Suddenly, Mick stopped and turned, grabbed Del and turned him around.

What were they looking at? They began walking the other way.

Then Kiera saw why. People. Who—?

For an instant, she saw two people standing farther down the tunnel. Then, a single person, shaking her head and scrubbing her hair with her hands.

Rachel!

The two goons wanted *her.*

Sixty-Nine

Angela walked past the body, giving it a wide berth. Josh focused on her rather than looking down. Her eyes appeared to be closed. Not a bad idea, but as he crossed to the other wall and slid past the corpse, he looked anyway. Josh tensed, the pipe poised to bash the corpse to a pulp if it moved. But it remained still, a horrific sight that he would never forget, one hand a messy bunch of stumps, the upper part of the face bashed in by hard contact with the stone floor of the tunnel. The final horror was the odd-shaped cross protruding from the chest. What was going on down here? His mind flashed to an image of Kiera lying somewhere with a cross sticking out of her chest, and he couldn't make it stop.

The others—Doyle, Katy, Dani, Robby and Jami, and Matt—followed. Just ahead, he saw light, glowing rays emanating from the cavern. Meanwhile, the light in the tunnel itself seemed to fade, grow darker, colder—even less hospitable, if that was possible. He no longer cared about the bar and the apartment. None of it mattered. He would never operate a tavern here again. Nope. He was taking the insurance money and running far, far away. He just needed to find Kiera and escape this tunnel of hell alive.

At that moment, he thought he heard someone call Kiera's name.

Then he heard her yell, "Rachel! Don't move!"

Holy shit! She was still alive!

Hearing her voice, Ghost took off at a tear.

Josh followed.

⋆   ⋆   ⋆

A wind swirled about Lachlan, intense at times, intent it seemed on toppling him.

Willow held firm. He could sense her presence working with him, growing stronger, strangling and stifling the darkness. He had found the sweet spot of perfect concentration and focus, pushing inexorably against his enemy, forcing it into submission.

He could do this. He would do this.

Avenge the death of his friend, and rid the world—already host to far too much evil—of a malignant remnant of an invocation cast five hundred years before by Anna Flecher.

Lachlan clenched his jaw and sweat dripped from his brow, his legs ready to spasm at the supreme effort and energy he directed into the breach. The earth vibrated beneath his feet. Wind roiled around him. He heard a sea of voices, souls lost to the darkness or the Geata de Ifreann, maybe both. It was, without doubt, the most mournful sound he had ever heard.

Enormous energy flowed through him, pushing, straining, struggling—

It wasn't working.

There was an imbalance, a growing, negative pressure from the Geata de Ifreann. He needed Rachel. The talisman she held—the arrowhead—controlled and held the Geata in check and, he suspected, prevented the darkness from drawing energy from it. He couldn't do this without her and the arrowhead present in the room. Close would not do. Letting his mind wander, he sensed her presence in the tunnel. Walking this way, he saw the danger from two dead men: Del Riemann and Mick Herzlinger.

Every time his concentration was disrupted, every distraction, every danger and worry—each weakened him and gave strength to his enemy. Kiera would have to handle this.

"Kiera! You need to protect Rachel!" His voice thundered like a god's in the cavern.

He hadn't been comfortable drawing Kiera and Willow into this, but they were adults, acting on their own volition. Rachel was a child and involving her was far more problematic. He knew she would adopt the same defense if challenged: she was acting on her own volition. Still, he wasn't comfortable with the idea. She did not understand the risks she faced, nor did she possess the maturity to accept them.

It was a moral slippery slope he was reluctant to slide down. Children had always been off-limits. Never used as bait, decoys, pawns, or shills. Yes, she was sixteen. In bygone eras, she would be considered an adult, a woman, no longer a child. Yet here he was, equivocating in an era that clearly deemed her a child.

It was too late to second-guess. She was coming and he needed her. They all needed her.

He couldn't keep the darkness from the Geata de Ifreann for much longer.

Seventy

"Rachel! Don't move!" Kiera bellowed.

Mick swiveled his head, and she yelled, "Hey, lard ass! Right here!"

Del and Mick stopped and regarded her, as if trying to decide if she was the greater threat. They turned and walked toward her with purpose.

Careful what you wish for.

With a low angry growl, Ghost came up from behind, stopped and glared at the men, poised in full defensive stance. As Mick neared, Ghost let loose a growl that gave Kiera chills and leapt like a small bear, mouth open, canines bared. With surprising speed, Mick swatted him aside.

Ghost yelped, rolled, and retreated, evidently thinking better of a second attack.

"You leave my dog alone, asshole!"

With Del close behind, Mick moved on Kiera, "Lard ass is gonna kill you, bitch!"

Kiera stood her ground.

When they were almost upon her—as Mick reached for her neck—she leapt. Grabbing his right hand with her left and yanking it to chest level, she slammed his hand backward into Del's chest. Kiera swung her right hand in an arc—the cross held in a death grip—her arm completing the sweep, the cross piercing the palm to the hilt, the pointed end lodging between Del's ribs as she let loose a primal scream.

The momentum of the maneuver sent both men backward. As they collapsed, Kiera fell onto their cold, mushy, greasy bodies with an intense spasm of horror.

"Ugggggghhhhhhhhhh!"

She threw herself backward onto the stone floor, banging her head, wiping her hands on her pants in involuntary disgust. The gesture did nothing to erase the awful texture of their skin, the sensation of their cold bodies, the stink of death. Empty stomach or not, she rolled over and vomited a thin stream of bile onto the tunnel floor.

Kiera didn't immediately realize that Rachel was tearing down the tunnel, her long hair streaming behind, sword leading the charge. Screaming like a banshee, the girl looked like a Valkyrie coming to wreak vengeance on the world. She flew over the bodies of Caleb and Owen with a mighty leap and thrust the sword out, stabbing it through Mick and into Del's body. In an instant, both men vaporized in a cloud of dust.

For a moment, Kiera and Rachel stared at each other with stunned expressions, speechless.

With no trace of humor, Rachel said, "Neat trick, huh?"

Kiera sat, stunned and incredulous. How did she know that would work? Who else was down here? Where did she get that sword?

The tunnel shuddered as another tremor shook small stones and dust loose from the ceiling. The tremors shook her from a trance; they worried her. She suspected they weren't of a geological origin.

With all the other brazenly impossible things she had witnessed in the last hour, she could only assume the tremors were emanating from the cavern. That brought her little comfort. She only hoped Lachlan could overcome whatever it was causing these distortions in reality. Tremors. Dead men walking. Magic swords. Maybe even the tornado, now that she thought about it. A wedge tornado of that size was virtually unheard of this far outside of tornado alley. A tornado that seemed to have been aimed directly at the tavern.

Lachlan called out, "Rachel! Hurry! In here!"

Rachel put a hand out and pulled Kiera to her feet and they turned back toward the archway. It seemed to be growing darker in the tunnel. She squinted, looking ahead, thought she saw a man in the tunnel beyond the arch.

No!

She couldn't do this again. She couldn't kill another of those awful dead things.

But the man wasn't shuffling.

Ghost barked and flipped in a circle.

It was Josh!

Seventy-One

Rachel charged into the cavern.

She and Lachlan locked eyes. Shaking and shocked by all she had seen, she ran to embrace him, throwing her head against his shoulder. He gave her a firm hug, infusing her with a deeper calm than any pill could provide.

"I'm glad you're safe," she said.

"And I you." Lachlan took her by the shoulders and looked into her eyes. "I need your help right now. It's dangerous—"

"I came to help," Rachel said with more confidence than she felt. "What can I do?"

His eyes lit on the sword, saucer-wide with awe. "Oh my. The legend is true. The *Sword of Stikla*. Where did you find this?"

"Buried. Under the barn. The Sword of Stikla?"

"Stikla was a maiden-warrior, a powerful Viking woman—"

"A girl warrior?" Rachel forgot everything else for a moment. Holding the sword of a warrior-maiden in her hands, the significance filled her with awe and pride. She had only ever seen female warriors in movies. This sword had been owned by a true warrior. A warrior and a woman. No wonder it spoke to her with such passion.

"Oh yes, she was fierce in battle, legendary in her time. May I?" He held his hands out.

Rachel reluctantly handed it to Lachlan, reasonably certain it had just saved her life.

Perhaps sensing her unease—he seemed particularly sensitive in that regard—he said, "I'll just borrow it."

He held it and it looked natural in his hands. It glowed softly like the gem in the arrowhead she held tight. He reached into his satchel and pulled a small flat gold talisman from it and handed it to Rachel. "Here, hold this and the arrowhead in the same hand. It will protect you, and the arrowhead."

He sprinkled more blue powder around her from an old wooden shaker.

There was a flash of cold, blue flame—brilliant but not blinding—when the arrowhead touched the gold talisman, followed by a weak tremor. He moved her to the left, then back five or six feet, and squared her into position, his hands clasping her upper arms.

"Stay right there, just like that. It's critical. Keep your hand tight around the talisman and the arrowhead." He looked into her eyes. "Are you ready?"

Rachel nodded. She didn't understand what was happening, what she should be ready for. She only knew it was much bigger than her. Possibly history being written in her presence. She had no idea how she should feel, nor whether she would get out alive. It didn't matter.

This moment was monumental, and she was a part of it.

She nodded. "Ready."

Seventy-Two

Kiera watched Rachel disappear into the cavern.

Walking toward her, Josh was barely visible in the dimming tunnel as his eyes opened in recognition. He looked bedraggled, haggard. Of course he did. She probably did too. They had all been through hell.

She waved to Josh, never happier to see anyone in her life, then reached down and rubbed Ghost behind the ears.

He raised an arm and waved, a group of stragglers from the bar behind him. She stopped at the archway.

A moment later, the earth shook slightly and there was a brilliant flash of light from the cavern. She covered her eyes as small pieces of rock fell from the ceiling, hitting her on the head. She slipped just inside the cavern for no reason other than she felt safer there. Ghost tried to squeeze between her legs.

She gestured at Josh and the others to hurry.

How would they ever make it out of this alive? She feared that any minute, the walls and ceiling would cave in. Or that something she could neither see nor feel would swat them dead like existential bugs. An agnostic, she believed in *something* but had no patience for religion.

She never dreamed a world like this existed beyond the imaginary worlds of books and movies—and nightmares. No frame of reference for this moment existed anywhere in her understanding of the world. To be jolted like this left her dizzy and overwhelmed.

Josh trotted the last few steps, put a hand on Kiera's shoulder, and breathlessly said, "What's going on here?"

"No time to explain," Kiera said brusquely.

"Seriously?"

Surely she had used every drop of adrenaline in her system, but suddenly overwhelmed by the past few hours, Kiera shouted, "Yes! Seriously! There is no time to explain! I don't even know how!" She gripped his hands. "If we get out of here alive, I'll tell you everything."

He exhaled loudly and nodded. "Okay."

She looked at the group gathered around them. "Where's Kyla and Bella?"

"They stayed in the basement. Kyla's claustrophobic, she wouldn't come into the tunnel. Bella stayed with her."

"Shit. We can't leave them there." Kiera thought for a moment, hatched a plan, and pointed down the tunnel. "Get everyone out that way. The tunnel is open. I'll go convince Bella and Kyla to come with me. Then we'll worry about Lachlan, Willow, and Rachel."

"Okay." He grabbed and held her, whispering in her ear. "Are you okay?"

"Yes, no—you can't imagine what I've seen." She shuddered, just wanting him to hold her forever.

"Oh, I have a fair idea," Josh said, looking off into space. He hugged her tighter. "I don't want to let go of you."

"I know. I'd rather stay with you, but we have to get these people to safety. It's our responsibility, and we can't leave Bella and Kyla behind."

Kiera faced the group. They looked drained and disjointed by the experience, and who could blame them? A violent tornado, earth tremors, and now, trapped underground. Thank God they hadn't seen the dead people. Then she realized with a start that they must have walked past Scott. Dead Scott with a cross buried to the hilt in his chest.

No wonder Josh had said *I have a fair idea.*

Jesus! She could barely believe it herself—and she had stabbed the guy.

"Listen everyone. I'm going to get Bella and convince Kyla to come as well." Pointing toward the farm, she said, "The tunnel is open. Rachel came in that way. Josh will lead you all out. Be warned. There are two bodies ahead yet."

She looked at Ghost. "You should go with them, buddy."

Leaning harder, he refused to budge from her leg, begging with the saddest dog eyes she had ever seen. "Okay, you're coming with me."

She hugged Josh. "I love you. Go, get them to safety. I'll see you soon."

"Love you too. Bella and Kyla are in the cooler." He held her tight for a minute, then he and Angela led the group down the tunnel toward the farmhouse.

"Hurry! While it's still quiet in here."

She choked a sob against her fist, wondering if she would ever see him again.

Seventy-Three

Kiera looked at Lachlan and then Rachel. She could see only the back of his head but could tell he was concentrating. Willow stood, eyes closed, seemingly mesmerized. Kiera gave Rachel a little hand wave and ran along the tunnel, leaping over Scott with Ghost at her heels. When they reached the end of the tunnel, she turned to Ghost and knelt. "Stay here, buddy. I'll be right back."

As she climbed, he let out a mournful howl.

"I'll be right back, sweetie."

The basement was mostly dark, other than a narrow crack of light between the ceiling and the basement wall. Just below, a joist had fallen and someone lay beneath, partially crushed by the beam.

Kiera gasped. It was Charlie. She shuddered, clasped a hand to her mouth and looked away.

Shit!

She found Bella and Kyla huddled in the cooler looking various shades of terrified. Their flashlight was dim, nearly out of power. Hers wasn't much better. She didn't have long to talk Kyla into the tunnel.

She stepped into the cooler. "How are you girls?"

Kyla just stared, pale and shaking. Bella, looking a bit more composed, said, "I'm okay. Scared, but okay. Kyla hasn't said a word. I'd kill to get out of here."

"You and me both." Kiera looked at Kyla and touched her hands, which were wrapped around her shoulders. She jerked back, startled, seemingly in a fugue state.

"Kyla," Kiera said, softly. "I know you're scared. I know you have claustrophobia. We need to get out of here. It's not safe. The tunnel is safer, and we can get outside that way."

Kyla seemed to soften a little. Kiera slowly took her hands, talking soft and gentle, trying to calm her and gain her trust.

"It's okay. Bella and I will walk you through, keep you safe. I promise." She could promise no such thing, but such thoughts weren't helpful. She had to project calm, a sense of security—

The floor suddenly shook with a single fierce tremor.

Part of the basement ceiling audibly cracked and, with an agonizing groan, an entire section of the fieldstone wall and a segment of the ceiling collapsed with an earthshaking clamor and a billowing blast of dust. Bricks tumbled and fell to the floor along the edges. Sunlight filtered in. The ceiling—also the floor of the bar—remained attached to the center support beam and now formed a large ramp, leading up and out of the basement.

Kiera stared, stunned. "Holy shit!"

Suddenly the path out was clear and beckoning to them.

A freaking miracle! And no less—the first one today.

"Oh my God, guys. No tunnel. Come on. Let's go!" They leapt out and followed her. Ghost barked a frustrated, angry bark from the tunnel.

"I haven't forgotten you, little buddy!"

Kiera reached the tilted ramp of flooring and jumped on the bottom edge, testing it. It didn't budge. Stepped up a little higher and jumped. Solid as steel. Perfect.

"Okay, ladies. One at a time. Go up by the wall there and right at the top to solid ground. Hurry!"

Bella went first, but slipped twice on the damp wood before finding her footing with a hand from Kiera. A moment later, she looked down, a wan smile on her face. "I'm good, but everything's gone up here."

Shit. Kiera had suspected as much. "Okay Kyla, you saw how Bella did it."

Kyla didn't hesitate but ran up the ramp with the conviction of a confirmed claustrophobe.

"Good girl!"

Thank God. Two safe. Kiera ran up the ramp and out to the sidewalk; stopped, stunned by the devastation around her. She had seen plenty of tornado damage in her lifetime but she had never seen it in *her* town. The sight of it almost made her sick. Tears ran down her cheeks as sadness overwhelmed her.

Quinlan's Tavern was gone. The bar, the tables, the oak back bar swept away. Two partial walls remained, the others reduced to piles of brick. A wide swath of Miller's Crossing had been flattened, literally. Other than snapped tree trunks and random standing walls, this side of town had been brutally and efficiently bulldozed into a bewildering roadbed of broken vegetation, buildings, cars and trucks, signs, furniture, garbage carts, toys, cans, clothing, shoes, bikes and so much more.

People's lives, swept away in seconds. It would take years to rebuild and some people would be forever changed by the storm.

There were flashing emergency lights scattered along the edges of the damage path. Here and there, people wandered in the rubble in slow dazed circles, trying to make sense of the insensible. She had seen it so many times and it never lost impact, a brutal punch to the gut. Everything underground had been so surreal, and now this.

In the western sky, the sun shone serenely upon the disaster, a light breeze carrying the stink of leaking natural gas, wet insulation, and chemical smells she could only guess at.

She turned to Bella and Kyla. "Okay. You two go very carefully and see if you can find help. A cop, firefighter, whoever. I'll need help checking the tunnel. There are people down there yet. Okay?"

Bella nodded.

Kiera pointed south. "Someone needs to go to that old farmhouse about a mile up on Martin Road. There are people there who'll need help as well. Can you do that?"

Bella said, "Yep."

Kyla grabbed Kiera and gave her a fierce hug. "Thank you, Kiera, thank you. You saved me."

With that, Kiera headed back down the ramp and into the tunnel to a barking, leaping, ecstatic Ghost.

Time to drag the others out of the cavern before the whole mess collapsed.

Seventy-Four

Josh led the way, around Caleb and Owen, and along the tunnel. Their flashlights were dying and the tunnel had grown dimmer. Their faces and the tunnel walls had faded to shades of grey. At least it had spared him a vivid image of the dead bodies as they passed them. The path grew more treacherous with cracks in the walls and the floor. Had the cracks been there or had the tremors opened them? He didn't know, he had never walked this far. Nevertheless, it felt dangerous and unstable. His fear and claustrophobia were nearly unbearable and he walked ever faster, silently praying for an end to this dreadful passage.

Jami Braugher had caught her foot in a crevice and twisted an ankle. Unable to stand on it, she now hobbled along behind them with help from her husband Robby and Doyle. In between, the others were doing their best to keep up.

Thereafter, whenever Josh stepped over a substantial crevice, he yelled, "Crack! Watch it!"

Nobody spoke otherwise. The only sounds were feet on stone and their increasingly labored breathing. On they walked for what felt like hours, lights failing, the tunnel nearly dark.

Josh saw a narrow shaft of light ahead and yelled, "Slowing down!" Suddenly, the light was a little better. He stopped to examine an opening in the ceiling. Angela, Abbie, Katy, Dani, and Matt gathered around as Josh probed the opening with a finger. In the distance, they could hear Jami shuffling along with Robby and Doyle.

"What is it?"

"I don't know. It just looks like a crevice in the rock."

Maybe because they had been underground so long, that little bit of sunlight was captivating even if it wasn't the way out. Josh looked ahead, but the tunnel was dark and his flashlight beam so weak that it just looked black and endless. How much longer could it be? Kiera said someone had come through here. How? On a bike? On skates?

The tunnel shuddered, shaking with an intensity that scared the living hell out of him. He lost his balance and fell against the wall.

Shit! They were gonna die.

Gravel and small stones fell from the ceiling and it was hard to stand. The crevice above widened slightly, but he wasn't waiting around to see if it opened farther. "Run! Let's get the hell out of here!"

He pushed Angela ahead of him and yanked Abbie's arm. "Let's go!"

He could vaguely see Angela ahead and, as the crevice and beam of sunlight fell behind, he could see faint light about thirty feet up. It was the end of the tunnel! A square opening in the ceiling beckoned. *Yes!*

A long crack opened overhead and for a moment, he didn't think he'd make it. Angela looked back and clambered up the vertical steps in the rock and disappeared. A moment later he followed, climbing fast despite extreme fatigue and threw himself out of the hole and onto the dirt floor of the basement.

They'd made it!

He got to his knees and clapped Angela on the back, and they high-fived each other before turning to help the others. The tremors grew more intense and the house was shaking in a way that made Josh nervous.

Abbie climbed out next, covered in dirt and dust, followed by Katy and Dani, who looked like miners crawling out of the pit.

The ground shook in one final convulsion—a horrendous rumbling, a grinding of earth and stone. A thick blast of dust rushed from the tunnel opening as the floor beneath them caved and sank ten feet farther into the earth.

Seconds later, the house collapsed.

Seventy-Five

Lachlan felt enormous energy flow through his arms as he held the sword, blade up. Problem was, he didn't really know how to exploit it. It was Stikla's sword and ultimately, might only be potent in her hands. Well, Stikla had been dead almost a thousand years. Better to go with what he knew, though perhaps the sword would provide him some protection. Everything about this moment was an unknown. He could only rely on his extraordinary senses, intuition, and vast previous experience. He prayed it was enough.

"Willow? Ready?"

She stood like a statue, eyes closed. She nodded and for a moment, Lachlan thought she looked like a goddess with her long flowing tresses and flawless complexion.

"Rachel?"

Eyes wide open, she nodded, looking surprisingly calm. Young, eager, innocent—a long life ahead of her—he would never forgive himself if anything happened to her.

He placed the sword at his feet, pointing outward, then slipped a thin amulet into his left hand, an ancient piece given to him by a

Romany sorcerer. Cast in gold, bearing the face of Wōden, it was his most powerful protector. He grasped the gold Celtic cross with both hands, gripping tightly, then looked around one more time. The cavern glowed an iridescent blue, the stone fluorescing with the energy in the room. The longship also seemed to glow. It was an ethereal, beautiful light that most people would never witness, more vivid than the Aurora Borealis.

Lachlan closed his eyes, the cavern slipped away, and his mind connected with the energies flowing through the cavern.

With the immense kinetic tension in the room, like giant metal bands bent taut, it felt like the world itself could be ripped asunder. A faint scent of ozone hung in the air and, in the sudden silence, a low frequency vibration coursed through his feet and the floor of the cavern. He shut that out. Cleared every stray thought. Imagined standing in a vast cathedral-like space, communing with the spirit of every person who had ever lived.

Lachlan rose to an altered state of consciousness, his mind elevated somewhere above his corporeal body, humming in perfect sync with the very center of the Caol Áit. The dangerous Geata de Ifreann remained closed, held in check by the jeweled arrowhead in Rachel's hand.

Energy rushed outward from the Celtic cross, reflecting off Willow and the arrowhead in Rachel's hand and returning to him, amplified, working mercilessly on the darkness—grinding, wearing, eroding, driving it into the ground. Finally, all the energies in the cavern were flowing in his favor, doing his bidding. He felt like a god on a mountaintop—a benevolent god, but a god nevertheless.

All of that energy encircled the darkness in a vortex of flow lines—in many things, nature found the vortex to be the most efficient means to transfer energy and momentum, from whirlpools in the ocean to hurricanes in the atmosphere. At its center, the rotating bands were filled with clouds, lightning, and thunder in a roar that grew ever louder.

Lachlan eased his grip on the cross and let go of it. The cross floated in air, held there by the energies. He slid the cargástriftr from his back pocket and held it up, above the cross. At his feet, the Sword of Stikla quivered and rose until it stood vertical, beneath the cross and the cargástriftr. At no time did he open his eyes. He didn't need to; he felt in perfect command of the cavern and everything within. The earth juddered with the enormous disturbance flowing through the energy fields. Try as it might, the darkness seemed no match for him.

The whirlwind, spinning in the center of the room, became an intense spindle, drawing tighter and tighter, rotating faster and faster, filled with vivid flashes of lightning, the sound of the wind growing until it sounded like a Boeing 747 tearing down a runway for takeoff.

Lachlan fought with every fiber of his being to maintain a merciless focus on the center of the room.

Chanting in Old English, he snatched the cargástriftr floating before him and fired it into the swirling maelstrom. The vortex flared and blazed brilliant as the base of it bored a hole into the rock of the cavern floor. The white-hot tip cut and bored, wider and deeper, until the entire swirling mass abruptly disappeared into the earth with a tremendous rush of air as a hurricane force wind blew through the room and followed the vortex into the ground.

It ended in an instant with surgical precision.

Silence fell over the cavern.

The sudden change was startling after the horrendous roar of the vortex. Eyes still closed, Lachlan probed the room for disharmony, evidence the darkness had somehow withstood the tremendous onslaught of energy directed against it.

He felt nothing.

Peace. Quiet. Serenity.

He had done it!

Beneath his feet, the ground vibrated, a faint tremor growing stronger in waves.

He tried to relax. His muscles spasmed from the effort. Waves of pain wracked his body. There was always a price to pay for summoning the forces of nature. A migraine threatened to split his head in two. Still, he was still alive. What was a little pain?

As the tremor intensified, he opened his eyes. Willow still appeared to be in a trance while Rachel looked around, looking confused but otherwise unharmed. The longship was rocking on the plinth in sync with the tremors.

A shadow of doubt arose.

Had he done it?

Had he really destroyed it? Or just sent it scurrying away into the ground? It had gone to ground in the rock once before, after that catastrophic explosion at the MacKenzie house. How could he be sure it was destroyed and gone forever this time?

As he pondered the question, the earth beneath his feet convulsed and threw him to the ground.

Seventy-Six

With Ghost loping at her side, Kiera ran down the tunnel in the fading light with a weak flashlight, nearly tripping over the dead body of Scott Robbins. She could hear a loud noise echoing along the walls, not unlike a commercial jetliner taxiing for takeoff. Brilliant blue light emanating from the cavern illuminated the way. Suddenly, a strong gust of wind swept down the tunnel toward the cavern, nearly knocking her off her feet.

As the cavern arch came into view, the ground shook again. She turned the corner and planted herself in the archway, remembering that doorways were the safest spot in an earthquake. Lachlan, swaying, seemed to be in a trance. Did he not notice the longship rocking on its moorings?

Rachel evidently saw the danger and bolted toward Kiera and the archway. The earth beneath their feet convulsed, throwing Lachlan to the ground.

Willow, a little slower in recognition, turned and froze, and the delay proved nearly fatal. The longship rocked in wider and wider arcs until, pushed past the point of no return, it tipped and fell in slow

351

motion. The wide gunwale of the ship slammed into Willow, knocking her against the wall, opening a gash on her forehead, nearly crushing her beneath the substantial weight of the vessel.

As the ground rumbled with aftershocks, Kiera yelled, "Lachlan! Willow! We have to go! Now!"

Willow stirred. Lachlan raised his head and looked around, dazed, as if waking from a trance. Moving slowly, he rolled sideways and stood, unsteady at first; shook his head and inched toward the door, fighting for balance. Halfway there, a rock fell from the ceiling, striking a glancing blow to his skull. Lachlan collapsed, unconscious, bleeding from the temple.

Kiera stood, frozen, unsure what to do. They weren't leaving him behind no matter how difficult it proved to pull him out. She looked at Rachel, who seemed very close to hysteria, her hands clenched in front of her mouth. Who could blame her? Focusing on something tangible— saving Lachlan, bringing him to safety—saved her from falling into hysteria herself.

Pulling Rachel into a tight hug, Kiera held her face-to-face by the shoulders and said, "We've got to help them, get them out of here. You help Willow. I'll take care of Lachlan."

She nodded and ran toward Willow. Sitting up, the woman was bleeding from her forehead, but smiling with an oddly serene expression, her eyes half closed in bliss.

Lachlan's pulse was strong and steady. Kiera shook him gently but he was unresponsive. The bruise on the side of his head looked serious. They would have to move him. The ground had stilled somewhat for the moment, but she felt certain staying here was too dangerous.

Rachel helped Willow to her feet. Despite the head wound and the blood, she seemed steady even with the floor shaking beneath her.

"Rachel! Come here and help me!" Kiera yelled over the ground rumble. "Willow! Move. We have to get out of here."

Kiera carefully hoisted Lachlan's right side at the shoulder and pointed to the left armpit. "Lift there, under his arm."

They dragged him to the archway. He was a slight man, otherwise pulling him might have been impossible. Willow followed with a dazed look as she gawked at the fallen longship. Ghost barked in a frenzy as if admonishing them to hurry. It was growing warmer in the cavern and what appeared to be steam hissed from a crevice behind the longship.

Kiera tried not to fret about Josh, hoping against hope the earlier rock fall hadn't trapped them, or worse, buried them. She didn't know, couldn't know, and she could only cling to an optimistic outcome. Periodic small spasms shook the ground. Mostly, Kiera remained focused on getting Rachel and Willow to safety and pulling Lachlan out of the tunnel. She felt an affection for the man she couldn't explain based on their brief friendship.

With a new wave of tremors, the shaking grew more intense. Cracks opened in the walls of the cavern and rocks fell from the ceiling. They dragged Lachlan along the tunnel which seemed to go on forever. Kiera's flashlight was dead and the natural light had dimmed to midnight black. They navigated by feel only. She could hear Willow shuffling along behind them.

Somehow, Kiera and Rachel drew on reserves of energy driven by panic and fear and pressed on, stopping twice to rest and to switch sides so they were supporting Lachlan with the opposite arms. While Kiera approached the point of exhaustion, Rachel carried on without a complaint, showing little sign of fatigue.

Light ahead! The end of the tunnel, about thirty feet away.

"We're almost there," Kiera said.

"Yep," Rachel said, eyes forward, jaw set and determined. Talk about stoic. The girl was amazing.

As they approached the stone steps, the earth heaved in a terrifying convulsion, a horrendous rumbling, a grinding of earth and stone culminating in a massive, thunderous rock fall behind them. The tremor threw all three of them to the ground. Kiera threw herself over Lachlan to protect him while Ghost panicked and tried to crawl beneath her. Thick out-rushing clouds of dust from the tunnel followed the collapse while grit and pebbles rained from the ceiling.

The temblor felt nothing short of cataclysmic and Kiera worried the cavern and the entire tunnel system had collapsed. Had Josh and the others gotten out? She had to believe they did, but she feared the longship had been destroyed. Willow had passed out and lay, covered in grey dust, near Lachlan.

Rachel, face darkened by rock dust, suddenly jumped up and yelled, "The sword! Oh my God! I forgot the sword!"

The dust had begun to settle and the tunnel behind them was blocked, closed off by a solid wall of boulders and rubble. Rachel ran to it and tried moving a couple of rocks before evidently recognizing the futility of her efforts. She let out a heart-rending sob. "Noooooooooo!"

Kiera grabbed her arm and pulled her into a hug. "I'm so sorry, sweetie. We had to get Lachlan and Willow to safety. We saved their lives."

Looking little mollified, Rachel gazed longingly down the collapsed tunnel for a moment, hitched a sob, and helped Kiera first drag Lachlan and then Willow the final ten feet to the steps. There was little debris here and sunlight filtered down from the basement. The tremors had stopped and Kiera felt simultaneously grateful, exhausted, and shell-shocked.

They would need help to get Lachlan out. Kiera said, "I'm going to find help. You stay with Lachlan, Willow, and Ghost. I'll see if Kyla and Bella found help. Is that okay?"

"Yeah. That's cool." Tears streaked her grey face.

Kiera gave her a hug. "Thanks."

Kiera climbed into the basement and up the ramp into the sunshine, the sun low in the west, birds chirping somewhere nearby. It was amazing how often this kind of pleasant weather followed severe storms. She stood at the edge of the basement debating whether to stay put or walk toward the nearest squad car. Then she saw Bella and Kyla walking through the debris with two guys who looked like firefighters.

She checked her phone, hoping to call Josh, but she still had no signal. Standing out here in the daylight, she had to believe he'd made it too.

The two good-looking guys who walked up to Kiera, name-tagged Sean and Justin, were volunteers, wearing black station pants and shirts with **Town of Miller's Crossing FD** logos on the pockets. Sean said, "How can we help, ma'am?"

"There's a man and woman in the basement who are injured, we need help getting them out."

"Show us where they are," Sean said.

They followed Kiera down the ramp and into the basement.

Kiera pointed into the tunnel. "Down here."

They viewed the hole suspiciously. "What is this? Some sort of storm cellar? Is it safe?"

"The tunnel goes to an underground cavern we were exploring. There was a cave-in."

Justin knelt down and looked around through the hole in the floor. "It looks safe." He climbed down, looked Lachlan over, checking his neck in particular. He carefully lifted him and lay him over his shoulder and climbed up into the basement, making it look easy.

Kiera said. "That was amazing!"

"All part of the training. Let's get him over here." He pointed to the granite-topped table. Kiera grabbed a sweatshirt and tucked it under Lachlan's head, then watched the other firefighter reach down and help Willow up into the basement.

Rachel appeared at the rim. "What about Ghost?"

Sean said, "Ghost? Is that someone's name?" On cue, Ghost started barking.

"Ah."

Kiera's eyes lit on the sling Josh had used earlier. She handed the rope end to Sean and said, "If I go down and get him into this, can you pull him up?"

He nodded. "No problem."

Kiera climbed down and pulled one end of the sling up behind Ghost's front legs and the other in front of his back legs. "Okay."

She held on as Sean lifted him, to be reassuring, but Ghost seemed to be enjoying himself, wearing a smug dog smile. She took one more look around, climbed into the basement and walked over to Lachlan. "How is he?"

"Pulse is strong but this is a pretty severe head injury," Justin said. "I have some EMTs on the way with a stretcher. The hospital here is full so they may send him to the trauma center in Auburn."

"Shit. Okay." Kiera glanced at Willow. She too was a dirty shade of grey with dried blood on her face. "You okay?"

Willow nodded and looked at Lachlan with sad longing. She gently stroked his forehead. A tear ran down her dirty cheek.

Rachel walked over, knelt by Lachlan, and held his hand for a moment, then locked eyes with Kiera. "I should go. Let my parents know I'm okay."

Willow pulled her into a hug. "You were amazing, kid. A maiden-warrior if ever I saw one."

Rachel gave her a sad smile. "I need to know Lachlan is okay. Will someone let me know?"

"I will." Kiera and Willow both spoke at once.

Kiera said, "How can we find you?"

"Rachel Nash. I live at 727 Chestnut Street."

"Nash. 727 Chestnut, got it." She gave her another hug and watched her walk away. A remarkable girl.

Kiera turned to Justin. "Did they tell you about the people at the farmhouse on Martin Road?"

"Yep. Someone will get out there in good time." Sean shrugged.

"In good time?"

"Have you looked outside?"

★   ★   ★

It was dark by the time Kiera reached the farmhouse on Martin Road, having hitched a ride with two volunteer firefighters heading there to help. She still hadn't heard from Josh.

Emergency lights flashed everywhere. Kiera gasped in shock when she saw that the farmhouse, lit by powerful work lights, had collapsed into a trench. Police officers, firefighters, and volunteers were coming and going, but no one seemed to be in charge. A large truck with a boom was backing into the drive and being directed to the pile of debris that was once a house. She then noticed the ground had caved into a long trench running north toward town.

No sign of Josh anywhere on the site.

She worked her way closer to the house and collared a firefighter. "What's going on?"

"There are a number of people in the basement, we don't know how many yet."

She yelled as loud as she could, "Josh!"

A moment later, she heard him, faint as could be, "Kiera!"

Thank God!

He was alive!

She sat and cried.

His voice was all she needed to hear.

Seventy-Seven

Ugh.

Kiera opened one eye and screwed it shut. The room was overly bright, her head fuzzy from a bit too much chardonnay.

Oh well. The wine and the Xanax were the only things that allowed her to sleep, to escape the incessant visions of the dead creatures in the tunnel, to silence the awful sounds in her head of the cavern collapsing, to numb the terror of her narrow escape from death.

The experience had been overwhelming and she knew the nightmares, the excessive vigilance—always looking over her shoulder—the sense of impending death, the feeling she didn't have long to live; they were all symptomatic of post-traumatic stress disorder.

Where the hell was she? She cracked an eye again, just slightly. The living room. Her sofa. The flat screen in the corner hanging over the gas fireplace was playing some ancient rerun with the sound turned off.

Ghost hopped down and barked until she sat upright. "Alright, alright. I'm coming."

Kiera shuffled to the kitchen, let Ghost out the back door and decided to make real coffee today. She poured water in the coffeemaker and opened a bag of fresh Columbian. Made a treat for Ghost of kibble and canned food. He came tearing in the door as soon as the food hit the dish.

A week had passed. She and Josh had hardly spoken since they had pulled him from the basement of the old farmhouse. Besides Josh, only Angela, Abbie, and Katy had survived. Doyle, Robby, Jami, and Matt were missing in the tunnel cave-in and presumed dead. Dani had been killed when the house collapsed. Kiera knew Josh was dealing with demons and post-traumatic stress of his own.

The tornado had killed forty-eight people and injured over two hundred more. Twenty-three people were still missing, including Professor Marshall and Owen Prosser. A third of Miller's Crossing had been effectively wiped off the map. Josh talked about moving one of the few times they had talked. He didn't mention her in those plans. Maybe it was just shock, maybe he felt she and Willow were partly to blame. He had loved Quinlan's and seemed to mourn more for the tavern than for their endangered relationship.

She took a leisurely shower. The fog in her head lifted. She dried her hair, pulled it into a ponytail, and applied minimal makeup. She was off to visit Lachlan. He remained in a coma with a head injury: brain swelling and a small subdural bleed. His prognosis was *guarded,* a euphemism for *we don't have any clue whether he'll live or die.* She went every day to sit with him and talk, hoping to see some response, some flicker of an eyelid. But his face remained set in stone and she feared he would float in limbo forever. Rachel had twice ridden along but said little and looked deeply melancholy. She seemed to bleed over Lachlan's condition and held a small flat gold object in her left hand as she talked to him like a child would to a father. Kiera recognized it as one of his talismans.

It was a grey day, the low flat blanket of stratus a mirror of her mood as she drove to Auburn Memorial. Kiera took the elevator to the third floor and walked to the end of the corridor and Lachlan's room. She set her purse on a chair and looked at him sadly. Nothing had changed. Then she noticed a familiar scent in the air.

A moment later, Willow breezed in the room and stopped sharply, caught unaware. "Oh."

Kiera quietly said, "Hello, Willow."

She merely nodded. A long, awkward silence followed. They hadn't talked since the day of the tornado. Kiera wanted to call but couldn't. She didn't know why. Willow hadn't tried to call her. The rift between them felt deep, almost insurmountable. Kiera still couldn't get past Willow shooting at her. It wasn't mindful, but mindfulness seemed like an abstract concept with all the ghosts wondering around in her head. Finally, Kiera said, "How are you?"

"Okay." She wouldn't look at Kiera. Instead, she walked to Lachlan's side and talked to him quietly. Kiera stood on the other side, also talking to him. Two could play that game.

Five minutes elapsed. Suddenly, Willow said, "How are you, Kiera?"

"Okay." Now Kiera couldn't make eye contact. Her best friend since third grade stood across from her and she couldn't look at her, couldn't talk to her.

Finally Willow said, "Can you ever forgive me?"

Kiera didn't know the answer to that question. It felt like no. She also thought she could try harder. Kiera said, "I don't know, but I think I should try."

They agreed to have lunch sometime but set no date. As she drove home, she felt certain of only one thing.

Her life would never be the same.

★   ★   ★

Josh stood at a workbench in the basement of what was once Quinlan's Tavern, cleaning and packing away the tools he had salvaged from the rubble. Outdoors, he'd spent two days sifting through rubble and debris and had found nothing worth keeping. It was depressing, soul-destroying work and he found himself in tears several times. He had loved Quinlan's—one of his life's dreams and the perfect bookend to his career in law. Now the bar was gone, and he didn't think he could face starting over again.

With the tools stowed, he turned to the staircase. A tow company had finally come and salvaged the car tossed there by the storm, hauling it away. He picked through the junk that remained: broken glasses and bottles, a bar stool, a flatscreen that had snapped in half, and ironically, one of Kiera's tornado pics. Besides the utter depression that had descended upon him since the tornado, there was a constant burning anger. At Willow for her part in the madness, but mostly at Kiera. His dream was gone and he blamed her. If she had just left well enough alone, if she and Willow had just stayed out of the tunnel, none of this would have happened. The storm, the sinkhole, none of it was natural. Somehow, rationally or irrationally, it all pointed back to Willow and Kiera and he didn't know if he could forgive either one of them.

Beneath the broken glass and debris, he found a photo of Kiera and him behind the bar, taken the night they opened. The frame and the glass were broken. He tossed it on the junk pile, loaded his tools and drove away. The insurance company could handle it from here.

He wasn't coming back.

★   ★   ★

Kiera stood at the bay window, looking out at a dull, grey day. Tinges of yellow and red colored the maples. The grass lay brown and dormant. It hadn't rained since the day of the tornado.

A month had passed and Miller's Crossing had lived through its fifteen minutes of international fame in the worst way possible: as victim to a double disaster, the site of a violent tornado *and* an earthquake.

Or a sink hole.

It depended on who you asked. One group believed the area lay over an *aulacogen*, a fancy word for an unresolved fault or rift deep in the earth's crust. Nonsense, said the sinkhole people. The area lay atop a large shield of limestone—the Niagara Escarpment—and a sinkhole seemed much more likely. As of her last read, the sinkhole faction was winning.

Kiera and Josh had had plans to meet for lunch yesterday; he canceled at the last minute. He had been drifting away since Quinlan's had blown apart. Maybe they just needed time, that age old cure that supposedly fixed everything. She was no longer certain even that would work. Disasters could bring people together, but sometimes, they tore them apart instead.

Lachlan remained in a coma. They were now calling it a *persistent vegetative state.* It sounded bad. She visited every day nevertheless and chatted with him. Rachel rode along more often and they were becoming friends. Back in school, she was a senior and thinking seriously about a career in archeology. Kiera advised her on courses and school choices while trying to keep her cynicism to herself.

She thought about working again with little enthusiasm. She had more interest in writing. About the cavern and the longship and the events of that day. Few people had experienced it as completely as she had, though the rumors and stories circulating were so fantastic no one believed them. Likely no one would believe her either. Part of her believed the longship and whatever remained should stay buried for an eternity. The things there, the thin place, the gate—maybe they weren't meant for mere mortals to experience.

She and Willow were doing better, their relationship on the mend. They were going to The Vinery for lunch today and things almost felt normal between them.

Of all the things she wondered, she wondered most if it was over. Finished. Resolved, the beast destroyed.

Had Lachlan *won*.

Obsessed with the issue, Kiera had since read every article written on Kenric Shepherd and the explosion at the MacKenzie house. She had an inkling of what they'd faced and how Shepherd died, for whatever that was worth. In the end, she had to believe it was over. Had to believe all that pain and destruction had accomplished something. But she also knew the darkness could hide underground and come back at another time, in another place.

At night, in the dark, Kiera feared she would never know that truth for certain.

Someday, maybe she wouldn't worry about it so much. Someday.

Willow arrived thirty minutes late. Wearing a cute blue tie-die maxi wrap and a floppy hat, with her wavy blonde hair and dewy complexion, she looked as lovely as ever.

"Willow!"

"Kiera!"

Willow threw her arms out, grabbed her, and gave her a vaguely indecent hug in her touchy-feely way.

"You look great!" Willow gushed.

"You too, sweetie."

They were back to their old routine.

"Glass of chard?"

"Duh."

Seventy-Eight

A few days later, Kiera sat at the kitchen table sipping Columbian coffee. Grabbing her laptop, she clicked on her email client.

A single email greeted her from Ari Thomas, the guy who was going to research the tavern's history.

Sheesh!

She had forgotten about that email, sent so long ago, in another life. He had attached a PDF.

Three pages long, Kiera skimmed the details. The last Quinlan to own the bar was Jack Quinlan who had died in 1969. A list of Quinlans who'd owned the bar prior stretched back to 1878. Curiously, the building had been purchased originally by Thorson Kuenlang who changed his name to James Quinlan soon after. Ari noted the name *Kuenlang* was Norwegian and probably pronounced *Kwen'lan,* the name change likely performed so Mr. Kuenlang sounded more American. Many immigrants had done the same thing.

The family also owned a farm south of town. Somerset Quinlan was listed as the owner. Thing was, he didn't exist. A trust had been set up to pay the property taxes and expenses in perpetuity. Something had gone wrong with the trust established for the tavern. The bank had seized it and sold it off.

The end.

Crap!

Kiera felt hollow, vaguely angry. This was the final injustice. No closure at all. Ever.

If the Quinlans knew the story of the tunnel and cavern, it was lost.

A secret the last Quinlan had taken to the grave.

*   *   *

Dana MacKenzie sat in her living room, dressed in comfy sweats. Curled up with her iPad, she was reading the news, a fascinating feature story about a tornado and earthquake in Wisconsin, not far from the ill-fated house her parents had owned. The story delved into the event in great detail, an EF-5 tornado, the most powerful category, and the collapse of a large sinkhole, possibly set in motion by the low atmospheric pressure near the tornado. It all sounded very logical and scientific and Dana wasn't sure she believed a word of it.

Such an event, occurring anywhere else on the planet, wouldn't have raised an eyebrow, but she had seen things at her parent's house that defied any explanation and all belief. Those events still bothered her deeply. Like most people who experienced trauma, she had developed a story, a story she told herself to explain everything, to help in the healing, to make it easier to carry on.

In the story Dana had written, her mother and a man named Shepherd had faced down some evil, the nature of which she couldn't even imagine. She didn't need to. She believed the story ended there when the house was destroyed in a devastating explosion, the remnants consumed by fire. Whatever evil they faced had died that night along with her parents and Kenric Shepherd. It was the only way she could live on without fear, without looking over her shoulder every moment of every day.

Dana finished the story, chewing on a nail, sipping on her favorite riesling. For the first time in months, she reached into her purse, grabbed the bottle of Xanax and washed one down with the last of her wine.

Some nights, it was still the only way she could sleep.

⋆   ⋆   ⋆

Two nights later, at 3 a.m., Leah walked into her bedroom. There was a loose board near the doorway and Leah's footstep on that board always woke her instantly. She had been Aunt Dana, but they had finally completed the adoption proceedings and Leah was now her daughter. Leah had started calling her Mom six months ago anyway. Leah had no memory of her mother, who had walked out on her, or her father, who had been killed in a car accident two years ago. Dana also assumed that Leah had no memory of the night her grandmother died.

"Mom? Can I sleep with you?" Leah said. "I had a bad dream."

"Sure, sweetie." Dana sat and helped her climb into bed and got her situated with her blanket. She rolled over and ran her fingers through Leah's hair. She lay there, barely visible in the wash of light from her alarm clock, wide-eyed and unhappy.

"What did you dream about, honey?"

"Lachlan. Do you remember Lachlan?"

Dana started. Lachlan? That had been months ago. She hadn't heard from him since.

"Yes, I do. What about Lachlan?"

"He's sleeping in a hospital. He doesn't think he's going to wake up."

"How do you know that?"

"He spoke to me."

Leah looked so much like Laura, her grandmother, sometimes it hurt to look at her. Her expression was still troubled. "Did he say anything else?"

"Yes." She looked into Dana's eyes. "He said we have to move."

At first, her tired brain couldn't comprehend. They had to move? "What? Why, honey?"

"He said we're not safe here anymore."

"Why?"

"He said the darkness is coming."

Thank you!

Thank you for reading *Quinlan's Secret*. As an independently published author, I rely on all of you wonderful readers to spread the word. If you enjoyed *Quinlan's Secret*, please tell your friends and family. I would also sincerely appreciate a brief review on Amazon.

Hayward's Revenge, the sequel to *Quinlan's Secret* and the final installment in The Elders trilogy, will be available early in 2021.

Again, thank you!

Cailyn Lloyd
http://www.cailynlloyd.net

Acknowledgments

A number of people had a hand in helping me finish *Quinlan's Secret*.

Many thanks to my editor, Lucy Snyder, for her tireless efforts and crucial and invaluable insights during the creation of this novel.

Also, thanks to Jennie Lloyd who read and provided valuable advice on each draft and Amanda Robinson who copyedited the final version.

This book is so much better because of their contributions.